D1520936

Books by Fran Stewart

The Biscuit McKee Mystery Series:

Orange as Marmalade
Yellow as Legal Pads
Green as a Garden Hose
Blue as Blue Jeans
Indigo as an Iris
Violet as an Amethyst
Gray as Ashes

Red as a Rooster
Black as Soot
Pink as a Peony
White as Ice

A Slaying Song Tonight

The Scot Shop Mysteries:

A Wee Murder in My Shop
A Wee Dose of Death
A Wee Homicide in the Hotel

Poetry:

Resolution

For Children:

As Orange As Marmalade/
Tan naranja como Mermelada
(a bilingual book)

Non-Fiction:

From The Tip of My Pen: a workbook for writers

Black as Soot

Fran Stewart

Journey of a Dream Press

Black as Soot
the 9th Biscuit McKee Mystery
Fran Stewart
© 2018

1st edition: © 2018 Fran Stewart

ISBN: 978-0-9897142-8-0

This is a work of fiction. Any resemblance to any person living or dead is purely coincidental.

This book was printed in the United States of America.

Journey of a Dream Press
Duluth GA 30096
www.JourneyofaDream.com

For Darlene

The final four books of the Biscuit McKee Mystery Series began with RED AS A ROOSTER. BLACK AS SOOT is the second of the four books, and will be followed by PINK AS A PEONY, and WHITE AS ICE. For your own enjoyment (and to prevent total confusion), read all four in the correct order, as the author makes no attempt to "bring the reader up to speed" with the story so far.

If you enjoy reading the usual "Author's Note" at the beginning of a book, you will find an all-inclusive one (and my list of acknowledgements) at the end of RED AS A ROOSTER.

My thanks to Vermont Castings for their permission to use their Defiant Flexburn stove on the cover of BLACK AS SOOT and in the pages of this story, and to Dr. Ciaran Toal of the Irish Linen Museum (Lisburn Museum) for helping me to understand how flax is grown, harvested, and used.

At the end of each of these four books you will find pertinent lists of geneaogies as well as who's taken shelter in Biscuit and Bob's house.

Wednesday, December 6, 2000

"**THE THIN UNHAPPY** moon," I quoted once we'd all returned to the attic from an extended bathroom break. We had a number of toilets here in this old house, but with twenty-one people, we had to do a lot of sharing. I was the last one upstairs, simply because Marmalade dove under the bed to retrieve her favorite blue mouse, and had insisted on a game of fetch—I throw, she chases, I fetch. Bob had given it to her a couple of weeks before, and she was still entranced with it.

It is fun only when you throw it for me.

Once we were settled, Ida picked up the diary of Mary Frances. "I'm going to back up a paragraph," she said, "to get us on track."

I was glad because, other than that one *thin unhappy moon* line, I'd sort of forgotten where we were.

I always know where we are.

I patted Marmalade and settled back, as much as I could manage, into the uncomfortable folding chair.

So the candle is out. Once he walked away, though, I opened the shutters as wide as possible and now I write by the light of the thin unhappy moon. When we leave tomorrow, I will allow my steps to linger behind the others. I must arrange to walk in the very back and then to drop far enough behind so that Hubbard and I might steal away in the confusion. I know he will be watching for me. Mister Silas Martin is sure to be riding on Devil at the rear of the procession, but of all the Martins, he would be the most amenable to letting me go, if I can only explain to him before he raises a general alarm. I am sure—almost sure—he will see reason. This means I will not be present when Myra Sue is buried far from Brandtburg, but I feel fair certain she will forgive me, for she knows—she is the only one who knows—of my secret marriage last night to Hubbard Brandt.

"It sounds even more like a plot out of Shakespeare," I said when Ida paused to take a breath. I could hardly wait to tell Bob about this. He loved Shakespeare, as was obvious from all the well-read volumes on our bookcases.

I like Shakespeare. Softfoot reads it to me sometimes. Sometimes his voice sounds like purring.

"Shakespeare," Charlotte Ellis said. "My college roommate and I took an English class our junior year that was nothing but Shakespeare."

She didn't sound like she'd enjoyed it very much, but maybe I was reading too much into her tone of voice. Maybe she'd liked the class so much, she was sorry it ever had to end.

"I hated it," she said.

Okay, so I was right the first time. "His plays are meant to be seen on stage," I said. "A lot of people who think they don't like Shakespeare change their minds once they see them performed."

Charlotte leveled a gaze at me that made me suddenly very aware that she was, technically, my boss now that she was chair of the library board.

Glaze laughed at me. "Quit preaching, Biscuit. Some people just don't like the same things you do."

The moment smoothed over, but I still felt a bit unsettled.

"Hold the fort," someone called out from downstairs, and we all turned at the clatter of footsteps. "Don't open anything until we get there!"

"That sounds like Esther?" Sadie's voice held a distinct question.

Sure enough, my third Petunia's fuzzy gray hair appeared, followed by her bright turquoise sweatshirt. "I hear you're having a party up here. Bob told us all about it. May we join you?"

Behind her, Sylvia Parkman beamed.

Glaze beamed right back at her mother-in-law-to-be. "Sylvia! We thought you were staying with the Johnsons?" There was as much of a question in her voice as there had been in Sadie's a moment before.

"We were," Sylvia said, "but it started getting way too crowded up there."

I was certainly happy to see Tom's mother and grandmother, but I wondered first, why they had come, second, how they had gotten here, and third, what I was going to do with them. Well, I didn't need to bother about number three, because I still had some unassigned bedrooms. As to my first question, if they were that crowded, they might easily have called for relief. Of course they had. And Bob had gone up the hill to bring them down here. I love it when I can answer all my questions.

I answer many of your questions, but you do not listen to me.

Sylvia turned to me. "I hope we're not imposing, Biscuit."

"Of course not. It's a big house, and you're completely welcome." The Parkmans could take the other room that had a double bed, and that left me with Esther. Maybe she wouldn't mind rooming with Amanda. I'd have to ask Amanda before I suggested it, but I thought it would probably be okay. I sure hoped they'd brought sheets with them. Otherwise, they'd be curling up in blankets. If I even had that many blankets.

"Bob came up and helped us get here. And we brought our own pillows and sheets."

She must have read my mind. "Good."

She leaned close to my ear. "I think the Johnsons were sad to see us leave."

I lowered my voice to match her tone. "Why?"

"That left them with …"

But her words were interrupted by the roar of a loud engine, several loud engines, outside. The attic windows were too high for us to look through without the benefit of the stool, but I could tell the noise came from right out in our front yard. When they cut off, one after the other, the silence left all of us wondering what the heck was going on. "I guess we'll have one more little interlude," I said. "Let's find out what the noise is all about." I headed for the stairs, followed closely by Glaze and Maddy.

Within what seemed like seconds—we were just passing the broom closet—we heard the engines start up again and zoom off into the distance. The front door opened and closed below us. Bob hollered up the stairs, "Biscuit! You might want to get everybody down here!"

"Especially Glaze!" Tom's voice held a note I'd never heard before. Excitement? Elation? What was it?

It is his happy showing.

The entryway was filled with people. Jam-packed as a matter of fact. And in the middle of the crowd were my mom and dad. They had the biggest smiles I'd ever seen, even though their cheeks were rosy red from the cold, and Mom was rubbing her hands to warm them.

"What on earth is going on?" I asked. " I mean, I'm really happy to see you, but what are you doing here? How did you get here all the way from Braetonburg? Why? Is everyone all right?"

Bob laid a hand on my arm.

Tom stepped forward and sank to one knee in front of Glaze. "Now that your parents and my parents and my grandmother have joined us, would you be willing to marry me tomorrow evening?"

Glaze cried out and flung her arms around his neck. "Yes!"

She is very happy to see SunsetLady and DreamMaker, and she loves Fishgiver very much.

Dave sang out a creditable, though slightly flat, rendition of the first few lines of Get Me to the Church on Time.

On time for what?

"It's a good thought, Dave," Tom said, "but we won't have to go that far."

What do you mean?

Dee let out a tremendous moan. "No church?" She and Maddy had planned to help me decorate it. No wonder she was disappointed.

"He didn't say that, Dee." Glaze smiled that radiant grin of hers. "A wedding will turn this old house into a church. Behave yourself, Dave."

"Bravo," Father John said. "A wedding right here!" And he began to applaud, soon joined by all the rest of the group, except for me. "We'll have a party."

Will there be fish or chicken?

"That's wonderful," Maddy gushed, "but if you do the wedding here, now—or rather, tomorrow—I won't have a chance to wear that great dress I bought."

I stifled a moment of insane glee. If I couldn't have the perfect matron of honor dress, since Maddy had bought it out from under my fingertips—so to speak—at least she wouldn't have the pleasure of flaunting it in my face.

Instantly—almost instantly—I was ashamed of myself.

Why?

Marmalade wound herself around my ankles. Lucky cat. She never had to worry about what to wear.

That is true. My coat is perfectly silky. It keeps me warm in the snow time and cool when the sun is hot.

I looked around for Korsi. With this many feet in the front hall, I wouldn't want to be a cat. But then I felt a surge of relief. If Korsi wasn't here, then everybody must be well.

He is still sleeping on the chair where GoodHands was.

"We'll have a big bash for our first anniversary," Glaze said, looking at Tom, who nodded his agreement. "You can wear it then."

Carol raised her hand, rather tentatively. "Could I wangle an invitation?"

"Absolutely," Glaze said. "Everybody here is invited."

"As long as we don't have another ice storm," Dave said, and was generally booed by everyone.

"Maddy, if there's another ice storm next year," Glaze said, swiping her silver hair back from her face, and cutting through the booing, "just remember to pack the dress in your overnight bag."

"Sounds like a plan," Ida said. "In the meantime, I think we all brought changes of clothing for a couple of days, so we can at least be fresh for your wedding."

"Yeah." Ralph laid a hand on Ida's shoulder. "Maybe we won't stink up the place too much if we change our shirts."

Ida slapped at his hand.

"What's wrong with that? We all know we can't take showers here."

Why not?

Even if we'd had electricity, our water heater wasn't big enough to handle daily showers for twenty-one—now twenty-six—people, and there had been a general agreement to avoid using too much water, just in case.

In case of what?

Of course, if we'd had electricity, we wouldn't be having this situation in the first place.

What situation?

Father John chuckled at Marmalade's increasingly loud meows. "It's only been in the last century that people began to think frequent baths were a necessity. What if we agree just to ignore any smells?"

"Or," Henry said, "think of them as a return to a simpler way of life."

Ida sniffed. "More like a necessary evil."

11

Mouse poop! I do not know what you are talking about.

Marmalade sneezed, and I put aside all thoughts of the indigo dress. After all, my sister was getting married, and I was determined to make it a lovely wedding, even without all the frills we'd planned for the church. We could push most of the living room furniture back out of the way and we'd all gather in a couple of loose semicircles. Henry could stand in front of the wood stove. No. That way we'd be looking at Glaze and Tom's backs through the ceremony. The bride and groom could stand in front of the stove facing us, and Henry would be the one with his back turned to the congregation—if you could call a bunch of people in sweatpants a congregation.

All those red silk bows I'd planned to attach to the ends of the pews were still in a box in the broom closet. Dee and Maddy could help me. We'd sprinkle them strategically around the room. They'd be color-coordinated with our bright red wood stove. Candles, of course. Lots of candles. And surely there'd be enough food to gather an appropriate wedding feast afterwards, although we'd be hard-pressed to figure out a cake. Maybe Tom could cook one on the wood stove. No, that wouldn't be right. He shouldn't have to make his own wedding cake. Anyway, I didn't think a wood stove would double as an oven, even a stove as nice as our Defiant.

I edged up close to Bob. "How did you manage this?"

"Why do you think I had anything to do with it?"

I wrapped my arms around his waist. "It has your indelible trademark all over it."

"Tom and I talked about it after breakfast." He raised his voice so the whole group could hear him. After all, that way he wouldn't have to repeat the story. "Doc and Reebok volunteered to help us get Tom's folks down here. We had a heck of a time getting up the hill, and it was even more treacherous coming back down again."

"I know. I saw you four leave here, but I had no idea where you were going. I thought you'd gotten a police call. But how did you manage to get Mom and Dad?"

"I just happen to know a couple of firefighters up in Braetonburg who have snowmobiles."

"Snowmobiles? In Georgia?"

"They take their families on winter camping trips up in the Blue

Ridge mountains."

"But, snowmobiles? When is there ever enough snow for snow-mobiles?"

He laughed at the indignation in my voice. "This week, I'd say. I don't know if they've ever actually used the things before this. They were mighty excited about trying it. Anyway, they agreed to try to bring your mom and dad down here, but we didn't want to say anything because they weren't sure the machines would be able to get enough purchase on the ice. If it had been too dangerous, they wouldn't have risked your parents' lives."

"What about Auntie Blue and Uncle Mark?" Glaze had a note of sadness underneath the joy.

"I'm sorry," Bob said. "There was no way, with only two snow-mobiles."

She ran her hand back through her silver hair. "That's okay, Bob. It would have been nice, but I guess there's only so much transporting you can expect friends to do."

"Mark and Blue said they'd watch the house for us while we were gone," my mom told us.

I like WaterWoman. She has a good lap to sit on whenever we visit.

"Speaking of the transporters," I said, "didn't you invite them in to get warmed up before they had to drive all that way back? We could have given them coffee or hot chocolate or—"

"Heck no. They were having the time of their life."

"Driving out in the open through freezing weather over treacherous ice is not my idea of a good time," I said.

"But aren't you glad they have a different attitude?"

Glaze pushed me aside, gently, and wrapped her arms around Bob's waist. "Thank you. This is the best present ever."

Tom slapped Bob on the back. "I can't thank you enough, my friend. As Glaze says, this is the best wedding present you ever could have given us." He pulled Glaze close to his side. "And now I'll get to marry this woman right on time!"

"Is that a chess board I see in the living room?" my dad asked. "I just may have to whip somebody's butt at cutthroat chess."

"Fine with me," Mom said, laughing, "but leave me out of it. I prefer more civilized entertainment."

"Good," Glaze said, "because we need to indoctrinate you new-comers into our attic society."

Dad looked faintly puzzled, but Bob slapped him on the shoulder. "Don't worry, John. It's a female thing. We'll explain it to you and Frank over a big mug of coffee."

"Sounds good to me," Tom's father said, and all the men headed for the kitchen while we women moved in a cohesive group toward the stairs, our attic group now increased by three more than we'd had this morning.

IT TOOK US quite a while to bring the newcomers up to date with everything that had been happening. I was gratified—but not surprised—to see how readily they got into the swing of things. By some sort of common consensus, we started with the first items we'd found—the penny whistle, the hobby horse, the boater, Ida's hat, and so on. Mom, who after all was born a Martelson, took particular note of the hatbox Ida's hat had come in. Prissy Martelson's hat. After she finished examining the childish writing that Prissy had inscribed, she and the others exclaimed over the wedding dress, with its elaborate invitation, and were especially impressed by the beautifully embroidered tablecloth, even though it had that tear in it. By the time we got to the newspaper article and the photograph of Sadie's father, I could tell our newcomers were totally on board the history boat.

They are not on a boat. They are here in the attic.

I had the feeling we'd left something out, something important, but couldn't think what we might have forgotten. Oh well, it would wait. The journals were the big thing. "You're not going to believe what else we found," I finally said, and Dee started an impromptu drumroll on top of the steamer trunk. Maddy pulled three more chairs into our circle and we—I have to admit it—made a really big deal of revealing the journals. "We found them at the bottom of that trunk," I said, pointing.

"You found them," Sadie corrected. "We'll give you due credit for the find of the century."

Ida indicated the stacks of hatboxes and told the newcomers, "You'll each get a chance to choose a hat, too." She fluffed out her limp white feather. "But nobody's going to find one as good as mine."

"Except for mine," Maddy said. "And mine is actually good enough to wear in public."

Ida swung her head from side to side, for all the world like a stubborn mule. "My hat has character, and yours doesn't even come close."

"Hey, you two." I flapped my hands. "No arguments. Let's read the diaries for them."

"I think I'd rather hear the diaries than choose a hat," Mom said.

Ida and I re-read as far as we'd gotten before Mom and Sylvia and Esther showed up. After all the inevitable comments, Ida said, "We're planning to read the rest of them in chronological order. Luckily they're all dated."

"Except for Hubbard's first entry," I said in the interest of historical accuracy.

"It's my turn to keep going." Ida straightened her shoulders, as if preparing for a siege.

What is a seege? Mouse droppings! Why do I even ask? You do not answer me.

After one big meow and a funny little sneeze, Marmalade jumped off my lap and began grooming herself. I never give her baths, since she's an exceptionally clean cat ...

Off course I am.

... but I've often joked with Bob that Marmalade's fur is covered with a lifetime accumulation of cat saliva.

I do not drool! My tongue is very dry.

Of course, her tongue is so dry and scratchy, maybe she doesn't deposit much of anything on her fur when she licks it like that.

Ida's voice interrupted my thoughts, her voice pitched at a dramatically low tone. "This is the end of that entry from April nineteenth. Now we're all on the same page and all of us are hearing this for the first time."

I felt like we needed another one of Dee's drumrolls. As if she'd read my mind, Dee started slapping her lap rhythmically.

"Hush," Ida said, and the drumroll stopped.

My Hubbard and I will follow the trail of the wagons many

days from now, perhaps even six months or more down the road. He assures me that the two of us will travel much faster than the lumbering wagons and we well may find them settled in some warmer clime. By that time I may be with child. If that is an accomplished fact, my parents will have no choice but to give me my few possessions, including the four other precious books, which I have well hidden in the one personal box I was allowed to pack. This volume I will keep secreted beneath my overskirt so it will be with me when I leave.

"Wait a sec," Pat said. "How could she possibly think the Martins would find a place to stay just six months down the road? They didn't get here until 1745."

"She had no way of knowing that," Dee said. "Did anybody even know how big this country was back then?"

"A lot of people knew," Maddy said, "but I doubt Mary Frances had any way to translate a schoolroom map—if they even had one—into practical knowledge of just how far away Georgia was."

"And we have no indication," Carol said, "at least not in the old accounts I've read, that they even thought they'd go as far as Georgia. All they wanted to do was head south to warmer weather and to get away from all the dissension in Brandtburg."

"It's a wonder they didn't mutiny along the trail if they were expecting such a short trip," Pat said.

"Maybe some of them did," Carol suggested, "and we just don't know about it yet."

"We'll never find out if you don't let me keep reading."

I will stop now in order to write a short letter to my mother. I will slip it into one of the food baskets before we leave tomorrow so that, when the wagons stop for the midday meal, she will not fear that I am lost. I know she will understand why I married Hubbard, even though I fear my father will not. She will understand why Reverend Atherton hoped to heal the rift between the two families that has torn this valley apart.

I have just had a thought. I will leave the note for Mother here on my bed as soon as I can write it and will go to the outhouse. Nehemiah is always so proper about such things, he will not think to follow me there. But I will skirt around the privy and go thus to Hubbard's house tonight.

"It really sounds romantic," Maddy said, "but we know something had to have happened, because she ended up married to Homer."

Melissa curled her lip. "How could she have married Homer? She says she married Hubbard."

"Maybe somebody killed Hubbard the way Ira Brandt killed Myra Sue," Rebecca Jo said. She looked at Carol. "Do you know anything about this?"

"Nobody killed Hubbard. At least not while he was still in Vermont. He and Ira left Brandtburg a year or so after the Martins left, and the two of them disappeared without a trace."

"Then how…" Sadie's voice trailed off.

"The next entry," Ida said, "is dated May 6, 1741."

I did a quick calculation. "About two weeks after Myra Sue died."

"After she was murdered." Maddy's voice was colder than I'd ever heard it.

"Wait," I said. "Do you want to hear this from Hubbard's point of view? He's got a couple more April entries."

19 April 1741 early Sunday morning. I write this by the light of the moon, for I do not wish to risk awakening my brother by lighting a candle. I am wed. I am a married man. This night after the moon rose, I met Mary Frances as she clambered out of her friend Myra Sue's window—such a sight that was—and we hurried to the church where Reverend Atherton married us with only his wife as witness. Afterwards we had but a few hours, spent I am sorry to say, in the loft of the minister's barn. It was not the sort of wedding night I had planned, but it was necessary, for we had no other place. Seeing my wife in the achingly bright light of the moon last night was almost more than I could bear. Words fail me. I thought I loved Mary Frances before this, but now—now there is no end to the depth of my feelings for her.

"Oh, that's so sweet," Sadie said. "I love a good love story."

"I don't think this one is going to turn out so well," Ida said. "Not if she ended up married to Homer."

"He keeps writing," I said. "Same day but a few hours later."

Sunday just after dawn. I write this quickly for I needs must be on my way to church in but a few moments. I find myself writing in quite small letters, for I want these precious pages to last, yet I must put down the happenings of this morning. I was little pleased with my brother this morning, and I could not help but let my irritation affect my hands. I tied the makeshift bandage around his arm far too tightly, but I was in no mood to be gentle.

Ida interrupted me. "Bandage? What bandage?"

"Like you think we know the answer?"

I couldn't help but agree with Maddy's sarcasm. "He'll tell us," I said, and repeated a few words.

I was in no mood to be gentle. 'It was Homer Martin, I tell you!' Ira kept yelling.

I cared not. Ira and Homer Martin had words at the public house on Friday night. I doubt not that Ira's quick tongue probably provoked that fight and this morning's foray was retaliation from one of the Martins for some insult or other.

"What foray?" Maddy's question was echoed by several others.

"No clue," I said, "but I'll keep reading.

Sunday, 19 April 1741
Brandtburg

IT WAS WELL past the middle of Saturday night when Mary Frances returned and climbed in the window, which Myra Sue had left ajar. She refused to answer any of Myra Sue's whispered questions other than to say that she was more determined than ever to stay with her love, with her husband.

"You truly did wed him?"

"Aye. That I did." She sighed. "Truly indeed."

Even in what little moonlight trickled in through the window as Mary Frances closed the shutters, Myra Sue could see that something about her friend had changed. Something indefinable. Was it the way she held her shoulders, the way her back looked … defiant and yet supple somehow? "Come to bed," Myra Sue finally whispered. "Perhaps not to sleep, but at least to warm yourself a bit." She inched closer to her sister to make room for Mary Frances.

But Mary Frances did not seem cold, as cold as she should have felt considering the brisk spring air outside. If anything, she radiated heat, as if she had pulled summer into the room through the window, and there was a subtle smell to her, something Myra Sue had never smelled before.

Myra Sue wanted to ask her friend about what had gone on. Had she truly been married? But the night was cold, the bed was warm, and Mary Frances seemed distant somehow, as if she had climbed out the window as one person and come back in as another. Myra Sue fell into a deep sleep before she could ask any other questions.

Too soon, the roosters crowed and dawn light crept in. Myra Sue had to shake Mary Frances to awaken her. The younger two girls had already dressed and gone, teasing their sister as they left about being a slugabed on her wedding day. She had no time to think about her upcoming wedding to Homer Martin, though. There was much to do in last minute preparations for the journey the next day.

"Mary Frances, can you not awaken on my wedding day?" Myra Sue watched her friend yawn and stretch and then suddenly grimace as if in pain. "What is wrong? Are you hurt? Are you ill?"

"No. I am not hurt. Not truly." Mary Frances pushed the quilt away, stood, and turned to reach for her overskirt.

Myra Sue's eyes widened as she looked at the shift Mary Frances wore. "You *are* hurt!" Halfway down it, Myra Sue saw a spot of blood. "It is the full of the moon," Myra Sue whispered, afraid that her parents might overhear her, but the sounds from the hearth area were loud and cheerful. "It is not time for your courses. What has happened?"

So Mary Frances told her, briefly, but with a great deal of quiet wonder. And Myra Sue went to her own wedding later that morning with far more knowledge than most of the married women of Brandtburg had possessed on their wedding days. Her mother had given her some information two days beforehand, but the few scraps of knowledge confused Myra Sue more than enlightened her. Now, at least she knew a bit more of what to expect. Myra Sue hoped that Homer Martin would be as gentle with her as Hubbard had been, according to Mary Frances. But when she stood beside Homer at the front of the church and smelled his ale-drenched breath, she was afraid that might not be so.

FOR HUBBARD BRANDT, the day could not come fast enough. This was the day he would claim his wife. His wife. He loved the very thought of those words. As soon as Myra Sue Russell was wed to Homer Martin, Mary Frances would be free to slip away from Reverend Russell's church to join him. All Hubbard had to do was get through a service of his own. Reverend Atherton, who served the Brandt community, was even more long-winded than Reverend Russell, who preached to all the Martin clan. Mary Frances had once teasingly suggested that she might refuse to marry Hubbard, for marriage would mean she would have to endure what Hubbard had told her were interminable sermons every Sunday, preached in Reverend Atherton's reedy tenor voice. At least Reverend Russell's voice was pleasing to listen to.

Hubbard was dressed and ready for church well before first light. Ira was not, of course. Not after the carousing and drinking and raving from last night. Hubbard cut off a goodly hunk of bread and reached for the butter. He sniffed it. Not rancid. Good. Ever since the death of Ira's wife Felinda, the unmarried women of the Brandt clan flooded Ira's house with offerings of food. That was fine with Hubbard, although there were times like this when he and his brother could scarce finish one set of meals before another arrived—in the hands of a hopeful young woman. Hubbard was quite willing to accept the edible gifts. At least he knew that when he built his own house, one for himself and

Mary Frances, Ira would be well provisioned. He could just envision this house piled—and smelling—with butter that had turned, bread that was stale, and meat that had gone badly by.

Surely, Ira would remarry as soon as Hubbard moved out.

He should, he supposed have already built a house for himself and Mary Frances, but he had not found the words to justify his moving away from Ira's household. If only Reverend Atherton had consented to marry them sooner and in public rather than secret.

He scooped up a sizable hunk of the butter and slathered it on the bread. Before he could take a bite, Ira stepped gingerly from his room. Even in the dim morning light, Hubbard could see the red rims of Ira's eyes. Despite Ira's capacity for copious liquor consumption, Hubbard was sure he would have a sore head most of this day. "I am surprised to see you up so early, brother."

"Have to take a little trip," Ira said carefully, and almost tiptoed for the door.

Hubbard stifled a grin—it served him right to have a pounding head—and bit into the bread. From outside, he heard Blaze nicker softly.

SILAS MARTIN LIFTED his face into the mild early morning breeze that had sprung up as they crouched there. He was glad that he and his brother were downwind from the cabin, and even more glad that Ira Brandt did not have a dog. Ira Brandt was the kind who would shoot first and inquire later.

He regretted having let Homer talk him into attending him on this fool errand, but something in Silas felt a need to go along in case he had to protect his older brother. In case of what? He did not know—but then, with Homer, anything could happen. This was nothing new. Silas almost always felt obliged to accompany his brother just to be sure Homer did not get into more trouble than he could get out of.

No one could remember why the first angers had erupted between the Martin family and the Brandts. It may have been over land. It may have been over women. It may simply have been that one family did not like the words of the other. But the fathers of their grandsires had come to blows, and one of the Brandts had challenged one of the Martins to another fight. The Martin had won, of course. At least, that was the way the story had come down to Silas and his brother, from the older Martin men. Then, too, there was the incontrovertible evidence of the murder long ago of Silas and Homer's grandparents, Albion and Lucelia Martin. That it had been the Brandts who had committed the crime was something no Martin ever doubted.

There was seldom a gathering of men from the two families where fights did not erupt. Most often they tried simply to stay out of each other's ways. But blood had been spilled on occasion. Usually only from a broken nose or split lip, but sometimes there were cracked pates and broken arms.

"You cannot get any closer without risk that they will see you," Silas advised his brother.

Homer used the tip of his knife to remove a glob of grime from beneath one of his fingernails. "Shut your mouth, Silas. I can track a bear into her den." He slipped the knife back into his belt.

Silas wrinkled his nose. "It may be she would not see or hear you, but she would smell you a league off."

His brother turned aside, scratching idly at his armpit. "Stay here if you are afraid. I am going closer. I want to do this before the sun is up, and I can manage it by myself if you are too cowardly."

Silas would not let himself be drawn in by his brother's obvious ploy.

Homer pulled up the kerchief that was tied around his neck to cover the lower part of his face and tugged his cap—one of the many their grandmother had knitted for the two of them—lower over his forehead. When Silas did not move, Homer shook his head and inched away, melting around the base of the hickory tree where they had been watching the side of the small cabin. Homer's plan to tip over Ira's outhouse was one Silas wanted nothing to do with.

Silas continued to crouch beside the hickory, and wondered about his brother. Homer would be wed to Myra Sue Russell in but a few more hours, at the end of the Sunday church service. Yet now he was readying himself to play a prank on Ira Brandt. It boded no good.

Silas was no coward. At least, he did not think he was. But he was sorry he had agreed to come with his brother on this particular venture. He had done it as much to keep Homer from making some harebrained mistake, but now that Homer had eased away from Silas, Silas felt sure that approaching the Brandt cabin was the most rabbit-brained of all Homer's ill-planned schemes.

He stretched his legs cautiously, anxious to be sure they would respond in case he had to run.

This Brandt cabin was well separated from the others. There was, of course, a wide expanse of open land around the cabin, but Ira Brandt's wife Felinda had died the previous spring, and Ira Brandt had farmed out his four living sons to his older sister, and his three daughters—all of them too young yet to cook for Ira—to Edward and Julia Dillingham, who had lost three of their eight children in a tragic house fire two years before. He had given Felinda's goats to Mistress Dillingham as well. Silas tried to imagine Ira Brandt having the patience to milk a goat. It was a scene he could not visualize.

Ira seemed unable—or unwilling—to get another woman to marry him, so there was no food growing in the clearing. Felinda's kitchen garden had long since gone to weeds, and the surrounding space was filled with the bright green grasses of a spring that had come earlier than usual. The grasses gave no cover, except where they sprang more abundantly at the base of the rickety posts of Ira's spindly fence. Two posts leaned precariously. The frost had been particularly deep this past winter, and all the fences had suffered. Ira should have reset his posts long before this.

Silas wondered why Hubbard, the younger brother, had not done the work. He need not wonder, though. Younger brothers sometimes refused to do an older brother's work for him, just as Silas had this day refused to help Homer tip the Brandt's outhouse. Perhaps he and Hubbard had more in common that they had differences between them.

He regretted that he had never taken the time to know Hubbard Brandt better. And now it was too late. After tomorrow when Silas left Brandtburg with the rest of the Martin families, he would never see Hubbard Brandt again.

He poked his head carefully around the side of the tree. Ira Brandt's horse, Blaze, whuffled from the far side of the clearing. He was a big, friendly gelding who was, from what Silas had seen, as even tempered as any horse could be, except perhaps for Devil, Silas's own horse. Fortunately, Blaze was generally quiet, which Devil almost never was.

Silas watched Homer creep along the fence line that passed a few feet behind the cabin's outhouse. In the distance, he heard a horse approaching, its hoofbeats distinct in the still morning air. Homer must have heard it as well, for he froze behind a tall clump of last year's Joe Pye Weed interwoven with heavy tufts of wild grasses. Silas was happy to see that Homer was showing some discretion, although this long before dawn, it would be hard for anyone who did not know Homer was there to distinguish him from the shadows of the thick weeds.

Silas heard the cabin door open and saw a wedge of candlelight spread across the yard. Blaze nickered once more. Ira Brandt, just barely visible, wove his way around the corner. Toward Homer.

Ira pulled on the outhouse door, which did not open readily. He swore and pounded on the warped planks, tried again, then turned aside and proceeded to unlace his pants beside the fence. Too loose, they dropped around his ankles. If he had stopped a few feet short of the fence, he might not have been hurt, but he let go with a healthy stream of urine directly onto the heavy clump of weeds that Homer hid behind. Silas watched in horror as Homer erupted over the fence, drawing his knife as he did so.

Even drunk, Ira was a formidable enemy, but in midstream and with his drawers constricting his legs, he was at something of a disadvantage. Ira shouted, stumbled, and fell toward the fence. Homer slashed at him. Silas saw the arc of dark liquid as blood spurted. Ira howled his rage, and Ira's brother spilled from the cabin. Homer vaulted across the fence and fled back toward the tree line where Silas had already risen.

If Silas had known Hubbard and Ira would both be awake and fully dressed this early in the morning, he might have been able to talk Homer out of such an ill-fated jaunt, but he did not take the time to reason that out. He joined Homer's retreat. Thanks be to glory that both young men could run like deer in the forest, far faster than the bulkier Brandt men, one of whom had to raise his breeches before he could run at all. Homer and Silas were lucky in that, for they had to circle far through the woods to reach the Martin cabin.

By the time the two brothers made it to their own house, they were winded, but there was no sign of the Brandts.

"He could not have recognized me," Homer said when he finally got his breath back. "Otherwise they would have come here directly."

"You think you are safe, then?" Silas was sure he sounded as incredulous as he felt. "Ira Brandt has never been known to ignore even a slight, much less an offense such as this." Homer shrugged, but Silas, almost too angry to speak, went on doggedly, all the while knowing that his brother would not listen to reason. He never had. "You drew blood. You expect him not to take some sort of revenge?"

"He could not have recognized me." Homer sounded sullen, but Silas could feel his brother's undercurrent of pride at having bested a Brandt. Homer began to laugh. "You should have heard him grunt when I appeared so suddenly."

"I did hear him. You mark my words, brother. He did not need to recognize you. He will blame all the Martins, and you as the purported leader of our family will bear the brunt of his anger. You may think it is humorous now, but I fear you will yet rue this morning's caper."

WHEN HUBBARD HEARD his brother's shout, he took a moment to swallow one more bite and then ran out and around to the back in time to see a man hightailing it toward the woods beyond the fence. He ran to Ira's assistance, appalled at the sight of so much blood already showing red in the growing light of dawn.

"Go get the bastard," Ira snarled.

"No! We need to wrap your hand lest you bleed to death."

"'Tis but a scratch. Go get him, I tell you."

"That is far more than a scratch, Ira."

"May I be of assistance?" The reedy voice from above and behind them startled them both.

"Reverend Atherton?" Hubbard wondered if he was merely imagining the man who had so recently—so few hours ago—joined him in holy wedlock to Mary Frances Garner.

"Your neighbor's child, Benjamin Grant, died just an hour after I …"—the minister looked closely at Hubbard—"after I … uh … retired last night. I have been sitting with the grieving parents. I needs must prepare for church services now, but I heard your shout as I rode past."

"Need you me to help dig the grave?" Hubbard served in that capacity at times, and it suited him well to help in this case, for the Grants had been good neighbors. Their oldest unmarried daughter, in fact, was the one who had set her cap most determinedly for Ira. It was her bread and her butter Hubbard had eaten only moments before.

Reverend Atherton skewered him with a stern look. "You know full well we cannot labor on the Sabbath. Tomorrow will be soon enough. They have placed the boy's body in the springhouse."

Hubbard followed his brother toward the house, wondering all the way about the identity of the assailant. Homer Martin, most likely. He was surprised that Homer was alone. Usually he hauled his brother Silas with him. Hubbard had always had the impression that Silas was a reluctant participant at best. Rather the way he himself tended to be a reluctant participant in Ira's schemes.

The more he thought about it, the more he realized that he and Silas Martin had a great deal in common. The man was a fine artist and an exceptional woodworker. He had an obstreperous older brother. He seemed always to be in his brother's shadow.

Hubbard regretted that he had never taken the time to know Silas Martin better. And now it was too late. After tomorrow when the Martins left Brandtburg, he would never seen Silas Martin again.

Ahead of him, Ira swore when the door did not yield to his shove. Hubbard stepped past him and lifted the latch.

Sunday morning, 19 April 1741
Brandtburg

SUSAN BREETON MAY have been only twelve, but she had always been one to go after what she wanted no matter who tried to dissuade her. There were only seven years between her and Silas Martin, and while Susan acknowledged that perhaps she was still too young to be considered of marriageable age, she knew time would eventually take care of that problem.

In the meantime, she hated Sophrona Blanchard. The Blanchards were part of the Brandt clan—Sophrona's mother was sister to Mister Ira Brandt. The Blanchards lived only a stone's throw from the Breeton's house. It had pained Susan to see the way Sophrona hung onto the arm of Silas Martin every chance she had. And now that Silas had distanced himself from Sophrona Blanchard, and no longer came to call on her in the evenings, Susan gloried in the possibilities.

Mother and Mistress Blanchard were always cordial to each other—perhaps they had to be since they lived so close by—and Mother had remarked once that Mistress Blanchard and Sophrona had the patience of saints to have taken in Ira Brandt's four boys, for of course much of the care of Ira Marcus, Ira Alonzo, Ira Prentiss, and Ira Samuel fell on the eldest daughter, Sophrona. "Ira Brandt," Susan's mother had once said, "has a swollen head indeed to give all four of his boys his own name, as if he seeks to enlarge himself somehow." Her tone moderated, though, as she went on to say, "How sad that Felinda Brandt died a-birthing. It is no wonder that Ira gave away his children, for he could not have cared for them."

Within two months of that pronouncement, Mother herself died in childbed. Susan had feared at first that Father might give her away, but Susan and MaryAnne were both of an age to take on the ordering of the household, unlike the small Brandt girls, none of whom was older than five.

Father said the Brandts and everyone related to them were evil. Susan tried to fit seventeen-year-old Sophrona into that category, but she had to admit that Sophrona did not look evil. Rather, she looked merely silly, always fiddling with those improbable curls of hers. Susan had no intention of ever doing anything that ridiculous when she was of an age. If she were honest with herself, she would have to admit that she would not be able to. Susan's hair, long enough that she could sit on it, was straighter than a dowsing wand. At least a dowsing wand had a slight bend to it. But Susan's hair had none.

Mother, just the day before she died, had said Susan's hair was her crowning glory. "But do not be vain about it, my daughter," Mother had said as she lay there, almost too weak to lift her hand.

Susan was not sure she needed to pay attention to what Mother had said, though, since she had overheard Mother tell MaryAnne not to be vain about her cooking, and Pioneer not to be vain about his hunting prowess, and even little Willy not to be vain about his way with animals. That seemed to Susan to be what mothers said before they died. "Do not be vain."

Well, Susan was not vain. She was jealous.

Silas may have scorned Sophrona, but Sophrona still had a

wooden plate that Susan coveted, for Silas had carved it for her—for Sophrona.

What made it so special was the design Silas had cut into it. Sophrona had bragged about it, how the SM for Silas Martin intertwined with the SB for Sophrona Blanchard. SB could just as well mean Susan Breeton, or so Susan told herself. And now that Susan's whole family would be leaving the valley on the morrow, Susan had decided she had to have the plate for herself.

She waited beside the brook, hiding behind the enormous willow tree that grew between the two houses. The arching wands curved down around her with their early spring green leaves serving as a screen. MaryAnne had not yet begun to gather in her two brothers to get them ready for church. Susan was already dressed and ready, as she had been careful to show her older sister before stepping outside, ostensibly to go to the outhouse. Far behind her, Susan could hear Willy romping with Lucky, his year-old black and white dog. He would pay no attention to what Susan was doing. If only those Blanchards would hurry a bit, Susan thought. How long could it possibly take to ready themselves for church? They usually left well before Susan and her family did. The Brandts and all their clan attended services at Reverend Atherton's sturdy stone church on the far side of the village. The Breetons went to Reverend Russell's church, much closer by, for it sat near the edge of the Martin's side of Brandtburg, the eastern half.

No one knew just when the two groups had separated into two disparate communities, each with its own church, and Susan did not really care to know. She just knew that the Blanchards had farther to walk and therefore had to leave earlier.

Mother—when she was alive—often spoke pleasantly to Mistress Blanchard, Sophrona's mother. Susan could not understand why the fathers all hated each other while the women seemed, for the most part, to get along well enough. Maybe once she was grown up herself, she would see the sense of it.

Behind her, she heard MaryAnne call to Willy and Pioneer to quit their larking around and come inside.

Within moments, Sophrona, her parents, and all her brothers and sisters, including the four Ira's—as everyone called the four boys who had been left motherless when Felinda Merchant Brandt died, just weeks before Mother died last year—exited through their front door and turned left into the lane that ran in front of both houses. Susan counted to fifty, giving them plenty of time to be well on their way. She slipped from behind the willow, ran past the Blanchard's privy, around the kitchen garden, and ducked through Sophrona's back door. It took her only moments—although it seemed like a lifetime to her—to locate the wooden plate. She had thought long and hard about how she would secrete it. Her sister MaryAnne would never have allowed her to take it, much less to keep it. So MaryAnne must not know.

As quickly as she could, she wrapped the plate securely in a long piece of cloth she had appropriated from the ragbag, raised her dress, and tied the rag tightly to her upper leg. She took a few tentative steps around the room, making sure the plate would not fall out of its improvised sling. It banged against her leg, but she could not arrange it in such a way to make it more comfortable. She tightened the sling one more time and then walked back to her house.

"There you are," MaryAnne said when Susan slipped inside. "I am glad you decided to join us."

Susan ignored the mockery. She did feel a little bit bad about having saddled MaryAnne with the chore of cleaning up both the boys. Pioneer could get himself dirty just walking across the room. He seemed to attract messes wherever he went. Susan laid a hand on his scrawny shoulder. Even though he was a year older than she, he still acted like a child half the time. "You look as if you have been rolling in the leaves," she remarked, and set to work combing his unruly hair, making sure all the while that her plate-burdened leg did not brush against him. It would not do to have him question the lump underneath her skirts. Within minutes, the boys were ready and Father led the way out the door, where they turned right and headed for Reverend Russell's wooden church building.

Throughout the service, the plate dug into the back of Susan's legs. Every time she tried to squirm into a more comfortable position, MaryAnne would turn her head and stare until Susan settled down. By the time the service was over, Susan's left leg was asleep, and she almost tripped trying to exit the pews.

Within minutes, though, none of that mattered. After the service, after the death of Myra Sue Russell Martin, nobody paid any attention to Susan, and she was able to slip the plate into the bag where she had folded her extra dress, her other apron, and the five pairs of her spare stockings.

2000

"THERE ARE JUST two—no, three—more paragraphs in this entry," I said. "Remember, this is Sunday, April nineteenth." It helped me to keep the timeline straight in my head.

"The day before the Martins left the valley," Carol said.

"The day after Hubbard married Mary Frances," Maddy reminded us all.

Despite my anger at my brother's ready intransigence, I cannot help but wonder who the man was who sliced Ira's arm. He sprinted away from the outhouse, as if he had been planning to tip it over. My brother and I pulled such a stunt ourselves when we were but gangling boys, laughing the entire time. Our father found us out, and made us build a new privy for the Grants, since the one we tipped came apart at the joints the moment it crashed to the ground. I was careful this morning not to let Ira see my amusement.

Sadie chuckled. "Things haven't changed much in all these years. Tipping outhouses was a favorite prank among the boys when I was a child."

It didn't sound like much fun to me, but I supposed boys might think it was hilarious. "It doesn't sound like it was a boy, though. Hubbard calls him"—I looked back a few lines—"*the man who sliced Ira's arm.*"

Nobody had anything to say to that, so I kept going where I'd left off.

The Martin—it was most likely Homer, for it sounds like what he might try even on his wedding morning. I cannot imagine how any bridegroom can want to endanger himself just before his wedding, but Homer Martin has ever seemed to think he is incapable of dying. He might have done us a favor had he been successful, for our privy hole is practically full, and we desperately need to dig another, but Ira keeps refusing to begin the project, and I have no desire to dig it by myself.

'Divest yourself of that bloody shirt,' I told him, 'and get yourself ready for church. Perhaps the elder Miss Grant will be willing to sew you another one, since this is badly stained and ripped almost beyond repair.'

Ira grunted, growled, and grumbled, but eventually betook himself off to complete his dressing for the day, and I take these few moments to record this small event for eternity. I am sorry Ira was injured, but it is so slight a cut despite the copious blood, I am certain his skin will forget it soon, even though Ira himself will no doubt nurse his anger over it for many a day. Still, Ira with his breeches around his ankles was a sight most droll. I will share it with Mary Frances when we are in a house of our own, and we will laugh about it, I have no doubt.

"If Mary Frances left the next morning," Maddy said, "she and Hubbard must never have had a chance to laugh about the outhouse."

"Maybe they did," Melissa argued. "Does he say anything else about it?"

"Nope," I said. "That's it for this one. Your turn, Ida."

"When's your next entry dated?"

"Hubbard's, you mean? April twentieth."

"Mine's not till May sixth," she said. "You go on reading so we can keep this in some sort of order."

Sunday, 19 April 1741
Brandtburg

CHARLOTTE ELLIS GAZED around the crowded church. She did not want to leave the next day on what she was convinced would be a doomed trek through the wilderness. If her husband had not died fourteen years before, if she had given birth to sons to support her instead of just the two useless girls, if she had known how to survive without help, she would never have moved into her sister's house. Sarah was kind enough, Charlotte supposed, but Charlotte did not care to be an object of charity. Charity was something one gave, when it was convenient, not something one should have to accept.

She watched as Willem Breeton and his motherless children filed into a pew across the aisle from them. Willem would be married again within the year, Charlotte felt certain. Men needed women to handle the household and the children. Charlotte could remember when Willem was just a stick-thin boy, six years younger than herself. Six years wasn't too large a gap.

What was she thinking? The last thing she needed was to disrupt her life. And she would rather be horsewhipped than to run after a widower, no matter how broad his shoulders, no matter how captivating his smile. Of course, if he chose to run after her ... She pulled herself firmly together and marshaled her thoughts to focus on the marriage service that would happen after the end of this day's sermonizing.

What a shame Myra Sue had to be saddled with an illiterate, pitiful excuse for a man like Homer Martin.

This marriage was all the fault of Charlotte's sister Sarah. Sarah wanted grandchildren, and she had been perfectly willing to sacrifice her daughter to get them. Well, Myra Sue was making her bed and she would have to lie in it.

Two pews ahead of Charlotte, Mistress Anthina Shipleigh sat like a brooding chicken, her voluminous, ill-knit shawls twisted around her scrawny shoulders. Beside her on her left were her six homely daughters, and on her right crouched her husband, Elias Shipleigh, whom Charlotte had never known to do a decent day's work. Their worthless son Colton was crammed into his seat beside his father at the end of the pew, with his arms crossed over his far too ample stomach. For such a young man to be so portly, he had to be as useless as his father, doing naught but eating everything he could get his mouth around. Charlotte blamed Mistress Shipleigh, of course. If she conducted her household affairs properly, she would have had better children. If Elias Shipleigh had married her, Charlotte, instead of Anthina, he might have amounted to something. Charlotte would certainly have kept him in line.

Elias turned his head suddenly and caught Charlotte studying him. He turned back around, but not before Charlotte saw the self-satisfied smirk on his face.

It was all Anthina's fault. Charlotte had been on the verge of getting Elias to propose to her when Anthina suddenly sprouted up like a garish toadstool in the middle of a patch of perfectly acceptable mushrooms. She had turned Elias' head so fast, Charlotte had hardly known what had happened. And now they had all those children while Charlotte had settled for Rupell Ellis and had only the two daughters. Of course, Anthina had become scrawny and ill-favored over the years, while Charlotte was pleased to know she had kept her own softly rounded shape and the smoothness of her own face.

On Charlotte's left, Sarah sighed, as if the wedding this day were a happy event. People getting married? That was never happy as far as Charlotte was concerned. Necessary perhaps, but seldom happy. They were fools who expected bliss in marriage. She had made the mistake of saying so once after Sarah was married to the Reverend Anders Russell and after Charlotte had come to live with them. The scene was from so long ago it seemed wreathed in smoke. Sarah had asked, "If no one married, where then would the children come from?"

The naiveté of the question, as if Sarah were dealing with a child with no knowledge of the world, had stung her to the bone. She had glared at her younger sister from under the thick ridge of her heavy eyebrows. "You would not speak to me like this if you were not married."

"But I *am* married," Sarah said, "and we are both dependent on the Reverend."

They were only thirteen months apart in age, but Charlotte always felt at a distinct disadvantage whenever she and her sister had a disagreement. Even on the few occasions when they were in accord with each other's opinions, Sarah always seemed to take the lead.

After all this time, Charlotte still felt as if Sarah expected her to grovel. She had been putting up with this arrangement for fourteen years. When her husband first died, she and her two small daughters had been taken in by the Reverend Anders Russell—because he was a minister and this was his Christian duty, she knew, and Charlotte's sister Sarah was the minister's wife, so they had to offer her a home. Charity, after all, was a requirement. Charlotte had thought the arrangement would be temporary. But the years had rolled along and Charlotte became a ready-made nursemaid as Sarah bore child after child.

Charlotte had never been one to fawn over sticky fingers and pudgy cheeks. She had treated Sarah's children well enough, and they had certainly turned out to be well behaved, but now Sarah's girls—especially the two younger ones, Anne and Edna—seemed to think Charlotte was an object of pity for having lost her husband so early on in life. And then, for Charlotte not to have remarried made her an object of their ridicule. Charlotte was sure her nieces thought no man would have her. It wasn't that. She had experienced enough of marriage with one man. Cruel as Rupell had been, she never wanted to risk another marriage, even considering it was the only way most women had to care for themselves. Husbands and children. None of which she had. Well, she had the two girls of course, but they hardly counted. She had no sons to take care of her in her old age. Which was still a long way off, thank the heavens.

Nor had she had any offers of marriage in all this time she had been widowed. She would have refused them, of course. But it would have been nice if she had been asked. She adjusted her bonnet and sat a little straighter. If she had to endure watching that slip of a girl, Myra Sue Russell, getting married, she could at least do it without looking uncomfortable. After all, Myra Sue was her niece.

The wedding was a simple affair. Ordinarily, as everyone knew, they should have gathered at the home of the bride's parents, had the ceremony, and then celebrated afterwards, but with the Russell house—and every other house—filled with crates of household goods, and with most of the food already packed, there was hardly any room for the bridal pair, much less for the wedding guests.

So here they were in church and now would have to sit on these uncomfortable benches even longer than usual. Thank goodness this week the Reverend Anders Russell's sermon wasn't as long-winded as it usually was. After a final prayer and the Amen, Homer Martin stood and Myra Sue walked up to stand beside him. They spoke their words, and Myra Sue's father brought out the parish marriage register for them to sign. She signed her new name, Myra Sue Russell Martin, and Homer made his mark, and it was done. It was about time. Charlotte's stomach had begun to make some uncomfortable rumblings. Charlotte, of course, looked over at her daughter Martha, as if to reprimand her for the noise.

Moments later, as they walked out of the small church, Charlotte saw Mary Frances Garner slip between Myra Sue and Homer. "She is mine for just one moment longer," the chit of a girl declared and threw her arms around Myra Sue. The two women hugged—they were both near tears, anyone could see that—and then held each other at arm's length. Behind Mary Frances, Homer could not even be bothered to watch. His unconcern reminded Charlotte disturbingly of Rupell, her own late husband. Apparently Homer Martin was as cold-hearted as Rupell had been.

At just that moment, Ira Brandt rode into the clearing, his hand wrapped in a blood-soaked bandage. "No happiness for you, son of a coward, and coward yourself!" he cried as he pointed his fowling piece at Homer Martin. The explosion came before anyone in the crowd could react. Ira wheeled around and spurred Blaze into a dead run away from town.

Homer Martin stood frozen on the doorstep of the church. Myra Sue, his new wife, lay crumpled in the dirt in front of him. Mary Frances flung herself on top of her friend's motionless body and screamed and screamed and screamed.

Charlotte had been momentarily stunned by what had happened, of course. But really! Could not anyone stifle Mary Frances Garner's frenzy?

2000

"MONDAY EVENING," I READ. Looking ahead a few words, I gulped and went back to the start of that entry.

Monday evening 20 April 1741. I can barely write. God forgive me, but I would willingly kill my brother at this moment, for he has thwarted my plans.

"Thwarted his plans?" Pat snorted. "Ya think he's talking about how Ira murdered Myra Sue Russell?"

"That sure would put a damper on his plot to sneak away with

Mary Frances," Dee said.

The two of them giggled a bit, until they sensed a wave of disapproval from the rest of us. "It's hardly something to laugh about," Ida said.

"But this was almost two hundred years ago," Pat said.

I clamped my jaws together so hard I almost bit my tongue. After taking a deep breath, I ran my gloved finger over that last sentence. "Do you think Hubbard really did kill Ira?"

"Not right away," Carol said. "Remember? I told you the two of them left Brandtburg eventually."

"It's hard to believe Hubbard didn't follow Mary Frances right away." Sadie indicated the diary I held. "Not after writing all that stuff about how much he loved her."

The inn and public house at Knowlton Lake in Random is now but an unattainable dream.

Again, I stopped reading. "Random? Where's that?"

"It's a town a few miles west of Brandtburg," Carol said. "It sounds like he was maybe planning to take her there?"

"Like a honeymoon?" Pat asked.

"If I were the two of them," Maddy said, "I'd want to get as far away from Ira as I could."

Yesterday just after the Sunday services, my brother shot and killed Homer Martin's new wife. I saw him as he bolted from town headed north. I followed him, not knowing what was wrong, but fearful that Ira might do himself some harm for he seemed in a most terrible frenzy. When I found him, he confessed the murder to me. Before I could coax—or bully—him into returning with me, we were overtaken by dark, and the next morning I woke to find that he was gone. Good riddance to him. When I returned to Brandtburg without him this morning, Mistress Ellis did her vindictive best to disconcert me by telling me of the fighting that erupted between the two families while I was gone. My heart is sore not only with the loss—for now—of my wife, but because one of my nephews was slain by a stray shot. If Ira ever has the courage to return home, I fear our sister will never forgive him, and I must say I agree with her attitude. She has raised those four boys of Ira's as her own for the past year, and this loss is most grievous to her.

"I wonder if they ever made it up," Rebecca Jo mused.

"Carol told us they left town together that autumn," Sadie pointed out, "so they must have at least been speaking to each other."

"That doesn't mean Hubbard forgave him," Ida said with finality.

"I meant Ira and his sister," Rebecca Jo said. "His murder of Myra Sue led directly to the fight where Ira's son—the one he'd given away to his sister—was killed. Am I right?" She looked around the room and waited for our nods. "Could she ever forgive him?"

Naturally, there was no answer to that.

Sunday, 19 April 1741
Brandtburg

HUBBARD AND MARY FRANCES had agreed, after their first plan was thwarted by Myra Sue's insistence that Mary Frances be at her wedding, to meet Sunday in the early afternoon, as soon as the midday meal was completed. "I will be able to slip away then," she had assured him. Hubbard intended to arrive early at the meeting place—a secluded glade in the nearby woods. From thence he would take her away to an inn near Knowlton Lake in the town of Random. It was a long ride, more than a dozen miles, and they would have to ford the North Branch of the Nulhegan River to get there, but Star was strong enough to carry them both, and Hubbard looked forward to having his wife's arms twined around him as they rode together. He wanted to be sure Star was fresh, however, so he intended to walk to church this morning, walk home, load Star with the supplies he had stowed away in the hayloft for this event—food, blankets, and a roll of canvas in case they had to take shelter from the weather—and leave the letter he had already written to his brother. He would still have plenty of time to be at the rendezvous well ahead of his beloved.

"If we stay away for a fortnight or two, there will be time for the consternation to die down," he had told her. Also, he had not wanted to spend the first nights of his married life in a house that was sure to be filled with the anger of his brother at Hubbard's betrayal, for so Ira would surely see it.

HUBBARD AND IRA always walked to church of a Sunday, but this morning, Ira had saddled Blaze and, despite Hubbard's objections, had doggedly insisted, "You may walk, brother, but I intend to ride."

His hand must be hurting much worse than he will admit, Hubbard thought as he walked briskly into town. Ira's head, more likely, was still pounding from the excess of drink the night before. Blaze had a steady gait that would not jostle a rider overmuch. At least Ira's hand had ceased to bleed. The bandage had still been relatively white as Ira had ridden away.

Hubbard could barely contain his impatience once he was seated beside his brother in the modest church building. Reverend Atherton's reedy voice went on and on in what the good reverend probably thought was a solemn tone, but sounded more like the pattering of early spring rain on a thin roof. Hubbard wondered if the minister was aware of how many of his congregation fell asleep during the service. Even now Hubbard could see a number of women using their shoulders to prop up their drowsing husbands.

Reverend Atherton spoke this morning of the responsibility of neighbors, leaning rather heavily on the story of the Good Samaritan.

Hubbard tried to envision just how and when he would see Mary Frances, his wife—his wife! They had planned it last night in the loft of Reverend Atherton's barn after they were wed. Not for long, as they had had other activities on their mind.

He could not suppress a wide grin of sheer delight, but ducked his head as soon as he noticed the parson's frown. He schooled his face as best he could, but could not help marveling that no one around him seemed to notice the light he was sure must be streaming from his eyes, from his hands, from his very body.

His wife. *She needs must be with her friend Myra Sue now*, he thought, and tried not to resent the time that Myra Sue's wedding ceremony and this Sunday service required him to spend away from Mary

Frances.

Beside him, his brother stirred uncomfortably. Hubbard could see from the corner of his eye that the bandage he had contrived was discolored with fresh, bright red blood. Ira's hands were clenched so tightly in his lap, Hubbard wondered if he would ever be able to move his fingers again. There would be time after the service, and before he left to meet Mary Frances, so he could change Ira's bandage. Would that Ira would take another wife soon so his care would be in her hands instead of in Hubbard's. Mayhap their eager young bread-baking neighbor would take over the care of Ira's wound once Hubbard was gone.

As soon as the service ended, Ira pushed his way through the milling throng of friends and relatives, and practically ran to Blaze. Hubbard could see him over the heads of the people around him, and wondered at his haste. He was himself anxious to get away, but did not want anyone to suspect anything, so he took time to greet neighbors and to say a few words to Reverend Atherton, who gave him a knowing smile, before he sauntered away from the church and headed for home, only to find Ira not there. The bandaging would have to be done by someone else, then, for Hubbard did not intend to wait.

He had barely strapped the blankets and the packet of food onto Star when he heard Blaze thunder toward the house. He had a glimpse of Ira's face—and the blood-soaked bandage around Ira's arm—before horse and rider disappeared, headed north, away from town, toward Gore Mountain. Without thinking, Hubbard vaulted onto Star and took off after his brother. Star was fast, but Blaze was faster. By the time Hubbard caught up with Ira far from Brandtburg, both horses were dangerously lathered. Ira stood beside a tall oak, knocking his forehead against the trunk repeatedly. Hubbard flung the reins any which way and barreled into Ira, knocking him flat. "What sort of fool thing are you up to now?"

"I killed her," Ira blubbered.

"What are you talking about? Get hold of yourself."

"I meant to kill Homer, but the shot went wide."

Hubbard felt icy fingers crawl along the back of his neck. Mary Frances had been at the wedding. She would have been standing next to Myra Sue. "Who did you kill?"

"The shot went far wide. She was not even standing next to Homer. There was one between them."

Hubbard already had his hands around his brother's throat before Ira choked out, "I killed Myra Sue Russell."

"IT WAS HOMER'S fault," Ira insisted as they made a hasty camp in the dark. These woods were not conducive to nighttime riding.

Ira had been in favor of leaving the valley altogether, but Hubbard knew his brother would have to pay for his crime. It could so easily have been Mary Frances. It could have so easily been *his* wife that Ira killed, rather than Homer Martin's wife. He was appalled at the thought that Ira might be hanged for the murder, but … but what if Ira had killed Mary Frances instead?

There was a simple answer to that. Ira would not have lived long enough to face a hanging.

Hubbard knew without a doubt he would have killed Ira in his rage and left his body here to be devoured by painters and whatever other animals roamed this forest.

But then Hubbard would have admitted his crime—how could he not?—and been hanged, the sooner to join his wife in … No. She would have been in Heaven, while he, as his brother's murderer, would have been consigned to Hell.

"It was Homer's fault," Ira said again, interrupting Hubbard's dire thoughts. He waved his bandaged hand practically in Hubbard's face. "If he had not knifed me, my aim would have been true. If my hand had not been injured, I could have held my weapon more steadily. It was Homer's fault."

Hubbard stopped listening. He hardly thought of anything else other than how to get to Mary Frances now that the community—both communities—would be up in arms. But Ira Michael was his brother. His badly injured brother.

And he knew without a doubt that Mary Frances would not agree to leave with him. Not now. Not yet. She would need time to mourn her friend, time to attend the burial. Surely they would bury Myra Sue today, now, this evening. Reverend Russell did not hold so firmly to the requirements not to labor on the Sabbath the way Reverend Atherton did. At the least, they would bury her the next morn before they left

Brandtburg.

As long as Hubbard returned to Brandtburg before the Martin families left on the morrow, he would be able to spirit Mary Frances away from them. He would. He knew he would.

The last thing Ira said before he wrapped himself in his blanket that night was, "It was Homer Martin's fault. I never intended to kill a woman."

Hubbard refused to give him the comfort of an answer. It could so easily have been Mary Frances.

When Hubbard woke the next morning well before dawn, Blaze was gone. The food and blankets were gone. Ira was gone.

Monday 20 April 1741

WHAT ELSE COULD Hubbard do but head for home? Ira had food and a blanket and Blaze. He would have to fend for himself. Hubbard could not risk going after his brother, for he had to be back in Brandtburg before the Martin clan left.

Surely by now Myra Sue's body would be underground and Mary Frances must be wondering where he was. He needed to be there to comfort her.

He straightened himself in his saddle. He needed first to go to the Russell's church and pay his respects at Myra Sue's grave. He might even find his wife there.

He had a moment's doubt—surely Reverend Russell would not let a lynch mob—no. He need not fear for his life. The Martins would all be angry, justifiably so, but he, Hubbard, had been nowhere near the scene of the accident.

His hands jerked so hard on the reins, Star threw her head upwards. "I apologize, Star." It was no *accident* that killed Myra Sue Russell. An accident perhaps that *she* had been hit rather than Homer Martin, but the deed was clearly murder. The identity of the victim did not change that. His brother was a murderer. His brother would be hanged.

The first person he saw when he rode into town was Charlotte Ellis, who motioned him angrily to the side of the road in front of the public house and told him the ghastly tale of the near massacre from the day before. It took the death of a child to stop the madness—for that was what it had been—but Mistress Ellis did not mention the child until her parting shot.

CHARLOTTE ELLIS WAS not that enamored of children in general—she had been cured of any such feelings through her years of caring for her own and her sister's offspring—and the dead child had been a Brandt after all. Not that she would have wished his death, but there was no telling what else might have happened if the boy had not been in the way of a stray bullet.

The boy was well known to this man who sat so high and mighty on his horse in front of her. She was sure she knew how to cut him down a peg or two. But she would wait to do it. The anticipation was delightful.

"I hope you are proud of that brother of yours," she snarled at Hubbard. "Not only is Myra Sue Russell Martin dead at the hand of your brother, but the resulting fight left Calvin Garner with a knife wound in his leg all the way down to the bone." Or so Augusta Garner had said. Charlotte had not seen fit to visit. Sitting with injured people was not her favorite activity, and there were plenty of other women who would be willing to do what they saw as their duty to sit and commiserate with Augusta.

"If you need assistance digging Miss Myra Sue's grave," Hubbard Brandt said, "I will help. It is the least I can do."

"We don't need the help of a Brandt. We do not plan to stay to bury our dead. We will take them with us and bury them at the first churchyard we find along the way." Charlotte settled her basket more firmly on her wide hip. "Far from Brandtburg and far from you murderous Brandts. I must go now. I have more important things to do than to waste my time speaking with someone like you."

"You said you would take *them* with you. Were there others who died?"

Charlotte thought he sounded distressed. As well he might. "We have many people injured," she told him, "and Mistress Geonette Black Surratt lost her father in the fight. She is sore distraught." Mister Black would not be much of a loss, Charlotte felt sure, even to his widow, but she need not mention that to Hubbard Brandt.

She watched the play of emotions on Hubbard Brandt's face. Almost as if the question were being torn from him, he asked, "What of the Brandts? Were there deaths in my family as well?"

"Only your mother's brother." Charlotte felt certain there had not been much love lost between Hubbard Brandt and his scurrilous Uncle Oliver Simon, so she was not surprised when he simply tipped his hat and turned to go.

HUBBARD TIPPED HIS hat to Mistress Ellis and touched Star gently with his heels. He was intrigued by the combination of venom and elation that Mistress Ellis had displayed throughout her diatribe, as if the story of such a tragic fight somehow elevated her in the telling of it. He was sorry indeed for the death of Mister Black, for the old man, as toothless as a newborn babe, had been an accomplished storyteller. The Brandt men who gathered in Robert Hastings' public house of an evening tended to go quiet when Mister Black began one of his tales so they would not miss a word. The old man had known, of course, how popular his stories were with the men of both families, and he had always spoken loudly enough for all to hear. Mister Black had so willingly shared his tales.

"Oh! Mister Brandt? I almost forgot to mention something."

He reined in Star and turned in his saddle to face Charlotte Ellis. "Yes?"

"You Brandts lost one other person that I know of." Here she paused as if to gain maximum effect.

Hubbard had not been that close to his Uncle Oliver, as Mistress Ellis might have been aware, but something in her tone warned him to tighten his stomach muscles.

"It was your brother's youngest son, Ira Samuel."

The blow was almost more than Hubbard could bear. Little Samuel was ever the jolliest of Hubbard's four nephews. "Who would kill a seven-year-old child?" The question burst from him before he could stop himself.

"It may have been but a stray bullet, most likely fired by one of you Brandts."

Her self-satisfied answer made him want to leap from Star's back and slam her head against the wall of the building behind her just as Ira had pounded his own head against the oak in his despair over having killed an innocent woman.

It took every ounce of self-possession Hubbard could muster. He would never strike a woman, never, but he was sore tempted in this case to make an exception to his own rule. He turned his back on Mistress Ellis and rode away through the strangely quiet town. He paid no attention to the silent people who went about their daily business, but who watched this Brandt turn west at the crossroads and ride toward Reverend Atherton's churchyard. Since Miss Myra Sue—Mistress Martin, he corrected himself—would not be buried in Brandtburg, there was no need for him to go to Reverend Russell's church, but there were three Brandt graves to be dug. Not only his neighbor's child, Benjamin Grant, but now Uncle Oliver, and young Ira Samuel.

Hubbard rubbed the palm of his hand hard across his chest, but could not alleviate the dull ache in his heart. If and when Ira returned to Brandtburg, he would have a great deal to answer for.

By the time Hubbard reached the church, men were already hard at work in the graveyard. He did not know the names of any of them. They were neither Brandts nor Martins, but newcomers to the valley who farmed on the outermost reaches of the town and did odd jobs when there was a call for it. Three piles of dirt, three piles of the large stones that always seemed to be present in the rocky soil. Reverend Atherton stepped forward, lifted a hand, and motioned for Hubbard to dismount and follow him to one side of the churchyard.

"Where is Ira?" The minister pitched his voice low lest the gravediggers hear him.

"I know not where he is, only that he is far north of the town."

"Let us hope he does not return this day. If he does, I cannot vouch for his safety."

Hubbard nodded. What was there to say, after all? When he had thought his brother had killed Mary Frances, he had been ready to strangle Ira. How could he expect anyone else, the Russells in particular, to forgive the murder of their daughter? "Mistress Ellis told me with great pleasure of the happenings yesterday."

Apparently Reverend Atherton liked Charlotte Ellis as little as did Hubbard, for his normally pleasant face lengthened into displeasure.

"Do we have only two dead?"

"For now," Reverend Atherton said, "but there are many sorely wounded and like to die soon without a miracle." He named them, but Hubbard's thoughts were on his nephew.

"Where is Ira Samuel's body?"

"Laid out at the Blanchard's house, with your sister like to faint away at any moment. We will postpone the burial—all of these three—until this afternoon, after the Martins have left the valley." He paused and seemed to grope for words. "I wish … I wish I had not counseled you to wait to marry nor to keep your marriage secret. There might have been …"

He ground to a halt, and Hubbard laid a hand on the old man's shoulder. "There might have been many different outcomes, but we needs must deal with what is. And what is, is deep enmity between these two families. It is perhaps best that the Martins leave right away."

The minister nodded. "I understand they will take their dead with them."

"So Mistress Ellis informed me. I had intended to visit Miss Myra Sue's grave and pay my respects."

"There will be no more Martin graves here in Brandtburg." Reverend Atherton worried his lower lip with his few remaining upper teeth and looked around, as if to be sure he was not overheard. "What of your wife?"

What indeed, thought Hubbard. "I must attend my nephew's funeral and try to give what comfort I can to my sister. She loved young Samuel as if he had been her own. As soon as Ira returns and we have dealt with him"—he came near to saying *after we have hanged him*—"I will go after the Martins and will claim my wife." He paused. "If she will still have me."

Reverend Atherton frowned but remained silent. One of the gravediggers approached and stood with his cap in his hand. "We are finished, Reverend. We would like to go home to our noonday meal and then will return to fill in the graves after you hold the services."

Hubbard certainly hoped he had never sounded that unconcerned whenever he dug a grave for someone.

THE MARTIN FAMILIES left Brandtburg late that morning to the sound of no applause, no rousing trumpet or bagpipe, not even an audience, at least not a visible one.

The day after the wedding of Homer Martin and Myra Sue Russell, the day after the murder of Myra Sue Russell Martin, and the deaths of those others, when all the Martin families—far more than half a hundred people—left Brandtburg, Charlotte Ellis sat as tall and as straight as she could in the back of the Russell's wagon. Unfortunately, she had to sit on Myra Sue's coffin, which was deucedly uncomfortable, but once they found a burial yard, she would have more room.

Sarah and some of the other women had laid out Myra Sue and wrapped her body preparatory to the trip. Charlotte was not interested in helping with such matters. Myra Sue would be buried somewhere along the trail, as soon as they could find a convenient churchyard. Charlotte did hope they would find one soon, lest the body begin to smell. Thankfully the weather was not yet too hot.

All this preparation had been a dreadful affair, and Charlotte had hardly slept from the tension of that and the flurry of last-minute arrangements for the journey. She had not been able to find her favorite brush that morning, for one thing, and had wasted precious minutes searching for it. If one of her nieces had borrowed it and then left it behind, Charlotte would find it hard to forgive. She would question them when they stopped this evening. She wondered when and where that would be. How far away, how long would she have to endure the rockhard seat of this infernal wagon?

Homer Martin looked angry enough to keep forging ahead all day and through the night as well, but even he would have to stop, considering all the livestock. And the children. He couldn't walk everyone to death, although he looked as though he wanted to.

The only joy Charlotte had experienced this whole day was in having been able to tell Hubbard Brandt of the death of his nephew, Ira Samuel. She knew her words had shaken him to the core. Good.

They weren't even outside the limits of the town yet, and she already wanted to stop and rest her feet—and that portion of her body where she sat. She should have placed two folded quilts atop the coffin rather than just one. Thinking about the length and the uncertainty of the journey ahead of her made her cringe. The bloodshed on the steps of the church and in the center of the town yesterday had been a bad omen. She felt that in her very bones. This journey was doomed.

She looked ahead of her, past the sturdy bulk of her sister Sarah sitting in the front of the wagon next to Anders, to where Homer Martin slouched on his bay mare at the front of the straggling line. Anders and Sarah's wagon came next, of course, right behind Homer Martin. Charlotte assumed Silas Martin was at the rear of the procession on Devil, that completely misnamed horse of his, making sure no one straggled.

As the minister, and the oldest of the heads of families, it should have been Anders Russell's right to lead the flock, but this whole scheme had been Homer's idea, from what Charlotte could glean from conversations she had overheard. Homer was so proud—far too proud in Charlotte's estimation—of being the oldest surviving Martin in the valley. For some reason, which Charlotte could never fathom, the rest of the men thought that lineage conveyed some sort of special favor on Homer. She sniffed and brushed impatiently at an errant hair that had straggled out of her tight bun and worked its way free of her cap. There was nothing special about Homer Martin; that was for sure.

If Myra Sue had lived, she would have been the one driving Homer Martin's wagon, because the mighty Homer had to sit on his horse at the head of the column, like some sort of general. He—or more likely his brother, for Silas seemed to have all the brains in that family—had recruited nine-year-old Lucius Hastings to drive their wagon, even though the child had a broken arm that was confined in a sling. The boy was puffed up at his own importance. Charlotte hoped he would not tip the wagon into a river, for that would slow down the entire party.

Anders would have been a better choice as leader, but he and Sarah were grieving the loss of their daughter, Myra Sue. Charlotte automatically bowed her head for a moment—a quick moment. Myra Sue was no great loss as far as Charlotte was concerned. Homer would have done better to have married one of Charlotte's daughters. In fact, she planned to suggest just that, after a suitable time had passed, despite her built-in bias against men in general. At nineteen and eighteen, her girls were both presentable enough. She glanced at the two of them, walking side by side to the left of the wagon. That was the way it should be. The youngsters walked. It was good for them. They had their heads together, most likely complaining about their lot in life. Louisa had always been a complainer, and Martha was not much better, taking her cues from her older sister.

As far as Charlotte was concerned, her sister Sarah had been foolish to insist that Myra Sue and Homer marry before they left. She could almost hear Sarah's whine. "It is not seemly for our daughter to go on such a long trail where we will not have the benefit of our own cabin," she had said. "She must be wed before we go." Charlotte knew what that meant. Sarah was afraid Homer would take advantage of his betrothed. If Sarah hadn't insisted, Myra Sue would still be alive. Not that Charlotte would ever say such a thing to Sarah—probably not. Unless Sarah provoked her. Myra Sue's death had, after all, truly been Sarah's fault—could not everyone see the truth of it?

The other Russell children, the surviving ones, walked on the other side of the wagon. Thomas, age twenty, Anne, nineteen, and Edna, sixteen. Abner, eighteen, had chosen for some unfathomable reason to walk behind the Russell wagon with the Garners. Chauncey Endicott, Sarah and Charlotte's father, sat in the wagon in back of Charlotte, on the other side of the coffin, his bony bottom cushioned by a folded-up quilt. He was mostly toothless and rather cranky, but he was a master at the making of fine ale. Charlotte's mother rode in Worthy Endicott's wagon, since Eunice, Worthy's wife, was the only one who could stand having her around.

Charlotte reached out and patted the basket that held her papers, carefully wrapped in a cloth she had soaked in beeswax to keep out the rain. She would not have left them behind even if someone had offered her money. She kept the family records. That was an important job, and she took it seriously. Of course, she also kept her ears open for any pieces of information she could add to her growing list of—how should she phrase it?—the *improprieties* of other members of the community. Tonight, she would place the precious packet into the bottom of her sturdiest wooden box. She would have packed it there last night, but there had been information to add, and then Louisa had woken early complaining of stomach pains. She sighed. Being a mother was a never-ending travail. And keeping a secret in too small a house was a never-ending burden.

Charlotte looked back over her shoulder. Immediately behind

the Russell wagon was the Garner contingent. Calvin Garner should have walked to the right of their wagon, but his leg had been so badly scored in the fight that had erupted after Myra Sue was killed, that he could not walk, nor even drive the wagon. His wife Augusta drove the team, while Calvin sat like a stump beside her. Stubborn man, not willing to show any weakness. He held his rifle, as if he could be any help in a fight. Charlotte decided that knife wound in his leg was not so bad as Augusta had claimed. Augusta was always one to expect attention.

Young Able walked immediately to the right of where his mother sat. Wilbur was in that line as well, but he hardly counted. Mary Frances, the older of the two daughters was behind Able, with her nineteen-year-old brother, Nehemiah, beside her. Abner Russell strode along behind Nehemiah, with Constance to his left next to the wagon. Charlotte wondered idly why Mary Frances was hemmed in like that. At least, that was what it looked like to Charlotte.

Robert Hastings—the innkeeper with the unfortunately large nose—and his pregnant wife Jane Elizabeth Benton Hastings, had three living children, fifteen-year-old Charles, Bridgett who was twelve, and young Lucius, an unprepossessing child if ever Charlotte had seen one—the one who was driving the wagon for Silas and Homer Martin. His arm was still bound up and held in a sling. He'd broken it a bare month ago. If Silas' team had not been so well-behaved, the boy never would have been able to control them.

Robert Hastings had said that very morning that he regretted having to leave his successful public house, but he knew that should he stay behind when the others left, he would be putting his family at risk. It was clearly a case of hanging together or hanging separately, as his great-grandsire was reputed to have said before he left England with his large family. Robert's elderly father and Jane Elizabeth's aged mother rode on the wagon seat with Jane Elizabeth. Robert's father, Richard Hastings, whose nose was as bulbous as his son's, had built the first tavern in Brandtburg. He no longer took part in the running of the inn, and Charlotte could not see that he was of any use whatsoever, not since his wife died some years before.

Call Surratt and his wife Geonette Black Surratt trailed behind the Hastings family, with their two young children, Nell and Edward. Geonette would be birthing her baby soon. Charlotte shuddered, thinking how glad she was that her own daughters had been born inside a house, unlike what Geonette—and Jane Elizabeth, too—would face on the trail. Call Surratt's father was a simple-minded man, still strong in body but not in brain. They'd let him drive the wagon. Charlotte sincerely hoped that wasn't a mistake. Call's mother and Geonette's newly widowed mother were piled higgledy-piggledy in the wagon. Geonette's father, of course, was in a pine box at the bottom of the pile, awaiting whatever burial place became available to him. Nobody in that family had any idea of how to pack a wagon properly. Charlotte would be willing to wager—if she were ever to indulge in the sin of wagering—that they'd lose half their possessions beside the trail along the way.

Charlotte could not see Geonette's young brother, Sergeant Black, anywhere. No telling where that rapscallion had gotten himself to. The first time they stopped for a meal, he would show up. That was one thing Charlotte was sure about. His sister Presila was bouncing along on the far side of their wagon. That girl never just walked anywhere. It was always like she was up on her tippy-toes. Not a brain in the girl's head, Charlotte felt certain.

The sixth family head was the broad-shouldered Willem Breeton whose wife, Mary Surratt Breeton, had died the previous autumn. She left behind four children, MaryAnne, Pioneer, Susan, and young Willy. MaryAnne, already a stickler for details at thirteen, tended to herd all the younger children, not only her own brothers and sister, but her young cousins as well. Charlotte felt MaryAnne was entirely too full of her own importance. There were no Breeton grandparents. That black and white dog of Willy's followed him around as if the two were locked together. Charlotte did not have much patience with dogs, but she supposed they were useful enough in killing rats. About the only thing they were good for as far as she was concerned.

All those young children were going to be something of a bother on the trail. Oh, they had their uses, gathering kindling and tending the goats and such, but as much as Charlotte disliked the Brandtburg schoolmaster, Mister Ormsby had been useful in keeping the children out of one's way throughout most of the days. She wondered what would be done about a schoolmaster when the company reached their destination.

The Endicotts, the Shipleighs, and two other families had agreed to go along on the journey, but Charlotte secretly believed they would not last for long. They were a questionable group at best, and their head, Worthy Endicott, despite his name, was one of the least worthy men Charlotte had ever known, with the possible exception of Ira Brandt. The fact that Worthy was Charlotte's brother had no bearing whatsoever on her opinion. And Worthy's wife, Eunice, did insist on spawning child after child. It was a good thing some of them died young.

Now, as she rode through the town, Charlotte could feel the tension quivering in the air around her, like a splinter burrowing down toward the middle of her body. Ira Brandt should have been hanged yesterday for the murder of Myra Sue. Everybody had seen him do it, but he had gotten away, and none of the Martin men had been able to find him.

They had to travel through the entire Brandt enclave on the western side of Brandtburg, for their southern journey began toward the west. They could not head directly south, for the Nulhegan River was not easily fordable, and of course the heavily forested and mountainous trail to the east would have been ill advised.

She could feel, sense, the Brandts watching them from behind closed windows. In fact, she saw several curtains twitch, but no faces appeared. Nor did any rifle barrels emerge from darkened doorways. That had been her real fear—that the Brandts would retaliate as the Martins left, while here she sat high on Myra Sue's coffin, a perfect target. Perhaps she should have let her daughters ride, one on either side of her.

But the entire town was eerily quiet, disconcertingly vacant. Until they came to the edge of the town.

Hubbard Brandt and Reverend Atherton stood beside the road, off to the right, their hands empty, their faces solemn. As the Russell wagon passed them, with the body of Myra Sue wrapped in linen, lying in a scrabbled-together box, the box on which Charlotte sat, the two men removed their hats and held them over their hearts.

Except for a quick glance, Charlotte kept her eyes straight ahead. She would not give them the satisfaction of looking curiously at them or even of acknowledging their presence. Maybe it was just as well that they were leaving. Brandtburg had nothing left to offer Charlotte Ellis.

Once they were behind her, she turned slightly and saw Mary Frances bolt toward the two men from the side of the Garner wagon, but Nehemiah grabbed her arm and held her back. Charlotte felt the same way as Mary Frances. It would be good to scratch out their sanctimonious eyes. She almost wished Nehemiah had not stopped his sister.

THAT NIGHT, HOMER Martin drank himself into a stupor. No one blamed him, of course, for had he not lost his wife to that murderous Ira Brandt? Any man would do the same, although, if truth be told, Homer seemed not to need the excuse of a murdered bride—or any other excuse—to overindulge.

Even with Homer's amazing ability to hold his liquor, he could barely walk the following day, so it was Silas, his younger brother, who led the Russells, the Endicotts, the Hastings family, the Breetons, the Garners, the Surratts, and the other families southward—well, westward until they could ford the North Branch and turn to the south—on Tuesday, April twenty-first, the second day of their journey toward they knew not what.

2000

"THE BEST-LAID PLANS," Ida said. "I'm sorry they didn't get to go on a honeymoon like they planned, but you'd think they would have realized it was inconceivable for the two of them to make it as a couple."

"They could have," Maddy said.

"You'd like them to have succeeded." Ida's voice was terse. "That doesn't mean it was particularly practical. Think about what they would have been up against."

Maddy sighed. "I guess you're right. The best-laid plans of mice and men…"

"And Brandts and Martins," Carol said.

"They weren't very good plans to begin with," Charlotte Ellis said.

She'd been so quiet, her words surprised me. I had to wonder if there was a story behind them. She sounded so intense.

1985
Atlanta

CHARLIE ELLIS BOUNDED through the kitchen door. "Mom! You won't believe what I did today!"

"What? Tell me."

Charlie loved the way Mom was always so willing to listen. Not like Charlie's friend Jennifer's mom. Charlie shivered. She hated going to Jennifer's house. It was always sort of gloomy. She shed her book bag and swiped a chocolate chip cookie from under the glass dome. "I'm writing letters to our state congressman—well, congresswoman—and I'm going to ask her to sponsor a bill for me!"

"Slow down a bit, sweetie. What's this bill about?"

"So we can eliminate homelessness."

"Eliminate it? That's a powerful goal, honey." She poured some milk for Charlie and a cup of coffee for herself. "How do you propose to do this?"

Mom listened carefully and asked some good questions. After their discussion was over, Charlie admitted it wasn't quite ready enough yet.

"That's okay, hon. You've made a good start just getting the idea in the first place. Did Miss Hope have some suggestions for you?"

Charlie shrugged. "She said about what you just told me. I've got a lot of thinking and researching to do."

"That's the way things get accomplished."

Charlie drained her glass. "When we moved here, I didn't know what it was going to be like. But now I'm really happy."

"You don't miss Martinsville?"

"Not really. Do you?"

"No honey. Not at all."

"I miss Grandma Masters."

"Yes, sweetie. So do I."

2000

IDA LIFTED THE Mary Frances diary. "Is that it?"

"Nope," I said. "There's a little bit more to this entry."

I saw my wife as she left Brandtburg, for Reverend Atherton and I rode out just beyond the town where there is a gentle bank beside the road and waited for the Martins to appear. Homer Martin's hand went to the stock of his rifle as he rode past us, but I daresay it was all for show. I barely noticed him, for my eyes were busy searching for my wife. Our ostensible purpose—Reverend Atherton's purpose—was to pay our respects to the Russells as their wagon went past, bearing the heavy load of their daughter's coffin, with Mistress Ellis sitting on top of it. I felt sorry indeed to see how Reverend and Mistress Russell mourned, but my true purpose was to see my wife and to reassure her with my eyes that I would follow her as soon as possible. The Garner wagon was next in line after the Russells, and Mary Frances tried to run to me as she walked by, but her brother Nehemiah caught her arm and berated her. I fear it may be a day or even two before I can leave here, but I doubt not that Mary Frances—my wife—will be ready to go with me as soon as I appear. Pray God I may spirit her away from their camp without further bloodshed.

"This doesn't make sense," Dee said. "How did she end up here in Martinsville married to Homer if Hubbard was planning on kidnapping her?"

"It wouldn't have been kidnapping," Maddy said. "Kidnapping is only if somebody doesn't want to go along. She tried to run to him like that, for heaven's sake. Isn't it obvious she wanted to stay with him?"

"But why didn't he just follow her and … and do something?"

"Obviously their plans didn't work out." Ida sounded impatient with Dee and Maddy's argument, which was borne out by her next words. "You'll just have to zip it and wait for the story to unfold."

Saturday, 25 April 1741
Brandtburg

HUBBARD BRANDT SHIFTED on the hard oak bench and studied the rest of the town council members. He was not truly a member of the council, for it was made up of the heads of each family in the Brandt's valley. Ira should have been here. But Ira was still gone, so Hubbard had been required to take his place. He had seriously considered refusing, but knew that Mary Frances might still need time with her injured father. He would never try to force her away from her family in their time of need, but he would far rather be there shadowing the Martin group than here accomplishing nothing.

If he heard one more person complaining about who could take over which house, he felt he was going to strike someone. The only building that was not up for dispute was the tavern. It had been sold to a young man who was newly come to the valley. He and his wife would, like the Hastings family, live above the public rooms and would undoubtedly fill those rooms in no time at all, for wasn't the woman breeding—or so it had seemed to Hubbard the one glimpse he had of her as her husband helped her down from the wagon they had arrived in.

And then there was the church. No one knew what to do with it. Reverend Abernathy had expressed no interest in it. What need had he for another church building when the one he had was larger to begin with, stone-built, and more than adequate? Hubbard imagined that the now-abandoned wooden church would slowly disintegrate, prey to the ravages of weather, for no one could live in a church, nor would anyone want the parsonage, which sat too close by the graveyard.

Two buildings left to rot, then. Perhaps men would eventually use the stones of the foundations for new houses as the town grew. The only hope to save the church and the parsonage would be if a second minister came to Brandtburg, but Hubbard sincerely hoped that would not happen, for he could see more division in the community should people choose to abandon Abernathy and take up with a new man.

The remaining houses were all a hotbed of contention. Every second or third son, unable to inherit his own family's dwelling place, since that was the right of the eldest son, wanted his own house and land, and the town council were hard-pressed to hear all their petitions and their complaints. Just now, Arthur Stanley had carped, "The Garner house was practically filled to bursting with wildflower petals strewn everywhere."

"Be glad they did not fill it with offal," Thomas Williams retorted.

Hubbard wanted nothing to do with any of this dissension.

All he truly wanted was to leave Brandtburg and go after his wife. All he wanted to do was see Mary Frances again, hold her, take her away with him.

But he had not been able to leave. The burials had needed to be attended. The council must meet each fortnight. And Hubbard needed to be at home when Ira returned. For come home he must. Surely.

2000

"GO AHEAD, IDA," I said. "Hubbard's next entry isn't until May seventh."

"Yeah," Dee said. "Don't leave us hanging here. Even after a couple of weeks, Mary Frances must have said something about what happened. Keep reading."

Ida indicated the box of tissues. "I may need another one of those things."

Maddy sent it on its way around the circle.

Ida took one and went back to the journal.

Wednesday, 6 May 1741

I feel so much anger I want to set the wagons afire. My brother caught me as I tried to flee the evening after Myra Sue's death. He did not know I was running away. He thought I was insensible with fear of the Brandts. When I berated him by shouting, "Why do we not stay and defend our homes?" he thought only that I was overcome with anger over Ira Brandt and the death of my dear friend, and Father's injury. But I wanted more than anything to be with my dear Hubbard Brandt. I am his wife. I want to be his helpmeet and the mother of his children. I have lain in his arms, even though that one night we had together was in the loft of Reverend Atherton's barn. The odor of hay will, I know, ever be one of my favorite smells.

I cannot tell anyone in my family. I fear their anger. I must find a way to leave.

Ida looked up at the rest of us. She set the book down on her lap and reached again for a tissue. "I may go through a whole box of these." She blew her nose, and so did a number of the rest of the women. I was surprisingly dry-eyed, more intrigued by the unfolding story than worried. After all, this had all happened almost two hundred years ago. On the other hand, I was moved by the way Mary Frances talked about the smell of hay. In two hundred years, people hadn't changed all that much. Would Hubbard ever mention the smell of hay in his journal? I wanted him to catch up with her fast, but knowing what I did about Martinsville history, I was really afraid to hear of him getting killed in the process. After all, Mary Frances ended up here in Martinsville without Hubbard.

Our company have now been more than a fortnight upon the road. Mother is in the wagon with Father. Constance, Nehemiah, and Able are playing a simple string game with Wilbur, and I write by firelight, trying to keep my tears from spotting the ink.

"What do you suppose that string game was?" Rebecca Jo asked.

"And why would it need to be simple? I like games with a challenge." Glaze had a point. There's nothing as boring as a puzzle that's too easy to solve.

Nobody had an answer, of course. We all waited while Ida took a couple more deep breaths.

I feel a need to set down what happened. I know that Hubbard, my dear husband, is safe, for I saw him as we left the town the day after the fighting. I tried to run to him, but my brother Nehemiah took hold of my arm so tightly it seemed I could feel his anger coursing through him. After those unnecessary deaths, all our menfolk were armed. They walked or rode encircling the wagons, where the smallest children were stuffed between boxes and bags, cautioned to keep their heads down and their mouths shut. All the women either drove the wagons or walked immediately beside them, except for the

Russell women. Charlotte Ellis refused to walk of course, and her—

Charlotte broke into Maddy's words. "Charlotte Ellis?"

"Oh, of course, dear," Sadie said. "I hadn't really thought about it, but this"—she pointed to the journal—"would be the woman you were named for." She looked at Charlotte quizzically. "But you must have realized that."

"Well ... sure. My mom always told me I was named for one of the founding mothers of Martinsville. She was pretty proud of being descended straight from the original Charlotte Ellis. I guess I was just surprised to hear that name ... my name ... in such an old book."

"Mary Frances sure doesn't seem to like Charlotte Ellis," Maddy said.

"I wouldn't take it that way if I were you," Pat said. "Maybe Charlotte—the original Charlotte I mean—had bad feet or a gimpy knee or something, so she couldn't walk."

"I can see we're going to get our Charlottes mixed up all the time," Carol said. "Did you ever have a nickname, Charlotte?"

"Well, my college roommate always called me Charlie."

"Then I think we should, too. If you don't mind, that is."

"Fine with me."

Sadie gave Charlotte—Charlie—a funny look. I wondered what that was about. "That's what your mother always called you," Sadie said.

"Yeah. Her, too."

"Okay. From now on," Rebecca Jo declaimed, "if we talk about Charlotte, it's the original Charlotte Ellis from 1741. When we say Charlie, we'll all know we're back in this century. Agreed?"

We all nodded, of course. Leave it to Rebecca Jo to find a sensible solution. My mother-in-law had more common sense than almost anyone I knew. Except maybe for her son. Maybe that was where he got it from. Maybe that was why I'd married him. One of many reasons. I could feel myself beginning to heat up.

You are not hot.

Ida interrupted both my thoughts and Marmalade's loud meow. "Now that we've solved that problem ..."

Charlotte Ellis refused to walk of course, and her sister Sarah Russell sat on the wagon seat as if her heart had been ripped apart by her daughter Myra Sue's death. She seemed to pay no mind to her two other daughters, who sat directly behind her, their arms around each other.

My mother drove our wagon, and my badly-injured father rode on the seat beside her. He insisted I walk directly behind Wilbur and Able, with Nehemiah to my immediate right.

Wilbur was next to the wagon, for should anything have gone awry, he would not have known what to do. Young Able seemed proud to be in line with the men, and looked ready to defend his older brother.

Ida rested the book on her lap for a moment. "There's your answer, Glaze."

"What answer?"

"You asked why the string game had to be simple. It sounds like Wilbur was challenged in some sort of way, what with"—she looked back at the page—"with young Able needing to protect his older brother."

I was glad she saw that. I hadn't caught the significance. I was obviously going to have to listen a lot more carefully.

"She's talking about Able," Ida continued.

He held his hunting knife in his hand, but I could not help but notice that his hand shook ever so slightly. Constance was directly behind me with Abner Russell beside her, his steady presence giving a feeling of solidity. I wondered at Abner's presence in our family group. I also wonder if I was placed in the middle of so many menfolk to prevent my trying again to run away. If so, it was an effective measure. Still, the wariness we all felt was almost like a thing alive. If I had managed to escape, would the Brandts have misinterpreted my action and attacked me?

There was, I am sure, great need of fear, for the brawl that erupted when Ira killed poor Myra Sue might have rid the town of all its men forever. Our menfolk chased Ira into the center of the town, and the Brandts responded as if we were attacking them. Ira Brandt escaped in the ensuing melee. Had it not been for Silas Martin and Mister Hastings on our side and Reverend Atherton on the Brandt side, they might still be slashing or shooting at each other.

These three men of peace, though, had been unable to stop the worst of what happened. I abhor Ira Brandt. If it were not for him and his hatred, I could have slipped away. I would be with Hubbard even now. Everyone would know that I am his wife. Before Mister Hastings and Reverend Atherton calmed the uproar, there were three more killed and many injured, including the deep knife wound in my father's leg.

"That knife wound can't have been good," Maddy said. "Those were the days before antiseptics."

"You had to be tough to live back then," Carol acknowledged. "And even then, something like this could fester, and you'd be dead before you knew it."

Dee shivered.

Soon after we left the edge of Brandtburg behind us, we came upon my husband and Reverend Atherton standing beside the road. They removed their hats as the Russell's wagon drove past, but I doubt whether Reverend Russell or his wife saw them. I tried to run to my Hubbard, but Nehemiah grabbed me in a vise-like grip and would not let—I find I am repeating myself and would not waste this paper in such a way.

I know my Hubbard will come for me. I readied myself to slip from our camp that night, but there were guards aplenty set round us. Each night I have waited for a sign that my husband has come for me, but I feel now that I must wait until we are farther along the road and feeling somewhat safer. My husband is ever one to plan ahead. He will not act precipitately, for we both must remain safe when he rescues me.

Perhaps even now he follows well behind us, biding his time.

I hope that Hubbard was not close to the Brandts who died. We lost Mister James Black, my cousin Geonette's father. He was shot in the chest. My father said that he died bravely. I do not know what that means. We buried Myra Sue's body and that of Mister Black that first evening far along the trail in a churchyard we found beside the way. Widow Black was distraught at first, but seems to have recovered nicely in these few days. She has set her cap now for the old Mister Hastings. Anyone with eyes can see what she is doing.

"Some things never change," Rebecca Jo said with a laugh. "Can't you just see Widow Black pursuing that hapless old man?"

Carol cut through our chuckles. "Back then, it might not have been thought funny. Women generally needed to be under the protection of a man."

"I thought widows had it better, though," Maddy said. "As long as they didn't marry, they owned the property or the business. Isn't that right?"

Carol pursed her lips. "True. Unless they had a son, in which case he would have inherited everything."

Pat made a rude noise.

Homer Martin has continued as the acknowledged leader of our group. The name of Martin seems to hold all the men of our party in a spell. Young as Homer Martin is, even my father defers to him. Reverend Russell probably should have been the leader by right of age, but he mourns too much to do anything other than twitch the reins now and again to keep his horses moving. My father, too, might have taken over the leading of the party if he had not been injured, but I know it pains him much. His leg is bound up, and I can see a dark stain even now on the bandage that my mother tends with much clucking and head shaking. She is worried, I can tell. His leg—indeed his whole body—is hot to the touch. Tomorrow I fear he will spend the day bouncing in the wagon on top of the bedding, between the baskets of food, for he is unable to put his weight on the leg without crying out.

"Blood poisoning, you think?"

I nodded at Dee. "Sure sounds like it. Some sort of infection, for sure."

"Blood poisoning isn't really a medical term," Maddy said. "It's septicemia."

Ida cleared her throat.

I have a touch of the grippe, which has afflicted me each morning for several days. This morning I vomited again while I was in the woods relieving myself. Yesterday it was after I ate a Johnny-cake, but I was able to get away from the wagon before Mother saw—or heard—me.

"What's a Johnny cake?"

I was glad Dee asked, because I had no idea.

Maddy, of course, was the one who answered. "Sometimes they were called journey cakes because they travelled well. They were sort of like fried pancakes made out of cornmeal and water. Sometimes they used leftover biscuit dough, but I think the cornmeal lasted longer without going bad."

"Oh. Thanks."

I have not told her of my indisposition, for I am reluctant to add to her burden. Fortunately, I always feel better afterwards. I hope it will not come again, for I fear I will not always manage to get far enough from the group to be sure no one will hear me.

I cannot seem to stop crying. I feel like Juliet in the play Mister Ormsby, our schoolmaster, read to us once, crying over the banishment of her Romeo and letting her father think she was distraught due to the death of her cousin Tybalt.

"A touch of the grippe? Throwing up in the woods?" Pat sounded particularly sarcastic. "If she's been diddling around with her dear Hubbard, I'll bet anything she's pregnant."

Maddy looked scandalized. "Did people do things like that back then?"

We burst into guffaws. "Where have you been living?" Pat asked. "In a cave?"

Sadie made a quelling motion. "It was an honest enough question." She turned and patted Maddy on the shoulder. "People have been doing such things since the dawn of humanity, dear. It's just that they talk about it more openly now than they used to. And maybe more of them do it a little earlier than they used to."

"You all seem to be forgetting"—Ida held up the journal—"that Mary Frances Garner wasn't playing around. She was married to Hubbard Brandt."

"And if she's pregnant already," Sadie said, "then Homer Martin wasn't the father."

"If she was pregnant," Sadie said with a particular emphasis on the *was*, "then she must have lost the baby."

"Why?" I think we all asked that.

"Because all our town council chairs descended from Homer and Mary Frances Martin, so she had to have another baby and Homer had to be the father."

"But she was already married to Hubbard."

"Obviously Hubbard died somehow or other," Rebecca Jo said. "So then she could marry Homer."

"We don't have evidence to support any of these theories. They're all just guess—"

"Wait a minute," Dee interrupted Carol. "Don't we get to find out who the two Brandts were that got killed?"

I pointed to Hubbard's diary. "Hubbard said one was his nephew."

Ida shrugged. "Mary Frances didn't name them."

Several voices spoke up at once. "Maybe it wasn't important to her." "They were only Brandts." "Keep reading; maybe she tells us later."

In the middle of all this chatter, Carol held up her hand. "Now aren't you glad you have a real live historian in your midst? They weren't *only Brandts*. They were my relatives, remember?"

I rearranged my butt on the folding chair. All this sitting was putting my legs to sleep. Maybe I should have brought a bunch of pillows up here. Other than the ones Maddy had been sitting on. Did I even have that many pillows? Ida closed the book. Dee stood up briefly and rubbed her rear end. "This is too much sitting," she said. "Tell us, and then let's take a break. I could use some hot coffee."

"Me, too," I said, "but I'll make mine tea."

"Good idea," Carol said. "But first, we need a drum roll here. The ones who were murdered ..."

Pat spoke up. "What do you mean murdered? It sounds like they were just killed in a brawl."

Carol looked at her for a long time. "This was all murder. These were real people dying real deaths simply because of their names and because my ancestor was too quick to pull a trigger. There was no good reason for any of this to have happened."

In the ensuing silence, Sadie coughed. "That was a long time ago. I'm sorry anybody had to die ..."

I do not want you to die.

She paused a minute to let Marmalade finished meowing. "But I do want to hear the rest of the story before I turn ninety. Let the good Dr. Mellinger speak."

The good Dr. Mellinger laughed. So did the rest of us. I glanced over at Ida. She was running her gloved index finger along the spine of the old diary. It looked like she felt a connection to it. No wonder. She'd been struggling with that backwards writing for a long time now.

I folded my similarly-gloved hands on top of Hubbard's journal. I guess I felt a connection, too. I was also extremely grateful that he wrote the normal way, from left to right.

"Okay," Carol said, as she sat back down and crossed her legs. "This is the way it was. After Myra Sue was killed, practically every man in the Martin clan stormed into town looking for Ira, just as Mary Frances mentioned. Someone fired a shot or pulled a knife and it was like the entire town went crazy. Ira Brandt's uncle on his mother's side was the first to die. Nobody missed him much because he was drunker than Ira most of the time. I have no idea how many Martins got hurt or even killed, but there were seventeen Brandts wounded, and three of them died later, after the Martin clan pulled out the next day."

Carol paused. She uncrossed her legs and leaned her elbows on her knees. "The other Brandt death during the fight was much worse. It was Ira Brandt's youngest son, who had been crouching off to one side, watching the melee. I'm pretty sure his death was an accident. It certainly stopped the fighting on both sides, and that's when Silas Martin, Reverend Atherton, and Robert Hastings moved in and brought everybody to order. In those days bullets never went very straight from those old muskets, and in all that chaos, it would have been easy for someone to shoot without thinking. There's no telling whether it was a Martin bullet or even a Brandt bullet that killed him. He was just in the wrong place at the wrong time. He was seven years old, and his name was Samuel."

As Carol said that, I happened to be looking at Sadie. She went absolutely white, and I thought she might be having a heart attack. I lunged up, hard to do because my right foot had gone to sleep, and tottered across to her. "Sadie? Are you all right?" And then I halfway remembered having heard something about the death of her son, Sammy, a long time ago, and knew that the name must have pierced her heart. An attack, indeed.

Ida came up next to me and said, "Oh Sadie, dear." Dee placed her hand on Sadie's shoulder, although I could tell from her expression she had no idea what was wrong. Pat reached over and touched Sadie's knee, murmuring something I couldn't hear.

I met Carol's eyes. The poor woman obviously had no idea what was going on, but she recognized that something she'd said had caused this flurry of empathy. I wondered how she was going to handle it. She must have been a psychic at some level. She walked right up to Sadie, knelt in front of her, and said, "Sadie, I'm sorry if anything I said brought you pain." She took a deep breath. "Did you lose a child named Samuel?"

Sadie's lips were pressed so tightly together they disappeared in her soft wrinkled face. She nodded.

"Have you ever talked about it?" Carol asked her.

I asked her, but she would not tell me.

The only sound was Marmalade's loud purring. Sadie sat perfectly still for a moment. I think she was holding her breath. I think we *all* were. Then she closed her eyes and shook her head. Her fingers tightened convulsively around a wrinkle in her yellow sweatpants.

Carol was probably the only woman in the room who didn't know that Sadie wore yellow all the time. "Would you like to tell me now?"

Sadie nodded her head, and we all let out a sigh.

"It was in 1955," Sadie said. We strained forward to hear her, even those of us who were right there close. "Scarlet fever it was, and a horrible reaction to the medications Doctor Garner gave him. I cared for him day and night." Sadie chewed on her lower lip for a moment. "He was seven. He was … only … only seven." She reached out for a tissue. "He was born when I was practically middle aged. He was the only child Wallace and I could ever have."

Sadie's hands fluttered in her lap, and she twisted the tissue until it ripped apart. Carol placed a hand over Sadie's gnarled knuckles. "What happened, Sadie?"

"It was a Thursday evening. I was so tired. I'd been up all night and all day. He'd been delirious with the fever, but right then he was quiet for a spell. I was sitting there beside him. He was on the wide sofa in the parlor. I'd carried him downstairs that afternoon so he could sit in the light from the big windows. His bedroom was on the other side of the house. The dark side at that time of day. He looked up at me …" She paused, and I wondered if she would have the strength, the courage to continue, but it was almost as if she had been waiting a lifetime for this chance. "He looked up at me," she repeated, "and reached out toward me. When I leaned closer, he touched my face. 'Mommy,' he said, 'would you put on your sunshine dress?' That's what he always called a pretty yellow housedress I had. It had soft yellow flowers all over it. Yellow was always his favorite color. When he was little he always drew with the yellow crayons. He drew yellow boats and yellow houses and yellow suns."

Sadie's voice had become a singsong, almost as if she'd told herself this story so many thousands of times, it had melted into her being.

"Later, when he started school, he asked for yellow pencils, and he drew yellow squiggles and yellow airplanes and yellow stars and yellow dinosaurs. One day I remember I asked him, 'Oh Sammy, won't you ever draw anything that isn't yellow?' And … he looked … so … so hurt." Sadie stopped for a moment. "I would give … anything," she said, "anything to be able to take back those words."

Sadie gently disengaged her hands from Carol's and rubbed her forehead. She patted an unruly gray curl back away from her face. "When he asked me to put on my sunshine dress, I … I was tired and I didn't want to walk upstairs. But also, I didn't want to leave him alone, even for a moment. He looked so … fragile. He looked almost translucent, like I could have seen … yellow sunshine right through him. So I told him … I would … wear it … tomorrow." She reached for another tissue to replace the limp pieces in her lap, and turned her head away while she blew her nose. When she looked back at Carol, she shook her head. "You see, dear, I truly thought there … would be … a tomorrow."

We all watched Sadie, as she folded her arms across her yellow sweater and began to rock gently to and fro. Marmalade jumped up into Sadie's lap and was enveloped in a hug so tight I wondered if her little ribs would ever be the same.

LooseLaces cannot hurt me. I can help by sharing her sad.

Carol let out a long breath and leaned back on her heels. She looked down at the floor. Then she reached out and slowly tied the loose yellow laces of Sadie's yellow tennis shoes.

The only sounds were Marmalade's loud purr and Sadie's quiet sniffles.

It was a long time before Dee quietly said, "Let's all wander down to the kitchen for some coffee, shall we?" She glanced at her watch. "The men should be ready for a break from all their games."

I glanced at Sadie, hoping she didn't think we were trivializing what we'd just heard. I knew these women, though—well, maybe not Easton, but she was still downstairs, so I didn't need to worry about her—and I had a feeling we all wanted to help ease Sadie's transition after such a devastating revelation. She still sat with her head down and her arms clasped around Marmalade on her yellow lap.

"Incoming," Bob said from the top of the stairs.

Behind him, Ralph spoke up. "It's been way too quiet up here. We haven't heard any rabble-rousing for a couple of hours and we thought you might all be napping."

Sadie swiped her hands across her face and then returned to hugging Marmalade.

She may hug me as much as she needs to.

"Nice of you to come check on us," Dee said.

"Naw," Ida said. "They're just curious to see whether we've found anything else."

"As a matter of fact,"—Sadie straightened her narrow shoulders—"Ida and Biscuit have been reading something you might find interesting."

So, our circle extended by quite a bit, the small book circulated as Ida explained about Mary Frances Garner's habit of writing backwards, and I showed them Hubbard's journal. Then we re-read those first entries. I was glad of a chance to hear everything twice. I'm not sure the import of it all had quite sunk in the first time around.

Finally, one of those inexplicable silences descended. A silence deep enough for us to hear Bob's tummy rumble loudly. There were quite a few good-natured jabs about hosts who never fed anybody.

"It's my own stomach crying out," Bob said. "Not yours."

"We just finished lunch not too long ago," Dee said. "I'd like some coffee, but don't you think there's such a thing as too much food?"

Ralph patted his stomach. "Nope."

I couldn't help but think about how jammed our fridge was, to say nothing of all the frozen food out on the back stoop. "Anyone who wants to eat is welcome to it. Let's head downstairs, shall we?" I set Hubbard's journal back on the pile and started for the stairs as Marmalade jumped down and Sadie stood.

I will go with you!

NONE OF US felt like going back up to the attic after we'd finished our various snacks. Unlike the various warm-weather barbecues we'd hosted or attended over the years, where most of the people walked around balancing a plate in one hand and a glass of iced tea in the other, traveling from one superficial, short-lived conversation to another, here—now—we seemed more willing to simply stay in one place. Not only at this meal—well, snack—but at the other one we'd shared a few hours ago here in our big kitchen. We just sat there and talked. Sometimes there would be three conversations going at once—the people gathered at each end and a separate one amongst the folks around the middle of the table. Sometimes, though, one person's voice would rise above the rest, and we'd all stop to listen.

Just like now.

Tom used a fork to clink against the side of his coffee mug. "Attention, attention," he said, and those of us who'd been turned away from him swiveled in our seats. "Glaze and I have been talking about how to organize this wedding of ours."

Oh my gosh. Here I'd been having so much fun in the attic, I'd practically forgotten about how I needed to decorate the house for the wedding tomorrow. The big red bows that I'd planned to put on the end of the pews, I could just lay them on tables around the living room and entryway. And tie them all the way up the bannister. Glaze and Dad would have to walk down the stairs—she'd make a spectacular entrance that way, although the fact that she'd be wearing sweatpants would detract from the picture somewhat. The bows were in a big box in the upstairs broom closet. Maybe Ida would help me place them. And Dee. And Maddy. It was going to be a time-consuming job.

"We were talking about it right after Mom and Dad got here," Glaze said, and I came back to the present hoping I hadn't missed anything vital. "We decided we'd like to be married in the attic."

"The attic?" I must have sounded aghast—and no wonder, because I was. Everyone turned to look at me. "Why the attic?"

"Seemed like the best place," Tom said. "There's lots of room up there and plenty of chairs."

"Anyway," Glaze said, "if the wedding were down here, we'd probably have to stand close to the wood stove ..."

That is the warmest place in the house.

"Much as I love your stove, Biscuit, it does churn out an awful lot of heat." She smiled, apparently thinking that would take the sting out of the way she was decimating my plans.

I had to admit she was right, but what was I going to do with all those bows? Staple them to the rafters?

"No sense having the two of us wilt in front of you," Tom said. "And anyway, we thought it would be more fun up above."

"Fun." I echoed his word, meanwhile seeing all my hastily rearranged plans going for naught.

"I'd be willing to bet nobody else has ever been married up in the attic," Amanda said. "This would be a first."

"You never can tell," Henry said. "There could easily have been several weddings up there. Although I've conducted most of my weddings in churches, there've been plenty in back yards, one at Nanny Goat Beach on Sapelo island off the Georgia coast, even one where the bride and groom stood on the roof of their oversized pickup-truck."

"Were you up there with them?"

"Well, Doc, the truck was big, but it wasn't *that* big." He patted his ample waist. "They stuck me in the tail end of the truck bed. Couldn't get much closer because of the rakes and shovels and wheel barrows. The groom ran a landscaping business."

"You'd think they would have cleaned it out for a wedding," Pat said.

"How'd the bride get up top if all that equipment was in her way?" Ida could always be counted on for a practical query.

"Up a step ladder by the driver's door."

"In a wedding dress?"

Henry shook his head. "In jeans and sweatshirt."

Ida curled her lip.

"She had a lace veil on her head, though," Henry said, "and her outfit was white."

"Humph! And that makes it okay?"

"Don't be such a traditionalist, Ida," I said. "On a stepladder, jeans would be safer than a long white dress."

"The only steps I want to climb," Glaze said, "are the ones up to the attic."

"That's fine with me," Henry agreed.

"Maybe we could put one of the wedding-in-the-attic invitations in the museum," Maddy suggested.

"How can there be attic invitations?" Dave asked. "They didn't even think about it until today. And what's this about a museum?"

Maddy shrugged. "Everybody seems to think I need something worthwhile to do." She pushed her glasses more firmly onto her nose. "Besides writing. So we're going to start a museum."

"And who cares if there aren't any attic wedding invitations for now?" Pat waved her arms around. "Once this storm is over, we'll have a limited edition of them printed up—one for everybody here."

"Plus some extras," I said. "Auntie Blue will want one, and my kids."

"Sharon and Margaret," Melissa suggested.

More suggestions came from every direction. "Don't forget the Johnsons." "Or the Olsens." "What about—"

"All right, already," Pat hollered. "We'll print a bunch."

"You're making me wish all these other people could be here," Glaze said.

Ida spoke up, with her unending practicality. "They wouldn't all fit."

"It doesn't really matter where the service is performed," Henry said, and I saw Father John nod. "Think of the countless weddings throughout history where no church building was available."

"Like the Martin clan on the trail," Carol suggested. "In four years, they must have had a lot of weddings."

"Exactly."

"Dave," Pat said, "why don't you take a couple of the guys upstairs and put some chairs out in a semicircle – enough for all of us. That way we'll be ready for tomorrow night." She seemed to be doing a mental accounting. "Twenty-four."

"Twenty-six," I corrected her.

"Twenty-four," Tom said. "Glaze and I will be standing."

"Twenty-three," said Henry. "So will I."

"Twenty," Dee said. "Maddy and Biscuit and I are attendants, so we won't get to sit down."

"You're complaining about it?"

"Watch it, Dave," Dee said, "or we might just make you sit out on the front porch."

"I'm sure he'll figure out a way to disrupt the ceremony from there," Pat said. She was grinning as she spoke, but her voice had a bit of an edge to it. I wondered what that was about. Oh heck. I knew what it was about. If I had to live with Dave's constant joking around, I'd probably want to flush him down the toilet.

"My wife knows me well," he said, and planted a resounding kiss on her cheek before he, Henry, and Doc headed for the stairs. Korsi stayed curled up on Doc's chair. That cat was sure on vacation from his regular job as office greeter. It was absolutely uncanny. Korsi never paid a bit of attention to anyone who was well—except of course, to Doc. If a parent brought a sick daughter into Doc's office, Korsi would sit in front of the kid or lean against her leg. If an ailing mom came in, accompanied by a child or two, Korsi would ignore the children and put a paw up on the mother's knee.

"Don't mess up our circle!" Pat's order brought me back to my senses.

Henry waved back over his shoulder. "Don't worry. Your circle is sacrosanct."

Sadie stood up from the table and put her hand on Easton's shoulder. "I think that I've had quite enough for one day. May I be excused from the cleanup detail?" Without waiting for an answer, she said, "I'd like a little nap. Would you help me up to our room, Easton dear?"

Easton took her arm and steered her through the doorway and toward the wide stairs. Marmalade followed them.

LooseLaces might need to hug me some more.

I saw Easton pick up Sadie's vibrant neon yellow suitcase and cart it toward the stairs. "I brought my own sheets," I heard Sadie tell her.

"Don't worry. We'll get your bed made up just the way you want it."

Easton and Marmy came back to the kitchen a few minutes later. "Sadie fell asleep almost as soon as we got her bed made up," she told us, and we heaved a collective sigh of relief.

"I'm so sorry," Carol said. "I feel like I opened a can of worms."

The men looked confused. So did Easton, but this wasn't the time to clue them in. Not yet.

Rebecca Jo shook her head. "Don't you be sorry one bit, Carol. That woman has been holding all this in for almost half a century. We all knew she wore her yellow dress to Samuel's funeral, and she's worn yellow ever since."

"It's been a town joke," Ida said. "I'm ashamed to admit it, but I laughed along with everyone else about eccentric Sadie in her yellow car and yellow house—she made Wallace paint it the summer after Sammy died. But this is the first time I ever heard the whole story. Did any of the rest of you know it?"

A chorus of no's came from every woman there. The men still looked confused, but there must have been something in the atmosphere that prevented any of them from asking us about it. That was okay. I'd tell Bob later.

Doc walked in, trailed by Henry and Dave. "Everything's all set up," he said as they rejoined the group. Korsi jumped down, waited for Doc to provide his lap again, and curled right back up.

Why is it that people always gather in the kitchen? It must have something to do with comfort. Not physical comfort, although my regular kitchen chairs weren't too bad. Emotional comfort. Comfort food. Food for thought. Thoughtful friends. Friends for … Okay, Biscuit. You can come back to earth now.

And scratch my head.

Marmalade pushed her head under my hand, and I spent several minutes massaging her ears.

Amanda watched us for a bit. "You know there are acupressure points on a cat's ears?"

"I think I read about it somewhere," I said. "Massaging her ears like this can be very healing, can't it?"

Amanda nodded.

And it feels good.

Marmy must have agreed because she purred her assent. The funny thing was, the whole process relaxed me as well. Sadie would get through this. After all, we were all on her side.

No you are not. She is upstairs and you are here.

On some level or other, I knew I should probably head up to the attic to set out the bows and place lanterns around in strategic places. I could always do it tomorrow, though.

How could I not be excited about my sister's wedding?

You still have some mad in you.

Why hadn't she asked me about holding the wedding here, instead of just announcing it to everyone like that? And getting married in the attic, of all places?

I stretched my arms out behind my back, grasped my hands, and pushed back on my shoulders as far as I could. This enforced inactivity was getting to me.

"Is it permissible," Father John said, "for a mere man to inquire what all that stuff was about Sadie and her wearing yellow all the time?"

"Yeah," Dave said, although he obviously didn't know anything, since he'd been upstairs when we mentioned the yellow. "Are you planning to clue us in, or are we supposed to play Twenty Questions?"

If Pat had been sitting next to him, I'm sure she would have kicked his shin, but she'd gotten up to refill her coffee mug. She answered his quip as if it had been a real question. "I think that decision needs to be someone else's." Pat turned to Rebecca Jo. "You've known her longer than anybody else here."

"It's not like she told us in confidence," I said.

Glaze rubbed the back of her neck. "I'd say it was more like a dam breaking."

So Rebecca Jo told the men, and Easton, too, for she hadn't been up there. We spent quite a while just poking at the crumbs of our snacks, cutting off one more slice of cheese, nibbling on a cracker, refilling a mug.

Finally Bob spoke up. "Thanks for telling us. You know, Sadie is an amazing woman. She worked as one of the original Rosie the Riveters during the war."

"I didn't know that," I said.

SADIE SLEPT FOR several hours, so of course, the talk eventually turned to the journal of Mary Frances. Doc and Henry seemed to have the most questions. It was funny, I thought, but both of those men were transplants—Henry from the Midwest and Doc from … from somewhere. Why had I never thought to ask? Or maybe he'd told me and I had forgotten.

The other men got caught up in historian fever, too, especially when Ida went back up to the attic and returned with the two journals so the men at Bob's request could hear the entries a second time. She brought the white cotton gloves, too.

It's hard to live in a town as steeped in history and mystery as Martinsville without developing a healthy curiosity about it all, and here was history playing out before our eyes, so to speak.

We took the time to clean up the dishes—not that there were many of them—but the men kept sitting there at the table while we worked—Bob had Marmalade on his lap—and we batted around a lot of ideas that the Mary Frances diary had stirred up.

"Do you think we could keep reading," Amanda asked, "even though Sadie isn't here?"

"I don't see anything wrong with that," I said. "We seem to be reading all the entries two or three times anyway, so we'll just do a repeat when she comes back downstairs."

Everyone nodded, so Ida opened her book. "My next entry is May seventh," she said. "That's the day after her last entry. What about yours, Biscuit?"

I thumbed over to the next page. "May sixth. I'll go next."

"Keep it in order," Carol said. "That's—what?—just over two weeks after Myra Sue Russell was killed on the church steps." As if any of us could ever forget that fact.

Wednesday, 6 May 1741. Yesterday Doctor Farrard took off my brother's right hand and forearm to stop the spread of the putrefying flesh. I have been too busy for too many days. I long to quit this place and go after my wife, but Ira is my brother. As much as I would like to damn him to hell, I cannot.

I let the journal sink back onto my lap. "That's all he says."

"Wow," Carol said. "I never knew Ira lost his arm. Poor guy."

Ida muttered something that sounded like *serves him right*, but I couldn't be sure.

Tuesday, 5 May 1741

HUBBARD HAD ALMOST lost his composure on the day after the bloody conflict. When Mary Frances tried to run to him that day a fortnight ago as the Martins left the valley, and when he saw how determined her brother Nehemiah was to detain her, and when he noticed in what dreadful pain her father appeared to be as he labored to stay upright on his seat in the wagon, he saw that her place for now was with her family. He was also painfully aware of the arms carried by all the men in the Martin's retinue, weapons Hubbard felt sure they would have used had he attempted to take Mary Frances away. He had tried to assure her with his eyes that he would follow her as soon as he was able, but his reasons—the funerals in his family, the disputes among his neighbors, and now, two weeks later, his brother's increasingly precarious health—seemed futile excuses indeed.

Ira was desperately ill. By the time he returned to Brandtburg on the twenty-fifth of April, after hiding in the woods for six nights, Hubbard was ready to dispatch him, but Hubbard took one look at Ira's fevered face and his anger turned to compassion. This was his brother, after all.

Ira had wanted to ride off after the Martins, but there were more graves to dig—four other Brandts had died over the past few days—and funerals to attend. By the time the last grave was covered over, the wound left in Ira's hand by Homer's knife had not only filled with pus, but ugly red streaks began to advance from wrist almost to his elbow. Although Hubbard, like Ira, had been afire to race after the Martins and retrieve Mary Frances, his brother's needs took precedence.

The doctor had been unable to stop the spread of the putrefaction and while Ira was out of his head with fever, the doctor told Hubbard, "It will have to come off."

"Is there no other option?" Hubbard knew his brother would be furious if he awoke with only one hand.

"Yes, there is another option."

Hubbard's hopes lifted, but only until the doctor added, "We can let him die."

They fed Ira as much whiskey as he could swallow, but even so, it took five heavy men to hold a screaming Ira down while the doctor amputated his arm just below the left elbow. When Doctor Farrard took a burning brand from the fireplace and stabbed the glowing end of it repeatedly against the stump to sear the flesh and seal off the bleeding, Ira fainted away.

"He stayed awake while you cut him into two pieces," Alvin Brandt marveled, wiping his neckerchief over his sweating head, "and then he faints like a woman at a little heat?"

Hardly a little, thought Hubbard, who had come near to passing out himself at the smell of burned flesh. "I misdoubt I could stand to be burned that much," he told Alvin. "I think I would sooner die."

2000

"OKAY," I SAID. "Your turn, Ida." I turned my attention to Marmalade, who had oozed up into my lap again.

You may scratch my ears

She needed a serious amount of scratching. I removed my white gloves. Her soft ears and silky fur felt so good. I wondered if she enjoyed being scratched as much as I enjoyed scratching her.

Yes.

I kept stroking her back, but turned my attention to Ida's voice.

Thursday, 7 May 1741
 Father's leg is worse, much worse. My mother can barely control the tremors in her hands. I know she fears for his life. And then what will become of us? Nehemiah is young to take on the responsibilities of being the head of our house, and Wilbur, only a year younger than Nehemiah but more like a child than young Able, is so dreamy-eyed most of the time, he would walk us off a cliff if he were in charge of leading the team. Thank goodness I have my sister Constance, but I cannot confide in her, and even though she is sixteen, she is not quite enough of a woman to share our mother's fears and mine.
 If only I were not ill, I could be of more help to my mother, but my stomach will not abide the smell of my father's oozing leg and I find myself vomiting, usually soon after I rise each morning. Even the smell of our burning candles turns my stomach, although the moose fat has not gone putrid yet, so I see not why their burning should make make me feel poorly. Perhaps tonight I will ask my mother if I can beg to sleep in the Surratt wagon, away from the smell. At least they use rush lights rather than candles.

"I never heard of moose fat candles," Father John said.
"Probably because you've never had many moose this far

south." Carol grinned as she explained. "They made candles out of any sort of fat available, especially when they didn't have enough beeswax. Unfortunately the animal fats went rancid fairly quickly and the smell, apparently, was atrocious."

Ida scanned back over the entry. "And these rush lights? What were they?"

"Rushes were a hollow-stemmed plant that people dipped in fat and burned." Carol twisted her mouth as she thought. "It sounds like they weren't as smelly as the candles, but if they were soaked in fat, you'd think they'd be just as bad."

"They must have been easier to make than candles," Sadie said.

"Mary Frances is dealing with morning sickness and her dad's leg is rotting off," Dee said when Sadie paused. "And the candles were stinky. Poor thing."

"Her dad probably had gangrene," Maddy said. "I think he's the one to feel sorry for."

"The pain must have been intolerable," Bob said. "I wonder why they didn't amputate it the way they did Ira's arm?"

"Amputation was a chancy thing back then," Carol observed, "with no way other than whiskey to alleviate the pain."

"Still, you'd think they might have tried it."

Ida must have been looking ahead. "Here's the answer," she said.

Saturday, 9 May 1741

Why had we but one doctor in Brandtburg, and he related to the Brandts? The Russell women are gifted at healing, and Mistress Hastings as well, but my father's wound needs more knowledge than those good women have between them. None of them knows how to bleed him. Yet I fear he is far beyond any help that bleeding might accomplish. His incoherent nightly ravings keep everyone in the nearby wagons awake, I am sure, although no one has yet complained. The yawns as people muddle through the breaking of our fast each morning, though, are enough to show how exhausted everyone is.

"This is really interesting," Reebok said. "I feel sorry for all of them."

Carol nodded. "They certainly went through a lot to get here, and at this point they're less than a month into the four-year journey."

"Do you think they would have left to begin with if they'd known how long it was going to take them?"

Rebecca Jo studied Reebok for a few seconds. "I wouldn't have."

"You might not have had any choice." Dee made a derogatory sound. "Or would you have stayed with the Brandts?"

Rebecca Jo looked across the table at Carol. "It might not have been too bad. At least some of those Brandts turned out okay."

Sunday 10 May 1741. I fear my brother will die. Doctor Farrard tells me that if the fever does not lessen soon, we will lose him. I sit here, even though I should be taking my rest since Ira is unusually quiet for the moment. I remember the time I crawled through the pasture fence and Ira hauled me out from under the curious noses of the three milk cows our mother kept. It is perhaps my earliest memory, looking up into Ira's face, while one of the large-eyed cows peered at me over Ira's bony shoulder. I doubt they would have trampled me, for they were all sweet-tempered, and I was ever fond of them, but Ira was convinced I needed rescue. He was brave indeed to confront his fear of the cows in order to save me.

I looked up from the page to see a rather goofy look on Carol's face.

"Maybe he wasn't completely bad?" She sounded wistful. I suppose I wouldn't want to think my ancestor had been a total loser.

Maddy wasn't convinced. "That was when Ira was a little kid. Too bad he had to grow up."

"Some kids don't change," Reebok said. "Sometimes they stay the way they were to start with." His voice hardened. "But sometimes they do change. He made a mistake. A bad mistake. But that doesn't mean we have to condemn him forever."

I must admit we all rather gawked at Reebok. I'd never heard him sound so forceful.

"Do you think he ever got over being afraid of cows?"

"He would have had to, Dee." Carol splayed out her fingers. "Everybody had a milk cow or two back then. If not cows, then goats."

I like goats, but I have never seen a cow.

"But didn't the women take care of the cows? I think I read that somewhere." Maddy's question was a good one, but nobody seemed to know the answer.

Finally, Carol said, "It probably depended on the individual family."

"The ones who were afraid of cows probably were the ones with the goats," Dee suggested.

Is HenLady afraid of cows?

For some reason I thought about Maggie Pontiac with her goats and chickens.

Ida made a shushing sound, and we all settled down, even Marmalade. "Two days later, this is what Mary Frances wrote."

Tuesday, 12 May 1741

Edna Russell, who is sixteen and should be far beyond the night terrors of a child, screamed even louder than my father last night, keeping the entire company awake. There were fearful mutterings among the menfolk. This morning we women found that it was not a nightmare that caused her screams but something more elemental. Her costiveness has been bad before but this time it is truly debilitating. We women—almost all of us, excepting only Charlotte Ellis—had a consultation, discussing all the various aperients that could be given her.

"What's costiveness?" Dee asked.

"Constipation," Rebecca Jo said.

"Aperients," Maddy said. "What are aperients?"

"Laxatives," Doc Nathan told her. I'm glad he did, because I didn't know what an aperient was either …

Neither did I.

… although I should have been able to figure it out from the context.

What is a kontex?

"Poor kid," Maddy said. "She must have been miserable to scream so—"

Dee zipped her fingers over her mouth. "What happened to her, Ida?"

Between us, we came up with so many potions and salves and poultices, it will be a wonder if the poor child ever leaves the woods again. At least they were effective.

"Well," Rebecca Jo said, "I guess that answers that. Wonder what they used?"

Personally I was wondering why Charlotte Ellis, the original one, hadn't helped the other women.

"There are two more paragraphs here." Ida looked around to be sure she had our attention.

I was startled this evening just before our meal when

Ida stopped, cocked her head to one side, and held the book out toward Carol. "What's this name? It's spelled S-a-y-r-l-e."

"He was one of the Endicott brothers," Carol said. "I've never heard of it anywhere else."

"How the heck am I supposed to pronounce it?"

"Beats me." Carol looked at Maddy. "Any ideas?"

"Say-er-lee," she guessed, emphasizing the first syllable.

"How about Serl," Sadie suggested, "like Earl but with an S on the front?"

"Maybe it was sar-ler," Dee said. "You know, the way people from England and Boston put r's in where they don't belong?"

Ida twitched her nose. "I'm going to go with Maddy's idea. It makes the most sense."

when Sayrle Endicott approached me and very gently maneuvered me off to one side of the group where we could not be overheard, but not so far away that I would feel uneasy. I have known for long that he favors me—it would be hard not to see—but he surprised me greatly when he asked for my hand in marriage. 'I am loath to mention this,' he told me, 'but the word is that your father may soon die, and I propose to be the one to protect you.' It was most sweet. Of all the despicable Endicotts, he is the only one who is in any way palatable, but marriage? Even were I free, which I am of course not, I would no sooner bind myself to the Endicott clan than I would to a bevy of venomous snakes. He further tried to entice me by saying that he had a number of books that I might enjoy. As if the lure of books would lend credence to his suit. When I told him as gently but as firmly as possible that I would not accept him, he tried to laugh it off, but I could tell I had wounded his pride.

He began to walk away from me, but then turned back and warned me to take care. 'My sister,' he said, 'has taken against you.' He said I should not accept any gifts from her, particularly no food. I know not from whence these warnings come, but as I do not like his sister Charlotte in the first place, I will have no difficulty in following his advice.

When once again I am with my Hubbard, I think I shall not tell him about this, for there is no need to burden him with the knowledge that another man desires me or that someone feels I might be in danger.

"She's planning to keep secrets from Hubbard?" Pat's tone left no doubt what she thought about that. "Husbands and wives shouldn't do that."

I looked at Dave, wondering if he'd say anything to his wife.

Apparently not. He was inspecting his thumbnail. I wondered if he'd even heard her.

The topic of secrets brought Susan Porter, Henry's daughter, to mind. I studied him briefly. He and Irene seemed to have ironed out all that drama that happened when his long-lost daughter showed up in Martinsville and set the gossip mill to turning. I was exceedingly glad that Susan hadn't taken refuge here. Come to think of it, she was one of the ones who'd bought a wood-burning stove. How Roger could stand her, I had no idea. Maybe they spent all their free time ballroom dancing. I wondered if he was at his parents' house now or if he'd sheltered at Susan's retreat center, the one she started when she bought the old Keagan Hotel. Hmm. I'd have to ask Esther. Or Henry.

Henry must have felt my scrutiny. "Poor Sayrle," he said. "I wonder if he ever recovered from the disappointment."

Pat let her breath out audibly. "He probably married somebody else within a month or two."

Tuesday, 12 May 1741

CHARLOTTE ELLIS STARED across the fire. Her brother Sayrle was acting strangely, even for him. He had always been so quiet that Charlotte often forgot he was nearby, but this night she watched him approach the Garner wagon after a surreptitious look around him. He was up to something. Naturally, Charlotte kept her eye on him.

After one more look around him he stepped close to Mary Frances, that silly chit of a girl, and seemed to draw her aside. Now, Charlotte's curiosity was piqued indeed. There was no way she could get close enough to overhear his words, for the slant of his head as he leaned toward Mary Frances told Charlotte that he spoke quietly.

Mary Frances looked surprised, then seemed to choose her words carefully. After a moment, Sayrle turned and stalked away, his shoulders held stiffly, his chin lifted.

What on earth was going on?

When he stopped and walked back to Mary Frances, Charlotte leaned forward and narrowed her eyes, as if the squint might help her hearing, but to no avail. A few moments later, Sayrle left the woman's side.

Charlotte would not have been surprised if it had been Joel who approached Mary Frances, for he mooned after her as if he were sick for her love. Lovesick. Disgusting. But Sayrle? What could he possibly have wanted?

2000

"MAY FIFTEENTH," IDA said. "That's her next entry." She glanced at me. "When is Hubbard's next one?"

I opened the book. "Not till the end of June, the twenty-fourth. Go ahead."

Friday, 15 May 1741

I overheard Reverend Russell speaking with Mister Homer Martin this morning. The Reverend feels that my father's leg must be taken off, but who among us could do that, even to save my father's life? Why, oh why must there have been such a bitter feud between our men and the Brandts? If not for the decision of Homer Martin to leave, we would still have access to Doctor Farrard. We would not be on this trail. My father would not have such a wound. I would be with my dear husband. I hate Homer Martin. No matter how much the men tried to tell us that it was a decision made by all of them, there is not a woman in this group who does not know it was Homer Martin's obduracy that persuaded their final resolution.

And what of the warmer weather we have been promised? Even should it be an easier life whenever or wherever we finally settle, is it worth the cost? What will become of my mother and Constance and Able and me and Wilbur after Father dies? Nehemiah is but nineteen, certainly old enough to have a family of his own if he would but marry, yet I think he may not yet feel ready to take on the leadership of this family.

Ida finally rubbed her eyes and closed the book. "I'm going up to check on Sadie."

Easton beat her to it. "I'll go."

"It's almost time for supper." I picked up the box of matches and started around the room lighting candles. "See if you can get her to come down for it."

"But if she won't," Rebecca Jo said, "we can take up a tray."

84

"Tell her we'll all invade her room and watch her eat." Maddy's grin was wicked. "So she might as well come downstairs."

"That's quite a threat." Easton flounced out of the kitchen.

Rebecca Jo patted her wide waistline. "I'm too full from lunch and all these snacks to face another meal for a while. Maybe quite a while."

I turned to Bob. "We may not feel like going outside later, so can we check the bird feeders now, to be sure there's enough food for them for tomorrow morning?"

"I'll help, too," Reebok offered.

So will I. I will notice every smell of every visitor to the feeders.

Once we hauled the bags of seed, the bucket of dried mealworms, and the packages of suet outside, we stopped almost without thinking. For a moment, before the birds descended, the only movement was the puffing of steam clouds as we breathed. The crystalline air froze the hairs inside my nose, but it was all just so gosh darn beautiful, I barely noticed the cold. The ice covering of the previous day had thickened to an even heavier crust. We scattered sunflower and safflower seed on top of it—plenty of extra so the raccoons and possums would be replete—and made sure the feeders were full. I was privately surprised to see the ease with which Reebok hoisted those heavy bags. Had he been working out?

Once enough seed was distributed, we retreated indoors. Even before we had the door closed, I could hear the *chicka-dee-dee-dees*, the trill of Carolina wrens, and the raucous calls of the cardinals behind us.

Melissa had set out a plate of cookies—as if we needed more food!—and everyone was still congregated around the table, munching and laughing. Sort of like the chickadees, I thought. Except for Charlie Ellis. Maybe she was still full—we had been eating a lot—but how could she resist cookies, especially my molasses chewies? I took one for myself. I was just about ready to go up and check on Sadie and Easton when Marmalade let out one of her gurgles.

They are coming.

I patted her and then looked up to see the two women wearing smiles and warm fuzzy bathrobes. Every bit of conversation stopped abruptly. Easton wore what I recognized as Sadie's practical bright yellow chenille bathrobe. It was way too short for her, and a pair of ridiculous-looking striped knee socks peeked out from underneath it. Sadie wore a soft blue bathrobe that brushed the floor. Around her neck was the blue and orange scarf that had looked so outrageous up in the attic, but that now seemed to brighten her path.

She walked the length of the kitchen and stopped in front of Carol Mellinger. "I think it's time for a change," she said, giving Carol a big hug.

Needless to say, the kitchen erupted with our cheers.

Eventually, Glaze spoke loudly enough for her voice to calm the rest of us. "Sadie? Tom and I would love it if you would wear that stunning marian blue ensemble to our wedding tomorrow evening."

Glaze was the artist in the family. Leave it to her to give the painter's name to that particular shade. I had no idea what marian blue was, except that it was right in front of me, draped around Sadie. Glaze had once referred to Sadie's house as cadmium. I should have looked it up. You'd think, with me as a librarian, I'd chase down every word I didn't know. All I'd registered, though, was that Sadie's house was incredibly bright. Happy-looking. I'd had no idea it sheltered such a broken heart.

"That's a great idea," Easton said. "The bathrobe can be the first item in your brand new wardrobe."

"But that will leave you without a long enough robe," Sadie said. "I've enjoyed borrowing this one, but I'll need to return it to you so you can keep your ankles warm."

Easton lifted one blue and white striped foot and rotated it. "You think these heavy knee socks you knitted for me last year won't keep me warm enough?"

"Looks like a trip to Mabel's Dress Shop is going to be on the schedule," Rebecca Jo said, "once we can get back on the roads. In the meantime, I have a green sweatshirt you're welcome to use, Sadie."

"You'll need to get yourself some purple Wellingtons for when you're working your hives," Bob suggested.

"Pink pedal pushers for summer," Ida proposed.

What are petal pushers?

"What are pedal pushers?"

"You're too young, Maddy," Ida said. "They're pants that only reach to mid-calf. What do they call them now? Capris?"

"Just think of all the colors you could begin to wear," Dee said. "Like cement."

We all looked at her blankly, until Father John started to laugh. "*Sea-mint*. That's good. How about *Baby, It's Gold Outside?*"

"You'll need some bright colors, too," Melissa said. "What about *Red Any Good Books Lately?*"

"Why don't you get some new tennis shoes," Henry said, "for running around town in? Maybe a nice shade of *In the Pink.*"

"Or *Tickle Me Pink*," Dee said.

"*Hi-Ho Silver?*" That came from Rebecca Jo.

"*Beige as a Bagel*, perhaps?" Dave looked exceptionally proud of himself for that one, although I privately thought it was a bit lame.

"Naw," Ralph said. "Beige is *Nacho Good Color* for Sadie. I think something along the line of *Navel Orange* might be better for her skin tones."

Ida scowled at her husband. "Since when are you a skin tone expert?"

"Since I heard you talking about it on the phone last week."

Anxious to head off any dissension, I suggested, "Maybe Sadie could wear *Laughender*."

"*I'm So Blue*," Carol said.

"You are?" Maddy looked concerned until Carol made a funny face.

"*That's Not What I Mint*," she clarified.

"*Existential Gilt*," Father John intoned.

"I know one." Reebok set down his hot chocolate. "*Come and Get Me Copper.*"

Bob raised his coffee mug. "You win the prize, Garner."

For what? I do not know what anyone is talking about.

Reebok's face flooded with a delicious shade of pink, rather like the heirloom peony that bloomed by the front deck each summer. I waited just long enough for the applause to die down a bit before I said, "Okay. There's time for more attic discoveries before supper. Let's head back upstairs."

"Once you get the kitchen cleaned up," Ralph reminded me.

"This wasn't a meal," Ida told him. "It was a snack, and you fellas didn't prepare it."

Bob stood. "Looks like we're all cleaning up." He pointed with his nose. "That end of the table gather the trash. In the middle, you clear off any plates or cups. I'll wash. The other four at this end"—he nodded to Doc and me on his left—"will dry." Then he looked at Maddy and Ida on his right. "You'll put things away. Sound like a good agenda?"

Not waiting for an answer, he headed for the wood stove to get the kettle of hot water.

"Fine with me," Ida said. "I'm not going to read anything for awhile. This old writing is hard on the eyeballs."

But your eyeballs are in your head.

For some unknown reason, Carol laughed. I hadn't thought Ida's comment was at all funny. She bent to murmur something to Marmalade, who had just let out one of her loud meows.

Ida stood and patted Ralph on the shoulder. "You're in the middle group, and I'm on the end. Bring our plates, and I'll meet you at the sink."

"Then can I sit and watch you work for once?"

"What do you mean *for once*?"

"You call it work? All that fun you've been having up in the attic?"

She studied Ralph the way she might have inspected a cockroach in her pantry.

"You're in trouble now," Dave said in a singsong.

But Ida surprised all of us. She laughed. "Actually, we *have* been having a great deal of fun. And it hasn't felt like work." She surveyed the women around the kitchen. "Has it?"

"Not to me," I said. "But while our end of the table is washing up, the rest of you can go get some more wood or something."

"If the ice weren't so thick, we could have a snowball fight," Father John said.

"And we'd pay for it in the morning with joints that won't bend," Henry reminded his friend.

"Scoot!" Ida flapped her hands the way Maggie Pontiac did when she was trying to herd her hens into the coop. Luckily, all of us people were slightly more cooperative than a bunch of chickens.

I will stay here at the table with GrayGuy.

Marmalade jumped back onto the chair I'd just vacated. When

she curled up, she looked like a pale—and much leaner—reflection of Korsi who was snuggled in Doc's chair.

1983

CLARA WAS GOING to kill him. Hubbard Martin knew that without a doubt. Meanwhile, Hubbard was going to kill Carl Armitage. Carl was usually so inefficient, he let everything slide, but this one time—first time ever—he'd gotten the council's agenda to the *Record* before the deadline, and they'd printed it, including the place that outlined the *Proposal by Clara Martin*. And Maggie and Norm Pontiac had read it. So had everybody else in Martinsville, including Dave Pontiac.

He looked around at the other council members. Not a one of them would meet his eye. He'd wanted to talk to Ralph Peterson before the meeting, but Ralph hadn't gotten there early, the way he usually did.

Maggie and Norm sat there in the third row among a bunch of their friends, but Hubbard couldn't help but notice that Maggie had saved two seats right next to her.

He shuffled the stack of papers in front of him and called the meeting to order. Maybe he wouldn't show up.

But he did.

Norm's parents walked down the aisle, sidled in front of a few folks, and sat down. Dave reached across the two women and shook Norm's hand.

Then he looked up at Hubbard and raised one eyebrow, leaving no doubt in Hubbard's mind that if Hubbard didn't side with Maggie and Norm, Dave would go straight to Clara and to heck with the consequences.

Surely he wouldn't. Surely he had too much to lose.

But Hubbard didn't dare take that chance. He gnawed at his lower lip and wished he was dead.

CLARA MARTIN STOOD at the council podium. She planted her feet firmly so she wouldn't fidget. This was too important a night to let nerves get the better of her. She was sure of Hubbard of course. He'd never do anything without her knowledge and approval. But there were two or three of the others that she hadn't been able to get a commitment from.

Her arguments were impeccably lined up, though, and her logic was unassailable.

Maggie Pontiac's chickens were a disgrace to the town. To say nothing of those goats of hers.

Clara wanted the chickens gone. Hadn't that rooster woken her up more than enough mornings as it was? But Clara hadn't been a politician's wife for nothing. She knew when to pick her battles and where to wage them. Too many people in town bought eggs from Maggie.

The chickens would have to wait their turn.

For now, the goats were her target. Once they were banned, she'd go after the chickens.

Goats are dirty, she told the council. They stink. They attract flies. Right in the middle of town. The goats were disruptive. People were always stopping along the sidewalk to watch them bouncing around all over the place. There had even been times when people came from out of town and parked all higgledy-piggledy on the street while the drivers and their passengers got out and took pictures, especially in the spring when there were baby goats bouncing around all over the place. What kind of image of Martinsville was that?

As she presented each point, she put a checkmark next to it on her list. Her long list.

Once every item was checked off, she moved to have goats banned from inside the town limits.

Clara had never supposed that Maggie Pontiac would be at the meeting, but some traitor had put the item on the agenda ahead of time, which meant that everybody read it when it was printed in the *Keagan County Record*. Not only was Maggie there, seated in the third row back, but it seemed like a quarter of the town filled the other chairs.

"I like the goats," one woman said as soon as Hubbard asked for comments from the audience. "I take my kids to watch them sometimes, and the goats are so friendly they always come over to the fence to talk to us—or that's what it seems like."

"Goats are not dirty," another person testified, "regardless of what some people think. I buy goat milk from Maggie for our little boy who's allergic to cow's milk."

"I buy it for the same reason." Bisque McKee—that traitorous librarian. Clara was going to have to get rid of her as well as the chickens. "Only it's for one of my granddaughters. And I drink it myself, since I know there aren't any growth hormones in goat milk."

"Maggie's milking parlor is impeccably clean," Ida Peterson said, and Clara knew then that Ralph Peterson would vote to keep the goats, especially after the meaningful look Ida gave him before she sat back down.

"And the goats don't stink," someone else argued. "Maggie told me it's because she keeps only female goats, and only brings in the males when it's breeding time. It's the males that stink."

Well, Clara couldn't argue with that, not the way she was so angry with Hubbard for publicizing this agenda item ahead of time. Males *did* stink. That Nick Foley, for instance. He sat there with the other council members nodding his head like he agreed with all these people. Clara had known Nick Foley would be trouble the moment he got himself elected to the council. He still held a grudge. She was sure of it. All those years ago, he'd asked her to go steady with him. She'd refused, of course. Told Nick he didn't have a chance because she planned to marry Cornelius Martin once the two of them got old enough. After Cornelius died, Nick asked her again. How many times did she have to say no?

Now, she knew, he was getting his revenge.

"The goats are kind of a Martinsville tradition," Sharon Armitage said.

Hmph. That did it. Carl would have to vote the way his wife wanted him to. Clara was going to cancel her next hair appointment. She'd travel all the way to Garner Creek if she had to to get her hair done. She was never walking through the door of Sharon's Beauty Shop again as long as she lived.

"They're cute," said Margaret Casperson. "And Fergus, their watchdog, keeps coyotes away from town."

Maggie stood then. "I'd like to correct a misconception, Margaret. Fergus couldn't possibly keep coyotes away from Martinsville. I think it's just luck that we haven't had any in town. But if they ever do show up and try to jump over our fence, Fergus will certainly protect his goats from them." That was all she said. She didn't even try to defend herself. She had the gall to smile at Clara before she took her seat.

After all the other council members voted to keep the goats, Clara didn't speak to Hubbard for three weeks, even though he'd abstained from voting.

2000

THE CLEANUP OPERATION didn't take long. Almost before I knew it, we trooped back up to the attic. Beside me, Glaze bent down to pat Marmalade. "Will you still come visit me when I move out?"

Out to where?

"That's good," Glaze said. "I can count on Marmalade."

I happened to glance up in time to see a quizzical look come over Carol's face.

SmellSweet did not listen to me. I asked her a question and she did not answer it.

Carol waited until Marmalade finished meowing and then asked, "Where are you moving to, Glaze?"

Thank you for asking that.

Glaze held out her left hand, and her engagement ring, a tasteful green sapphire surrounded by a ring of small diamond chips, glinted in the soft attic light. "I'm glad you'll be attending my wedding. My fiancé, Tom, owns a restaurant here in town."

"A marvelous restaurant," Melissa said, and the rest of us seconded her.

"I'll be moving into his house a couple of blocks from here on Second Street."

Oh.

"Does Marmalade know where his house is?"

Yes. Fishgiver is a good friend of mine.

"She sure does."

"Marmalade has a regular route," I said. "She visits most of our friends."

That is because they are my friends, too.

"I always give her a little dish of cream," Sadie said.

I enjoy it, LooseLaces.

"She gets chicken when she visits me," Melissa said. "Or whatever else I have on hand."

Yes. Thank you, GoodCook.

"Tomatoes when they're in season," Rebecca Jo said.

Several of the women gasped. "Tomatoes?"

"Remember Annie McGill?"

I remember TomatoLady.

"She told me once that Marmalade liked fresh organic tomatoes. So, once Annie was gone, I decided to keep up the practice."

I like your tomatoes, too, BookLady.

"And Tom always seems to have some salmon for her," Glaze said.

I am very fond of fish.

"It's a wonder she doesn't weigh a ton," I said.

"All that walking around town must be what keeps her trim," Carol said. "I'm glad she'll be able to continue to visit you, Glaze."

Yes. Thank you for the information.

Carol glanced down toward Marmalade and, for some reason, said, "You're welcome." She pulled the hand-drawn map of the Metoochie River Valley out of her pants pocket. "Can you imagine what the breakup of families must have entailed back in the 1700s? Nowadays, even if you moved to Garner Creek or Russell Gap, Glaze, you'd still be able to visit back and forth easily. But imagine the first Martinsvillians—"

"Is that a word?"

"I doubt it, Maddy, but it gets the idea across, wouldn't you say? Anyway, imagine when some of them left to go back up the valley to start their own homesteads and those new towns. They'd have to leave behind everything, everyone they knew."

We were silent for a few moments. "Even when they left Brandtburg in 1741," Rebecca Jo said, "at least they still had the entire Martin group. Who do you suppose was the first to leave here?"

"Probably a younger son," Carol said. "The eldest usually inherited the family farm or the family profession, and the younger ones would have to either work for their brother or find some other place. I imagine the available farm land around here was claimed fairly quickly, so they'd almost have to move north."

Maddy shook her head. "It was probably the Endicotts," she said. "They must have left in order to found Enders."

"No," Glaze said with decision. "One of those other families probably bailed out along the way first. Didn't you mention a Fountain family, Carol?"

"Yes. Peter Fountain."

"Isn't he the one who had a dozen children?"

"Only eight," Carol said.

"Well, with that many children, if they'd stuck to Homer, you'd think there would be a whole slew of Fountains hereabouts, but I've never heard of any."

"Me either," said Sadie.

"Or me," put in Rebecca Jo, "although there are some Endicotts here and there."

"It makes sense that the Endicotts would have been among the last to leave the group," Dee said, "since they ended up so close by."

"Unless there were other families that left at the same time and went back to the north instead of south," Glaze pointed out. "Does anyone know if there are other towns immediately north of Keagan County?"

I searched the faces of the group. Everyone looked as blank as I'm sure I did. "I never looked at a map with that in mind." I headed for the stairs. "Be right back."

Keagan County and the Metoochie River Valley are difficult to find even on the most detailed map, and the one I had was no exception, but when I spread it out across our card table, right over the letters Sadie and I had sorted into piles, we saw that the land north of the valley, all the way into North Carolina, was a craggy collection of deep, narrow, presumably wooded, valleys. I love maps that show the contour lines. "I'm sure a few individual small farms can be found there," I said, "but the slopes are so rugged you'd have to be a mountain goat to get around easily."

I like goats.

"That still doesn't mean a family might not have left. Just that they most likely didn't found any towns along that stretch of the river."

"With all the things that could go wrong," Dee said, "I think I would have wanted to stay with the big group."

My mom was usually the most patient of women, but she put a stop to all our guessing. "I want to get started. Just point us toward a trunk." She stopped when Esther held up her hand.

"Not yet. I want my own hat."

Carol reached up to a stack of hatboxes on one of the piles of military footlockers.

Those flat metal trunks were probably filled with uniforms, and I didn't feel like I could face that at the moment. All those thoughts of war. "I can't believe how many hatboxes are still unexplored," I said.

Carol handed the top one to Esther. "How about this?"

"Looks good to me."

"I'll take the next in the pile," my mom said.

Mom's hat was rather ordinary looking, but Esther's was a gorgeous white knit piece with five rows of heavy ribbing turned up around the edge. Above the ribs, two full crocheted white flowers nestled in a bed of small green crocheted leaves. Tasteful. Elegant. Esther looked rather stunned as she lifted it from the box. I don't think she even noticed the envelope that fluttered to the floor until Glaze stooped to pick it up.

"Wait," I said, doing a mental count of bodies. "We're missing somebody. Pat! You won't want to miss this."

Pat and Charlie were bent over the same trunk halfway down the attic. They both straightened so fast they bumped their heads together, and there were a few moments of confusion as they got themselves straightened out.

"Charlie, too." I'd forgotten about her.

"This is the most gorgeous hat I've ever seen," Esther said once everybody was assembled.

"I think you're right," Maddy said. "I thought my indigo hat was pretty wonderful, but this one's exquisite."

"Not quite as good as mine." Ida fluffed her white feather and chuckled at Esther's incredulous stare.

"There's a story here, Esther," I said. "We'll clue you in later. Meanwhile, why don't you try it on?"

"And then, you can read the letter that was in the hatbox with it," Glaze said, handing her the envelope.

Esther peered at the stamp. "England. My, my, do I have a genuine British hat here?"

"Apparently," Glaze said. "Read it. Maybe it'll tell us where it came from."

"It sure looks like your hat's never been worn," Amanda observed.

"Either that, or someone took very good care of it," Rebecca Jo said. "I wonder why it ended up here in the attic? I can't imagine a hat like this would go out of style anytime."

Esther slipped the hat into place—it might have been made for her—pulled a chair up beside Sadie's and my card table and opened the envelope.

```
            9 April 1912
            Tuesday
            South Western Hotel
            Southampton, England
Amelia Stockton Hoskins
Beechnut House
Martinsville Georgia
USA

Dearest Amelia,
```

"Wait!" Melissa's voice blared through the attic. "Amelia—wasn't that the name of the woman in the photograph? The one looking back over her shoulder?"

"You're right," Maddy said. "I think it was."

"I know it was. Do you think this could be the same person? When was that photo taken?"

Maddy unwound herself from her pile of pillows and rooted through the museum drawer. "Eighteen-ninety. So Amelia must have married Young Gideon Hoskins, the one she gave the photograph to, and here she is twenty—no, twenty-two years later, living in Beechnut House."

"And wearing this hat, apparently," Esther said. "The next line says …"

I do hope you will love this hat as much as I do. I bought it a fortnight ago at a quaint millinery shop in London that was almost within sight of Buckingham Palace, and the hat, I feel, is grand enough for a queen, which is why I am posting it to you. I have simply no more room in my trunks.

Esther looked up and grinned. "So, it definitely is a genuine London hat! And from near the palace, too."
"Keep reading," Sadie said.

I have no doubt I will be home in Martinsville long before the hat arrives, for we leave England tomorrow, and should arrive in New York harbor the morning of the 17th. Can you imagine how fast we will be steaming there—but five days to cross the entire Atlantic Ocean? I do not know how long the Royal Mail Service will take, but I would imagine it will be somewhat longer than our voyage. From New York we will travel posthaste via train to the Tallulah Falls depot in Cornelia where, as you know if you have received my other letters, we left our automobile, so it will not take us long at all to travel those last miles back home.
I cannot wait to watch you open this package and hear your cries of delight.
By then I will have enthralled you with stories of our journeys through Paris and London. This has indeed been the trip of a life-

time, and I plan to recount it for as long as
I live to anyone who will listen. John has
paid slightly more than ten pounds apiece for
our second-class tickets on the ocean liner. I
begged to go first class, but John, ever thrifty
as he is, would not pay eight times as much
just so we might have twenty-three courses for
each dinner instead of a mere three.

There will be more than 2,000 passengers
on the ship. Can you conceive of that many? I
have already met one of our second-class companions, a delightful young woman named Ed-
wina Troutt. She travels alone and assured me
last evening when we met her at dinner that
she was happy to be sailing in two days rather
than waiting for the ship she was scheduled to
board. It has been delayed because of a coal
strike. She feels certain the Titanic is a
much lovelier ship, but even if it were not so
grand, she looks forward to arriving home sooner than planned.

"The Titanic?" Esther dropped the letter into her lap. "She was on the Titanic?"

"That's sure what it sounds like," Carol said.

"Maybe they missed the ship and made it home some other way?" Maddy didn't sound too hopeful.

"No wonder this letter got saved," Rebecca Jo said. "It's prob-ably the last thing Amelia ever received from whoever wrote this."

Esther checked the signature. "Her cousin Mary."

"Except the hat," I said. "Can you imagine how horrible it would have been to get the hat after she already knew her cousin was dead?"

Esther swallowed hard and continued reading.

Give my regards to your husband. I wish

him well with all the animals he cares for. And please bestow an enormous hug on Perry, although I doubt he will appreciate it, his being a terribly grown-up eleven years of age.

I know you must wonder at the type-writing of this letter. I never knew of a hotel that provided type-writers for the use of the guests. I have had great fun experimenting with it, and even note that I have not misspelled a single word. You would love the South Western Hotel. It is truly beautiful. I hope that someday you and Gideon will be able to trvel here.

Oh dear! There is my first type-writing mistake, leaving the a out of travel.

I look forward to seeing you soon,

Your loving cousin,

Mary

post script: If you have not found occasion to use the opera glasses I sent you last spring, you will soon, for John has informed me that on our next trip to New York City, I may take along a companion. You will love the opera!

"No wonder Amelia never wore the hat," Esther said.

"I know that woman she referred to in the letter," Maddy said. "I read up a lot on the Titanic when I was researching one of my books. I planned to have a homicidal maniac loose in the halls of the ship, but the story just never came together."

"I can see why not," Dee said, and Maddy growled at her.

Why are you growling, CurlUp?

"The woman," I reminded her.

"The Troutt woman survived. She lived to be a hundred years old if I remember correctly."

Quietly Esther returned the letter to its envelope and removed the hat. "I think this needs to be in the museum rather than on my head."

It was looking a little dim up here. The sun must have gone behind a heavier-than-usual cloud. I lit a couple of lanterns. Sadie went to her usual seat at the card table, but turned her chair around so she faced our informal circle. "Let's start with the next journal entry."

"First," I said, "I have a question, Sadie."

She looked an inquiry at me.

"While you were napping, Bob told us you worked as one of the Rosie the Riveters during the war. I'm really curious. Could you tell us about it?"

"Oh, Lordy, I hardly ever even think of those times anymore." She smoothed out a non-existent wrinkle on the blue bathrobe she still wore. "Wallace was gone, you see, on his way over the ocean, and I had nothing to hold me here. Sammy wasn't born yet. Wallace's brother-in-law had been one of the first Americans to die in the war, and that left his sister Cathy alone living in Omaha. We tried to talk her into moving here, but she didn't want to be too far from her husband's grave, so I went to her."

Her eyes took on a slightly unfocused look. "Those troop trains were packed to the gills with servicemen, mostly young fellows headed to training camps, but somehow I managed to get a ticket. Each train I boarded, there was a serviceman who'd offer me his seat. I always wondered if those young men—boys, they were, really, even though I wasn't much older than some of them—I wondered if they survived. I'd like to hope they did, but we lost so many."

Gradually all the other attic women had taken seats around the circle. "So," Ida said, "you went to Omaha." I could tell from her inflection that it wasn't a question. She must have heard this story before, but there were a lot of us who hadn't.

"When I got to Omaha, Cathy already had jobs lined up for us. You'd think with her being a new widow, she'd want to sit home and grieve, but nothing could have been farther from her mind. *I want to be sure other men survive so there won't be more widows like me*, she told me that first evening after I got off the train. *We're going to do our part.* Omaha, like most of the cities and the towns as well, was seeing a big drain on their manpower, so the manufacturers agreed to use woman power. That's what the poster was all about."

"Poster?"

"Yes, Amanda. The Rosie the Riveter poster. Surely you've seen a photo of one—the woman wearing a blue blouse with her dark hair tied up in a red bandana."

"Flexing her biceps," I said.

"That poster convinced a lot of women to go out and fill the jobs their husbands had held before they enlisted. That's what Cathy had done, and of course as production demands mounted with the war effort, they needed a lot more manpower. Woman-power, I guess you'd say."

"Rosie sounds like pretty effective propaganda," Amanda said.

Sadie nodded, but there was a sadness I couldn't quite place, so I asked, "What did you do once you were hired?"

"Oh, there was a training program first. I worked in a plant that built airplanes. And yes, I put in rivets that held the wings together, among other things." She grinned. "It was an assembly line, but we took pride in our work, and I always hoped that one of the bombers I helped put together would stop a German advance that otherwise might have killed my Wallace."

"Did you ever doubt he'd come home?"

Sadie studied Carol for a moment before answering her. "I don't think I did. Maybe in the middle of the night, but time has sort of blurred the memories, and, after all, he *did* come home."

When she was quiet for several long seconds, Ida prompted her. "And?"

"He had terrible nightmares."

It was such a simple statement, but I recalled all too clearly the nights I'd held Bob when he woke from dreams—nightmares—of Viet Nam.

Sadie sat quietly again, and I became more and more sure she had something else that needed saying. "What is it, Sadie?" I finally asked.

"We built B-29s. Bombers. They were called the Superfortress." She spread her hands and looked at the backs of them, then turned them over and inspected the palms. "One of the planes that came from our plant turned out to be the *Enola Gay.* I've often wondered if my hands set some of the rivets in that particular plane."

She raised her shoulders and dropped them. "Of course, the planes didn't have names when we were building them, so there's no way to know."

We all seemed to take a deep breath at the same time. "Do you hope," I finally ventured, "that you did, or hope that you didn't?"

"When I remember that it led to the end of the war in the Pacific, I hope I helped build it. But when I see the photographs of the devastation, I hope I didn't." She looked around the circle. "Does that make any sense at all?"

Esther Anderson cleared her throat. "Does anything connected with war make sense?" I remembered that her husband, Tom's grandfather, had been killed in Korea.

We went back to our various trunks and boxes in a rather subdued mood. War stories tended to do that to me.

Do what?

Pat went back to the trunk she'd been examining earlier. It wasn't two minutes before she found another old envelope. But this one held a black-bordered death notice with a penny tucked inside.

"Maude Singleton?" Pat checked out the circle that had formed around her. "Anybody know of a Maude in, uh, 1913?"

Nobody did.

1913

YOUNG GIDEON HOSKINS set down his pen and ran both hands through his hair. "What is it, Perry? What's that you have there?"

"It's a Lincoln penny! Mr. Breeton gave it to me in change at the store." He handed it to his father.

"I read about these in the newspaper three, maybe four years ago, but this is the first one I've seen." He checked the date stamped on the coin. "Nineteen-aught-nine. We'll need to keep this. That's the year the first ones were minted."

Amelia walked into the kitchen at that moment. "What about mint? Are you brewing tea?"

It took the veterinarian a moment to interpret his wife's comment. "Not the herb. The one-cent Lincoln coin."

Perry quickly lost interest and wandered away, but Amelia studied the bit of copper. "His face looks most thoughtful. I've never seen one of these."

"Neither have I. That's what I told our son." He looked back at the several papers he had spread out on the kitchen table. "It has taken four years for these pennies to find their way into our town, but not even a month for the federal government to find us and send us"—he gestured to the forms—"this notice about the new income tax."

"Oh, dear." Amelia sank into the chair next to him and lifted the paper closest to her. "A full page of directions? How complicated this looks."

"Turn it over. Look at page number three."

She studied the other side of the paper. "Deductions? Do we have any?"

"We haven't any debt, so we haven't paid interest on any loans. And no losses due to shipwreck. I do believe lines three—that's the school tax—and the last one, number six, are the only ones that apply to us."

She ran her finger several inches down the page and read number six aloud. "*Amount representing a reasonable allowance for the exhaustion, wear, and tear of property arising out of its use or employment in the business.* What wear and tear?"

"I thought I might list the number of items of mine the Surratt's goats have eaten."

She laughed at his droll tone. "You bought several implements during the past year. Surely they could be listed on line number one." She picked up the other page and studied both sides. "Four pages altogether. Why did they have to make this so complicated?" Amelia screwed her face into that patently fake grimace he loved so much. "One per cent," she read. "That does seem excessive."

"Be glad we did not make $500,000, for then we would have to pay ..."—he leaned over and bumped his shoulder against hers and she joined him in reading the amount for that category—"six per cent."

The Lincoln one-cent piece sat enshrined on the middle of the table until the following week when Amelia received the black-bordered notice of the passing of her cousin Maude. She had never been that close to Maude, but Maude had a four-year-old son who would now be motherless, and for that Amelia felt extremely sorry.

Her eyes rested briefly on the coin. The boy had been born in 1909. Someday he would appreciate having the coin, but he was too young for now. She tucked the penny into the envelope and set it aside. Another ten years and she would send it to him.

Three years later, though, the boy and his father were both killed when their buggy overturned on the sharp curve of the road between Braetonburg and Martinsville.

2000

"THIS IS RIDICULOUS," I said some time later. "These papers are so jumbled up. That one"—I pointed to the letter Sadie had read earlier, the one about *another* boy from Lovina to Melanie Hoskins—"was from 1827, while this one," and I held up a brown-stained sheet of paper, "was in the same bundle, but it's dated February 14, 1746, almost eighty years earlier."

Dee held out her hand, and I passed the letter to her. "Valentine's Day? More than two hundred years ago?"

"I don't think Valentine's Day had been invented that long ago," Ida said. "Wasn't it a Victorian thing?"

"You're partly right," Carol said. "St. Valentine's Day was a feast day in the Middle Ages, but the tradition of sending fancy cards didn't come into vogue until the nineteenth century."

"How do you know so much?" Ida didn't sound peeved at having been contradicted. If I could have attached an emotion to her words, it would have been something akin to awe. I was pretty much in awe of Carol myself, even though she hadn't known anything about liability laws. I guess you can't know everything.

"So," Mom said, "what does it say?"

"Here." Dee handed the letter back to me. "You read it. I have trouble deciphering this old handwriting."

Friday, 14 February 1746
My dearest MaryAnne, if I may be so bold as to address you in such a way,

Surely you cannot be unaware of my feelings for you, but I fear that you may be completely unaware of the depth of those feelings. As you well know, I am unable to express myself with ease. My fault of speech has long been a burden to me, but never so much as when I find myself near you, wishing to speak with ease and clarity, but having no way to curb my wayward tongue, which seems always to be tied in a knot.

"Oh," Maddy said, "that's so sweet."

"Tied in a knot," Dee said. "Tongue-tied? Do you think that means he stuttered?"

"Well," Rebecca Jo said, "he obviously had some sort of speech impediment. Keep going, Biscuit. I want to see how this turns out."

I am therefore reduced to plying this undertaking of mine in a written missive, this precious sheet of paper having been supplied to me by the most generous Mister Silas Martin, although I misdoubt he knew for what purpose it was to be employed, for I was unwilling to broach the subject of my heartfelt hopes to anyone else before I had unburdened my heart to your dear self.

"He sure is wordy," Ida commented, "and that sounds like it was all one sentence."

"If he stutters," Dee said, "maybe he feels like this is his only chance to express himself."

Maddy drew her index finger and thumb across her lips. "Shhh!"

I have loved you ever since that day when, heedless of the danger to yourself, you flung yourself into the path of that murderous painter in your desire to save your brother. As I saw you leap forward, my heart constricted, for I knew at that moment that I could not bear to lose you. Had that dead hickory not fallen when it did, had it not struck down the painter in mid-leap, I feel certain you would have at-

tacked the cat barehanded, for such is your courage.

"She attacked a mountain lion?" Sadie sounded incredulous and I could see why.

A lion?

"This is what's so intriguing about an attic like this," Carol said. "There are all these stories that we may never fully understand, but the glimpses we get into the lives of these people is something I find absolutely fascinating."

"Me, too," Sadie said, "but could a tree really have fallen on the mountain lion?"

Another lion?

She looked around the circle, and most of us shrugged. Even Marmalade seemed to join in Sadie's query. "I don't know," I said, "but I suppose stranger coincidences have happened."

Maddy bent over my shoulder and studied the letter. "It sure sounds like MaryAnne, whoever she was, was a fireball."

"The only MaryAnne I recall from the original lists was Mary-Anne Breeton," Carol said, "and she was only thirteen when they left Brandtburg."

"The date on this letter is 1746—do you realize the United States hadn't even been formed yet? We were still the Colonies. I wonder if anybody says anything about King George in here. Wouldn't that be a find? Anyway, in 1746, if this was in fact your MaryAnne Breeton, she would have been"—Maddy counted on her fingers—"eighteen by this time."

"Certainly of a marriageable age," Carol said. "In fact, girls back then were considered marriageable when they were only fourteen or fifteen."

"I wonder why she waited so long," Dee said.

"Maybe she was waiting for somebody," Ida waved at the letter, "to get his tongue untied."

Melissa seemed to be thoroughly intrigued. "Keep reading," she said.

Dare I hope that you will allow me to ask your father for permission to court you? Dare I hope that you might be willing to accept my suit if only I can prove myself worthy of you?

Please know that, should you agree to become my wife, I will provide for you until my dying breath. Should you refuse me, I will remain unmarried, for I cannot in good conscience marry another when my heart is forever in your keeping.

Needless to say, we all sighed ...
He sounds as nice as SoftFoot.
... even Marmalade. I finished reading the final two lines.

With deepest hopes, I remain your ever faithful
Thomas Russell

"Russell?" Sadie reached out for the letter. "I was born a Russell. Do you think this could be my great-great and so on grandfather?"

Ida wiggled her fingers at the letter. "There's something on the back of it. Did he write a P.S.?"

Sadie turned the paper over and shook her head. "This writing's in a different hand, but the same date."

14 February 1746

If you think to hide behind a letter, Thomas Russell, you must disabuse yourself of that notion immediately. I will not be proposed to in writing. I expect you to speak to me yourself.

Sadie looked up with a grin. "That's pretty clear."

"She must be your ancestor, then," Ida said.

"Why?"

"Because you have just as much spunk, which you obviously inherited from her."

Sadie looked inordinately pleased. Eventually she began to chuckle, and the sound was so infectious, I couldn't help but join in.

"I don't know what's so funny," I finally said, "but this has been a really good laugh."

"It's probably funnier to think about than it will be to explain it," she said.

Amanda appeared at my side. "Laughing is really good for you. It massages your internal organs."

Sounded like a good idea to me, and it didn't cost anything. I'd spent a fair amount of money going to Amanda on a regular basis—and didn't begrudge a cent of it because I always came off her massage table feeling so much better than when I'd walked in the door.

"The best part is that you can get the laughter treatment any time of the day or night, and you don't have to pay for it." She must have been something of a mind reader.

"What was so funny, Sadie?" I asked.

"I just thought that I've spent so much time trying to learn about my ancestors, and all I had to do was come look through the trunks up here to meet them practically face to face."

I waited for a moment, wondering if there would be a punch line of some sort.

"Like I said," she added, "it's not as funny when I say it out loud."

It is not funny to me because I do not understand it.

"I've never been that interested in genealogy," my mom said from the other side of the white dresser. "I keep track of about two generations back, but beyond that it seems like I can never get to know those people, to know what they're really like, so I just haven't bothered."

She peeked out from behind the dresser and must have noticed my cocked eyebrow, because she added, "You don't feel like I neglected your cultural education, do you?"

"Not at all." The wind gave a particularly vicious moan right then. "Everybody with a wood stove probably has a jam-packed house," I said. "I wonder who's staying at the Johnson's."

"Don't you remember, Biscuit? I told you when we got here about who all was there."

"No you didn't, Esther." I know I tune out periodically, but I would have heard something like that.

"Oh," Esther said, "that's right. That was when the snowmobiles showed up and made so much noise."

"And brought such wonderful gifts," Glaze said.

Esther seemed not to hear her. "Some people just can't seem to get along. Seems like everyone up there has been sniping at each other ever since they walked in, and they're probably still doing it, which is one reason why I think the Johnsons were sorry to see Bob take us away."

"I guess I'm glad everybody has a place to shelter from the storm," I said, happy that the people who'd ended up here were nice folk. Of course, if this storm went on for another day or two, would we begin to get on each other's nerves?

"You guess?" Glaze was laughing at me, and that made everybody else laugh, too.

That was probably just as well. It kept me from having to explain my thought processes.

On a happier note, I contemplated how lucky it was that so many people had bought those wood stoves. I envisioned little pockets of people all over Martinsville, keeping toasty warm as they huddled around the fire.

"Well," Mom said, "let's keep looking." She lifted a lidded, dark brown basket made of wicker—it looked like a picnic hamper—from the top of a flat-topped trunk. "Maybe we'll find something special in here." She studied the outside of it. "Interesting hasp."

Naturally I had to go over and look closer. "Is that a bone?"

"Sure looks like it. A turkey leg bone, Maybe?"

I echoed her. "Sure looks like it."

Dee sidled up beside me. "Why on earth would anybody …" She left the question dangling.

"It looks clean enough." Mom worked the bone out of the leather loop and opened the basket.

Four pewter cups, four pewter plates, and one light blue glove.

"I get the cups and plates," Mom said. "But one glove?"

"Maybe—"

Before Maddy could say anything more, Dee interrupted her.

"Don't make up a story, Maddy. We'll never know why."

Maddy pulled her arm away from Dee's grasp. "It's fun to guess, though."

Amanda reached around Dee and touched the glove gently. "It's so soft. What do you suppose it's made of?"

"Kid, maybe?" Mom sounded tentative.

"Kid? A baby goat?"

"No, Amanda," Sadie said. "Kid gloves were made from lamb-skin."

"Baby lambs?" Amanda made a face, and I remembered she was a vegetarian.

Carol spoke up from the other side of the attic. "They made gloves out of just about any type of skin. There was a whole industry that built up around glove making. The glovers were true artists."

"Thanks," Amanda said, "but I'll take my knitted mittens any day."

"How long have gloves been around?" I really did wonder. I guess I'd never thought about it. "Wait! Wasn't Shakespeare's father a glover? That was around 1600."

"Right," Carol said, "but the profession's a lot older than that. They found gloves in the pyramids."

"That's definitely a picnic basket." Sadie must have thought the glove discussion was senseless. "When did people start doing picnics?"

"Forever," Maddy said.

Carol spoke at the same time. "Ages ago. Originally it meant an outdoor meal where wine was served, but the French royalty formal-ized the idea of the pique-nique back in the 1600s." She gave the term a French pronunciation.

"I'd rather have beer and watermelon," Dee said.

"Amen" came from several of us around the room.

"And just think about it," Maddy said. "If a picnic is a matter of eating out of doors, then the Martins had one long picnic from 1741 to 1745."

"I can just imagine," Mom said. "I think eating outside like that would have gotten old in a hurry."

"Couldn't be a picnic," Rebecca Jo said, "if they didn't have a picnic basket."

"Why not?"

"Well, just think about it, Dee. Isn't a picnic much nicer when you lift each item out of a lovely basket like this one?"

"I can't imagine how this came to be in a picnic basket." Mom held up the blue glove. "Did you ever see anything so delicate? I can barely get one finger in up to the second joint, much less my whole hand."

"People were smaller back then," Carol said. "Shorter, lighter, narrower."

"I know that, but"—Mom raised her hand with her index finger pushed as far as it would go into the glove's index finger. The rest of the glove dangled limply along her palm—"this really brings it home."

"That's why they say showing is more effective than telling," Maddy said. "That's a lesson we writers have to learn early on."

"Ivy," Sadie asked my mom, "are you sure there's nothing in there to indicate who it belonged to?"

"There isn't. I've looked all over it."

"Under it? The picnic basket I mean."

"And under it. No notes, no initials, no handy-dandy labels."

"The only reason I can think of"—Maddy sent a quelling glance in Dee's direction, as if daring her to interrupt—"is if a young man took the other glove. You're always reading about lovesick fellas snitching one glove. Wasn't there something about that in *Little Women*?"

"First of all," Dee said, "I don't think people used a word like *snitching* back then—"

"You know what I mean."

"Yeah, I do, but I think the idea was that the gloves would get reunited with one another once the two lovebirds got married."

"Uh …" There was something burrowing around in the back of my brain, but I couldn't quite grab hold of it. I knew it was important. "One glove." It had something to do with that.

Everybody waited for me to quit thrashing my hands around.

"One glove! Didn't Mary Frances say something about one glove in that hundred-year letter of hers?"

Maddy scrambled to find the letter, picked out the relevant passage, and read it to us.

111

As he lay dying, Emeline told him through her Tears that she knew he had taken one of her Gloves. 'You may keep it forever, if only you will live,' she told him time and again, and he will indeed keep it forever, for when we prepared the Body for the Burial, the Glove was found, only slightly fire-damaged, in Jason's Pocket. Emeline tucked it between his Hands before we wrapped the Shroud around him.

"So," Maddy looked at the glove still dangling from my mom's finger, "these two never got together. How sad."

"We'll never know for sure," Carol said, "that the blue glove belonged to Emeline—"

"Seems pretty clear to me," Maddy grumped.

Carol ignored that. "Unless there's a more specific letter in there somewhere." She nodded toward the trunks, and we all dispersed, ready to find more treasures. And, we hoped, a few explanations.

Saturday 2 July 1814

EMELINE RUSSELL TREASURED the sky blue kid gloves her father had given her just last year when she turned sixteen. "I'll never need another present as long as I live, Papa," she had told him at the time, and she still felt that way. She wore them to church every Sunday and slept with them under her pillow.

Today, as she packed a picnic basket to take to the meadow, she decided she would wear the gloves, even though it was a Saturday. No, perhaps she would simply take them with her, for the weather was unusually warm. Her cousin Rose, who was married now to Baxter Hoskins, had agreed yesterday to accompany them as soon as she found out that Jason's older sister Luella, who was a particular friend of Rose, would be along as the official chaperone.

Emeline ran over the list of food she had packed, more than enough for Jason, for herself, and for Rose and Luella.

Emeline knew that within a year or two, or possibly three, she and Jason Martin would marry. He wanted to be sure he could provide for her, and she was clear-headed enough to know that was important, but sometimes she felt the two of them could have survived—thrived even—on only the deep affection they felt for each other.

She wrapped a loaf of bread in a linen towel and slipped it into the basket next to the stone crock of fresh butter she had just retrieved from the springhouse. She and her mother had baked the bread only that morning, and the yeasty fragrance filled the house. They would need to eat quickly, before the butter melted, for the day already promised to be bright, sunny, and hot, as it generally was in early July. The crock was still chilled, though, for the springhouse behind the parsonage was quite cold.

She wrapped the leather loop attached to the hinged top of the basket around the protruding semicircle of wicker and thrust a thin wooden dowel through the wicker hoop to hold the lid tightly closed. There. It was done.

Except for the flutter in her stomach whenever she thought of Jason, she was completely poised and ready when Rose and Luella appeared on the doorstep of the parsonage, followed closely by Jason.

Rose and Luella gathered some of the meadow's bright summer flowers to decorate the picnic blanket Jason and Emeline had spread on a soft bed of pine needles in the shade of one of the towering trees along the meadow's edge. They laughed and talked as the food appeared, Luella commenting on how good the bread smelled, Rose saying how glad she was the crock was still cold—"for we would not want butter melted all over the blanket"—and Jason praising the smell of the fried chicken.

"I included one of the turkey legs from last night's supper," Emeline told Jason. "I know how fond you are of roasted turkey."

"You know the way to my brother's heart," Luella said. "Feed him, and he will be forever in your debt."

Emeline set her gloves to one side of the blanket, just between her and Jason.

Eventually Luella and Rose made their excuses and strolled around the meadow, not too far as to negate their duty as chaperones, but not too close to interrupt the giddy conversation between Jason and the girl he so clearly loved.

When it was time for them to pack up the basket, Emeline folded the linen towel—the four of them had consumed the entire loaf—while

Luella tucked what little other food remained back in the basket and thanked Emeline for such a lovely luncheon. Rose, ever the practical one, used a bit of string from her apron pocket to tie the mullein leaves she had gathered into a bunch.

Emeline was always amazed that Rose, who used her left hand rather than her right, was able to tie such a tidy knot. If Emeline had attempted a backwards tying like that, the results would have been a hopeless tangle.

Jason lifted Emeline's gloves, waited until the three girls had their heads together in some sort of conference about whether the remaining butter would be safe to use at the evening meal, and replaced one of the gloves in the basket. The other one, he tucked tidily into his pocket. It was so tiny it hardly took up any room at all.

Emeline, of course, knew precisely what he had done, for she had watched Jason all the while she and the other girls were talking. She would miss wearing the gloves to Sunday services. Perhaps she would simply carry the single remaining one. After all, she would be reunited with her second glove once she and Jason wed.

When Jason lifted the basket, though, the dowel gave way, spilling half the contents out onto the pine needles. They all four bent to retrieve the remains of their picnic. Emeline's hand closed around the single glove before Jason could grab it. His glance at her was a question with no need for words. Her reply was a smile that needed no interpretation.

After a close inspection revealed that the dowel had broken clean in half, and each remaining piece was too short to pass through the loop to hold the basket closed, Jason stepped off to the other side of the large pine where they had thrown the bones as they finished with them. He brushed off the ants that had already begun to clean what was left of the turkey leg—not that it needed much cleaning, for Jason had chewed off every bit of meat he could. Using his knife, he cut off the gristle from one end of the bone, removed the knob on the other end, and thrust the remaining straight shaft through the wicker loop. "There," he said. "That should serve us well."

Luella, Rose, and Emeline laughed, and they all trooped down the hill to Fifth Street, where they turned and headed toward the parsonage. On the way down the hill, they waved at Daniel Garner, who stood with a bucket of water close to hand as he burned a load of garbage within a ring of heavy stones.

GORDON SURRATT HID behind one of the wide-girthed maples along the path down from the meadow and spied on Emeline as she picnicked with Jason Martin. Gordon's grandfather, Barnard Surratt, had always told Gordon he could have his pick of the women in the town. "You can have anything you want, grandson," Grandfather said, "but only if you are willing to fight for it."

Grandfather should know. He was the strongest man Gordon had ever seen.

"You come from the finest stock," Grandfather told Gordon often, "for I was the first baby born in the Martinsville barn after the settlers arrived."

Gordon had heard that Grandfather was the third of the babies, but he knew better than to bring up that thought in the presence of his grandsire.

Gordon had never in his nineteen years managed to grow shoulders as wide as Grandfather's or arms as long. Instead, he had decided early on that he would make up in cunning what he could not achieve with strength.

Jason had something that Gordon wanted. Emeline Russell, the daughter of the minister. Gordon was not foolhardy enough to fight Jason Martin, for Jason was a full head taller than Gordon and probably outweighed him by two stone. If he could not fight Jason for her, he would think of something else.

He stayed well hidden as they finished their picnic, then trailed his four unsuspecting targets down the hill, planning his strategy. Everyone knew how close Emeline was to her father. And everyone knew how much Reverend Russell loved the old church building with its doors hand-carved by Homer Martin and its new leaded glass windows.

If Gordon could bully his brother into breaking one of the windows, Gordon could catch him in the act and then would look like a hero to Emeline. No, Gordon thought, that would not work, for his brother would be sure to tell it had been Gordon's idea to begin with.

What else could he do though, so Emeline would see him as strong and brave?

Just as he wondered that, the quartet ahead of him waved to Daniel Garner, who was almost obscured by heavy smoke pouring from a fire ring in his side yard.

That was it! All Gordon needed to do was set a small fire in the Old Church, rouse the town with his shouts, and then extinguish the fire as soon as Emeline was there to see him do it. He would save her father's church, and she would be so grateful to him that she would forget about Jason Martin altogether.

This evening. He would do it this evening, for he knew that Emeline and her family generally took a walk shortly after their evening meal. He had followed them often enough to be sure of it.

That evening, he waited behind the large tree on the church lawn until he spied the Russells leaving their house and heading downhill. He ducked into the church and watched through one of the leaded glass windows until they came abreast of the tree. Then he tipped over his lantern, making sure the flame came in contact with the sprinkling of straw he had already placed beneath it. Once it was well and truly caught, he dashed from the front door yelling, "Fire! Fire in the church!"

If he had not waited to be sure Emeline recognized him, he might have been able to extinguish the flames. If he had thought to fill two buckets with water rather than just one, he still might have stopped the conflagration.

But Gordon waited for Emeline to see him, and then the one bucket of water was not enough. By the time he ran back outside to escape the flames and smoke, people had begun to gather, the bucket brigade had been formed, and he watched in disgust as Jason and Henry Martin saved the doors Emeline and her father loved.

AS SOON AS Gordon had his twentieth birthday, he asked Emeline to marry him, but she refused, contending that she would never marry, for her heart lay in the grave with Jason Martin. But of course, she changed her mind about marrying. She kept the picnic basket, with its turkey bone clasp, until her twenty-second birthday, the day she married Corbin Garner, the day she offered the picnic basket to Luella who did not want it, and then to Rose, who took it as a keepsake of that lovely July afternoon in the meadow and promptly asked her son Arthur to put it away in the attic, before her husband Baxter could preach against the frippery of picnics.

TWO YEARS LATER, Gordon's older brother Henly married and had a daughter, whom he and his wife named Grace. As Grace grew, she came to dislike her Uncle Gordon intensely, although she was never sure of why. When she married Arthur Hoskins, she found that Arthur distrusted her uncle as much as she did. Arthur may have had a touch of the blarney stone about him from his Irish grandmother, but his instincts were good, and she trusted him. They never invited Uncle Gordon into their home on Beechnut Lane, even though as a widower he would have appreciated a free meal.

2000

"JUST THINK OF all the marriages and births and funerals that have occurred here since 1745," Maddy said.

"Here?" Ida looked around the attic.

"I don't mean *here* here. I mean"—Maddy swept her arm as if to encompass the entire town—"*here* here."

What are you talking about?

"I'm sure this attic reflects only a small portion of them," Sadie said, "but I'm not sure I could deal with learning about every single wedding. It would get awfully old after a while, wouldn't it? And all those funerals..." Her voice drifted off to nothing.

"I agree up to a certain point," I said. "But there are a few events I'd really like to know more about."

"Like what?" Ida had finally removed her white-feathered hat, and she picked up another hatbox.

"Like that *you'd better propose in person* couple. Wouldn't you love to know how their wedding turned out?"

Monday, 13 July 1752

MARYANNE BREETON did not like the fact that Father had insisted on inviting all of the original families, as they had begun to call themselves, to her wedding. The only good thing she could think about her father's decision was that the Endicotts had left the group before Homer Martin led the rest of the company to this valley, so she would not have to put up with those Endicott brothers and their asinine behavior. But yesterday Nell Surratt had stopped her on the way into the dry goods store to say that she and her parents and her brothers would be so pleased to attend the ceremony. "Of course, you knew that, I am sure," Nell had said, with breezy certainty, even though MaryAnne thought of Nell as an uncertain friend indeed. Father should not have issued such a broad invitation.

It was on the tip of MaryAnne's tongue to ask Nell not to bring Barnard, the noxious seven-year-old, for she knew he could not sit still for even a short marriage service, but just then Mistress Garner had walked by with a warm greeting, and then Reverend Russell had stopped to comment on the unusual warmth of the day, and her opportunity to bar the disruptive boy was lost.

MaryAnne had wondered then if Reverend Russell knew that his wife had taken MaryAnne aside not two days before and told her of what she could expect on her wedding night. No, she decided, surely the minister would not have been able to speak to her so pleasantly if he had been aware of the information Mistress Sarah Russell had imparted. Constance, Father's wife for the past eight years had hovered in the background while Mistress Russell spoke. Perhaps Constance had not felt competent to explain such alarming details, for she was barely four years older than MaryAnne herself.

Now, Willy and Lucky had been chasing each other around the inside of the Hastings house and then out into the two lanes that bounded the front and side yards, and back inside again. MaryAnne was close to the end of her wits. Bridgett Hastings and Edna Russell had walked over early that morning to help arrange the food on tables in the front yard—the house was far too small for this many guests—but MaryAnne was not as comforted by their presence as she usually would have been. She liked Bridgett and Edna, but today as she took this irrevocable step, she felt unwilling to pass the time in idle chatter. She found herself more nervous than she could recall having been in many years—not since the aftermath of that day the painter tried to attack her brother.

She had no doubts about Thomas of course, but she could not shake the feeling that something would go wrong. Thomas had told her only last week that he was worried about whether or not he would be able to speak his vow.

"Surely," MaryAnne had said, "you will be able to manage saying *I will*." When he looked dubiously at her, she had placed her hand on his arm. "Even if it takes you twenty minutes to say it, Thomas Russell, I will be happy to wait."

"P-p-perhaps you w-w-w-will," he said, "b-b-but wh-wh-what about th-th-the other p-p-people?"

"Are you marrying them?"

"N-n-n-no." He had smiled his sweet smile then and touched the end of her nose with the tip of his finger.

"Then what could possibly concern you?"

MaryAnne smiled at the memory, flicked away an impertinent fly, and shifted a loaf of newly baked bread from one end of the table to the other.

"Leave it," Bridgett told her. "Come inside to the back room and I will re-braid your hair for you. Willy! Come here and keep the flies off the food. And don't you be eating any of it!" As soon as she was certain the dog would settle down and the boy would comply, she turned back to MaryAnne. "Your guests will arrive soon, and you do not want them to see you with your hair sticking out every which way from beneath your cap."

"Nor do you want them to see you before time," Edna cautioned.

"That is a silly convention," MaryAnne objected, but she let them lead her away from the front of the house where she could hear her father greeting the first guests as they began to assemble. Soon the yard would be awash with—she sighed—everyone from the town, including Nell and the obstreperous Barnard.

"I am glad you washed your hair yesterday," Bridgett said with a giggle as she tied a wide ribbon around the fine end strands of Mary-Anne's copper hair. "Are you going to let Thomas unbraid it for you tonight?"

MaryAnne hated it when she blushed, but she could not stop the wave of red that rose almost from her feet as she remembered what Mistress Russell had told her.

"Certainly she will." Edna adjusted the fall of MaryAnne's full skirts. "If he is not so overcome with awe of your beauty that he is struck motionless."

MaryAnne pushed playfully at her friend's shoulder. "He will do what he needs to do." And then she blushed even harder as both her friends dissolved in peals of laughter. She felt fairly certain that they did not know what she knew, but everyone knew that … something … happened on a wedding night.

2000

"**THE ONLY WAY** we're going to find out about some of those marriages is to find more wedding invitations or letters or diaries," Pat said.

Rebecca Jo rubbed her hands together briskly. "Then let's get busy."

I didn't really expect anything. After all, what could possibly be more informative than the Mary Frances and Hubbard diaries? But I dutifully opened a different trunk and began to rummage through it. A quilt, some rather ragged placemats, a few boring greeting cards, half a dozen purses that had seen far better days—why had anyone bothered to keep them?

I straightened my back, feeling every vertebra creak. "Anybody found anything yet?"

A chorus of *nopes* and *unh-uhs* came back from all around the attic, interrupted by a tentative voice saying, "Maybe."

I was happy to leave my useless trunk and join the crowd congregating around Amanda. "What is it?" several of us asked.

She held up a stack of paper, maybe ten or fifteen pages, each folded neatly in half and the whole stack tied tidily with a rough string. I lifted my eyes away from the papers to see that everyone had created a double circle around her and the trunk she'd been searching through.

"They're letters," Amanda said in that soft voice of hers, so well-suited to her job as a massage therapist. We had no trouble hearing her, though, for we were all holding our breaths. We parted, like the Red Sea, as she moved toward the nearest card table.

"Maybe we should get a photo of this," Carol suggested, and I took up my camera to oblige her with a couple of closeups. "Use the gloves," she reminded Amanda.

Still completely quiet, we waited while Amanda untied the string and unfolded the first letter. She studied the page for a moment and fell even more silent than usual. I was astonished at the absolute stillness she displayed. "It was written in October of 1768," she finally said, "and it's addressed to Myra Sue."

"Myra Sue?" Dee sounded as surprised as I felt. "Myra Sue, Homer's first wife? His dead wife?"

Amanda lifted her shoulders almost to her ears. "There's no last name on here."

"Maybe there was another Myra Sue in town?" I didn't believe it, since that was such an unusual name, but thought it just might be a possibility.

"There's nothing wrong with writing a letter to somebody who's deceased," Sadie said with finality, and I had to wonder how many letters she must have written to her brother Eustace or to her small son, Samuel. Or, for that matter, to her husband Wallace, whom she'd lost so recently.

Almost as one, we all turned to Carol, asking if there had been another Myra Sue in the Martin clan.

"Not that I know of. Not unless another woman by that name joined the company on their way south."

"Or maybe somebody named a baby girl after the dead woman," Sadie said. "After all, it's been almost thirty years since she was killed."

"Read it," Melissa ordered.

Tuesday, 18 October 1768

My dear Myra Sue,

Mister Silas Martin gave me a dozen precious pieces of paper last April, but I have been loath to use any of them until now. I have decided to write to you once a year for the next twelve years, or perhaps I can limit myself to one side of each page for a letter, in which case these cherished sheets will last me twenty-four years. As I am already forty-four years of age, that means I must live to be sixty-eight, a goal that may be beyond my capacity to attain.

At forty-four, I am now more than twice the age you were when you died.

"When you died," Amanda repeated, hardly more than a whisper. "She's writing to a ghost?"

"Who's writing to a ghost?" Pat, coming back upstairs from a potty break, elbowed her way between Maddy and Carol. "Who signed it?"

Amanda dropped her gaze to the bottom of the sheet. "Mary Frances, writing to Myra Sue. And I can read this writing. It's not backwards like her diary is."

"Maybe because it's a letter," Dee suggested.

Amanda looked like she was going to continue reading, but Maddy held up a hand. "If we're going to read the Hubbard diary and the Mary Frances diaries in chronological order, we ought to do the same for these." Without waiting for us to agree or disagree, she told Amanda to re-tie the string.

"Can't we just read the first one," Sadie asked, "so we'll know what we're getting into?"

"Nope. She's liable to say something that will completely confuse us, and it's hard enough to keep everything straight as it is." Maddy held out her hands, and Amanda dutifully placed the bundle in Maddy's safekeeping. "The top drawer," Maddy said, placing the letters there as she spoke. "Amanda, you're in charge of remembering October of 1768."

"As if I could forget," Amanda muttered.

"When we get that far in Ida's diary, you remind us, okay?"

"Spoilsport," Pat said, but Carol spoke at the same time.

"That makes perfect sense, Maddy. Thanks for keeping us on track."

Pat was obviously not assuaged. "This storm's going to have to last a long time for us to get through all those years."

Ida ignored Pat's moan, but when Dee objected also, Ida turned firm. "You know it's better to do this in chronological order."

What does that mean?

"Reading things in the order in which they were written is always a good idea," Carol said.

Ida spread her hands. "Yeah?" But Carol just shrugged.

"If the ice melts," I said, "you can all come back." Good grief. What was I getting myself into?

With a heavy sigh of resignation, Pat sank into her chair, but she winked at me when I caught her eye. Maybe that was why she got along so well with her constantly-joking husband. She was just as willing as he was to pull somebody's leg.

Whose leg? She is not pulling anyone's leg.

Carol tilted her head when Marmalade let out a loud meow. It almost sounded like a question. Or a complaint. "What'll it be," I asked. "More diary readings or more trunk exploration?"

"Trunks," Ida said. "I'm not ready to tackle that backwards writing quite so soon."

"You're the boss," said Carol, and we all dispersed.

IT WASN'T THREE minutes later that Dee called to us to gather around. "It looks like a business card case," she said, "but it's different, somehow."

"It's bigger," Carol said. "The standard size nowadays is, I think, a couple of inches tall and three-and-a-half inches wide."

"You're just a font of useless information." Ida's grin took the sting out of her comment.

Dee held up the case she'd found. "So why is this one bigger? Maybe it's not even a business card case."

Amanda looked at it rather dubiously. "It's pink."

Dee studied it for a moment. "No clue what it might be, though, if it's not for cards."

"They didn't call them business cards back then," Maddy said. Before Ida could snicker, she added, "Yes, I was researching one of my historical horror stories. They were called calling cards, and people left them to indicate they had visited someone."

"I've read plenty of Anne Perry and Georgette Heyer," Rebecca Jo said, "with all their fancy Victorian and Regency society stuff, and I can't imagine anyone in Martinsville sporting a calling card case. Not in a town where everybody knows everybody else."

"I don't know everybody," I said, although I did know most of the people who had library cards.

"Maybe not now, but I imagine the town's grown quite a bit"—Rebecca Jo pointed to the case Dee held—"since then."

"Maybe that's why this is in the attic," Amanda said. "Nobody used it."

"Well," Sadie said, "Somebody ought to use it. What about you, Amanda? For your massage therapy practice?"

Amanda shook her head. "I don't hand out many cards."

"Of course you don't," I said. "We're all your clients—as are half the rest of the town—and I daresay we keep you pretty busy."

Sadie scanned all our faces and eventually turned to Carol. "What about you? Could you use it?"

Carol beamed.

Sadie started chuckling again. "You could have special, larger cards printed up."

"Why?"

"So there'd be room for your full name."

Carol grimaced. "Christmas Carol Mellinger, Ph.D.? I don't think so."

1816

LYDIA HASTINGS SHEFFIELD added yet another knitted scarf to the multiple layers she had already looped around her neck. Over the past few months she had become somewhat immune to the pervasive cold. It came near to freezing the water in the china washbowl that sat on one of the dressers in their room at the Dakota Hotel. Of course, she was immune only as long as she was bundled up enough to make it difficult to bend in the middle.

Pray God that Curtis would end his business dealings soon. They had been here for months, and Lydia longed to be home in Martinsville, even though she knew the volcanic explosion that had caused winter to descend on New York had also sent the temperatures plummeting in the Metoochie River Valley.

She had already dated the letter, but now she added a sentence just below the date.

The Dakota
New York City
Monday, 27 May 1816
Who would have thought this year would have no spring?
Mister Reuben Hastings
Beechnut House
Martinsville, Georgia

My dear brother,

She laid down her pen. This letter of rights ought to be sent to her niece, Rose Hastings Hoskins, for Rose—as the oldest of Reuben and Astaline's daughters—would be the logical one to distribute the gifts to her twin sisters, but Reuben needed the letter. He had been so out of sorts for the past ten years, ever since his lovely Astaline died, and now he seemed to be failing more with each passing month. Lydia tried to write to him and to send him small gifts as often as she could, and of course when she and Curtis were in Martinsville—as she sincerely hoped they would be soon—she visited her brother often in his house on Beechnut Lane.

Perhaps seeing these whimsical calling card cases would bring a smile to his lips.

There was, after all, another very good reason to send the cases to Reuben rather than to Rose. Lydia was sure that any packet addressed to Rose would be opened first by that narrow-minded husband of hers. Baxter Hoskins had always been so prudish, Lydia could not imagine why Rose had married the man. Lydia guessed—more than a guess—she felt certain that Baxter would toss the cases down the privy hole rather than let his wife and her sisters enjoy them.

She did not think, though, that even Baxter would have the audacity to open a packet clearly addressed to his father-in-law, for did not Baxter's Good Book enjoin him to honor his father and mother. Did that apply to fathers-in-law as well? She certainly hoped so. She knew, however, that he would be curious about the contents of the package, which was one reason for her inclusion of an aromatic handful of pipe tobacco that had already spread its odor throughout the hotel room and would, she knew, permeate the entire gift package.

I hope you are surviving this cold spell, and I hope the weather is not so cold in Martinsville as it is here in New York City.

As you can see, I am including small gifts for Rose, the twins, and Lilian, and I depend on you to see they are delivered safe into the intended hands. I will send the boys' gifts directly to them, since they will have no problem receiving packages. I could have sent the other girls' presents direct to their homes, but I wanted you specifically to see the whimsical nature of the gifts.

Reuben would understand what she meant. He would pick his time carefully to be sure that husband of hers was away from the house before he gave Rose her present.

I fear you might not recognize what these cases are intended for, since there is no need for calling cards in little Martinsville. Here, the society dames carry their cards in outrageously decorated cases in order to leave one or two—one for the wife and one for the husband— at the homes they visit on their daily calls. The higher the social rank of the caller, the more likely that person's card is to be placed on the top of the pile in the silver salver that receives them.

For the twins I have chosen the most colorful, the most fancy cases I could afford to buy, and I can imagine their pleasure as they exclaim over the flowers (for Emma) and the butterflies (for Caroline). I assume they will share them as they do everything else. Please explain to them that the cases are one-of-a-kind, so I could not buy two that were alike. The hummingbird case is for Lilian. The heavily-nubbled pink silk on the case for Rose is luscious indeed, is it not? I had debated sending her a case with two elaborate swans, their necks intertwined around the knotted clasp, but I chose this one instead. Should Baxter glimpse it, I hope it will be less likely to incur his self-righteous piety.

Was that too pointed a declaration of her distaste for Baxter Hoskins? No, Lydia decided. Reuben knew how little she liked the man with his insistence upon plain living to the point of denying his wife any pleasures at all. Lydia had often thought that Baxter had a decidedly convenient way of determining what would offend God and what would not. Lydia knew, because Rose had told her, that Baxter had insisted Rose give up the lovely silver pendant that had been her mother's, while he—Lydia could not help but notice—flaunted such an expensive pocket watch, always pulling it out to check the time or to wind it when people were watching him. Now that she thought of it, though, Lydia had not seen him winding his watch for some time, maybe even for several years. She would have to ask Rose about it privately once she and Curtis returned home.

I hope your leg is bothering you less, Reuben, although I fear this cold weather must be a painful time for you. Do take care, and let Rose pamper you. I do not envy your having to interact with Baxter over the dinner table each day, but I know you enjoy the company of your loving daughter. I hope you enjoy the small gift I have included for you as well. I know it is a favorite of yours. And I trust you will not open this package when Baxter is within the house! Your new tobacco will provide the excuse for such a bulky package should Baxter inquire—as I know he will.

With great affection, I remain
Your loving sister,
Lydia

She completed her letter with some haste and included it in the package she had already prepared, with the four calling card cases and Reuben's special tobacco. She wanted to send it in the morning post, but also she longed to go downstairs to the dining hall and order a hot cup of tea, one she could wrap her frigid fingers around.

REUBEN HASTINGS KNEW to the moment the exact time each day when Baxter Hoskins left the house. The man was nothing if not punctual. After the front door closed, Reuben waited an extra two minutes before he made his halting way downstairs, just to be sure he would not encounter his sanctimonious son-in-law. At times he regretted having deeded this house over to Baxter, but with this game leg of his, and his failing health, he was unable to maintain the place. Rose had been more than happy to return to the house she had been born in to care for her ailing father. He grinned to himself. He was not nearly as close to death's door as everyone assumed him to be, but he had wanted to keep an eye on Rose for as long as he was able.

"Good morning, Father," Rose called to him from the foot of the stairs. "Are you ready for your breakfast?"

"That would be delightful."

"You have a package from Aunt Lydia. It was delivered just as Baxter left."

"He did not open it, did he?"

Rose looked pained, and Reuben regretted that he had yet again revealed so blatantly his dislike of the man Rose had chosen.

She handed him the still-sealed package and he carried it to the breakfast table in the large kitchen that stretched along one entire side of Beechnut House. "Well, well, well," he said. "What do you suppose your aunt has sent this time?" His sister Lydia was a dear. She seemed determined to brighten his days, and indeed she managed quite well.

"I hope she sent you more of that tobacco you liked so much from her last package."

Reuben raised the package to his nose. "I do believe she did."

"I do believe you are right. Baxter sniffed the package quite avidly before he left."

Rose handed her father a knife and he cut the string carefully. Lydia had, as was her wont, dropped sealing wax on the knot to hold it firm, which made that part of the string virtually unusable. As Rose wound the unwaxed portion of the string up in a small ball and placed it in the drawer where she kept various odds and ends, Reuben unwrapped the heavy brown paper and extracted the letter contained therein. He skimmed it quickly. "Your aunt sends her love and a gift for each of you girls," he said and read her the words contained from the third sentence in the second paragraph through the question mark in the fourth. There was no need to pain her further, although he knew that Rose was aware of Lydia's opinion of Baxter.

He folded the letter away into his shirt pocket. He would read it again more carefully in private. He took the fragrant packet of tobacco he had wanted and handed the other four small items to Rose.

"Oh, Papa!" Her use of the pet name she had called him when she was a girl—before she married Baxter—delighted Reuben. "How cunning these are!"

He had not heard her so excited in years and he watched with great pleasure as she exclaimed over the paper flowers and butterflies of the first two cases, the hummingbird, and the heavy silk of the fourth case. He would have to write to Lydia right away to share with her how much joy her gifts had brought.

"Will you be all right by yourself for an hour or so, Papa? I would like to take these directly to Caroline and Emma. And to Lilian. I will need to leave quickly if I am to visit with each of them and be back in good time to prepare the noon meal." She paused for just a moment. "Would you like to come with me?"

"Not on that ice. My leg will barely hold me here in the house." His leg was feeling much better of late, but he delighted in being able to use it as an excuse whenever he did not want to do something. "You take care out there."

Rose donned layers and layers of outerwear and picked up three of the colorful cases.

"Aren't you taking yours to show them?"

She pressed her lips tightly together. "I think mine needs to be upstairs in the attic before … before we eat."

Before that husband of yours comes home, Reuben thought. "Would you like me to take it up there for you? I think this leg of mine will appreciate the exercise."

"Oh, Papa, would you? I would be most grateful." She bit her lip and turned away, but not before Reuben saw the gleam of a tear in the corner of his beloved daughter's eye.

For just a moment, Reuben wished his son-in-law a lingering death. Baxter was not a bad man, but—confound it!—he found no joy in anything. Not even his wonderful wife and his beautiful children. Reuben was gratified once more that he was there to help his daughter as much as he could.

2000

"IT'S DEFINITELY A case for calling cards," Carol said. "As Maddy said, they were particularly popular during the Victorian era when women called on each other."

Dee raised an eyebrow. "But why is this one here in Martinsville? This isn't England, and I doubt there were ever any big society circles here."

"Well," Carol said, "there's always the possibility that someone bought this in New York or Philadelphia or Charleston and sent it here as a gift."

"If so, they probably didn't know much about little bitty Martinsville."

"A gag gift, perhaps," Dee said.

"Way back then?"

"Sure, Maddy. People have always delighted in jokes."

"You know," Pat said, "it's almost boring finding these things and not knowing where they came from. It's frustrating never knowing the story behind what we're finding. Maybe we need to go back to Mary Frances and Hubbard's diaries."

Rebecca Jo had been silent for so long, I'd almost forgotten about her. "Some of the most boring things have a lot worth saying," she said.

Pat shifted sideways in her seat so she could look at Rebecca Jo. "Like what?"

"Like this." Rebecca Jo held up an old notebook. Its pasteboard cover looked cheap, with a mottled black and white pattern on it. "It's an accounts book that was kept from 1908 to 1932 by," she glanced at the first page and enunciated each word, "Nancy Geonette Harrison Hoskins." She pronounced the second name with four syllables—Gee-oh-net-tee.

"Geonette? I've always loved that name," Sadie said, "but I think it was said more like *Jenettie*. It sounds so old-fashioned, but I had a friend named Geonette when I was in grammar school."

"*Had* a friend? It sounds like you didn't stay close," Dee commented.

"No we didn't, dear. She died when she was ten."

"Oh."

"It's all right. There were so many deaths back then. It was the

Spanish flu epidemic."

Carol cleared her throat. "I was under the impression that strain of the flu killed healthy young adults, but not so much the children or the elderly the way other diseases did."

"You're right," Sadie said. "Geonette was the only child in Martinsville who died of Spanish flu during those three or four years. It was awful while it lasted."

Her tone of voice said that her comment had been a dreadful understatement.

"Most of our young men," she continued, "if they weren't killed in the Great War, they caught the Spanish flu and died."

Amanda reached out a hand to her, and Sadie grasped it, patted it, and let it go. "If I remember rightly," Sadie said, "your Nancy Geonette," here she inclined her head toward the book Rebecca Jo still held, "was my Geonette's aunt. She lived up on Fifth Street."

"If she lived on Fifth Street," Glaze said, "why do you think the book ended up here?"

"Somebody died or somebody moved or somebody married," Maddy said, spreading her hands.

"Back to the account book?" Dee, who was sitting across the card table from Rebecca Jo, craned her neck to look more closely. "What sort of accounts?"

"Just household records of what she bought and what she sold." She flipped to a random page and pointed. "In April of 1910, for instance, she says she spent $7.07 over the course of the month and brought in $13.59."

Dee ran her finger down the column of figures. "That's a long list for only seven dollars. And seven cents," she added.

"Most of the purchases were only five cents each—for soap, matches, tomato seed, soda, and something she called b-l-e-w-e-n."

"Bluing," Sadie said.

"Oh." Rebecca Jo widened her eyes. "Of course."

"What's bluing?" The question came from several people at the same time.

"I haven't thought of that stuff in years," I said. "We used it when I was a kid."

"We used to have to add it to our whites when we washed," Rebecca Jo explained. "It made them look whiter."

"Then you should have called it whiting," Amanda said.

"No," Sadie said. "It was a lovely deep shade of blue. It came in powder form, and you bought it by the box. If you added too much, the whites ended up looking blue."

"It sounds like you're speaking from experience."

Sadie grinned at Amanda. "Unfortunately, yes."

"And there was a liquid form, too, in a blue bottle," Rebecca Jo said. "In fact, I might still have some left in my laundry room, although it's probably totally dried out after all these years. It was designed to work on cotton clothing, but now that most of our clothes are..."—she looked down at her cardigan—"are something else, there's no need for bluing anymore."

"First we clean out Biscuit's attic," Dee said, "and next we'll tackle Rebecca Jo's laundry room shelves." She looked around the ragged circle. "Does anyone else have any project requests?"

"I would say my attic," Ida said, "except that I'd be embarrassed to look at what's up there myself, much less expose it to public scrutiny."

"Sort of like the way I felt about this attic for years," I said. "But think of the treasures we could find."

"My house isn't as old as yours," she retorted. "Probably just junk up there. I could throw out the whole lot and be done with it."

Carol made a sound like she was strangling. "You can't do that!"

"Yes I could," Ida said. "It's my junk."

"But what if it's..." Carol stopped as she finally realized Ida was teasing her. It takes a while to get used to Ida's sense of humor.

Amanda let out a humming sound. "What else is on that accounts list? Anything interesting?"

Rebecca Jo ran her finger down the list. "She spent seventy-five cents for sugar and ten cents for buttons. A hat cost her twenty-five cents." She looked over toward the towering stacks of hatboxes. "I wonder if this hat is somewhere in that conglomeration?" She ran her finger farther down the list. "She spent another twenty-five cents for *rubnomes*." She looked at Sadie. "Any idea what those were?"

Sadie chuckled. "I don't have a clue. It's probably something logical but misspelled, sort of like the b-l-e-w-e-n."

Rebecca Jo shook her head and ran her finger farther down the list. "Her big purchase for the month was two dollars and sixty-four cents for *44B dom.* Would the B stand for bushels? And what's a *dom*?"

"Another mystery," I suggested, "but two-sixty-four seems expensive for 1910. I hope the *doms* were worth it, whatever they were. How about the income?"

Rebecca Jo counted a number of lines. "She sold twelve different batches of eggs. That would average three batches per week. Her batches ranged from two dozen to—wow!—thirteen and a half dozen, for a grand total of $13.59."

"She must have had a lot of chickens to lay that many eggs," Dee said.

"Do you think her rooster"—Pat flapped her elbows and I almost expected her to crow—"was as noisy as Doodle Doo?"

"That's Maggie Pontiac's rooster up the street from here," I explained to Carol.

"I know. I heard him the morning after I arrived."

Sadie smiled at Carol's droll tone. "Thirteen and a half dozen may sound like a lot, but she would have had to have a good many more than that. The ones she sold were just the excess eggs. She also had to have plenty to feed her own family. That was a time when people ate enormous breakfasts."

I like to eat a big breakfast. Especially if it is salmon or chicken.

Glaze guffawed. "Not like Maddy with her coffee and cinnamon rolls, huh?"

"Seven dollars out, thirteen dollars in," Melissa said. "Not bad." She raised her tea mug in a toast.

"But then in August," Rebecca Jo said with a cautionary note in her voice, "she spent $15.39 and sold only $4.48."

Melissa crossed her eyes. "I've had months like that."

Dee by this time had scooted her chair around next to Rebecca Jo. She reached across and pointed at something. "Look here. In July she bought *Blueing* for five cents, spelled with a b-l-u-e. So that earlier entry about b-l-e-w-e-n must have been something else."

"Don't confuse us," Amanda said with a shake of her head.

"And a corset at the enormous cost of fifty cents." Rebecca Jo shuddered. "My mother called her girdle a *foundation garment.* I don't see why we ever wore those things. Thank goodness they went out of style."

I thought back to a store display I'd seen the last time I was in Atlanta. "I hate to be the one to tell you, but in some places they seem to be coming back in."

Melissa reached for the little book. "May I?"

Rebecca Jo handed it to her. Melissa took the empty chair on Rebecca Jo's right, picked up an old envelope and started jotting what looked like a list as she turned from one page to the next. I hoped the envelope didn't have any particular historical value. "What are you doing, Melissa?"

"I'd like to know how much she made in a year." She indicated the two columns. "Expenses per month and income per month. Add them all together and you get, uh, let's see..." She figured silently for a few moments. "This would be easier if she'd used decimal points for the cents." Eventually she leaned back in her chair. "Looks like she lost $28.42 over the course of that year." She closed the book and slid it back across the table to Rebecca Jo. "That's too bad."

"You didn't have to do all that adding. She kept a reckoning herself on the last page." Rebecca Jo compared Melissa's figures to those of Nancy Geonette. "You got the numbers right, though." She opened to another page and pointed to a line. "In December she bought herself an organ for $37.35."

"If she hadn't bought the organ, she would have made money," Melissa noted.

"If she hadn't bought the organ," Pat said, "she might have died of boredom. I bet they all gathered around it and sang in the evening."

I like to sing.

Tuesday, 13 December 1910

March 1910

1 Plow	12.50	Eggs	3 doz.	54
Thread	35	Eggs	8 doz.	1.44
Soda	5	Eggs	7 doz.	1.26
Coal oil	60	Eggs	7 doz.	1.26

Shoes	1.25	Eggs 7 doz.	1.17
Garden seed	1.25	Eggs 5 doz.	85
Thread	5	Eggs 11 doz.	1.65
Coffee	20	Eggs 12 doz.	1.80
Vinegar	25	Eggs 7 doz.	1.05
1 barrel flour	6.60		
1 ticket	1.16	Milk	75
1 Couch	12.25	Milk	37
Slippers	1.75		
Buttons	10	Cow	15.00
Potatoes	10		
Ticket	2.20	Butter	90
Pattern	10	Butter	50
Linen	30	2 hens	70
Soda	10	Made a dress	75
Ben	10		
SPENT	$30.46............MADE		$29.94

NANCY GEONETTE HARRISON HOSKINS looked up from the March page of her accounts book. She'd taken the time to look through her lists, as she did every few months, to tally just where she stood with her income and expenses. And now here it was a cold December morning, only a few weeks left in the year. Over the course of the year, according to her meticulous reckoning, she had spent twenty-eight dollars and fourteen cents more than she had made. The upcoming year should be better, though. Next year, if the good Lord was willing, she would not have so many major expenses. There had been gifts for her only surviving daughter, Isabella, when she married that obnoxious Moses Garner. Nancy begrudged every penny of the seven dollars and thirty-two cents she had spent, for Moses was as tight-fisted as a cinnamon fern in the early springtime. The difference was that he would never uncurl his fronds the way the cinnamon ferns inevitably did. She smiled when she thought of another comparison. Moses Garner was as tight as Isabella's braids. She almost laughed aloud when she thought of the way Isabella's braids stuck almost straight out from the side of her head when she was a child, and they still had a tendency to do the same thing, even now that Isabella was a married woman. Married to Moses Garner.

She set those thoughts aside, for they would bring her nothing but grief, and went on considering her expenses. The plow that Hubert had needed so badly had cost her twelve and a half dollars. And the couch she bought that same month, for another twelve dollars and twenty-five cents. She had thought long and hard before buying it. For such an exorbitant amount, she could almost have bought another cow to replace Buttercup.

Of course, they hadn't needed another cow. They had needed a couch to replace the one Cousin Troy set on fire when he dropped that smelly cigar of his and didn't even notice it until the flames started shooting up. If she hadn't had a pot of soup heating on the potbellied stove right there in the middle of the parlor, the whole house might have caught fire. It was a waste of a good pot of soup, but at least the house had not been lost. Only the couch. Maybe she should be thankful to cousin Troy. She had never liked that couch. It was one Mother Hoskins had bought the year she was married. Nancy had put up with it because she hadn't had any other choice. Even after Mother Hoskins finally died, Hubert would have thrown a fit if Nancy had suggested changing it. Everything in the house had to stay just as it had been the whole time he was growing up.

Everything except the attic, she amended. She'd seen a lot of messy attics in her day, what with her five brothers and seven sisters. It seemed like she had helped every single one of them settle in their various houses after they got married. And every house in Martinsville seemed to have an attic full of useless stuff.

Except for Alva's house up on Fourth Street. That woman had taken one look at the chaos her new husband had brought her into, and she had started the very next week throwing things out. Every day while he was working up in the field, Alva would head upstairs and spend a little bit of time gathering a load to take down to the barrel out in the backyard where she would burn it.

Nancy chuckled to herself. Herschell had come back early one day and asked Alva what she was doing out there. 'I'm about out of soap,' Alva had told him as smoothly as a snake-oil salesman. 'I need more wood ash to make more lye.' And he had believed her!

She sighed and looked back at her accounts. May had been a good month, because of the four dozen hens she had been able to sell.

She turned a page. June was when some rats got into the hen house and ate seventeen of her baby chicks. But by then, Rosie, Buttercup's calf from two years ago, was producing more than her share of milk. It was just a balancing act, she thought, like the one in the circus that had come to the valley in 1898. That was the year she had bought a pair of clamp-on roller skates for Isabella. She still remembered how Isabella had insisted on wearing the key on a string around her neck. It was a wonder the child hadn't wanted to take her skates to the circus as well. She smiled as she remembered how her daughter Isabella had put young Obadiah Martin in his place over his spitting. And then she and Isabella had gone into the Big Tent and seen the tightrope walker.

Everything was a balancing act. Obadiah Martin would be the chair of the town council sometime within the next five years, if Nancy Geonette's instincts proved correct. She hoped he wasn't too young to take on the responsibility, but Morgan couldn't hold on much longer. Vinegar. And garlic. That was what he needed more of in his diet. She made a mental note to mention it to his wife. Not that the woman would pay any attention to her advice.

She was the one who had panicked just seven—or was it eight?—years ago when the sun began to disappear. Nancy Geonette knew it was a solar eclipse. All the rest of the town had known. Had the newspaper not warned everyone? Morgan's wife either did not read the papers or did not believe them. She had run screaming through the streets, certain that the end of the world had arrived. If Morgan had not chased after her, she might in her panic have run straight into the Metoochie River.

Nancy Geonette turned back to her accounts listings. Some months were up, some months were down. "Just a balancing act," she repeated to herself.

Six pages later her finger lingered over one particular entry, near the beginning of her list for December.

Organ   37.35

She had always wanted an organ, ever since she was a little girl and heard the one in the Old Church. Of course, hers wasn't nearly as grand as that one. Hers had only ten stops rather than the fourteen the church organ had, and only one foot pedal rather than two. Hers didn't have the lovely scrollwork or the detailed painting. It didn't have room for two hymnals at a time on the music rack. But Nancy loved her organ.

And she had made enough money over the previous eleven months that she had been able to justify the expense to Hubert. He had not been real happy about it to begin with, but during the past week, ever since the wagon from Breeton's store had delivered it, she had seen Hubert tapping his foot whenever she played of an evening.

Just this morning, as he dressed for a day of work, she'd heard him humming the first few lines of that new song *Oh You Mister Moon*. He'd forgotten a number of the words, but he had grinned at her as he remembered just a snippet of them. *We love the moon-light / Don't know why / No one is near us / No one can hear us / Only you, Oh Mister Moon.*

His voice cracked a bit on those last two high notes, but he had laughed at himself and wiggled his eyebrows. Nancy Geonette felt a deep contentment with her life.

The sheet music she bought was well worth the money if it could get Hubert to singing.

She browsed through the accounts book one more time. She still had a few more purchases to make before the end of the year. She had promised the children some firecrackers for celebrating the New Year, and their Christmas stockings needed a bit of candy and perhaps some nuts. She had her own pecan trees, of course, but she wanted to buy them something they would not see ordinarily. She needed matches, and another two spools of thread for quilting. To offset those expenses, though, she would have butter and eggs to sell.

All in all, she felt good about the past year. She supported a family of six selling milk and butter from her cows, eggs from the chickens, as well as the hens and geese she sold and the dresses she made for other women in Martinsville. Hubert spent a good deal of time tilling his fields, but so far she had seen little income from them. Even so, she would not belittle his work, for he did work hard, but she had her large vegetable garden, fruit trees, and grape vines, all of which resulted in more food on the table and more money in the jars underneath her bed.

There was a bank just opened up in Garner Creek. The First Community Bank of Keagan County, but Nancy Geonette had not made up her mind about it yet. There was something comforting about having her own money right where she had ready access to it.

She looked again at the list she had tallied of what she had spent so far this year. Two hundred and forty five dollars and thirteen cents to feed, clothe, and supply six children, a husband, and herself for almost this whole year. That was not an inconsiderable accomplishment.

Capping the inkwell, she carefully cleaned her pen and set her accounts book aside.

There was still enough time to play one song, maybe two, before she would need to set the potatoes to boiling for dinner. She lifted the top of the organ bench to retrieve one of her favorite pieces of sheet music and saw Isabella's roller skate key. Funny how she had kept it even though Isabella didn't skate anymore.

WHEN HUBERT DIED in 1913, Nancy Geonette refused to stay with her daughter Isabella and Moses Garner, whom Nancy Geonette had never learned to like. Instead, she went to live with her nephew, Young Gideon Hoskins and his wife Amelia and their six children. The organ accompanied her, of course. Nancy Geonette was the only one in that extended family who enjoyed playing, for she had been unable to interest Amelia or any of Amelia's children in learning the notes.

When Nancy Geonette died the following year after an extended illness, and Isabella, with nary a musical bone in her body, had refused the offer of the organ, Young Gideon corralled two of his neighbors to help him move it into the attic. They piled his aunt's collection of music on top of it and covered it all over with a large sheet. Amelia gave the hymnal to the church.

2000

"**I WONDER IF** the organ she bought was this one." Melissa's voice almost echoed in the cavernous space. She waited until we were all looking her way, and then she pulled on the corner of a yellowed sheet, causing a number of pieces of sheet music to cascade to the floor. She and Dee bent to pick them up.

The organ, with its stops and pedal and discolored ivory keys, was somewhat dilapidated but still beautiful.

"Does anyone play?" Carol looked around at the assembled women.

I waited a moment and then stepped forward. "I'm not very good. In fact, I haven't touched a piano for decades, but I'll give it a try."

I pulled out the stool and fingered the keys gently. Nothing happened.

"You have to pump the pedal," Sadie said. "That gets the air flowing."

"I'm supposed to coordinate feet and hands?" I made as if to stand up, but Sadie put a hand on my shoulder.

I pumped the pedal a few times and tried out a couple of the keys. They sounded a bit wheezy, but much better than I'd expected.

Melissa plopped a faded sheet of music in front of me. "We all ought to know this one."

"I've never heard the verse," Pat said, "but I know the chorus."

"I know the verse, too," Sadie said. "Remember? I'm older than mass-produced marbles."

I played the last few bars and then went back to the beginning. Sadie's voice was strong.

```
My darling I am dreaming of the days gone by,
When you and I were sweethearts beneath the
summer sky;
Your hair has turned to silver, the gold has
faded too;
But still I will remember where I first met
you.
```

Then we all joined in on the chorus.

```
Down by the old mill stream, where I first met
you,
With your eyes of blue, dressed in gingham too,
It was there I knew that you loved me true,
You were sixteen, my village queen,
By the old mill stream.
```

Then, of course, we had to try *Let Me Call You Sweetheart*. We were halfway through that one when Bob called out from the top of the stairs, "Sounds like a music hall up here. Mind if we join you?"

Doc, with Korsi tucked under his arm, crowded up the stairs

behind him. "You need some bass and tenor on that one."

"And baritone," Henry said. "Don't forget us baritones."

Maddy waved her hand. "Come on in."

Easton appeared next to Reebok. She'd been downstairs for such a long time, I'd forgotten about her.

Sadie started to move aside, but Dave stopped her. "The short people have to stay in the front so they can read the music."

"Humph. I grew up singing this music. I probably know every single word." But she grinned up at him and sidled back to stand just behind my shoulder.

After a reprise of the first song, we went on to *It's a Long, Long Way to Tipperary* and *In the Shade of the Old Apple Tree, Take Me Out to the Ball Game* and *Alexander's Ragtime Band.*

Maddy found a piece called *Halley's Comet Rag.* I took one look at the complicated score and threw up my hands. "That's way beyond my key-plunking ability."

Then Dee came up with *Honey I Will Long for You.* Sadie hummed a phrase or two. "Those lyrics were so syrupy, I'm glad it never became popular."

"Here's one," Glaze said. "It's called *Oh You Mister Moon.*"

I waited, half expecting Sadie to start humming, but all she said was, "I never heard of that one."

"Enough of this." I pushed back the stool and stood. Reebok helped Dee cover the organ, and the men—and Easton—retired below.

"Don't forget to feed us pretty soon," Dave said on his way out the door.

Pat tilted her head. "Like you're starving?"

He looked incredulous. "Of course!"

"Just a little longer," Sadie said. "Then we'll be down."

Rebecca Jo went back to leafing through the account book, and the rest of us returned to what we'd been doing before. We worked in relative silence for a while. I was just beginning to think Dave might have been right about food-time when Glaze spoke up.

"Look at this, would you?"

There was something in her voice that drew me out of my seat and over to where she sat at the third card table with her stacks of old greeting cards. She'd been methodically taking them out of the flat-topped trunk beside her for what seemed like hours.

"What's up?"

She refolded a yellowed piece of paper and handed it to me. "Can you make any sense out of this? It was lying between two pasteboard boxes of greeting cards."

It was a letter unlike any of the others on the table. Folded into quarters, the sheet had a round dark green stain on it.

"That's sealing wax stain," Sadie said. I hadn't even heard her come up next to me. The others gathered around.

Glaze held up the envelope the letter had come in, and we could all see the broken blob of green sealing wax on the back of it. Only a tiny bit of wax remained attached to the envelope, but the stain showed that it must have been a substantial size to begin with, a little larger than a quarter.

"The wax must have leached through the envelope onto the paper," I said, and several of the women nodded. I sniffed at it, and an unmistakable scent flooded my nose. "It still smells like beeswax!"

"How on earth can a smell linger for this many years?" Ida asked.

"Being locked up in a trunk probably helped," Maddy said, "with no circulating air."

"Read it," Glaze directed, so I unfolded the paper. Like a lot of the old letters, the paper felt heavier, more substantial than what we use nowadays.

I glanced at the first few lines and looked back up. "It's another one addressed to someone in Beechnut House."

"You've missed the point," Glaze said. "Look at the rest of the letter."

Dee craned her neck to peer over Sadie's shoulder. "Read it out loud, Biscuit."

I read out the date. "Eighteen-fifty-six. This letter was written before Lincoln was president. Amazing, isn't it?" I turned the page over to look at the signature at the bottom. "It's from somebody named Dolly. I wonder who she was."

Glaze held up the envelope. There wasn't a return address that I could see. "It's right here," she said, opening the envelope as wide as it would go.

"Of course," Sadie said. "I remember my mother telling me that paper was scarce when she was a girl, and people often took an envelope apart, refolded it inside out, and used it again."

"That practice stopped after the Civil War," Carol told us, "once paper and mass-produced envelopes became more plentiful."

"Can you read the name," Maddy asked, "without damaging the envelope?"

Glaze studied it for a few moments. "It's addressed to Mistress Delilah Surratt Kibby, Kibby House, Brothersville, Georgia. Delilah? That must be the Dolly who wrote this letter."

"I've never heard of Brothersville," Melissa said. "Does anybody know where it is?"

Maddy pushed her glasses more firmly onto the bridge of her nose. "In case you hadn't noticed, this is a big state with a lot of towns. It could be anywhere."

Melissa stuck her tongue out at Maddy, and we all laughed at the childish gesture.

"Keep reading," Dee said.

As soon as I read the first line, *I am in receipt, as you can see, of your letter*, Maddy interrupted.

"*As you can see.* Of course! The reused envelope would have told Grace that Dolly had received her letter." She shook her head in wonder. "Who woulda guessed you could learn so much from just a few words?"

"Go ahead and read it," Carol said, "but I need a potty break. Save it for me and I'll read it for myself when I get back up here." She headed for the stairs.

I nodded and read on.

17 February 1856
Kibby House

Mistress Grace Surratt Hoskins
Beechnut House
Martinsville
Georgia

My dearest Grace,

I am in receipt, as you can see, of your letter of the fifteenth of January. Thank you for all your encouragement in the matter of which we have so frequently—and so secretly—written. I pray daily that I may continue to be of some service to those who desperately need our succor and our active aid in finding their way to freedom in the North.

Maddy held up her hand. "Is she talking about the Underground Railroad?"

"Sure sounds like it," Dee said.

"Maybe," Melissa temporized. "Why don't you keep reading, Biscuit?"

As far as I am aware no suspicion has descended yet on Elijah or me, for if it had, I feel sure we would have been arrested immediately. Living as we do far out from the busyness even of small Brothersville, we have been able to send almost two dozen people on to the next station. Others turn up on our doorstep with a regularity that is both distressing and pleasing. Distressing because of their very desperate need for our services and pleasing because we have been able to help them in our own small way.

As to the secret room you inform me that you and Arthur have prepared—however did you hide its construction from your son? Gideon is from everything you have said about him completely intolerant. I hope you and Arthur take great care never to let him know about the room. While I appreciate the thought and I am fully aware of the difficulty its preparation must have entailed, I cannot see how it could be of service. I know how hard it is to get both into and out of that valley of yours not only because I followed that tortuous route along the river after I was married to Elijah, but also because I travelled back along it for myself when I visited you after your wedding—has it truly been thirty-four years since then? Even with the rather precipitous and hidden paths up the cliffs and the multitude of caves across the small river, you are hardly in a place where anyone is likely to search. I doubt they could find your <u>town</u>, much less the hidden room you now have in Beechnut House. You are not even close to any of the direct *lines that have been used so successfully, and I see no reason why anyone would wish to traverse the length of the valley only to have to reverse their course in order to "follow the drinking gourd." Your heart is true, my dear sister, as is Arthur's, but while we cannot make use of your room, would you consider sending quilts? I will explain herewith why I need them.*

"Quilts?"
Dee shushed Pat. "She says she'll explain."
"But…"
"Shhh!"

Not even a fortnight ago we drove a wagon piled with various household goods that we were prepared to say were gifts for his newly married grandniece in Augusta. Of course, you know that Elijah and I do not even have a surviving grandniece, but he and I both felt that the untruth would have been a justifiable minor sin. As it was, we did not have to explain our trip—who would suspect an elderly man such as my dear husband?

As you know, I have a hard time controlling my tongue, and Elijah insisted that he would tell anyone who stopped us that I was addled in my brain and unable to speak due to my advanced age. I think he privately hoped that we would be detained, just so he could tell such an outrageous tale. I do admit that I secretly practiced looking incompetent. I find that I am able to drool quite convincingly.

"She sounds like a hoot," Pat said. "Wish I'd known her."
"She'd make a great addition to our attic society," Glaze said.
"Shhh!" Dee repeated.

Our dear old mule, who used to be called Sling, but whom we renamed Slingshot, because she can shoot her foot out faster than Melanie's Zenus used to be able to sling a stone to scare off a wild dog—

or did I already tell you the story of how Slingshot saved our milk cow from a black bear only last summer? I cannot remember. Slingshot made the fourteen miles to Augusta in fine time, which was a blessing because one of the things we carried, underneath a rocking chair and several cast iron cooking pots, was an enormous wooden box of quilts. Hidden within the quilts was a woman and her six-year-old daughter.

When the woman reached us, her back was covered in open welts from the most recent beating her barbaric master had given her, and the quilts both under her and over her absorbed a good deal of her blood as we did not feel it would be safe to try to keep her with us for any length of time. We left Brothersville in the late afternoon so as to arrive at the next station, one of the Baptist churches, well beyond the setting of the sun. Thus we were able to use the cover of darkness to unload the wagon and its precious cargo. We left the rocker and the bloody quilts there, and returned home—we did not encounter a single obstacle, so there was no excuse for me to drool—with my cooking pots rattling around in the bed of the wagon. Slingshot was noticeably appreciative of the decreased weight of the load on the return trip, for she brayed enthusiastically as if in answer every time the skillet and the stew pot clanked together.

I daresay the inhabitants of the houses we passed on our journey are still cursing that infernal noisy mule.

Now that spring is upon us, I have not so much need of the quilts, but would value any you might be able to send before next winter—and in case we have such need of them again. Needless to say, I cannot admit to any of my neighbors that I am suddenly without extra coverings for our beds.

None of us knows the location of stations beyond the next one past us on the line, the one we have direct access to, but the conductor there told me that the next station was too far for Juneah—such a lovely name, is it not?—to travel in her condition. He assured me that she and her daughter would not be sent farther on until her back was healed enough for her to travel safely, although by what means they will either hide them or convey them I do not know. Juneah told me that she will take on the last name of Brown, for she refuses to be known by the last name of the man who was her master for most of her life. I heard two of the people in the church mention Baltimore, although they curbed their tongues as soon as they noticed that I was within earshot of their conversation. I do pray that Juneah Brown and her daughter might eventually make it that far.

"I hope they made it," Rebecca Jo said, and I found myself wishing fervently for the same thing. How, though, would we ever know the outcome?

Elijah informs me that I am a fool for writing openly of that which we must hide in our everyday life, so I will not refer to our doings in any subsequent letters to you. I will write to you of petty things, of jams I have put by and the state of my garden, of a dress I have sewn or yet another shirt that Elijah has ruined with those infernal cigars of his—at least the smoke from them does somewhat alleviate the peskiness of mosquitoes. But I will no longer write of the activity that is closest to our hearts. I thank the Lord that Elijah and I are of one mind in this. If I do happen to mention Elijah's non-existent niece in one of my future letters, you will know that we have helped another dear soul along on their path. If I mention your raisin pudding—which I long for, by the way—it will mean that we have a resident in our own secret room.

Know that you are in my heart always.
I remain ever
your affectionate sister,
  Dolly

"That's—" Pat started to say, but for once I was the one telling her to hush.

"Shhh! There's more."

Post Scriptum – For some reason beyond the fathoming of mortal mind, our august state of Georgia has chosen to change the name of Brothersville to Hephzibah, I daresay because of the seminary

147

that is here and the longtime association of the town with the Baptist Church. I can barely spell the new name, and will I am sure have a difficult time remembering to write my address so. You must remember when next you write to me, although it might be best if you put both town names on the envelope. I long for your letters, and for the quilts I know you will send. Do not delay in letting me hear from you.

Post Scriptum #2 – I have told you about my ongoing battle with Abigail, my youngest granddaughter, Almira's girl. I must admit I have been defeated. I have finally given up on trying to teach that child to knit. How any kin of mine could have such wayward thumbs I will never know.

"She sure is wordy," Dee said, in the same words she'd used to criticize Thomas the stutterer's letter.

I rested the letter on my lap.

"But just think about it," Maddy said. "Letters were really precious back then. People took the time to pour their hearts into them."

"I wonder if Abigail ever learned to knit."

"It goes on," I said. "There are three more additions. Maybe she'll tell us."

Post Scriptum #3 – Although it may be unnecessary for me to mention this, for you know our sisters as well as I do, I urge you not to tell Elspeth about your hidden room. She has a brain the size of a walnut and can remember to keep a secret no longer than a squirrel. Have you told Melanie yet? I hope not, for she will be sure to share it with Zenus, and he will, I am sure, see fit to give you unwanted advice.

"Melanie and Zenus," Maddy said. "Weren't those the names on the wedding invitation with that gorgeous brown dress?" She wandered back to the museum drawer and pulled out the invitation. "Yep."

Post Scriptum #4 – Never fear, my dear. I will end this letter eventually. The next time you write, though, please tell me more about the lovely cheval mirror Arthur gave you. It sounds exquisite. And how sweet of him to include such a loving thought as a part of his gift.

"The mirror?" Dee looked over her shoulder. "I wonder if she means that one?"

"It sure looks old enough," Sadie said.

Maddy indicated the letter. "Does she say anything about the—what did she call it?—the loving thought?"

"No." I'd already silently read the end of the letter. "Just one more addition."

Post Scriptum #5 – Elijah suggests – and I must concur with him – that you should burn this letter upon receipt.

"Burn it?" Dee's voice went up an octave. "Burn it?"

"Well of course, dear," Sadie said. "Something like this would have been dangerous—even deadly—if it had gotten into the wrong hands."

Melissa reached out and touched the letter softly with her index finger. "I'm surprised Elijah let Dolly mail it in the first place."

"I'm surprised too," Rebecca Jo said. "I'm so glad Grace ignored her sister's directive and kept the letter. Here, Maddy. Why don't you put this with the hundred-year letter from Mary Frances. And the Titanic letter."

"It certainly qualifies." Maddy opened the drawer of the wobbly white dresser. "Once the storm is over, I may do some research down in Brothersville—"

"Hephzibah," Melissa corrected.

"Hephzibah. And see if I can find any trace of Grace's sister."

"Maybe we could all take a field trip," Dee suggested. "If the Kibby House is still standing, that is."

"What I'd like to know," Glaze waved a hand over the stacks on her card table, "is how such a letter got mixed in with all these greeting cards."

"What I'd like to know," Maddy said, "is where that hidden room is."

We looked at one another for several heart-stopping seconds and then fanned out like bees bursting from a hive on the first warm day of spring.

I know where it is! I will show you.

We must have worried Marmalade with all our thumping around because she retreated to the back of the attic and yowled several times.

Yowled? Look back here!

"It could be under the floor," Dee said, "in the space between the attic and the second floor." She began to stomp around, stopping occasionally to peer at the wide hardwood floorboards.

When ListenLady comes back, she will hear what I am saying.

"Maybe it's behind one of these big cabinets," Melissa said from the end of the room, near where Marmalade was still meowing over something or other. "Here, Biscuit. Come help me move this." We tried unsuccessfully to shove an enormous armoire away from where it rested in the corner formed by the front wall of the house and the end wall of the attic. "How on earth did they ever get these heavy things up those stairs?"

"And why," I asked, "would they do it in the first place? I'm tempted to take this behemoth down to the bedroom. Wouldn't it be lovely?"

She raised an eyebrow. "You only think that because of the lamplight. It makes everything look romantic. In full sunlight this thing would look pretty disreputable."

I had to admit she was probably right. Still, maybe I could refinish it. Out of curiosity, I opened it, to find it jammed with old dresses and cloaks. These would bear investigating, but now wasn't the time.

Even after we moved everything—except the monstrous armoire—away from the walls and thumped on every available surface, no hidden room appeared.

"Maybe they dismantled it," Pat said, "after hearing from Dolly that it would never be used."

"I don't know about that," said Glaze, walking slowly around the perimeter of the room.

Sometimes I can't figure out my sister. "What are you doing?"

"Counting windows," she said.

The eyebrow windows set high on the attic walls were a distinctive feature of number thirteen Beechnut Lane—I changed my thought—of Beechnut House. Thank goodness for them. They lit the room, which may have been the only thing that kept it from being totally gloomy. The ones on the front of the house still had the original leaded glass panes, but the ones on the back were plain old ordinary window glass—not nearly so interesting. Even with the heavy cloud cover outside, there was still a fair amount of daylight coming in.

"Nine, ten, eleven, twelve," Glaze said. "Twelve windows on the front and twelve on the back."

"You'd better count again," I said. "There are thirteen of them."

"Twelve," she insisted.

"Glaze, I can't tell you how many times I've counted them. I've always wondered why they put in a baker's dozen, when most builders would have stopped at twelve."

"Where were you when you counted them?"

I looked at Glaze in surprise. "Standing on the front walkway, of course. Looking up."

"You're sure there are thirteen?" Maddy sounded excited for some reason that I couldn't fathom.

"Absolutely sure."

"Then that means," she strode toward the ponderous armoire against the far wall, "we may have found the room."

I have been telling you it is here.

It took five of us, tugging and shoving and grunting and swearing, to move the tall cabinet far enough away from the wall that we could get behind it. And that's where we found the little door. We probably wouldn't have noticed it if we hadn't been looking for it. The edges fit tightly against the surrounding panels of the wall.

"Nothing shows on this side," Maddy said, as I pushed against it. We all gasped when the door swung into an empty space beyond.

I told you so.

Carol rejoined us just then. "Told them what?" she asked, just as Marmalade started meowing up a storm.

Summer 1860

BABYLON COULD NOT hear the dogs anymore. That wide stream had helped. He had lost his footing a couple of times on the slippery stones in the fast-flowing water, but the nighttime breeze—that and his running—had dried him out pretty much. It was too much to hope that he had fooled those dogs for good, though. They had noses as keen as the smell of his momma's peach pies, but maybe he had slowed them down some. He was gonna need the extra time. He needed to rest, but he did not dare stop for long. Running all night had worn his feet to a frazzle, but he had to keep going. He stood stock still, trying to slow down his heaving breath.

You better stop right here, his momma had told him just a few minutes ago. Ahead of him was a treacherous cliff with no way to climb down it, and anyway there were houses spread out below him. It would be dawn soon.

Lucky for him he hadn't walked right over the cliff edge in the dark, but he had spotted the light from a candle or a lantern in one of the houses below. That and the feel of an early morning breeze pouring up and over the cliff had saved him from a fatal fall. The light and the moon and the breeze and his momma's voice.

He had heard it, like it was carried on the wind.

Don't you stop too long, though. Dogs is smart. Specially them dogs. They'll find you real fast once they pick up your scent.

I just need a few minutes to rest, Momma, he thought. My feet hurt.

More than your feet is gonna hurt if they catch you, son.

She had been gone for more than a year now, but he still heard her, usually when he was about to do something stupid, like talk back when he was not ever supposed to do that, or step off a cliff in the dark night.

You take care now, Babylon. I want you to grow up free. You take care. You have run this far. You better not get caught now.

Babylon was his basket name. Not the one the master called him. The one his momma gave him when he was born twelve winters

152

ago. She never used the name the master gave him. Out loud, when the master was around, she called him anything else, but never Fred'rick like the master did and never Boy like every other white person did. Just between the two of them, she called him Babylon, so he would never forget his true name.

There had to be a path around here somewhere.

He heard a light laugh, too high to be his momma's voice. And coming from the wrong direction. Momma's voice was always sort of inside him, but this one came from off to the side, coming up on his left between the towering trees along the top of the cliff. That's where the path must be. But now his way was blocked. He scooted a few yards back in the direction he had come from, ducked behind some thick greenery, dropped flat on his belly, and froze. The full moon spread shadows across the path.

"We have not done this since our courting days, Arthur." The woman's voice was awful quiet, but it carried on the early morning air.

A man's voice, deep and resonant, answered. "Tá do dheis mo chroí, bean de ghrásta."

Babylon did not understand a word of it. He risked a peek through slitted eyes, and glimpsed an elderly man and a bonneted woman before he ducked his head back down. In the soft moonlight of pre-dawn they would most likely not see him, but he preferred not to take the risk. He breathed through his mouth to make sure they would not hear him.

"You are correct, my love—I *am* right," the woman said. "You do not think I would forget such an early morning walk as this, do you?" The man did not answer, and the woman kept speaking. "You have not called me *bean de ghrásta* in several years." She sounded soft somehow, but Babylon knew better than to assume that a soft voice in a white woman meant a soft manner.

"But you are indeed a *woman of grace*," her husband said. "And lucky I am that you have never forgotten the language I courted you in."

"Nor have I forgotten that you have always had a touch of the blarney from your Irish great-great grandmother."

"Ah, I never met the dear woman, but she did leave a trace of herself in all of her offspring."

"And lucky I am to have a part in that family, my husband."

"Ah, Grace, what would I do if I did not have you by my side?

Here, let us sit and watch the moon as it travels, and then wait for the sun to rise."

"We will be sitting a long time, then, Mister Hoskins."

"We have the time, Mistress Hoskins." His voice had a laugh in it. "Our son is on his wedding trip, the house is dark, and this early moon-bedecked morning is mild."

Babylon dared to take a peek between the leaves of the shrub. The man spread his cloak and the two settled themselves on the flat rocks at the edge of the cliff. Their backs were to him, but he saw that there was no way he could get past them unseen to reach the path and the sanctuary of the woods.

"Arthur?"

"Yes, my dear?"

"Do you recall how Dolly told me that we should not have built the room?" Without waiting for an answer, she continued. "That was four years ago, and in all that time, we have never made use of it."

"I know, my dear, but I do not regret building it. The time may come, and I would rather have a secret room and not need it than to need one and not have it ready."

"Do you think Dolly might have let the other conductors know that we are ready to serve as a station?"

Conductors? Station? Babylon could not believe his ears. Could it be so? Could he have stumbled on a haven? Did he dare trust these two white-haired, pasty-faced people?

Where was his momma's voice when he needed her advice?

The man called Arthur put his arm around the shoulder of his woman. "I doubt your sister would have told anyone about it, since she believes we are too far off any trail." He turned and pointed to his left, up into the sky. "See, my dear. The drinking gourd is there, shining as clearly as can be. Surely someone will come this way, someday."

Far behind him, Babylon heard the baying of the hounds start up again. They must have picked up his trail on this side of the river. He should have stayed absolutely still, but his fear of the dogs made him start to his feet, and he dislodged a small stone as he jumped up.

The man heard the sounds as well. He turned and saw Babylon in the soft light of pre-dawn. "Friend," he said. "My young friend, we have a place ready for you."

Go with them, Babylon. Go fast.

The woman was already gathering her skirts to rise. "Come quickly." She looked over the cliff. "Before people are up and about their day." She did not add, *before the dogs reach us,* but Babylon could hear the unsaid words behind the urgency in her voice.

The man held out his hand. "Fear not, child. The North Star in the Dipper, the Drinking Gourd, has led you on the right path to us. Let me carry you down the path. That way the dogs may lose your scent for a bit. We need not make it too easy for them."

As they hurried down the trail, the man called Arthur whispered to his wife. "Get into your nightdress quickly, Grace. We needs must look like we have been sleeping if those most unwelcome visitors come to our door."

"No, husband. I will lead the dogs astray."

"It will not be safe for you."

"You know if there are dogs, there will be more danger for the child than for me. There is no time to argue."

At the bottom of the path, Grace quickly removed the tattered rags that covered the young boy's feet. Babylon was surprised when the man's eyes filled with tears. Babylon knew his feet looked bad, but he had never known a white man to cry over blood like that.

Missus Grace wound the rags around a long stick she found lying beside the path and used it like a walking stick, tamping the bloody rags against the ground with each one of her steps. At the house, Elijah carried the boy inside while Grace continued down to the river. Even with the dry spell they were having, there still was a steady flow of water. She threw the rags into the Metoochie. Once they were caught by the current, she tossed in the branch as well.

She turned to her right and walked beside the water downstream for a bit, waiting only to be sure the rags and stick were swept far away by the current. Then she turned between Breeton's dry goods store and the millinery shop to go uphill. As she walked, she rehearsed her story, that she had spent the night with an ailing widow and was only now returning home to prepare breakfast for her man. Behind her she heard the dogs yap in confusion as they lost the trail at the water's edge.

"Durn him!" One man's voice drifted to her on the breeze. "He's taken to the water again."

"Don't worry none," the other voice said. "We'll find him soon enough."

Grace could imagine the two of them heading upstream, toward the north, which, of course, was the direction a runaway would take.

She smiled to herself and walked the rest of the way home to cook a substantial breakfast for three. She would serve one of those meals in the secret room. She was sure the youngster would devour her famous raisin pudding. It was good she had made such a large batch of it just yesterday.

She quickly reviewed the supplies she would need for treating his feet and that wound she had seen on the side of his head. Bandaging, hot water, perhaps some of that salve she had recently concocted of comfrey, rosemary, and yarrow.

Her assurance faltered when she thought about her son Gideon and his older two sons from his first marriage. They were not to be trusted. She and Arthur had been hard put to keep the construction of the room from them. Fortunately the boys were out and about during the days and Gideon's work kept him from home for long stretches. On the few instances when he had caught either Arthur or herself coming down the stairs from the attic, he had accepted their explanation that they were cleaning it out. Fortunately, he had not offered to help. But then again, Gideon never offered to help.

When Gideon and Eliza returned from their wedding trip, Grace would have to sound out Eliza carefully. She was a charming young woman, but Grace knew better than to assume that charm could be equated with compassion. Gideon's first wife, his late wife, had been of a like mind with Grace and Arthur. Grace had missed Leonora every day since her death. She only wished she had been at home that day. She might have prevented Leonora's drowning.

She adjusted her cap, as if in moving it about, she could dislodge these sad thoughts from her brain.

By the time she reached the path to her door, she had begun wondering if she would ever have a chance to tell Dolly about this morning's work. Ah! She could write to Dolly and tell her of the batch of raisin pudding she had made. No, she would have to be more specific so Dolly would know she was using the code Dolly herself had devised. She would write that she had enjoyed a large bowl of raisin pudding as she lounged upstairs. And she would inquire after the health of Dolly's grand-niece. That would do it.

2000

"WHY," MELISSA ASKED as she looked around the narrow room, "would they have left a chamber pot and a mattress in here if they knew they were never going to use it?"

"Maybe they hoped they would," Sadie suggested.

"Not hardly," Rebecca Jo scoffed. "Not with that heavy cupboard in front of the door."

"I think they did use it." Pat stood beside the bare mattress. "Look. You can see the imprint of where somebody slept."

"That's ridiculous," Ida said. "A mattress wouldn't hold a dent like that for this long."

Pat bent down and poked at the edge of the crude fabric, which rustled under her fingers. "It's not stuffed with memory foam, Ida. It's straw."

It hadn't taken us more than a few minutes to squeeze behind the armoire and crowd ourselves into the long narrow room. It ran the entire depth of the house, but was barely six feet wide in the other direction. A window at each end let in some light and, thank goodness, kept the room from feeling like an enlarged coffin.

There was a pile of blankets on the floor just inside the door. I ran my hand across two substantial oak bars that were obviously designed to slip into the heavy brackets on either side of the tight-fitting door. "This sure would be an effective lock, in case somebody moved that heavy armoire aside."

"I doubt it would stand up to an axe," Dee said.

"This doesn't make sense," Pat said. "They would have needed a way to bring food up here to whoever was hidden away. They couldn't go moving such a heavy piece of furniture back and forth, and it would have meant bringing extra people—or at least two big strong men— up here every time they needed to empty the chamber pot or deliver a meal."

Maddy's head whipped around and she plunged through the

door. We all just stood there listening to the rustles and thumps, wondering what the heck was going on. Finally, she gave a shout of delight. A moment later, she crowed, "I found it!"

"Found what?"

"What are you talking about?"

"What are we missing?"

Maddy stuck her head back through the opening. "They didn't need to move the armoire. Come out here and help me shove it farther from the wall so you can all see."

We did as she asked, but I have to admit I was totally mystified until Maddy went around to the front, stepped over the piles of clothing she had obviously removed, and swung the back of the armoire toward her on carefully concealed hinges. "See," she said, "somebody could open the back of the armoire, push open the little door in the wall and, once they were sure the door was barricaded from inside with the oak bars, they'd close the back of the armoire, replace the clothes, and nobody would be the wiser."

Glaze high-fived Maddy through the secret panel. "How did you ever think to look for a secret door?"

Maddy pushed her glasses higher onto the bridge of her nose. "I used something sort of like this in one of my first thrillers. I got the idea from *The Lion, the Witch, and the Wardrobe*."

Is there a lion in there? I will protect you.

"You know what this means," Ida started to say, but Marmalade let out a truly ferocious growl, her fur bristling.

I bent to pick her up, but she jumped past me into the armoire and then let out a bewildered-sounding warble.

There is no lion here.

Carol said, for no apparent reason, "The lion is just in the name of a book."

Oh. Thank you, ListenLady.

I couldn't decipher what she was talking about, so I decided to ignore her. "Don't ask me what Marmalade's meowing about," I said to the room at large. "What were you about to say, Ida?"

"I think this room and the armoire's secret entrance means that a Martinsville Museum is going to have to be located here in your attic."

"I'll have to think about that," I said, "and I think the answer's going to be a big fat resounding *no*."

"Maybe we could build an outside entrance," Pat suggested.

"Wait a minute!" I held up my hand. "This is my house, my home. Not a public thoroughfare."

"Just an idea," Pat said, but I didn't like the glint in her eye.

"It *was* built to be an inn." Sadie had a mischievous sparkle in her eyes as well.

"Not on my watch," I said. I couldn't imagine people tromping through my house at all hours of the day or night. Well—that wasn't fair—surely the museum would have posted hours.

What are you talking about?

"It's too bad we don't have a museum in town." The feather on Ida's hat drooped disconsolately. "Some of these things would look real nice on display."

"But we don't know anything about them," Glaze said. "Don't museums have to have everything labeled and identified?"

"That would be the ideal," Carol admitted, "but sometimes it's just not possible."

I ignored them and turned around to head for the stairs. "Bob's going to want to see this."

"And Ralph."

"And Tom!"

Maddy stepped in front of me. "First, let's move the armoire back in place and see if they can find it."

"What a good idea, Maddy. Sort of like a treasure hunt."

We swung the hidden room's door back into place—it took us several tries, since the thing didn't have any handles on this side of it—wrestled the armoire to where it had stood originally, and made sure the hinged back would open correctly. Then we replaced all the cloaks and dresses.

Maddy dusted her hands. "Ready."

I took the letter downstairs with me. Ralph and Reebok had a heavy game of cribbage going on, while Dad and Father John were hunched over a chessboard. The rest of the men—and Easton—were gathered around the kitchen table, but they set their cards aside when I told them I had a letter to read to them.

As soon as we explained that we'd found the secret room, the whole entire temporary population of Beechnut House trooped upstairs.

They fanned out across the attic, all except Bob. He stood near the top of the stairs, just letting his eyes roam around the place. I could see the wheels turning, but had no idea what his thought process was.

He does not have wheels. He is thinking very hard.

Maybe, since he was the host, he was letting all our guests have the fun?

No.

I had just reached that conclusion when he let out a deep breath and strode between the trunks and the chair circle to the far wall. He laid a hand on the armoire. "It's behind here," he said.

Ida was indignant. "How did you do that so fast?"

"I counted the windows," he said, and beside me I heard Glaze mutter something unintelligible.

"Windows, Chief? What do the windows have to do with it?"

"There are twelve visible windows along each side up here, but there are thirteen windows on the outside of the house."

"Oh."

Glaze elbowed me in the ribs.

Why?

I ignored her.

Why?

Bob nodded at Reebok. "It makes sense that this wall must have been added later, and the only place a door could be hidden would be behind this big piece of furniture."

Even Bob was surprised, though, when we showed him the hinged back. I was afraid the clothes were going to be somewhat the worse for wear after having been dumped on the floor several times in one day, but we did try to be careful with them.

I spotted what looked like a homespun shirt, child-sized. Could it possibly have lasted so long? I wanted to look more closely at it once we'd finished with the hidden room, so I set it off to one side, on a small table, but not before I wondered if there was any way this could have belonged to one of the people we'd met in these letters and diaries. Maybe Mary Frances had put it up here when John outgrew it. No, that was impossible. She'd never lived in this house. But even so, I couldn't resist lifting it to my cheek. It was soft, obviously well-worn. The stitches were closely spaced. There was a patch near the hem and other signs of repairs here and there. Definitely hand-sewn.

1853

THE SHIRT SHE held was somewhat the worse for wear. Leonora turned it over, tallying the places she would need to mend. Young Gideon was such a quiet child, she failed to see how he could be so rough on his clothing.

Ah! Here was the answer. Smudges of mud along the hemline as well as a hole almost the size of her son's fist. A tiny piece of wet twig caught in the bottom of a damp sleeve, a willow leaf, and was that—yes it was—a charcoal smear. He'd been down beside the river yesterday, probably drawing pictures of frogs.

She sighed. The dedication of the new wing of the schoolhouse was set for just a scant hour from now, and Leonora despaired of getting Young Gideon cleaned up enough to be presentable. The new wing was a popular addition, and there had been much approval when Mister Ketchum Martin suggested the change to the leaders of the town. The old schoolhouse may have been sufficient for the past fifty years, but with the town growing so much, the students were now crammed into an insufficient space.

There was no telling where Young Gideon was at the moment, but she was fair sure it involved dirt. She and Mother Grace laughed often together about the boy's propensity for connecting with mud.

Luckily, the boy's father was out of town yet again on business, so Leonora felt safe in taking Young Gideon along with her and her mother-in-law to the ceremony. Her other children were less than enthusiastic about the building addition, but Young Gideon would be of an age to begin classes this year, and Leonora intended to encourage him as much as she could. He would be younger than the other children, but Leonora knew her son was thirsty for knowledge despite his father's scorn for it.

She stepped outside and called his name. Loudly. Repeatedly.

When at last he came running, she saw that the shirt he wore was in worse condition than this one she held in her hand.

"Mother! Look!" He stretched his hands out. They dripped with honey from a bright yellow comb he had obviously wrenched out of a hollow tree. Fortunately Young Gideon had never been bothered by bee stings—he certainly got enough of them every summer. Lucky, too, that the bees had not followed him home.

"I never saw wax of such a color, Mother!"

Always ready to encourage his questing mind, Leonora asked her son, "Why do you suppose this is so yellow?" It was, indeed, a most vibrant shade.

His eyebrows, already too full for his young face, drew together, and Leonora stifled an impulse to kiss her son's forehead. "The yellow poplars are blooming, and I have seen bees aplenty swarming over the blossoms." He thought another few moments. "Could that be why?"

Leonora did not know. The yellow poplar had always been a favorite tree, with its heady blossoms of yellow and orange and green, filled with the brightest of yellow centers. "Perhaps your schoolmaster will know the answer."

"The older comb was white, the way it always is, but this—this was new honeycomb. So it must have been the yellow poplar."

"Might have been, my son. Might have been."

He grinned impishly at her. "Yes, Mother. Might have been."

But Leonora could tell he was convinced he was right.

Later, at the schoolhouse, Young Gideon showed the schoolmaster a small section of the comb he had carefully drained of honey and rinsed in water from the rain barrel so it was hardly sticky at all. Leonora could not help her smiles when the schoolmaster confirmed that the yellow poplar was the most likely culprit in the mystery of the yellow honeycomb. Young Gideon was such an endearing child. And so very bright. Even though he was her own, she felt sure her opinion was correct.

She and Mother Grace exchanged knowing and loving smiles as they watched the schoolmaster try to wipe the stickiness from his fingers once Young Gideon's attention was captured by the array of books on a nearby shelf.

2000

THE MEN SQUEEZED one at a time through the door into the secret room. Speculation ran rampant as to who might have left that tantalizing indentation in the mattress once Father John raised the question.

Ida, who had gone in with Ralph, climbed back out with a smile on her face. "Good news," she said. "The chamber pot in there is clean. If you discount a hundred and fifty years of dust."

"Why is that good news?" Reebok asked.

"It means …"

Carol cleared her throat, and Ida looked at her and frowned. "Okay. I get it, Carol. A clean chamber pot *might tend to indicate*"— she stressed each of those four words—"that whoever used that mattress got out of here safely."

Maddy nodded vigorously. "If somebody had come in here and found the hiding place, they wouldn't have bothered to clean out the pot, right?"

Henry cleared his throat just as Carol had done, but I didn't think he was indicating disapproval. "I should think," he said, "that if somebody had broken in and found the hiding place, they wouldn't have moved the armoire back into position so carefully, either."

Carol smiled. "I think we're right. Whoever used it was safe here."

Pat tugged on Dave's sweatshirt. "Come here, honey. And everybody else, I guess. There's something else I want you to see."

I had no idea what she was talking about. I was about to follow the group when Father John touched my arm.

1995

CLARA MARTIN HARDLY ever touched her husband. There were just too many years of resentment between them, and the gulf seemed to get wider as the years passed. And now, after he'd made such a mess by inviting someone from out of town to be the new librarian, she was more inclined to clop him upside the head than to reach out like this. But sometimes, softness worked.

"It's just such a strange name," she told him, trying to keep the venom out of her voice. "Who on earth would name a child after a breakfast item?" Not that she ever baked biscuits for breakfast or any other time, but still. It just wasn't dignified.

"It's a nickname," he said, and Clara hated his reasonableness.

"That's as stupid as calling somebody Jelly or Beef Jerky or ..." she groped for something appropriate, "... or Corndog." As soon as she said it, she knew she'd made a mistake. That had been Hubbard's nickname for his brother, the one who died, the one who should've been the council chairman, the one Clara would have married if only he'd lived.

She saw Hubbard's jaw clench, and that vein on his temple started throbbing.

Still, she wouldn't quit trying. "We'd be better off with somebody local being the librarian. They'd be more likely to know what I want. I mean, what we want."

"Nobody local applied for the position."

"Anita didn't?" Clara couldn't believe it. After all she'd done for that woman, and how she'd encouraged her to submit her application.

"Nope. Just this Biscuit McGee or McKlee or something like that."

"Well, you certainly need to grill her about that name of hers. We can't have anyone setting such a bad example for the town children."

"Don't you think there are other things I should worry about?"

"Nothing that important." Clara turned away from him. She felt like she'd made her point, and as long as he asked the questions she'd led him to ask, she knew she had him right where she wanted him.

Now, all he had to do was blackball the woman, and everything would be set. She'd call Anita in the morning and get her to put in her application. So what if there'd been a deadline? Deadlines were just suggestions, after all.

At the meeting, as soon as Hubbard said he was opposed, Nick Foley spoke up in favor of the appointment. So did Carl Armitage and all the other council members. When Bisque McKee was given the job by those traitors—Hubbard's vote was the only dissenting one—Clara set her jaw and decided she would simply make life miserable for that uppity woman.

Bisque McKee looked entirely too much like Clara's older sister.

Bisque even sounded like her. The last thing Clara needed was to be reminded of her sister every day of her life.

2000

"**COULD I TALK** with you in private for a moment?"

I was surprised. I couldn't remember many conversations with Father John. At least, not without Bob or a bunch of other people there. "Sure." The rest of the group had gathered around Pat near one of the trunks, so I stepped aside, to where we were partially shielded from view by a folding screen. "Will this do?"

"I know you're really filled up here, but is there a room you won't be using as a sleeping place?"

I'd assigned Father John and Henry to one of the small bedrooms at the far end of the hall. It had twin beds and two windows. I hoped the curtains were heavy enough to keep out at least some of the icy chill.

"It doesn't have to be sizable," he went on. "Just enough room for a chair and maybe a little table?"

I thought about the twenty-four-hour prayer chapel at St. Theresa's. "You're not going to sit there all night, are you?"

"No. But I generally say my rosary in the middle of the night, between one and two o'clock, and I don't want to disturb Henry."

"I doubt you'd disturb him," I said. "He's up every morning from two to four, but then you'd know all about that."

Father John looked faintly surprised.

"Surely you don't think the whole town doesn't know about how Henry goes to St. Theresa's every morning to pray?"

"It wasn't supposed to be public information," he said.

"It's your 24-hour prayer chapel, right?" He answered me with a nod. "Some of us take early morning walks, and we've seen him sneaking in there."

"I don't think he exactly sneaks."

"Well, I didn't mean it that way. It's just that it's an open secret that he's part of your prayer team."

"Not exactly," Father John said. "He does come during that time to pray, but because he isn't Catholic, he cannot truly be a guardian of the host. The diocese would never allow it. The adoration chapel is … is much more than a prayer chapel. It's sacred in a way that non-Catholics can't possibly understand."

The implications of what he was saying went far beyond me. He must have recognized my confusion.

"Henry doesn't know this, and I would never tell him, but while he's praying for those two hours every morning, I'm there as well, sitting out of sight behind one of the tapestries."

"But the couple that has the shift right before Henry's—they never mentioned that."

"I swore them to secrecy. They would never leave if the chapel were attended only by someone who is not of our faith. I'm happy to know they've abided by their agreement. And apparently the couple who serve from four to six have kept the confidence as well."

I decided not to tell him that the four-to-six team were the ones who'd snitched on Henry to begin with. "I don't understand. Why do you have to be there if Henry's there??"

"Henry is a good man," Father John said, "and being of service is important to him. So when he asked to help St. Theresa's—to help me—by filling that time slot, I could tell he was going through …" He paused as if selecting his words carefully. "… through a difficult time himself."

I nodded. I didn't have all the details—in fact I didn't have any details—but everybody in town knew there had been some rocky times for Henry and Irene and their daughter. Daughters.

"I thought, perhaps, that two hours of prayer each morning in our beautiful chapel might help bring him peace of mind."

From the far end of the attic, a raucous burst of laughter interrupted my train of thought. Father John glanced that way and smiled at the happy sound.

"I still have a couple of empty bedrooms."

He shook his head. "I'd rather not be tempted. If I start yawning, I'd hate to have a comfortable resting place nearby."

"I thought resisting temptation was a good thing."

His grin was impudent. "Not getting into a tempting situation is even better."

"There's a windowless room under the attic stairs," I said. "I'm sure it was intended to be a storage closet, what with all the shelves in there, but we've got so much storage space in this house, all I use it for is a broom closet. There's certainly more than enough room in it for a chair or two, and a little table for a candle. You'll need the light. Maybe you and Henry could both use the space."

He smiled again, and I thought how very kind his face was. "I'll tell Henry about it. He's welcome to it from two to four, since he's used to those hours, but I plan to sleep then."

"But you just said you pray from one to two and then you're hiding in the chapel from two to four. That's three hours of sleep you miss every night."

He smiled once more, and this time it spread into a huge grin. "This ice storm is my chance for a real vacation."

"So, if you're not supposed to leave the chapel unattended," I said, "what about now, during the storm? Aren't you supposed to have someone there twenty-four/seven?"

"I called everyone on the schedule and told them to stay home and stay safe. Although I doubt the Vatican had *the ice storm of the century* in mind when they set down the rules, there is provision for times when no one is available. I lock the host, with great ceremony, in the tabernacle, which is a secure vault behind the altar."

"Well then, why don't you count on sleeping late tomorrow? There'll be plenty of breakfast food around for whenever you get up."

"That sounds like a marvelous idea. You women are handling most of the work. Except for a little bit of cooking and stoking the wood stove, there's not much we men are doing. In fact, our cooking is more a matter of assembling what's already there."

"I'd noticed."

He laughed at my dry tone. "Henry and I can take turns napping during the day." His smile turned rueful. "There's only so much chess I can stand."

"You could always play cribbage," I said, "if Reebok and Ralph will give up the board."

We shook hands, as if we'd made a pact of some sort. "Why don't you take one of those extra folding chairs with you when we go downstairs? There's already an old crate in your prayer closet. For that matter, the shelves are pretty much empty. Between the shelves and the crate, will that do you for a table?"

He nodded.

"You can lean the brooms up in the back corner of the room, and it'll be ready." I thought for a moment. "I hope it doesn't have too many spider webs in there."

It does not. I ate them already.

We rejoined the group just in time to get in on the tail end of some sort of joke. Dave seemed to be in good form, but I didn't ask to hear what we'd missed. If it was worthwhile, Bob would enlighten me. If it was one of Dave's usual repertoire, I wasn't interested.

"Why don't you all come downstairs in about five minutes," Dave said. "We'll have supper on the table in a jiffy."

The other women looked as surprised as I was. "You already cooked it?"

"Yep," Dave said, but Bob cleared his throat, and Dave dropped his gaze to the floor.

"Let me guess," Pat said. "You're going to lay out sandwich fixings, and we'll have to put them together ourselves?"

There was muttered mumbling from the rest of the guys, so we knew Pat had guessed right. I wondered why Tom hadn't intervened with his culinary skills. Maybe he considered himself on vacation as well.

"I have a good idea," Glaze said. "From now on, starting tomorrow, how about if you men take care of lunch, and we women will handle the evening meal?"

"Good idea," Ida said. "I need some real food at least once a day."

"Sandwiches are real food," her husband Ralph said. "And there's soup, too."

Ida scoffed. "Soup that Biscuit cooked, so don't try to take credit for it."

ONCE THE SANDWICHES had been disposed of, we settled in over coffee and tea and hot chocolate. I had to smile as I watched Henry fill almost half his mug with milk before he added the coffee. He must have sensed me watching him. "I asked Bob if it was okay. He said there was plenty of milk."

"Not a problem at all," I said, wondering if there were any coffee taste left after he finished doctoring his cup.

"Henry likes a little java with his milk," Father John said.

"Yeah, and you'd just as soon drink sludge," Henry countered.

I liked the easy camaraderie between the two men. I doubted either one of them ever had a chance to talk, really talk, to any of the other men in town, what with Henry being a minister and Father John a priest. Maybe that was why they always met for coffee—or milk and coffee—at the Delicious once a week. They always sat at the same booth way in the back.

"I have a feeling we're missing so much information," Rebecca Jo said, bringing me back to the current situation.

"Me too," said Dee. "I wish people had put their names or at least a date on everything up there."

"We know the year the secret room was created," Bob said, "but you're right, there's too much else with no history to it."

I fingered my silver pendant. "It's not that there's no history. Everything is rife with history. It's just that there aren't enough labels."

"It's a shame we can't at least uncover all these things in chronological order," Maddy said. "That would make it so much easier to organize later on."

"That's what we're hiring you for," Pat said.

"Hiring her?" Henry's mouth was full of cookie, but he asked anyway.

"As the director of the Martinsville Museum," Pat explained. "That is, if she won't mind working for free."

"At least the journals are in chronological order," Sadie pointed out.

"Chronology always helps," Henry said. "Besides the secret room, have you found anything else good?"

Yes. Many things.

I didn't know what to say, but luckily Marmalade interrupted with a string of meows.

Carol laughed. "Obviously Marmalade thinks it's good stuff. Biscuit found a kid's homespun shirt."

I didn't realize she'd seen me with it.

"Pass that plate of cookies, Tom," Dee instructed. "Before Dave eats them all."

Tom took a cookie for himself and passed the plate to his left. Charlie gave it to Maddy, who held it up out of range when Dave reached across the table for it. She nabbed her own cookie and sent the plate on its way.

Sadie propped her elbows on the table, leaned her chin on her fists, and watched the cookie platter making its way around the table. It was a good thing I'd made so many of them.

Reebok drained his mug of hot chocolate.

"Looks like it's time for the weather report." Doc Nathan stood and walked toward the counter where the battery-powered radio perched, munching on his cookie as he went. "We've been limiting our airtime to save the batteries," he explained, "but the weather reports are pretty important."

"I don't know why you'd think that," Dee said, and all the men laughed appreciatively at her little joke. Only I could tell she wasn't joking. I glanced around at the other women and could see similar thoughts in their expressions.

"We haven't been worrying about the weather," Rebecca Jo said. "We have history up there with us keeping us warm." She picked up a cookie and munched it slowly.

"If it warms up much more," Doc said, trying to fine-tune the dial, "we'll be able to get out of each other's hair in another day or so."

A burst of static precluded any comments. "… is warming up," Radio Ralph announced, "and the temp should continue to rise tonight and tomorrow."

"Then I guess we'll be leaving," Carol said.

A chorus of negatives greeted her comment.

Father John's voice took precedence. "Hasn't anybody clued this woman in?"

"Clued me in? To what?"

"Radio Ralph's weather reports," Bob explained, "are something of a joke here in the Metoochie River Valley. If he says cold, we bring out our polo shirts; but if he predicts bright, warm, and sunny, we know sweater weather's coming up."

"Sometimes," Ralph said, "I wonder if he knows darn well what the weather's going to be and just reports the opposite."

Carol looked aghast. I guess all the weather forecasters in Vermont are on the up and up. "Why would he do that?"

"Oh," Ralph said, "just pulling our leg for the fun of it."

Nobody is pulling your leg.

"Why does the station keep him on, then?"

We gave one big collective shrug. "He runs the station," Henry said. "He owns the station, does all the broadcasting—"

"Not quite all of it," Ida said. "He lets his nephew give the sports news."

"That's right," Henry admitted, "but WRRT ought to be called the voice of Radio Ralph Towers."

"So," Carol said, "if he says the temps will rise tonight, then we'll all be here for another week?"

"Not exactly," Bob said. "Even if a heat wave hit us—which just might happen despite Radio Ralph's report—all this ice is going to take a while to melt, and in the meantime, wet ice is truly treacherous to try to travel on. It doesn't really matter what Radio Ralph predicted. I think you'd better plan on another two days at least."

"If this were Vermont," Carol said, "the snowplows would have been out four days ago."

"Snowplows," Doc mused. "Has anybody here ever seen a snowplow in this valley?"

"Doesn't work that way in Jawja," Ida said, giving the name of our state its super-southern pronunciation.

"This is good." Maddy spread her hands wide above her head, as if to encompass the enormous attic two floors above her. "I hope the storm lasts for days so we'll have time to search through a lot more trunks."

"And read more," Ida said.

"And try on more hats," Easton offered, as if she hoped to be back up there with all the rest of us women.

Fat chance.

"Maybe not right now, though," Sadie said. "I'm way too comfortable sitting here."

"I hope the food lasts," Ralph said. "If it doesn't, I'm moving to the store."

"And we'll all be right there with you," Dave assured him.

While we munched, I gave everybody their room assignments.

ONE THING ABOUT not having electricity, as the dark of evening crowds into the rooms, it's easy to get sleepy. Even as we talked and ate, there were surreptitious yawns all around the table. After the kitchen was clean we all meandered into the living room and sat around the wood stove listening to the hissing of the wind outside. Maddy lifted her slipper-shod heels onto the edge of the couch cushion and drew her knees up tight against her chest. I wondered how many years it had been since I'd been able to sit that way.

Eventually the silence lengthened so much that I thought about heading upstairs just so everybody else would, too. I remembered my father-in-law—my first husband's dad—who used to wrap up a party by saying *It's time for me to go to bed so all you nice folks can head home.*

I did wonder whether, after the revelations of today, Sadie would even want to sleep on her yellow sheets. I didn't have to wonder long. She said goodnight to everyone and headed for the stairs, flooded closely by Easton. I heard voice drift down from the landing. "Maybe you and I could trade sheets? If you don't mind sleeping on yellow flannel?"

I couldn't hear Easton's response, but I didn't need to. What do they call it when someone undergoes a total transformation? A sea change?

Charlie was the next one up the steps, and it didn't take long for the others to follow. Bob and I waited around just long enough to make sure everyone was settled. Not that I cared by that time of the evening. Before I headed up the stairs—in fact, my left foot was already on the bottom step—I noticed that Reebok was still downstairs, standing by the wood stove.

"Bed time?"

"I'll be sleeping here on the couch, Ma'am."

"Why? We have enough rooms and even a few to spare. Don't you like the one I gave you? You could always move into—"

"That's okay, Ma'am. I thought I could make sure there's enough wood in the stove."

"That's really sweet of you, Reebok, but the coals should last the night."

"Not enough to send the warmth upstairs." He sounded much more definite than his usual self-effacing voice.

Bob was already all the way up the stairs, but it didn't seem polite to leave Reebok on the couch. "Are you sure you'll be comfortable?"

"Don't you worry about me, Ma'am." He always sounded so earnest. "I'll be fine here." He pointed to a blanket and a pillow I hadn't noticed. "The Chief gave me this. It's all I need."

What he needs, I thought, is a girlfriend. I'd have to ask Bob if there really was something in the works between Reebok and Melody, the town clerk. That would be sweet. They both liked hot chocolate as far as I knew. It wasn't enough to base a marriage on, but it sure was a good place to start.

Wednesday, December 6, 2000
    Five things for which I am grateful:
        1. The warmth of the wood stove
        2. The warmth of friendship – how good it is to have so
        many wonderful women—and men—with us now
        3. All the people who have left a legacy in this house
        4. Carol – without her, we'd be missing so much
        5. Bob beside me and Marmalade purring to her little
        heart's content. I wonder if Marmy enjoys being brushed
        as much I enjoy brushing her. I love it the way the birds
        pull her leftover hair out of that wire basket under the
        porch roof. Only in the spring, of course, while they're do-
        ing their nest building. Good grief, Biscuit, go to sleep!

I am grateful for
Widelap and SoftFoot
SmellSweet and Fishgiver
LooseLaces and GoodCook
ListenLady
this soft warm bed
the birds who use my hair to line their nests

BOB CRAWLED INTO bed beside me, lay there quietly until I'd finished writing in my journal—which took quite a while what with everything we'd discovered in the attic, and of course, I couldn't forget my daily gratitude list—and then waited until I blew out the candle.

"Come here, Woman," he said and opened his arms. I snuggled against him, enjoying his warmth, and felt Marmalade move under the comforter into her usual position at my back, between me and the edge of the bed. Sometimes, lying here between the two of them, I feel like the cheddar inside a grilled cheese sandwich. Very comforting it is. I'd put on my thick flannel pajamas over my silk long johns and added a pair of fuzzy sleep socks. With an extra blanket over the down comforter, we wouldn't freeze. I had a feeling I might be truly glad of all this extra insulation before the night was over, since we slept with our door closed, and there was no way the heat from the wood stove could circulate. I wondered briefly how the Martin families had managed through the winters on the trail. Brrr. At least we had hope that the power would come back on soon.

"This is good," Bob said, pushing my hair gently away from his face. "I like all our neighbors, but it sure is hard finding a place that isn't overrun."

I can always find a quiet spot.

"You can say that again. I'm glad we didn't have to install anyone on a pallet here in our bedroom. I'm surprised Reebok wanted to sleep in the living room, though. We still have a couple of empty rooms up here."

"He asked me if there were any chores he could help me with, and I told him the only concern I had was being sure the fire in the wood stove would last through the night, so he volunteered to be the caretaker."

"He really is a sweet young man."

"And a darned good police officer, too."

"Well, this means we still have more room if anyone else shows up."

Bob groaned. "That's the last thing we need." He stretched his neck, and I heard it crackle. We'd both been sitting too long all day. "I guess it's a good thing we bought such a big old house."

"You can say that again," I repeated.

He did not say it again.

I ran the name over my tongue like melted cheese in a fondue. "Beechnut House. We need to make a wooden sign to mount by the front door."

"I wonder if we can figure out exactly when this house was built? That way we could put the year on the sign."

I yawned. "Maybe there'll be something in one of the trunks. Oh! That reminds me. I found an old pocket watch I thought you might enjoy."

"Does it work?"

"I don't know. I didn't even try to wind it."

"When do I get to see it?"

"If you think I'm getting out from under these covers now you've got another think coming."

He laughed. "I suppose I can wait until morning."

"Just remind me. It's in the pocket of that fleecy vest of mine."

"You're really getting into this, aren't you?" He traced the scar over my right eye, and I could almost feel his gratitude that I hadn't lost my eye in that encounter.[1] I was pretty grateful, too. Then he ran his hand through my hair, almost the way I stroke Marmalade.

I like it when you pat me.

"You have no idea how fascinating it is," I said as Marmalade wormed her way over my hip and wiggled in between us. "Looks like we need to pay attention to this sadly neglected cat."

You pay attention to me. The only problem is that you do not hear me.

"Neglected? That'll be the day." He laughed and ruffled Marmy's head as she gurgled happily. "Do you think she enjoys what's going on in the attic?"

Of course I do, SoftFoot. I like being with Widelap and Smell-Sweet and LooseLaces and GoodCook, even though I could not find the lion, but ListenLady said it was not there.

I stilled my hand halfway down Marmalade's back. "She certainly has made herself at home up there. All those new things to sniff at and climb on top of." I arched my neck backwards and listened to the bones crackle as they shifted. My neck was even noisier than Bob's.

---

1 *Gray as Ashes*

Bed sure felt good after so many hours in uncomfortable chairs. "We've all enjoyed it," I said.

"It looks like you'll have plenty of time to enjoy it a lot more. The weather warmed up enough today to melt the top layer of snow..."

I was so caught up in the attic drama, I hadn't even thought about the weather. Or not much at least.

"... but the forecast on Public Radio says the temp will drop to ten degrees or so tonight."

"So it'll freeze all that melted water into an even thicker ice layer," I said. "Brrr!"

"We'll need to get up extra early to be sure the birds have enough food."

They will appreciate that.

I resumed stroking Marmalade's back. She was as soft as that old shirt I'd found upstairs. Softer, in fact.

Thank you.

I sure hoped there was some sort of marking on it to indicate who'd owned it.

"Other than that hidden room, which was quite a find, and the pocket watch you mentioned, was there anything else interesting up there?"

"Quite a few things, as a matter of fact. Several of the women think we should start a Martinsville Museum."

"Maddy mentioned that. It sounds like a great idea."

"You might change your mind when you hear that they want to set it up in our attic."

There was a lengthy, charged silence.

"I know," I said. "I think the very same thing."

You do?

"At least we'll have plenty of time to think about ways to quash that idea," I added.

"Right," Bob agreed. "This ice storm may take a month to go away."

Really?

I groaned to think of having a house full of guests for that long. It couldn't last a month. It just couldn't. And while we had a whole boatload of food, I doubted it would last with the way the men were eating.

Surely the ice would melt within a few more days.

"I know the perfect way to overrule the museum idea, my dearest. There's a two-letter word that is most effective."

What is it?

Bob covered the back of my hand with his warm palm as Marmalade purred in contentment. "Not to change the subject, but would you take Easton upstairs with you tomorrow when you go back up there?"

"Easton? Why?" She'd chosen to stay with the men, even when they had to do cleanup. Good riddance to her, I thought, although a little piece of me recognized the uncharitable nature of that attitude.

"I think she'd like to join you, but she doesn't know how."

"All she has to do is walk up the stairs," I said with some asperity.

"Yes, but would she be welcome?"

"Well, of course she … Oh." I considered all the ways Easton had alienated the women of the town by flirting repeatedly and obnoxiously with our husbands. "Well," I admitted, "maybe she wouldn't exactly be."

Then I wondered why nobody had objected when I ordered Easton to stay downstairs with the men. You'd think we'd all want her up where we could keep an eye on her. She was like a squirrel, I thought, except instead of collecting acorns, she collected men. Now that I thought about it, she even walked like a squirrel, always flitting around and twitching her rear end.

I yawned and considered what sort of animals the other people could be compared to. I'd have to think more about it tomorrow.

"That's what I thought," Bob said. "But she puts a damper on what we feel like we can talk about downstairs."

I leaned back and studied him in the faint moonlight that leached through the curtains. "What *do* you talk about downstairs?"

"Man stuff." I felt rather than saw him gesture toward the ceiling. "What do you talk about up there?"

I got his point. "Woman stuff."

"She's a woman…" He let his voice trail away.

"I can see you noticed."

He pulled me even closer to him in one of his delicious hugs …

Oof!

… causing Marmalade to grunt an objection.

I like hugs, but I do not like to be squashed.

"Bisque, it's your turn to deal with Easton. I've had quite enough of her to last a lifetime."

"Fine," I said, feeling as if I were being consigned to some sort of corporal punishment. At the same time, I felt glad indeed to hear his assurance. And he never called me Bisque unless he was making a very important point.

"What's this?" He fingered the pendant I'd forgotten to remove.

"Just something I found up there. You'll have to look at it to-morrow when there's enough light to see by." I described the exquisite little portraits. "There's no indication, though, of how old it is or who it belonged to—other than the initials, and I'm not completely sure about them. Unclasp it, will you? I don't want to damage it, and I doubt it'll be comfortable to sleep in."

You sound very sleepy.

Once I finished yawning, he did as I asked, then reached across me to lay it on the bedside table. I turned onto my left side so my back was snuggled against him—well, against him and Marmalade—and the last thing I heard was his whisper.

"If I have to be stranded in an ice storm, you're the one I want to be stranded with."

I like being stranded with both of you.

The last thing I saw before drifting into sleep, as Marmalade purred behind me, was an errant reflection from the surface of the tar-nished silver pendant.

REEBOK GARNER PULLED the folded piece of fax paper out of his pocket and studied it in the wavering light cast by the flames behind the glass door of the wood stove. He had a whole file of cold cases. Cases that other jurisdictions had asked about. He knew he wasn't likely to solve any of them, but wouldn't it be an accomplishment if he could?

These bones, for instance. He could just imagine how awful it would be to go walking through the woods and come across something like this. He was surprised the bones hadn't been more widely scattered. Or maybe they had been and these were the ones the searchers had been able to recover from the surrounding area. The fax didn't say.

He knew he should go to sleep, get some rest in case a call came in during the middle of the night, but he kept reading and re-reading the fax, studying the pictures, envisioning himself collaring whoever had killed this person. And finding out who this person was. There weren't many clues.

WITHOUT EVEN DISCUSSING it, Ida and Ralph shoved their twin beds together. They hadn't slept in the same bed for ages, but now didn't seem to be the time to stay on opposite sides of the small bedroom. Working together, they stretched the sheets across the two mattresses. It left an awkward bump in the middle, but Ida was pretty sure staying warm was more important than being completely comfortable. She found a couple of towels in the small dresser and used them to pad the space where the two beds came together. She knew she'd be the one sleeping on the bump, the one in the middle, the one to compromise.

Ralph was a good man. He just never seemed to think about what life was like from Ida's point of view. She probably should speak up for what she wanted, but somehow it didn't seem very nice to say, "I'd like to be the comfortable one—You sleep on the bump." She crawled in and prayed it would warm up soon.

From the room next door, she could hear muted voices. She supposed the house hadn't been built with sound-proofing in mind. Sadie and Easton were quiet people, though. Ida doubted they'd raise any sort of ruckus in the middle of the night. She had a momentary temptation to put her ear up against the wall to see if she could make out what they were saying, but then she laughed at herself. First of all, she didn't want to crawl out of bed.

"I hope Sadie won't try to listen to our conversation," she told Ralph.

"Huh?"

"Can't you hear them talking there?"

Ralph pounded on his pillow a couple of times before he crawled under the covers. "Nope. I'm not listening." He turned to face away from her. As he usually did.

Ida lay there for a couple of minutes, trying to stop shivering. It wasn't his fault. She knew that. She'd just never figured out how to let him know what she needed. What she wanted.

She sighed. For now, what she wanted was to be warm. So she inched over closer to his back, fitting herself against him. Despite the mattress bump, she was soon asleep.

"CHARLIE ELLIS," SHE said to herself as she looked at her reflection in the mirror. This room Biscuit had stuck her in was minuscule, but at least there was room to turn around. The candle gave precious little light, but it was enough so she wouldn't stub her toe on the scaled down dresser under the window. It was cramped, but at least the mattress, which she'd already pushed and prodded, seemed soft enough, even though the bed was way too short. Despite the slightly warm air that had seeped in from the hallway during the day, she didn't feel like undressing. Biscuit had told everybody to keep their doors open for the air to circulate, but she wasn't about to do that. Put herself at risk just for some warm air? No way. At least she couldn't see her breath coming out in little frozen puffs the way they had outside. Still, it was chilly, so she climbed in fully clothed, except for the fuzzy slippers she'd remembered to pack. Those she set right next to the bed, ready for the morning. It was always good to plan ahead.

As soon as she'd heard an ice storm was predicted, she'd packed a suitcase, not knowing where she'd go, but fairly sure she'd have to go somewhere. She'd lived through ice storms before this, and they were no fun. She wished she'd bought a house that had an alternate heat source, but her rather basic house on Second Street was the only one she'd been able to orchestrate. There just hadn't been any other houses on the market when she arrived here three years ago.

It was a good thing she was looking out her front window when Melissa and her B&B guests trudged by this morning. When she called out to them, they hadn't said where they were going, just to *come on along, there'll be plenty of room.*

She'd debated with herself whether or not to pack the one treasure she had—the old papers from the original Charlotte Ellis. The packet was fairly bulky, but her suitcase had a sturdy lock, so she'd wrapped it in her favorite college tee shirt and tucked it beneath her undies. She felt better having it with her. Things had changed, though, now that everybody knew about Hubbard Brandt. Those diaries were a real problem.

She wished she could have found them first. If she'd known what was in them, she'd have made sure they went in the throwaway pile.

She wasn't sure how she felt about staying here in the house of someone who was—not exactly an employee, but certainly someone who'd have to answer to her, now that she was the chair of the library board. It had felt a little awkward right at first when she discovered where they were taking shelter, but, heck, in an ice storm some things had to slide a little, right?

This room might be the size of a large closet, but at least she didn't have to share it with anyone. She heard murmurings from the room next door and put her ear to the wall. It was that Sadie, the woman who looked like a fire hydrant. A yellow fire hydrant. She hated the way Sadie looked at her, like she expected something and was constantly disappointed.

What right did an old woman like that have to judge her? She wasn't going to put up with it.

Before she got into bed, she pulled out her suitcase, unlocked it, and removed a couple of extra layers. It was cold in that attic, and tomorrow, she'd be better prepared. Her college tee would go over a turtleneck and her sweats. Some heavier socks, too. Those would help.

"I HOPE YOU won't be disturbed if I have to get up in the middle of the night to go to the bathroom," Sadie told Easton. "I'll try to be quiet." She plumped her pillow and made sure her reading glasses were right beside her on the bedside table. It was really more of a small dresser, with two wide drawers.

Easton wrapped her arms more tightly around her middle. "I'm more than likely to be the one who wakes you up. I've been having to go a lot more often lately."

"Oh dear. That's happened to me several times over the last"— she laughed—"the last five decades or so. I hope you don't have an infection of some sort." She made sure the tissues were within reach. On second thought, Easton might need them, too, so she pushed them back to the center. "In the meantime, be sure you drink lots of water."

"Won't that just make me have to get up more often?"

"You need to flush your system and you can't do that without plenty of water."

Easton didn't look convinced, so Sadie reached across the gap and patted her on the arm. "Trust this old lady, Easton. I've been there, done that, and—how do they say it?—got the tee-shirt."

Easton grinned. "Okay. And I'll try not to wake you up."

Before she went to sleep, Sadie had a few pleasant minutes thinking about just what that tee-short would have printed on the front of it. Naturally, a tee with a message like that would have to be yellow. She tried to stifle the giggle that erupted, but she needn't have worried. On the nearby twin bed, Easton was already snoring softly.

PAT PONTIAC HAD seen very few ice storms this severe. None, in fact. After all, up until she married, she'd lived in south Florida. Moving to Georgia had taken a real adjustment on her part. Even here in the valley, where the winters were, according to the natives, fairly mild compared to the rest of the state, she'd found herself longing for the all-pervasive heat, the unremitting sunshine, the flowers year-round, the beaches, the sea.

She'd still be there, if it hadn't been for the whirlwind courtship so many years ago that had swept her, like the winds of a hurricane, like Dorothy's tornado, into a story-book marriage, a whole new world. Munchkin land.

She listened to her husband snoring. He slept so soundly. Maybe that was what success did for a person. He'd never had any trouble falling asleep.

Early on, from the time she'd met him in the hotel where she worked and where he was heading up an early-December conference, a celebration of the success of his growing company where he showered his employees with elaborate gifts—the employees who'd sold the most—she'd loved the even more elaborate gifts he showered her with. It was like he'd seen her, made up his mind that she was going to be his, and then let nothing stand in his way until she had a ring on her finger the size of a small birdcage. A Christmas present that first Christmas. He hadn't left the hotel, hadn't gone back to work, really, once the conference was over. Not until she agreed to marry him. And, with a ring that spectacular, how could she not?

The feeble light leaking in through Biscuit's totally inadequate curtains let her see the reflections glinting from her fourth finger. Really, she was always knocking the ring into something. It was a wonder she'd never damaged it in all these years.

Sometimes she wondered what her answer would have been if she'd dated Dave for three years instead of three weeks.

Still, she did love these cashmere sweaters. Everybody else in the attic wore sweatpants and sweatshirts, while she sported color-coordinated cashmere and silk scarves, silk long johns and silk blend socks.

Dave let out a particularly loud snort, and Pat tensed her shoulders. It was worth it. It was.

DEE CRAWLED INTO the big double bed first and scooted over next to the wall. "This is a far cry from your fancy four-poster, isn't it? Do you miss it?"

Rebecca Jo chuckled. "I'd rather be here with at least a little bit of warmth seeping up the stairs than at home freezing to death. That bed of mine may be fancy as all get-out, but frozen bedding isn't my idea of how to get a good night's sleep."

"Still," Dee said, "you deserve a regal-looking bed. Those lion heads on the top of the posts are spectacular, you have to admit." She kept her voice low, aware that with the door open, she might disturb others.

Rebecca Jo settled in next to her well-loved daughter-in-law. "I'm glad my husband inherited the bed—it's been in his family for well more than a hundred years—but all the *spectacular* in the world never kept anybody warm."

"A hundred years? Really?"

"I'm not sure anybody knows exactly how long it's been in the family, but it's definitely an antique. His great-grandfather bought it soon after he was married. Or so the story goes. Maybe it was his great-great-grandfather." She sucked in her breath.

"What's wrong?"

"I just realized I can't remember the details." Rebecca Jo sounded bereft. "The number of times he told me about the history behind that bed—usually when we were in it—and now I can't remember."

"You probably had your mind on other things if you were in that luscious bed," Dee teased, trying to lighten the mood. "It was probably handed down from a bootlegger way back when."

"Thank you, my dear. I needed that." Rebecca Jo yawned. "Bootlegging. Hmm. You never can tell, I suppose." She yawned again. "My law-abiding husband would turn over in his grave if he thought it was something like that."

1802

WHEN THE FLOOD hit Martinsville that Saturday night, a number of structures were washed away, all of them having been built, with what everyone soon would know was lack of foresight, too near the edge of the usually placid river. For most years the Metoochie resembled nothing more than an amiable little creek, but in 1802, heavy winter snows in the Appalachians and the Smoky mountains to the north of the valley, combined with almost ceaseless spring rains, joined forces to swell the creek into a river, the river into a torrent, and the torrent into a full-fledged flood that sent water almost a quarter of the way up the hillside, wrenching buildings from their foundations and sending the remains of the one bawdy house in Martinsville—ill-situated directly on the edge of the river—washing down to be smashed to pieces among the boulders at the mouth of the narrow gorge to disperse finally in the lake at Enders. The irony was that no rain had fallen on Martinsville in almost two months, and the ground was bone dry, nor did any fall the night of the flood.

Eliza Moon watched with dismay as the thriving business she had built up over the past several years was decimated. The coincidence of two tragedies in one evening was almost more than she could bear, but she set her shoulders and made up her mind. She had escaped, for she had been pacing on the balcony outside her bedroom and had seen the approach of the floodwaters. Her instinct for survival was strong, and she had thrown her ample red hair back over her shoulder and had gone from room to room rousting the clientele and issuing orders. Not a single life was lost. Not only the clients, many of whom were members of the Martinsville Town Council, but all her ... employees ... had gotten out of the house as well.

Such was the power of Eliza Moon's personality, that once she knew imminent flight was necessary, she had railroaded the clients into hauling out her roll-top desk, three very fine gilt mirrors, Eliza's dresser that contained her extensive and costly wardrobe, the crystal chandelier—which they had to rip from the ceiling—and even the four-poster bed which Eliza used for herself alone, the one that had lion heads carved at the top of each post. The bed to which she invited only a few carefully selected guests.

She took an important few moments to retrieve her quite ample fund of cash, tying the bags around her waist beneath her overskirt.

She waded through the swirling flood waters, which by that time had advanced above her front steps, and pushed the men to carry her valuables a third of the way up the hillside, for she felt certain the flood waters would not rise so far as that, and to deposit them in the middle of the lane, for she had access to no other house. The men had obediently trudged up and down the hillside to complete the jobs she had assigned them, for she had taken the precaution of removing their breeches from each room as she rousted them out.

Her employees had been instructed to carry with them the most valuable of her assorted lamps, her own magnificent bedding, her elaborate but tasteful dresses, and the full-length portrait of Eliza that hung above the central fireplace. The artist was not famous, but the brush strokes were fine indeed and Eliza's full head of knee-length red hair was shown in its full splendor. She did allow the women then to save their own clothing and whatever small personal items they hoarded in their rooms.

The men dispersed as soon as Eliza's attention strayed from them to the women who had so recently entertained them. By that time, Eliza had returned the customers' breeches.

Already Eliza could hear the women grumbling about leaving. "She cares more for her precious furniture than for us," she overheard one of the women mutter.

Eliza reached into the everyday drawstring purse at her waist and handed the woman the coins she had earned for this night's work. She pointed to the north. "It is not raining," she said, "and not like to, for the sky is clear. The moon is full. You should have a pleasant enough walk to Braetonburg."

She raised her voice enough that all her women could hear her over the creaks and groans as the underpinnings of Eliza Moon's house collapsed and the house itself was swept downstream. "The house will not re-open. I will pay you the wages due to you and will instruct Tomas"—that was her general handyman and occasional bouncer—"to drive those of you who wish to leave, north as far up the valley as you wish to go."

She turned to the first woman, the one who had complained. "Even you may join the wagon-load."

Not a one of them chose to stay in Martinsville. Eliza paid them all as they mounted Tomas' wagon. She prided herself on being fair.

As the wagonload of women left, Eliza looked around her at the devastation. The moon flooded the hillside with light—a good thing, for it gave her a chance to inventory her possessions as they sat near the town green in the center of Juniper Street where the clients had deposited them. The few other buildings that had been destroyed by the flood lay down the hill from her in broken desolation, sagging off their foundations, with their roofs collapsed, their porches crumpled, their steps buried underneath assorted rubble. All of those establishments had been businesses, and their owners were even now still asleep, blissfully unaware of the desolation that awaited them on the morrow. She was rather looking forward to their expressions when they discovered her here in the middle of the intersection of Juniper and Second Street. She supposed she would be unable to sleep to midmorning as was her wont, once the early-risers of the town were up and about.

Eliza removed her soaked shoes and stockings, her overskirt, and her petticoat, and climbed onto her four-poster bed. She tucked the money bags down near her feet, pulled her magnificent down-filled comforter over her, spread the lava-like red hair for which she was famous—or infamous as some thought—across her pillow, and lay there thinking of the other tragedy that had impaled her just after she had eaten her supper.

She had suspected for several months, but this evening for the first time, she had felt a most-unwelcome movement within her belly. The babe would most likely be born in late summer, before the harvest. She had three months, four at most to establish her new business before her condition became obvious. Moon's Furniture. Moon's Fine Furniture.

She lay now on the first item she would sell. Surely someone would want such a magnificent bed. The purchaser might even be the man who had fathered this babe, if he were the sentimental sort. She wondered briefly which of the two it might be. Would it not be lovely if, between the pair of them, they drove the price of the bed up as high as the nearby cliffs?

2000
Matthew Olsen's House

MATTHEW OLSEN CALLED his son, Buddy, just before bedtime. "Wanted to make sure you were okay up there."

"Garner Creek isn't the end of the world, Dad. Of course I'm okay. Lewis and Bethany were delighted when I showed up. He's put me to work being the one to feed the wood stove all night long."

"Good." Matthew was smart enough not to say that this way Buddy would get an idea of what it was like to have a family to care for. He was still hoping Buddy would marry and supply his old dad with grandchildren to spoil.

"Their generator wasn't working, but I fixed it."

"Yeah?"

"Gave it some percussive maintenance."

Matthew grinned. He was the one who'd taught Buddy that sometimes a good kick worked wonders. Shook something loose that needed shaking.

The conversation didn't last much longer. It never did with Buddy. He was a good son, though. Matthew scratched Mr. Fogarty's head and covered his cage. Here in the warm living room, Mr. Fogarty would be fine. With all the heat that stove was turning out, the little parakeet might even think he was in a tropical setting, where all his ancestors had lived.

He rolled himself up in a blanket on the smaller of the two sagging couches, hoping the other one would be long enough for Nick Foley's lengthy frame.

Matthew had over the years gotten used to the fact that his wife was no longer with him. The heartache he'd felt at first, after she died, had gradually faded to resignation, but doggone it, he still missed her. Even though they'd slept in separate beds, they'd slept in the same room. He missed her more than anything.

Beside the stove, Mr. Fogarty let out a small cheep and Matthew felt somewhat comforted.

NICK STOOD WITH crossed arms, listening to Anita prattle on and on about something or other. He almost never paid attention. He'd learned long ago that most of what she said was just drivel, something to fill the air around her. He waited until she climbed into bed—he didn't trust her with the candle—and then he blew out the flame and went back downstairs.

This couch of Matthew's was uncomfortable, no matter whether you were sitting on it or trying to sleep on it. Nick squirmed, trying to get more settled. Damn ice storm. Completely inconvenient. Now that he didn't have work to look forward to, he didn't know what he was going to do after the storm was over. Retiring wasn't looking like much fun. Not that it was true retirement. Having to sell his dental practice had been a real pain. Still, it was his only option now that the Board knew. He could willingly kill the guy who had snitched on him, but it wasn't necessary, not with *H. Martin* completely batty like he was. Nick was going to be forced to give up his license. They were only doing the investigating at the moment, but he knew what they'd find when they dug deep enough, so he'd put out feelers for someone to buy the practice. Found somebody after just a week of looking. Lucky.

He hadn't told anyone yet. Anita knew, but she didn't count. He'd told her he planned to retire come the new year, but then she told him she'd opened that letter from the Board. He'd had to explain, but he told her not to say anything. What happened in the Foley house stayed in the Foley house. He had till after the holidays. That was when the new guy—well, gal—was taking over.

CLARA MARTIN MOVED her husband's wallet from his front pants pocket to the pocket on his pajama shirt. Ever since he became Council Chairman he'd always slept with his wallet right there next to his heart. Early in their marriage she'd wondered if he kept a picture of an old girlfriend in there, but she'd looked once, while he was taking a shower, and there had just been all the usual stuff. Diver's license, a couple of credit cards, some spare checks, and money of course, although he never seemed to carry much cash. No pictures. Not even one of her.

Every day it was the same routine. He'd take the wallet out of his pajamas pocket each morning and put it in his right front pants pocket. Then he'd reverse the routine at night. Out of his pants came the wallet and into his pajama top.

Obsessive compulsive. She'd read that term somewhere and she wondered if it applied. Of course now, since the … the accident, she had no way of knowing if he still worried about where his wallet was every minute of the day. Probably not. But there was that one time last week when she hadn't put it in his pajamas at night, and somehow or other she'd known he wasn't happy until it was there. After that, he went right to sleep.

Now, she studied his inert form for a few minutes before she blew out the candles and climbed into the twin bed on the other side of the small bedroom. She'd insisted that Matthew and Nick bring the bed down here so she could be close to Hubbard in case he woke. The last thing she'd wanted was to sleep in the same bed with him. They hadn't shared even a bedroom, much less a bed, for years, and she wasn't about to start now, although Matthew and the Foleys didn't need to know that. What happened in the Martin home stayed in the Martin home.

Thursday, December 7, 2000
Day #2

REEBOK HAD NO intention of forgetting his mother just because he was holed up here for the duration of the ice storm. Right from when he first left his home, he had called her every morning. Of course, that was usually to let her know he was going off duty and he'd made it through the night. He called her most nights, too.

He was still on duty. Here, the station, his cruiser. Did it matter? No, it didn't. He crept into the kitchen. Nobody would hear him.

"Ma? It's me. … Yes, I'm fine. … How are you getting along? … That's good."

When he finally said goodbye, he realized that this phone conversation was almost exactly like every other one he'd had with her every single morning. And night. That disturbed him faintly. He hadn't told her anything about all the wonderful things the women were finding in the attic. Or about filling up the bird feeders. Or playing out front on the ice with Dr. Mellinger.

He gave up worrying about it and called Melody.

He told her everything.

I SLEPT SURPRISINGLY well, considering that the house—except for someone snoring down the hallway—had been almost disconcertingly quiet, what with no furnace kicking on and off. I never heard the generator for the fridge and the water pump, and I sure hoped it was still working. The last thing I wanted to deal with was spoiled milk. The first item on the agenda, though, was a kiss. Bob set his journal aside long enough to do justice to it—he gives the best hugs and kisses.

He hugs me, too. Sometimes. He does not kiss me, though.

Just to keep everything balanced, I scooped Marmalade out from under the covers and gave her a quick kiss on the top of her soft head.

Thank you, but I would like to stay warm some more.

Marmy crawled back into her little cocoon, and Bob picked his journal back up. "What are you laughing about?"

I reached out and stroked his soft beard. It had already sprouted a fair amount. "You're going to be as fuzzy as Marmalade if this storm keeps up for much longer."

"I'm going to appreciate this beard when we go outside to feed the birds."

"You can say that again."

Why would he do that?

Beside me, under the covers, I could feel Marmalade begin one of those total-body stretches that cats do. I tried to do one myself, but was somewhat hampered by the heavy coverings. Also, I didn't want to let in any cold air. Oh, this was ridiculous. I threw back the covers and swung my legs over the side. Brrr!

I dressed quickly. It was almost agony to pull on my heavy socks. They were so cold to begin with I thought my feet would freeze. "Tonight," I said, "I'm going to put my clothes under the covers so they won't be quite so frigid in the morning."

You may put them with my mouse.

Marmalade meowed from under the comforter.

My mouse is not cold.

I watched the moving lump as she crawled up from under the covers. She had her felt mouse in her mouth. "You gave it to her," I said. "You throw it for her."

Marmalade dropped the mouse into his outstretched hand.

"Thank goodness she's not a dog," Bob said.

I am not a dog!

"I agree, but why?"

"Dogs get their toys all slobbery, and I wouldn't want a sodden mouse in bed with us."

"Good point."

I do not slobber.

"Don't forget your pendant." He reached for it and cradled his hands around it.

"What are you doing?"

"Trying to warm it a bit before I put it around your neck."

"Thank you!" I sat beside him on the edge of the bed, and lifted my hair off my neck, but after a moment of inaction on his part, I turned to look at him.

He was studying the pendant. "I think I can make out these letters."

"They must be the initials of the people pictured inside it. They look to me like A, S, and R. And maybe an H as well."

He kept tracing the design with his little finger. "You're right." he finally said. "RH and AS." He fastened the chain for me. "Whoever they are, they look great around your neck."

"Thanks, but I'm about to hide them under a layer of fleece."

When I donned my vest, I felt something clunk against my side and remembered the pocket watch.

"What a beauty," he said as soon as I handed it to him.

"It's scratched," I pointed out, "and even dented a bit on that one side."

"So? It's still a beaut. I bet there's a whole story behind that dent." He wound the watch carefully, and it began to tick. "Too bad it can't tell us what happened."

1853

"DO NOT MAKE so much noise," Ellen Hoskins warned her younger sister. Seven-year-old Rachael could not tiptoe if her life depended on it. And it just might. Ellen knew if Father caught them sneaking up to the attic, he would whale the living daylights out of them.

Ellen had noticed a long time ago, last year when she was only eight, that Father acted like a different person when he was out about the town. He was nice to everybody out there. Here at home, though, Father demanded complete obedience. And one of his strictest rules seemed to be that there would be no laughter.

Ellen knew what joy was. Her friend Fiona could laugh just at the thought of the sun coming up or a daisy blooming or her dog dancing on its hind legs. Ellen hardly ever laughed. Except when she was with Fiona. And then, only quietly.

Several months ago, Ellen and Rachael had discovered the attic, a place that had been forbidden to them. They always waited until Mother and Grandmother were hanging the laundry to dry on the lines by the back garden. And until Father was gone completely from the house.

They had just reached the top of the steps, when their smallest brother popped into view ahead of them. "What are you doing up here?" he asked.

"I should ask you the same question." Ellen tried to make her voice stern, the way Mother's voice often was. But Ellen knew her mother loved her—just as she, Ellen, loved her little brother, so her voice held more curiosity than anger. She had not known Young Gideon hid in the attic, but this explained the many times she had been unable to find him.

"I came up here to draw. You won't tell Father, will you?"

Even at six years of age, Young Gideon was an accomplished artist. Ellen had often marveled at the secret sketches of bugs and rabbits and dogs that he had shared with her. "I would never give you away, Young Gideon. But now you must promise not to tell about Rachael and me."

His wide solemn eyes, on either side of his protuberant nose, blinked in a wordless avowal of silence. He secreted himself once more behind a barricade of boxes. Ellen peeked at him. He had gathered an old inkwell she recognized as one their father had thrown out. He had scraps of paper and three bright yellow candles, although the candles were not lit. There was more than adequate light streaming in through one of the small windows.

The two girls left him to his drawing and went to the special box they had found just a few weeks before. They pulled it out from behind the large dresser where they had concealed it. When they did so, somehow they dislodged a heavy pocket watch that must have been hidden away back there.

Ellen turned it around and around, admiring the silver. It looked very old. Before she could comment on it, they heard Father's voice down below. "Leonora! Where are you?"

Even at six, seven, and nine, all three children knew by the tone of those few words that they had best be out of the attic before he came upstairs. In her hurry to leave, Ellen dropped the watch. Father was yelling again. Hoping his voice would cover the sound, she kicked the watch back behind the dresser and fled after her sister and brother to the stairs.

2000
Matthew's House

CLARA HAD BEGUN to dread each morning ever since Hubbard's … accident, but especially now that she was here in Matthew's house. There was so much to do just getting him ready for the day. At home, it had been easier at least. She could leave him in his pajamas all day and it didn't seem to matter, but here she felt like she had to dress him.

He was awake. She could tell from the pattern of his breathing. Without saying anything—what use was it talking to him when he never replied?—she laid out a warm pair of sweatpants, took his wallet out of the pocket of his pajama top, and slipped it into a shirt pocket. It would make a lopsided bulge, but this was hardly the time to worry about such things. She had a hard enough time getting him into the oversized sweatpants, and she certainly wasn't going to try to put nice slacks on him just because they were guests in somebody else's house.

Biscuit's House

THE TICK OF the old watch was reassuring. Amazing that something that old could be set to working again just by being wound up. It reminded me of that poem, something about an epitaph for a watchmaker. I wished I could remember the exact wording—about how he'd be wound up and "set a-going in the world to come." Okay, so I remembered six or seven words.

I left Bob studying the watch face and headed for the top of the stairs, but detoured when I heard quiet murmurs and clickings from somewhere near the attic steps. The door to the storage closet was propped open. Now I saw it held three folding chairs. Ida and Ralph sat in two of them, their backs to the doorway, and Father John in the other, all three of them speaking quietly in unison. Father John held a rosary, and I assumed Ida and Ralph did as well. The three sets of beads clicked gently in a susurration almost as timeless as ocean water sliding over beach sand. Speaking of timeless, that's what Father John looked like, his fingers moving effortlessly, the planes of his face—above his beard line—lit from the side by the flickering candle. He was supposed to have slept in, but maybe his parishioners needed him? I knew so little about the Catholic faith.

I paused for only a moment. Then, not wanting to intrude, I tiptoed back the way I'd come. By the time Marmalade and I reached the stairs, I felt thoroughly awake and refreshed. In fact, I was looking forward to another day of discovery in the attic. Reebok looked a bit rumpled, though. He stood when I started down the last flight. I noticed he had folded his blanket carefully and placed it across the arm of the couch. I didn't spot his pillow. It was probably tucked in back.

"Did you sleep well, Reebok? I worried about you. That couch couldn't have been very comfortable." Actually, I thought the couch was perfectly comfortable.

Marmalade jumped up on the couch and deposited her blue mouse there.

I like this sitting place.

Marmalade and I had taken plenty of afternoon naps on it, but I wasn't as tall as Reebok. He must have felt cramped. To tell the truth, I hadn't even given him a second thought from the moment I walked into my own bedroom last night, but now that I saw his bleary eyes, I felt bad for him.

"I was perfectly fine." I could tell he was lying. Of course, this had been his own choice—according to Bob. "And it was plenty warm enough, what with the stove cranking out so much heat. We made sure the rack was full yesterday, and look. There's hardly any wood gone." He picked up the mouse and tossed it. Marmalade pounced. "It's a great stove."

"Hopefully this ice won't last much longer and you can get back to your own bed."

"Yes, Ma'am," he said, but he didn't sound like he believed it would happen very soon. "The Chief gave us all a lesson yesterday on how to manage a wood stove. He said the first one up each morning was responsible for it."

"Thank you. No wonder it's so cozy in here." I knew from past experience that a certain number of the coals would hold overnight, just as Bob had said, but they wouldn't generate enough heat even to twirl the fan very fast, much less to have much effect upstairs. "How many times did you have to get up to replenish the wood?"

"Only once, Ma'am. Even then, there were plenty of coals left."
He retrieved the mouse and threw it again. "If we hadn't been heating the upstairs, too, I wouldn't have needed to add anything until this morning, but I wanted to be sure nobody froze up there."

He sounded like he loved the bright red Defiant almost as much as I did. A good dependable dog. That was what kind of animal Reebok was. If Easton was a squirrel, Reebok was a dog. One who was happy to be there and be helpful. It reminded me of a dog our neighbors had when I was a kid. Sammy, that was his name. They trained Sammy to fetch the paper every morning, and he'd always pick it up in his mouth and trot back so proudly with it. Except on Sundays, when the paper was two or three times heavier than usual. Those days, Sammy would go coursing back and forth, turning his head from side to side, carefully skirting the area of the driveway where the paper lay. Looking and looking, but never finding it. We always used to laugh about it, but I didn't think Reebok would ever skirt an issue the way Sammy did. Not if he could help.

"And don't worry." Reebok's voice interrupted my reminiscence. "I got right back to sleep afterwards."

"That's good."

It was good, too, that Bob was delegating, rather than trying to handle it all himself. Rather like what I was doing up in the attic. I never could have tackled all those trunks and all those hatboxes by myself.

"Miss Biscuit? Could I ask you a question?"

"Of course."

"Do you think Dr. Mellinger is planning to be here for a long time?"

"Not too long, I hope. The storm should be over soon."

"That's not … What I meant was, how long will she be staying in Martinsville?"

I had to think about that for a moment. "I'm not sure. I know she's on sabbatical—how long do those generally last?"

He shrugged. "I don't know. I was just wondering if I needed to start an index card for her."

"Index card? What do you mean?"

"I keep a file of index cards for everybody in town."

Bob had told me about Reebok's obsession with three-by-five

cards, but I'd forgotten about it. I tried to school my face so I wouldn't embarrass him. He must have thought I was confused. "That way I know what's going on."

"Right."

"It's a big help."

"I'm sure it is." I thought about Annie and Wallace and Diane Marie. And the Russell boy who'd been beaten to death so recently.[2] I felt something nasty crawl up my spine.

As if he'd read my mind, he said, "If anyone dies, I put their card in a special box I bought after all those fires. It's lined with dark blue material, and it has stars on the outside."

"What a sweet thing for you to do, Reebok." Impulsively, I stepped closer to him and gave him a quick hug. "Come on into the kitchen. I'll make you some hot chocolate and then get the coffee pot started. The others should be down here soon." I'd better make plenty of extra. Glaze liked hot chocolate almost as much as Reebok did. Actually, she liked milkshakes best of all, but this was definitely not the weather for frozen drinks. Bob was already up, writing in his journal. I always wrote at night, while he liked to do it first thing in the morning, but I didn't think Reebok needed to know all that. He probably simply thought I let his Chief grab a few extra minutes of sleep each day. Or maybe he thought Bob had already been up for hours. No way to know. Nor did it particularly matter.

As I crossed by the front door, I could hear Reebok's distinctive footsteps behind me on the wide hardwood planking. Tip-tap, tip-tap, almost as if one leg were a tiny bit shorter than the other. I probably would never have noticed it, except that Bob had mentioned it once. Said he could always tell when it was Reebok coming down the corridor at the town hall.

I had a sneaking feeling that I'd forgotten something, but couldn't for the life of me remember what it was.

You forgot to throw my mouse and you forgot to feed the birds.

"Miss Biscuit? We, uh, didn't have any calls last night? Police calls, I mean?"

"No," I said, leading the way into the kitchen. "I'm sure you would have heard the phone in the kitchen if we had. We turned the volume down on the ringer, so it wouldn't wake everybody up, but down

---

2 *Gray as Ashes*

here, you'd probably hear it anyway." I was so tired last night, I might not have heard the one right next to Bob's side of the bed, but I didn't need to tell Reebok that either. "I hope that means everybody is safe and warm and well fed."

I pulled a gallon of milk out of the fridge.

"Could you teach me how to do that?"

His question baffled me. "Do what?"

"Make the hot chocolate." For some reason, he started to blush.

"You really want to learn?" Dumb question. If he hadn't wanted to learn, he wouldn't have asked.

His *yes* was muffled by a yawn. Maybe he'd need a nap today, too. I wondered how Henry and Father John had fared with their middle of the night praying. It couldn't have been comfortable. Now with three chairs in there, it was fairly crowded. I could understand, though, why Father John might not have wanted to use one of the empty bedrooms for praying in. The long utility closet seemed almost chapel-like.

As I walked Reebok through the steps, one-half of my brain thought about the wagons the Martin family must have transported all their earthly goods in. Talk about crowded.

After the hot chocolate was underway, I grabbed the percolator from the drain board, but then detoured to the bay window and parted the drapes slightly—not enough to let in much of the icy cold. There was an utter ice-encased stillness outside. Behind me, from the living room, I could hear the faint whir of the fan on top of the wood stove. Within seconds, the inside of the window fogged up, and I whimsically traced my initials again. The only movement outside was the fluttering of wings around the almost empty feeder. Oh my gosh! I'd forgotten about the new layer of ice. Poor birds. I sure didn't want them to starve. I closed the curtain quickly.

They are hungry, and you promised to feed them early.

"Hush, Marmalade" I headed for the pantry. "I know it's time to feed you, but you'll need to wait until I get some birdseed out there."

Mouse droppings! You listen but you do not hear me.

"I'll help, Miss Biscuit, if you'll tell me what to do." Reebok paused and looked at Marmalade, who had just sneezed. "Is she okay?"

I am quite well, thank you.

"I'm sure she is. She just makes those funny sounds once in a while."

Funny?

Bob walked in as Reebok and I hauled twenty-pound seed bags out of the pantry. Well, they weren't quite twenty pounds anymore. I was glad I'd bought extra last week. "Glad you're here," I said. "We could use another set of hands."

Without speaking, he turned to get his heavy boots, and I followed suit. He and Reebok each hoisted two bags—sunflower and safflower, peanuts and mixed seed—while I took a stack of suet cakes and a screwdriver to knock off any enveloping ice cover. It took a bit of effort to wrest open the back door, which had frozen shut overnight. The hinges were as squeaky as ever, of course.

I noticed Reebok looking askance at the door. I guess he'd never noticed the squeak. Of course not. We always used the front door, since the back yard was fenced in.

We were mobbed by the birds as we slipped and slid across the frozen stoop and down onto the yard. Bob ended up stomping a foot—it was hard going—through the heavy layer of ice at each step, and Reebok and I followed behind him, like a band of Cherokee masking their numbers by treading in the footsteps of the people in front of them. Marmalade pranced and slid along next to us, her weight too slight even to dent the surface.

I want to sniff the bottom of the feeder to see who was here last night.

While Reebok and I filled the feeders, Bob detoured over to his beehives. We had ten of them, all clustered near the back fence. Four over in the far corner, three sort of in the middle, and the last four in the northeastern corner of the yard.

I loved those bees. They always made such a friendly sound. We'd left them with plenty of honey to sustain them through the winter, while the excess honey we'd taken from the hives looked like sheer gold in the pantry. "Are they okay?"

Yes they are. Can you not hear their winter song?

"They're doing great," Bob said, interrupting Marmalade's loud meow. "I can hear them buzzing like crazy." Bees form a living ball, called a cluster, in the middle of the hive during the winter and keep from freezing by constantly rotating from the outside toward the inside of the conglomeration. The queen, of course, is in the middle of the cluster, and the workers shiver to warm themselves and to warm her as well. It's quite an effective system. I'd never seen it, of course, since it wouldn't be fair of us to open the hive in cold weather, but I've seen pictures and read enough about the phenomenon to be fascinated yet again with these friendly little pollinators. The mason bees and bumblebees were all—hopefully—hibernating away in safety, although I wasn't a hundred percent sure if they hibernated or what. Surely the library had a book about pollinators. Or, for that matter, maybe Bob had one. Or Sadie.

Before Bob left the hives, Reebok lowered his voice and leaned closer to me. "I'd be happy to oil those door hinges for you, Miss Biscuit, once the weather warms up."

I tried not to laugh. I didn't want to hurt his feelings—it had been a kind offer after all. "We leave them squeaky on purpose, Reebok. That way we can tell whenever anyone opens the back door."

He thought about it. "Sort of like a burglar alarm?"

"Sort of."

He didn't look completely convinced, but by that time, my ears and fingers were too cold to care. The air smelled deliciously fresh, but I could feel the hairs freezing inside my nose.

"Ten degrees or so," Reebok said. He ran his gloved hand over the light brown fuzz of his beard and wiggled his nose the same way I'd been wiggling mine.

I was too cold to ask why he sounded so sure about the temperature. I hurried to spread extra seed over the ice layer.

By the time we made it safely back inside, there was quite a mob in the kitchen watching us through the foggy bay window and commenting on the number of birds that had already descended on the feeders. A bowl of scrambled eggs—it was one of my wide mixing bowls—sat in the middle of the table, and my stomach growled noisily. I noticed that all the women looked bulkier than they had yesterday. It was warm enough—just barely—in the attic, but extra layers seemed to be on everybody's mind. Pat had wound a scarf around her neck. It looked artsy and fashionable, and warm. Wish I'd thought of a scarf. Charlie had added a voluminous college tee—who on earth had chosen such an ugly color combination?—on top of her gray sweatshirt from yesterday, and

Sadie wore a green sweatshirt, although it looked like she had layered it over the warm yellow sweaters she'd had on when she arrived.

Somebody had started the coffee, and the smell permeated the house. Glaze handed Reebok a big mug of hot chocolate as soon as he took off his gloves, and his face lit up. I wondered if she realized he was the one who had concocted it.

He leaned closer to her and looked around as if he didn't want anyone to hear what he was about to say. Naturally, I sidled closer.

"Will you let us know when you discover something else up there?"

"You're welcome to join us," Glaze whispered back at him, and I watched his face with fascination as delight contended with horror. "That's okay, Ma'am. I'll just stay down here with the men. With the, uh, the other men," he corrected.

You may feed me now.

I took a moment to fill Marmalade's bowl.

After everyone had gathered at the table, Henry said a short blessing.

"Sounds good to me, pardner." Dave was, apparently, a would-be cowboy this morning. Dave the bear. Burly and always hungry.

Henry looked askance at him, but didn't say anything other than, "Pass the scrambled eggs, would you, pardner?"

What was Henry? An elephant, maybe? A little bit ponderous, but always careful where he put his feet. And where he stuck his nose.

AFTER BREAKFAST I stood and put on my loud voice. Not loud enough to carry upstairs and disturb Father John and the Petersons, though. "Time to go upstairs," I said. "There's no telling what we'll find today. Who cooked breakfast?"

"We did," Maddy, Carol, and Dee said at the same time.

"Then," Sadie pronounced, "have fun cleaning up, fellas."

"Reebok made the hot chocolate," Glaze said.

How did she know that?

"So I think he should be exempt from clean-up for now," she added.

"That's okay, Miss Glaze. I don't mind."

"And it'll be your turn to put lunch together, fellas," I reminded them. "Don't forget."

"I'm ready to make the sacrifice," Bob said. "What do you say, men? Shall we put on a lunch spread that will leave these women awestruck?"

"I'll be happy if it's simply edible," Rebecca Jo said to the room at large, but I noticed she gave her son a wink, and he grinned in return.

"Oh ye of little faith," Henry intoned, and motioned us women toward the stairs.

There was a general flurry of movement as women disengaged from their various spouses. The men began gathering utensils and plates, without even complaining about it. Funny how quickly you could train a whole bevy of people. I was going to have to rearrange my whole kitchen once the ice storm was over, though. No telling where they were putting everything once the dish drying was done. "You, too, Easton," I said, and didn't give her time to object. "Let's go."

Melissa held up her hand, reminding me of a picture of one of those meerkats who stood on their hind legs and watched for predators. Where on earth had that image come from? She was nothing like a meerkat. This whole animal analogy process was getting to me. I'd have to stop before I went nuts.

"Where's Ida?" she asked. "We can't proceed without her."

Just like a meerkat, wanting to keep the tribe together. Stop it, Biscuit.

Stop what?

"I'm right here." Ida walked in, followed closely by Ralph and Father John. "Go on up. It won't take me long to eat." She looked over the selection on the table. "Just don't find anything good until I get there."

"We can't have attic time without you," Glaze said. "I have a feeling we're going to find more wonderful things today, and you wouldn't want to miss out."

Without much thinking about it, we all settled back into our seats and watched the three latecomers fill their plates. Father John said a quick blessing and Ida started to take a bite. Before the food reached her mouth, though, she looked up at her impromptu audience, and said, "You know what I'm going to miss this week? The Sunday morning church signboard."

I cringed inwardly at her casual assumption that the ice would last another three days, although, after having been outside this morning, I knew it was a pretty safe bet.

"But you're Catholic," Maddy pointed out.

"That doesn't mean Ralph and I can't read it when we walk past the Old Church on the way to St. Theresa's each Sunday."

Henry poured himself another cup of coffee. "I have to admit I had some reservations about that signboard when Roger first suggested it."

"You also have to admit it's entertaining," Melissa said.

"Yes." Henry drew out the word, as if he didn't really mean it. "I'm not sure I like the trend of turning a church into an entertainment center. And some of those sayings Roger comes up with are …" He let the sentence peter out.

There was an awkward pause.

Bob, ever the diplomat, spoke into the silence. "I liked the sermon you preached about the sign a couple of months ago—I WENT TO THE HOKEY POKEY CLINIC AND TURNED MYSELF AROUND." I could almost hear the capital letters in his voice.

"I'd planned a sermon about the twenty-third psalm," Henry said, "but Roger's sign set me to thinking in a whole nother direction."

"I've always wondered if *nother* is really a word," Maddy mused.

"Only if it's preceded by *whole*," Bob said.

I do not understand you. What are you talking about?

"But you were right, Henry," Glaze said, reaching a hand out to Marmalade. "We can turn ourselves around, but we usually need help to do it."

I wondered if she was thinking about all those years before her bipolar disorder was diagnosed. She looked up at me at that moment, and I could see in her expression that I was right. I'd been no help at all to her during that time, because I hadn't known what was wrong. Fortunately, she'd forgiven me my ignorance.

She loves you.

I came back from my reverie in time to hear people listing their favorite signboard sayings.

"The one I liked best," said Dave, "was WHAT IF THERE

WERE NO HYPOTHETICAL QUESTIONS?"

"That couldn't be your favorite," Tom said. "You still lived out of town way back then. You weren't here to see it."

Dave put on an expression of blank innocence, but Pat blew his cover. "Maggie called us almost every week with a full report."

"Ah," Bob said, "a spy in our town. I'll have to investigate." He refilled his coffee cup and passed the carafe to his left. "After the ice storm."

"Maggie had a favorite," Pat told us. "It was MY SUPPORT GROUP FOR PROCRASTINATORS HASN'T MET YET, but she never did tell us what you preached about that week."

Henry shrugged. "About the only thing I could come up with was the parable of the loaves and fishes."

"What on earth," Ida asked, "does that have to do with procrastinating?"

"An awful lot of people must have forgotten to bring food with them to the Sermon on the Mount." Henry made a wry face. "Neglecting to plan ahead is sort of like procrastinating. I thought it was appropriate. Kind of."

Father John suggested THE FIRST FIVE DAYS AFTER THE WEEKEND ARE THE HARDEST—leading us all to tease him about checking out the competition. He spread his hands wide. "I'm just being ecumenical."

"That's a silly one for you to like," Ida said. "You work on the weekends."

"And every other day, too," Henry said, which garnered an appreciative look from Father John.

"Personally," Maddy said, "my favorite was EVERYBODY WHO BELIEVES IN TELEKINESIS, RAISE MY HAND." For that, she received a round of applause. That had definitely been my favorite, and I was happy to see that others seemed to agree with me.

"How on earth," Carol asked, "did you preach a sermon about telekinesis?"

"I wondered the same thing," Father John said.

Henry chortled a bit. "I didn't even try."

"If I remember right," Bob said, "you preached that day about Doubting Thomas."

Henry shrugged. "Come to think of it, it does sort of fit."

We all laughed, and Dee applauded.

She finished her enthusiastic clapping before she said, "There's one more that was pretty good. THIS MAY BE CHEESY BUT I THINK YOU'RE GRATE." She looked at Carol. "That was g-r-a-t-e. But Henry didn't say a word about cheese that week."

"No, but I talked about the meaning of feasts of food versus feasts of spiritual nourishment. Wasn't that good enough?"

"There was another one I liked," Father John said. "A DEAD END IS MERELY A GOOD PLACE TO TURN AROUND."

"You would like that one, Sharkey," Maddy said with a mischievous grin, and Father John grimaced.

"Sharkey?" Several of us asked at the same time.

"He used to steal all my marbles."

"Not so," Father John objected. "I won them fair and square. Squidling," he added with just as broad a grin.

"No fair! You said you wouldn't tell anybody."

He laughed at his sister. "You weren't supposed to tell anybody about Sharkey either."

"Oh." She scanned the faces of everyone at the table. "I wouldn't trust his poker playing if I were you."

Bob laughed. "I doubt we have to worry. He's lost quite a bit so far."

"What are you playing for?" I asked.

"Pretzel sticks. It's too icy outside for cold cash."

Another round of laughter—and a few groans—during which Ida stood and took her empty plate to the sink. "Now it's time to go."

"When you make lunch," Pat said, waving over her shoulder, "try not to use every single dish in the house."

"You don't really think they'd use every dish?" Amanda sounded scandalized. I could imagine. With her simple lifestyle, she probably cooked with a minimum of fuss.

Pat scoffed. "Not if my husband has anything to do with it. We might not get fed at all. He'd sit around jawing all day rather than cook." She seemed to rethink what she'd just said. "On second thought, if he gets hungry enough, he'll probably join in the effort."

"If they feed us soup"—Sadie's voice drifted down the stairs from in front of us—"they don't get credit for cooking, do they? After all, we're the ones who left it bubbling on the wood stove."

"Ralph will think it's cooking if he opens a loaf of bread." Thank goodness there was humor in Ida's voice. I didn't want to think how uncomfortable it would be if any marital squabbles broke out while we were all stuck here inside.

I LOOKED AROUND for Melissa. She must have taken a bathroom break. All of the rest of us, except Easton, were working in small groups—Glaze, Dee, and Maddy at one trunk—Rebecca Jo, Ida, and Carol beyond them sorting through a disreputable-looking footlocker—Amanda, Charlotte, and Pat on yet another steamer trunk, quite unlike the flat-topped wooden one Sadie and I had tackled. My mom, Esther, and Tom's mother were clustered around a collection of mismatched lamps. I'd hear an occasional low comment—"What a bunch of junk. Why would anyone keep something like this?" "Oh! I had a puzzle just like this when I was a child," "Whoever stashed this away really believed in tons of wrapping paper"—or a question about indecipherable handwriting, or snatches of a soft tune hummed below someone's breath, but for the most part we'd been silent for ten or twenty minutes. When Easton's explosive cheer came from over at the side of the attic, it surprised all of us.

"Look what I found!"

You'd think she'd found treasure, but all it turned out to be was a huge stack of old-fashioned white handkerchiefs, most of them monogrammed and edged in lace. I hate tissues—it seems a shame to cut down a tree just so I can blow my nose—but I also don't particularly like those super-delicate hankies, so I always make my own handkerchiefs from soft old worn out tee shirts or flannel sheets, which provide me with enough hankies to last a lifetime. I cut them up into generous sized squares that last a lot longer than those flimsy lacy things. When I blow, I want something substantial to blow into.

What are you talking about?

Marmalade must have felt the same way—she echoed my thoughts precisely.

I did?

But everyone else got as excited as Easton and gathered around her. The only reason I stood up was that my butt was going to sleep in that folding chair.

"Here," Easton said, and I finally understood the source of her excitement. "Look! This one on top has my initials."

It did indeed have an E, but it was a lot bigger than the H and the B, which meant, I was pretty sure, that E was the last name, not the first or middle. I didn't point that out, though, since Easton Hastings seldom got excited about anything except other women's husbands. Cancel that thought.

What thought?

I'm trying hard to be nicer.

I think you are very nice.

Even Marmalade told me to behave myself.

That is not what I said.

"But what are you going to do about that B?" Rebecca Jo asked.

Easton almost caressed the handkerchief. "B is my middle initial."

"I didn't know that," Sadie said. "What's your middle name, dear?"

I never thought I'd see Easton Hastings blush, but blush she did. "Blessing. That's my middle name."

I guess even Easton couldn't miss how incredulous we all looked. "My mother chose it," she said.

"And I can certainly see why," Sadie said after only the briefest of pauses. "Why don't you pass the hanky around so we can all see it?"

There was a heavy ridge of tatting all the way around the outside edge of her hankie. It looked incredibly scratchy. "This is a marvelous find, Easton." I felt rather proud of my forbearance. "Where did you find them? What was around them?" When she gave me a blank look, I added, with a great deal of patience, "Was there anything that might give us a clue as to who put them there? Or when?"

She reached behind her and pulled a long blue ribbon out of the trunk. "They were tied up in this."

"Lots of help that is," said Pat. "Are there any other initials in the bunch?"

"Who knows?" Easton waved her hand dismissing the question.

After all, she had her own initials. "Why doesn't everybody take one?"

I took one, but only because I spotted a soft cambric embroidered with a tiny bouquet of flowers on one corner. Half the fabric was stained, faded to a soft brown. It was a wonder anyone had saved it, but I could tell it had been washed carefully and ironed meticulously, most likely with an old flatiron, maybe even with one of the ones we'd found earlier.

"These are museum quality," Carol said.

"Mine isn't." I showed them the stain. "It's been through a lot, wouldn't you say?"

"It needs some bluing," Amanda said.

Dee made a face. "Only if we can find it in Rebecca Jo's laundry room."

"That looks like an old dried bloodstain," Maddy said.

Dee reached out to give a gentle tug on one of Maddy's brown curls. "Don't mind her, Carol," she said. "She's always looking for a murder or two."

Melissa walked back into the attic just in time to hear Dee's comment. "Not one or two. She'd be happier with five or six."

April 1799

HOPE BLACK'S WEDDING day dawned stormy—well, it wasn't even dawn yet, but Hope could hear the wind raging outside, along with occasional growls of distant thunder, and it sounded like the storm was not going to go away any time soon. It was depressingly cold, too cold for her sprigged muslin gown, even if she wore her heaviest shawl over it. She refused to wear something sensible, though. Maybe if she put on an extra petticoat, it would keep her knees from knocking together. And she had her long heavy knit stockings. They weren't in the least attractive, but on a frigid day like today—even if it was her wedding day—she'd rather be warm than stunning. Anyway, the stockings would not show, for her boots laced up almost to the middle of her lower leg. Still, her muslin was lovely. She and Violet had both labored long over it throughout the darkest days of the winter, planning for the warm weather ahead, and planning for Hope's wedding day.

April was supposed to be sunnier than this, she thought, as she wiggled to gather the quilts tighter around the two of them. Beside her, her sister stirred and yawned. Hope had a delicious moment of wondering what it would be like to waken the next morning beside a man, her new husband, instead of next to Violet, with whom she'd shared a bed from childhood. But she wasn't sure she was supposed to think about such things.

Her mother had pulled her aside several days before and told her all sorts of highly suspect stories about what went on in a marriage bed, but Hope was not sure she believed any of it. She had seen animals breeding, of course, but surely people had a different way of … of …

Hope pushed the covers—and her thoughts—aside. She didn't want to think about such things. There would be plenty of time for her to find out on her own. After all, a new century would be dawning in just nine more months. She might—might—have a child to usher in the year 1800. She *did* know that babies came into the world about that long after … whatever it was that happened … happened.

Behind her, Violet shivered. "Come back to bed, Hope. The roosters have not even crowed yet."

"You expect me to lie about like a lazybones on my wedding day?" But she snuggled back under the quilts all the same. "Just a few more minutes, and then I have to be up and about."

"Oh?" Violet sounded sleepy and mischievous at the same time. "Is there a particular reason?"

Hope rolled over, laughing, and pinned her sister against the wall. "You will miss teasing me when I am gone!"

"I will have the quilts all to myself and will not ever again have your cold toes against the back of my knees!"

"You do not have to sound so jubilant. You will miss me. Admit it."

It was still too dark for her to see her sister's face, but Hope sensed the tears before she heard them.

"I *will* miss you." Violet let out a most unladylike sniff and tugged on the quilt. "Very much indeed."

"Don't blow your nose on the quilt," Hope said. "Use the sleeve of your nightdress. It is considerably easier to wash."

Violet chuckled through her tears. "In truth, I will not sleep here alone. Polly is already planning her move into this room as soon as you become Mistress Endicott."

"That is fair," Hope said. "They have been three to a bed for the past twelve years, ever since Polly left her cradle."

"Polly will probably have cold feet, too."

Violet sounded thoroughly despondent, but Hope couldn't help laughing. "I hope Marel's feet are warm." She hoped she was not being too brazen to voice such a thought.

The sisters giggled together for a moment until Violet sat up. "I have a wedding present for you and Marel." She paused a moment before she admitted, "Really, though, it is just for you. Not for him at all."

Off in the distance, the Black's rooster began its predawn warm-up with a few croaks and an anticipatory squawk.

"What? What kind of present?"

"Something I made."

"May I see it now, or do I have to wait until the wedding?"

"You cannot see it now—it is not light enough."

"You know what I mean."

"You might not like it."

"How can you say that, Violet? If you made it, it will be precious to me. You ought to know that."

"We have to get up then."

"Why? I thought you wanted to laze about."

"I hid it beneath the mattress."

Making a big show of shivering as the earliest light limned the window in a pale aura, Hope threw on her dressing gown while her sister rummaged beneath the bedding. She saw a glimmer of white as Violet held something out to her, and she ran her fingers over the soft fabric, feeling the stiff tatting around the edges and the delicate needle-work on one corner.

"You embroidered a handkerchief for me? And tatted it as well?"

Violet's teeth gleamed as the morning light gained in intensity. "You should be able to see it in a few minutes."

Hope ran her index finger carefully over the fine lines of thread. "Oh, Vi, these are my new initials."

"That's right. I made the E for Endicott bigger than the H for Hope and the B for Black. You don't mind, do you?"

"Of course not, dear. I will be a married woman, and very proud of my new name. You *will* come to visit me often, will you not?"

"Of course, Hope Black Endicott." Violet giggled as she used her sister's full new name. "It is only a mile if I walk along the top of the cliffs. I just wish you did not have to live in Enders."

"But the Endicotts have always lived there."

"I do not see why," Violet pouted. "There is still plenty of room here in Martinsville."

Hope touched the end of her sister's nose and answered Violet's thought rather than her words. "I will miss you, too." She moved over closer to the window. "Now the light is strong enough I should be able to see my favorite sister's fine needlework." Hope could not help noticing that the E was a little crooked, but otherwise Violet had done a fine job. "It is beautiful, Vi. I will keep it with me always."

"If you ever decide you do not want it, I will take it back."

"But the initials would be wrong for you." She stepped back a pace and eyed her sister. "What? What are you planning? I can tell when you are up to something."

"Nothing." Violet's voice was overly casual. "It is only that ... that Marel's brother Hezekiah ..."

"Oh, sister, he is a fine young man—but would you not want your own initials on a handkerchief rather than his? And the B is all wrong for him, after all."

"For now," Violet proclaimed, "the H is for Hope. If I ever marry Hezekiah Endicott, I'll embroider my own handkerchief with a big V E. Or maybe"—she looked doubtfully at Hope's handkerchief—"I will stick only to flowers, since my letters are not completely straight."

"You will have to embroider your own, as I would never give this one back. And I care not what the letters look like, so long as you were the one who stitched them with such love." A sudden peal of thunder drowned out Hope's next words, and she had to repeat herself. "I would love to have you living near by me in Enders, which you would certainly do if you married Hezekiah Endicott."

Violet scrunched her face into a pout of distaste. "I hope Marel will be a good husband to you."

"He will be."

"How can you be sure?"

"If he is not, I will brain him with the flatiron."

Violet gasped for a moment before she saw the humor. "Men think they are so powerful with their muskets and knives, but we women have girdles and flatirons and spurtles, do we not?"

"And the men never suspect that we are well-armed."

On that rather gruesome note, Hope and Violet Black threw back the shutters, dressed in their warmest petticoats, their lightest muslins, their longest woolen stockings, and their heaviest shawls, went through their morning chores as quickly as possible, and then walked with their entire family to the church, where most of the town of Martinsville waited to celebrate the wedding of Hope Black to Marel Endicott.

FOUR YEARS LATER, almost to the day, Hezekiah Endicott fainted as he stood at the altar with Violet Black, just moments after he said, "I will." He struck his head on one of the tall iron candlesticks as he fell. It took them several long minutes to revive him, during which Violet held her new husband's head in her lap and blotted the blood from his temple with the soft handkerchief she had embroidered with flowers as soon as he proposed to her.

No one thought anything of the dizzy spells he suffered almost daily for the next fortnight. Violet was distraught when he died on the fifteenth day after their wedding. Despite the urgings of her sister and the rest of her family, she never remarried.

When Hope died years later, Violet took back the handkerchief she had embroidered so lovingly with Hope's monogram and saved the two handkerchiefs together until Hope's eldest daughter married one of the Hastings boys.

2000

I TUCKED THE flowered hanky into my sweatpants pocket. Even though it was stained, I thought perhaps Glaze might want to carry it for her wedding. Something borrowed, maybe. Or something old.

What does that mean?

Maybe she wouldn't mind the stain. After all, somebody had loved it enough to iron it and fold it so carefully.

"I need a change of pace." Glaze pushed aside her stack of boring cards, walked past the gramophone she'd fiddled with earlier, and headed for a battered wooden box. I could tell from here, all the way across the attic, that it hadn't been put together very carefully, or maybe the wood had just warped over the years, because there were definite gaps between some of the boards that comprised the sides of it.

"What are you expecting to find in there, Glaze?" I'd been ready to say, *a body*, but changed my mind at the last moment. No need to bring up those stories—not until Carol knew us a little better. "A treasure of some sort?"

"In this battered box? Not a chance. But it does look interesting, don't you think?"

I walked over to join her.

She reached for the lid, but then pulled her hand back. "The anticipation is almost better than—"

"No it's not," I said. "Open it for heaven's sake."

She laughed at me. "Curiosity killed the cat."

Oh, no!

She stopped when Marmalade let out a howl.

"But satisfaction brought life back," I reminded her.

From behind us, Pat spoke up. "Ignorance killed the cat. Curiosity was framed."

"You've been reading sci-fi, I'll bet," Maddy said to Pat.

"Sci-fi? No. Why do you say that?"

"C. J. Cherryh wrote that thing about ignorance and curiosity. She's a sci-fi writer."

"I didn't know that." Pat squinted. "Guess I'll have to be more careful about giving credit where credit is due."

"I wonder who first said that one," Pat mused.

"I think I'll open the box," Glaze said, "before we get stuck in a quotation bog." She lifted the lid. "Oh, phooey." She knelt on the floor beside it and rummaged a bit. "Looks like it's nothing but old rags."

Before she could lower the top, though, Carol intervened, and I thought maybe the tawny-haired Carol would be a lioness. A hunter—went along with being a historian—and the one who led the pride, no matter what the male lion thought about his own role. I wondered if she'd ever considered marriage. And what would Glaze be? A snow leopard, perhaps? With that silver hair of hers, it certainly would fit.

"You never know what's going to be in there," Carol said. "Let's at least spread them out and take a look."

"You're kidding, right?"

"Nope. People didn't throw out garments or fabrics when they became stained or torn. They saved them so they could use bits and pieces of old cloth for quilts or cleaning rags. The rag bag, or in this case the rag box, was a good resource. We might find an old dress or a christening gown or even a worn out hand-stitched quilt."

"If you say so." Glaze began lifting out hunks of fabric, some of it folded carefully, some of it bunched up in an untidy lump. Carol helped her, and they assembled quite a display of frayed, stained, and torn remnants. "Who on earth needed this many cleaning rags?"

"Obviously somebody thought they wouldn't need them any more," Ida said. "Otherwise, they wouldn't have put the box up here in such an inconvenient location."

"I just realized something," Glaze said. "There's not a bit of plastic anywhere up here."

"Yes there is." I pointed to the hula hoop leaning near where the back wall of the house met the false wall of the hidden room.

"I don't want anything plastic in the museum," Maddy asserted.

A monkey? Would Maddy be a monkey, always investigating everything? The way she curled up whenever she sat, I could almost see a prehensile tail wrapping around her legs.

CurlUp does not have a tail.

"You're right," Carol said, but she seemed to have something of a question in her voice.

"Better hang onto it," Dee said, lifting down another hatbox. "A hundred years from now people will be marveling over old-fashioned plastic."

Dee was definitely a giraffe, with her long legs and long neck and inquisitive face.

"I haven't seen a hula hoop in years." Melissa the meerkat headed toward the far wall. "Wonder if I can still make one work?"

"Go right ahead," Ida said. "If you throw your back out of commission we've got Doc Nathan downstairs and Amanda, our very own massage therapist, here to fix you up again."

Melissa stuck out her lower lip and gave a resounding raspberry. "I'll have you know I was hula hoop champion in fifth grade." By that time she'd reached the hoop. "It's smaller than the ones I remember," she said, picking it up and carting it back toward the rest of us. "And it's not plastic," she added.

Rebecca Jo took one look at it. "That's not a hula hoop."

1788

I OUGHT TO have been a boy," Astaline Shipleigh muttered. She did not have to keep her voice quiet, for her brother Franklin and his friend Reuben Hastings were far up the street, and for once there was nobody in sight on Beechnut Lane. The stiff breeze that swept down from the cliffs carried the sound of the boys' metal rods clanging on their metal hoops. Astaline's wooden hoop made practically no sound whatsoever. She would much rather have had the clang. She liked noise. She wished she could run and jump and swim and holler the way boys could, but her mother and father insisted that she behave like a lady. And she did. For the most part. When Mother and Father were watching.

She made a disparaging sound and grimaced, the way she thought highwaymen must do when they challenged the coaches of wealthy barons. Not that she had ever seen a wealthy baron, or a highwayman either for that matter—and there were no fancy coaches in Martinsville—but Astaline's imagination let her be anything she wanted to be, do anything she wanted to do. Anything, she had to admit, except be a real boy. And spin a loud metal hoop.

She gave her hoop a particularly vicious swipe that sent it spinning into a tree. She hoped for a moment that it would break, but then she immediately regretted that hope and ran to retrieve the hoop. She knew her parents would never replace it if she broke it—certainly not with another wooden hoop, but even more certainly not with the metal wagon rim she coveted. The only reason her brother had a metal hoop was that he had already had it when their cousin George Shipleigh lost his leg. All because Reuben Hastings' metal hoop ran into a tree. A tree that George had unfortunately just begun to climb. The gash left by the metal had festered and George's leg had begun to rot.

Astaline shuddered. She could still remember George's screams when Doctor Garner went to his house. She wondered what Doctor Garner had done with the leg after he cut it off, but she was not allowed to ask that question. And they never would have given her an answer anyway. If she had been a boy, she could have found out.

When she passed George's house, he called to her from the porch where he spent most of his waking hours. She leaned her hoop against the stairs and sat on the porch floor beside him.

"Have you heard about the liberty hoops?"

"No." She eyed him cautiously. Did he think she had forgotten the nasty tricks he had played on her in the past, urging her to climb a low-branching tree that he knew had been invaded by hornets, or telling her that if she flapped her arms fast enough she could fly like a bird from the top of the hayloft? She had not been pudding-headed enough to fall for that one, but she still had occasional nightmares about the hornets. "What are liberty hoops?"

"You are just a girl," he said, which caused Astaline to bristle, but he did not appear to notice, "so you would not have heard. My father told me that now that the War of Independence is over and the United States of America has been formed, some of the boys are cutting notches in their hoops, one notch for each state."

Astaline glanced sideways at the empty leg of his trousers. Her mother had said she should feel sorry for him now that he was crippled, but Astaline did not consider the loss of a limb to confer any extra status on someone who, in her opinion, had not deserved it before the loss. "Why are you telling me this?"

His face took on a look of bland equanimity, reminding Astaline of the blank stare of the more unapproachable barn cats. "Your brother cannot cut notches in his metal hoop. If you cut thirteen big notches in yours—one for each state," he added, as if he thought she would not know how many states there were, "then you will have the kind of hoop he cannot have." He smiled at her.

She studied him, wondering if there were a hidden trick, but she could not think of what it might be. He was right. Metal hoops could not be notched.

"How do you notch them?"

He gave a derisive laugh. "Surely even a girl can steal her brother's knife."

She could, she knew that. Franklin often left it lying beside his bed.

She had to wait four days before she had her chance. When Franklin and Reuben left to go swimming in the deep pool in the Metoochie River, she took her hoop and Franklin's knife out behind the woodshed. The job turned out to be harder than she had expected, but she was nothing if not determined. She planned to cut small notches, but the knife seemed to take on a life of its own. The first notch cut almost a quarter of the way across the wooden band. She gripped the knife more tightly, determined to curtail the depth of its cut, but even so, the second notch went halfway into the width. The third and fourth cuts were more reasonably sized, but now the hoop looked somewhat lopsided. Still, she had not sliced off a finger nor stabbed into either her arm or her leg. Mother would not have been happy if Astaline had gotten bloodstains on her apron.

Carefully, she counted each notch as she completed it. Carefully, she used the tip of the knife to scratch her first name along the inner edge of the hoop. Carefully, she returned her brother's knife. Carefully, she hid her hoop under the bed she shared with her big sister, proud that she now had the only liberty hoop in Martinsville.

She had not counted on her sister finding it. Martha Cornelia Shipleigh tapped her foot with that big sister kind of tap. "Why did you ruin your hoop like this?"

"It is not ruined," Astaline countered. "I turned it into a liberty hoop, with a notch for each state."

"You do not have as much sense as a baby goat," Martha Cornelia said in exasperation. "Look at how deep these gouges are. The first time you use it, it will shatter into pieces."

That was when Astaline remembered the slightly feral quality of George's smile.

The hoop remained under the bed.

George asked Astaline once why he never saw her spinning her hoop anymore. She told him, with haughty reserve, that she had outgrown such childish games. After that, she avoided walking past his house as much as she could. But she had discovered that if she ran beside a picket fence with her hoop stick extended, she could make a truly horrible, wonderful noise, louder and longer lasting than the clang of her brother's metal rod on his silly metal hoop.

YEARS LATER, WHEN Reuben Hastings began to court Astaline, she admitted to him that she had a liberty hoop. The look of envy in his wide-set eyes—wide set because of the size of that Hastings nose between them—was a deciding factor in her decision to accept his proposal. At the reception after their wedding, and after Ruben had given her a particularly beautiful silver pendant engraved with their intertwined initials, AS and RH, she gave him the hoop. He was so excited he knocked over his wine, spilling it on the rose-embroidered tablecloth that had been a special wedding present from Reuben's sister Lydia and his grandmother.

Everyone laughed so hard, nobody thought to mop up the wine or dilute it with water. The problem was that by the time they were able to remove the cloth, the wine had dried, and everyone knew dried red-wine stains on linen were irremediable, even when one used salt and boiling water. All the ladies, particularly Astaline's mother, clucked at the ruin of the fine linen.

Reuben carried the hoop proudly to the house on Beechnut Lane, the house where he had been born, the house where Astaline and Reuben would raise Mary Etta, their first child to survive infancy, Electa, Rose, and the two twin girls, and the girl and two boys that came after the twins.

Astaline tried numerous times to remove the stain, but eventually gave up and decided to use the tablecloth only at the dinners when enough people were invited and enough dishes were served to spread across the entire stretch of cloth and therefore cover the stain. Reuben was at first embarrassed to be reminded of his clumsiness, but after Astaline repeatedly told him the stain did not matter to her, he began not to be bothered by it, even when his brother Ethan teased him.

The last time the tablecloth was spread was the day of Astaline's funeral, the day Reuben slashed the tablecloth with the bread knife and cursed God for taking his wife.

2000

"**HOOPS WERE POPULAR** during the Victorian era." Carol's voice came from behind me. I turned briefly to look and found her standing at the cheval mirror, running her finger around the frame. "Victorian hoops were made of wood or iron. Wood for the girls usually and iron for the boys. Some of the older ones, from the seventeen hundreds, were made from the rims of wagon wheels."

"This one sure doesn't look like a wagon wheel," Amanda said. "So are you saying it's Victorian?"

"Not all of the old ones were wheel rims. There's really no way of knowing the age," Carol said. "Hoop toys have been used for thousands of years."

"Like marbles," Maddy said.

"I think," Ida drawled, "we can safely say this one's not that old."

"It looks like it's in pretty good shape." Melissa ran her hands around the hoop. "Except for these gouges."

I heard Carol's indrawn breath from behind me. "Gouges?"

"Uh-huh. And they seem to be fairly evenly spaced."

"How many are there? Are there thirteen of them?"

Why, I wondered, did Carol sound so excited?

I do not know.

"Thirteen?" Melissa cocked an eyebrow. "You've got to be kidding."

Maddy stepped closer to the hoop. "Why would you expect thirteen?"

"I'm not expecting. I was just hoping. Excuse me." Carol squeezed past Sadie's chair. "When the U.S. was first founded, a lot of boys notched their hoops to reflect the number of the original states. As states were added, sometimes people carved more notches, but that practice soon died out. The notched hoops tended to break more quickly than solid ones, so there aren't many left."

Melissa's eyes widened. She held the hoop with her left hand and started working her right hand around the rim. "One, two…"

By the time she reached four, we were all counting along with her.

When we reached seven, Melissa stopped. "Look at this! Something's carved inside the rim." She ran her finger slowly over whatever she'd found. "It's really rough here." We followed her as she walked closer to one of the eyebrow windows and held the hoop up to the light. "A-s-t-a-l-i-n-e. Asta-line? Or is it Asta-leen? Is that a name?"

Naturally, we all looked at Sadie and Rebecca Jo.

"I think she might have been one of the Shipleighs," Sadie said.

Rebecca Jo just shrugged. "No idea."

"If that's who it is, I'm pretty sure she married a Hastings, which might explain how it got here into Biscuit's attic."

Astaline Shipley. Why did that ring a bell? I pulled my silver pendant out from under my vest. "What was her husband's name? Do you know?"

Sadie drew her breath in through clenched teeth. "I ... No. I can't remember, but I'm sure it'll be somewhere—maybe some records in town hall?"

"Could it have been Robert or Richard or something like that? Something that starts with an R?" I undid my necklace and passed it to Maddy. "Hand this to Sadie, would you? Bob and I think these initials are AS and RH."

Maddy pushed her glasses more firmly onto her nose. "Sure looks like it." Her eyes went sort of unfocused. "Astaline Shipley and Tweedle-de-dee Hastings."

"That would be Riddle-de-dee," Pat said. "With an R."

What is a nar?

Once the pendant went round the circuit, I opened it to show everyone the two portraits.

"He has to be a Hastings," Sadie said. "Just look at the size and shape of his nose."

"Genetic trait," Carol offered.

"You bet."

Since there didn't seem to be any way to prove the man's first name one way or the other, we started the notch counting on the hoop all over again.

"Thirteen!"

When the cheers finally died down, we heard Bob's voice ringing up the stairwell. "Everything okay up there?"

"Sure," I called back. "We were cheering. Come on up and see a real treasure."

You can throw my mouse for me while you are here, Softfoot.

"And get Dave up here, too," Pat yelled.

"Ralph, too," Ida hollered. "He'll want to see this."

"And Reebok," Glaze called. She winked at me. She must have known I'd listened to her early morning exchange with Reebok.

"Okay," Bob said.

I walked to the top of the stairs and called after him. "Bring everybody!" I hoped they wouldn't expect anything as exciting as another hidden room. His footsteps receded.

When the men eventually trooped in, the attic looked crowded once more. I did a quick head count. All the men had joined us. I'd be willing to bet they'd gotten tired of their endless card games, and surely they had to know that anything we found up here was a potential treasure.

Marmalade put her front paws on Bob's leg and dropped her blue mouse at his feet. Sweet man that he is, he tossed it up in the air for her and she practically did a back-flip catching it.

That was fun.

"So," Ralph said, "what was so exciting you had to cheer about it?" I happened to be watching him when Melissa brought forth the hoop. Ralph Peterson was usually so nondescript. A very nice guy, but not talkative at all. As soon as he saw the hoop, though, his eyes widened appreciably. "I had one of these when I was a boy!" He stretched out a hand and touched it almost reverently. "Or rather, my dad had one that belonged to his father. He let me play with it a couple of times." His shoulders lifted almost to his droopy ears. "I smashed it into a tree and broke it." He glanced around at the group and rubbed his posterior. "Got a whale of a licking over it."

"Serves you right," Ida told her husband as the rest of us laughed.

Everyone had to count as Melissa held the hoop and explained the meaning of the thirteen notches.

"My dad's hoop didn't have any notches," Ralph said. I thought he sounded a bit envious.

When I asked about the name scratched into the edge of the hoop, none of the men recognized it. Wasn't it a shame, I thought, that people could so easily disappear after just a few generations. Whoever this Astaline was, she must have treasured her liberty hoop to have kept it safe. Of course, she was long dead, and there was no way of knowing who had consigned her hoop up here to the attic. She must have lived through the revolutionary war. I wish she'd left a diary for us to read. Maybe we'd find one. I sure hoped it wouldn't be written backwards the way Mary Frances Garner Brandt had written hers.

The men were less enthusiastic about the handkerchiefs and the hats and the tablecloth, but we still managed to spend twenty minutes or so gaily describing our miraculous finds. Glaze didn't mention the boring greeting cards, but I noticed that Bob picked up a couple and examined them.

"I'M GLAD THEY liked the hoop," Maddy said once the men left. "That's going to be one of the major exhibits in the Martinsville Museum." She looked right at me. "In the meantime, keep it safe, will you? It won't fit in the dresser drawer."

"It could be the oldest thing up here." Melissa's voice fairly sang with awe.

"Maybe, maybe not." Ida held up her index finger. She looked sort of like an orangutan. "The hobby horse could be older." A second finger joined the first. "The marbles, maybe?"

"We have no way of knowing how old a lot of these things are," Sadie said.

"That doesn't matter," Maddy said. "We don't have any details about the horse or the gown or the handkerchiefs—or the marbles—but this hoop can have a real nice placard with a story of why there are thirteen notches."

"Let's leave it back where it was to start with," I said. "We know it's lasted well back there, and I'd hate to have us bump into it or drop something on it if it's over here close to the stairs."

"I wish we knew who it belonged to," Melissa said as she carried it back to the far end of the attic.

"Astaline," Maddy crowed. "It belonged to Astaline."

"Lots of help you are." Melissa didn't even bother to turn around. "I meant a last name."

"Shipleigh," Maddy said.

"That's only a guess."

"Fine with me." Maddy's words were abrupt, but her tone was light, thank goodness. I hate arguments. "Grump about it if you want to," she went on.

"Well," I said, "since that wasn't a hula-hoop, we're back where we started. We still don't have anything plastic up here."

"You're wrong." Glaze walked past me to the gramophone she'd been inspecting earlier. She flipped open the lid of a sturdy cardboard box, revealing a whole collection of ancient records. She pulled out a couple and passed them around. "Vinyl's a type of plastic, isn't it?

What are vynils?

"Beats me," I said.

"I wonder if it still works?" Dee set down the hatbox she'd been holding for some time, reached for the hand crank on the old machine, and gave it a few turns.

Glaze slid her record out of its sleeve. "Caruso," she said. "That should elevate the tone of our endeavors."

The scratchiness was a bit painful to listen to, but even with the poor quality, I could tell why his voice had been lauded for so many years. The record I held was less impressive—Polka Music of the World, performed by a group that, according to the picture on the record jacket, consisted of three accordions played by earnest-looking men with wide smiles, and two trombones played by men with fat cheeks. They all wore plaid jackets and bow ties. I thought maybe I'd pass on that one.

"Well, I'll be jiggered," Sadie said. She held not an unwieldy thick gramophone disc but a much smaller 35 rpm record. "The Ames Brothers. I always did like them. Are you and your brother related to them, Maddy?"

"Not that I know of. I can ask him next time we go downstairs."

"Don't put it back in the box," Rebecca Jo said. "Once the power comes back on, we'll be able to play it. I still have my old record player somewhere."

"Probably in your attic," Dee said with a distinct drawl. "Or your laundry room."

"Why can't you play it on the gramophone?" Maddy asked.

"The grooves are much smaller on the newer records," Glaze explained, "so that heavy gramophone needle will damage them."

"It sure will bring back memories," Sadie said. She held up the record. "This one is *The Naughty Lady of Shady Lane*."

Those of us who were of a certain age burst into laughter. The younger women just looked blank.

They'd have to hear it to understand. Once I caught my breath, I asked, "What's on the flip side?"

Sadie turned it over, took one look, and burst into song. She still had a surprisingly clear soprano voice, without any of the shakiness so often associated with advanced age.

"I saw Esau, sitting on a seesaw," and Rebecca Jo joined in on the second line. I picked up on line three.

Once we finished—including the final *Hey!*—Dee looked like she thought we'd lost our minds, but she said, "Sing it again."

So we did.

> *I saw Esau sitting on a see-saw*
> *I saw Esau with my girl*
> *I saw Esau sitting on a see-saw*
> *Giving her a merry whirl.*
> *When I saw Esau, he saw me*
> *And I saw red and I got so sore*
> *So I got a saw and I sawed Esau*
> *Off that old see-saw, hey!*

"I don't know about you," Dee said after we finished with all the giggling, "but I'm ready for another hat."

"You're always ready for another hat," Maddy complained, but I could tell she was just teasing.

I delved back into my trunk and handed Sadie a small ribbon-wrapped stack. "Did these people never throw anything away?"

"We should be glad they didn't," Carol said from behind me, and I had to admit I agreed with her.

1802

ROSILLA GARNER MILLICENT lived in the largest house in Martinsville. She had a husband who was wealthier than the husbands of any of the other women. She had more servants than anyone in town.

When it came to the task of clearing out the attic of the Millicent mansion, though, the responsibility fell squarely on her broad shoulders, for only she could be relied upon to make the difficult decisions. What to keep? What to throw away?

She surveyed the expanse of boxes and trunks spread before her. Why did anyone think a single one of these artifacts was even vaguely interesting? She fingered a stack of journals, raising a flurry of dust in the process.

Everything would need to be cleaned first. Then she could decide what was to be saved—precious little of it, she thought—and what needed to be thrown out.

Maybe I could ask Astaline to help me make some decisions, she thought. She knew her friend Astaline was as clear-minded a woman as any in town.

Brushing her fingers against each other, she turned and left the attic behind, delivering instructions to her staff as she descended the wide staircase.

Once seated at her writing desk, she composed a brief note.

Millicent House
Tuesday 15 June 1802
Astaline Shipley Hastings
Beechnut House

My dearest friend,
I am in dire need of your assistance. I have just returned from a journey into the dark reaches of my attic, and I must say I am a bit overwhelmed with the task before me. I intend to clear it out.
You know that I would never dispose of a single book, for those are of the greatest importance. Then again, there are no books in the attic, as they all reside on shelves throughout the house.
Hatboxes, though? Letters? Diaries?
I have no need of those things, but am loath to commence such a daunting task alone. Even as I write, Mrs Surratt has set her housemaids to dusting and mopping three floors above me. Perhaps on Friday next, would you be willing to help me? Mrs Surratt, my housekeeper extraordinaire, is above such work, and the housemaids are

far too intimidated by me, although I am sure I have never given them cause to be.

Do I ask too much? Once we have accomplished this task, will you still consider me

Your dear friend,

Rosilla

She posted her note at the same time another was delivered to her. A letter from her sister, Almira Garner Fountain, who had moved away from Martinsville, against the considered and pointedly expressed advice of Rosilla. She read it, considered throwing it out, but then decided to share it with Astaline on the coming Friday. Astaline would appreciate the irony of such phrases as—she looked back at the letter and lingered over the words—*I have had six long years now to regret that I did not listen to you when you begged me not to marry Prattrick.* Rosilla Garner Millicent was not one ever to say *I told you so,* "but really, Almira," she said aloud to the empty room, "I did tell you so."

Fortunately, she finished speaking before one of the maids rolled in the tea trolley.

IT TOOK ROSILLA and Astaline almost no time at all. When the goal was to purge the attic, the instructions were easy. This goes, this goes, this goes. Astaline objected to a few of the items, such as a set of spoons with delicate patterns on their handles. "Are you sure you do not want these, Rosilla?"

At which Rosilla waved an airy hand and said, "Take them, take them. I have no need of any of this." When one of the maids found a stack of thick leather-bound books, Rosilla looked at the name imprinted on the top cover. "Garbage," she declared.

Again, Astaline intervened after she examined the first page. "These may not be regular books, Rosilla, printed ones I mean, but surely you don't want to throw out journals kept by one of your husband's ancestors."

"Garbage, I say. Or you may take them with you. I never did like the old bat. And she wasn't an ancestor. She was only his aunt. She died young."

Then she was not an old bat, Astaline thought, but she kept that opinion to herself.

The housemaids were kept busy indeed trundling box after box down the narrow servants' staircases to the ground floor and out the back entrance to the incinerator behind the house. There had been thunder for the last three days rolling down from the north of the valley, but fortunately there was no rain to interrupt the destruction of the numerous boxes. Astaline was almost afraid to think what might happen when the rain finally did begin to fall on Martinsville. The ground was so parched from months without rain, that when it did begin, she feared the roads would be awash with water that the dry earth could not absorb fast enough.

Already the Metoochie River was swollen. Snowmelt and excess rains far upstream, Astaline supposed.

After the attic was taken care of, as they sat over tall glasses of lemonade, Rosilla showed Astaline the letter from her sister. Together, they commiserated over the folly of Mrs. Prattrick Fountain. When Astaline went to hand the letter back to Rosilla, Rosilla waved it away. "I am purging my house of anything useless. Keep them, share them with Reuben, throw them away—I care not."

So Astaline took them home with her, along with the basket of odds and ends she had saved from Rosilla's purge, and it ended up in her own attic. "I really should not add to all this mess," Astaline told herself before she tucked the letter into one of the trunks and placed the basket on an old bed frame. Before she left the attic, though, she removed the spoons and took them with her. They would look lovely on her embroidered tablecloth for the upcoming dinner.

At the bottom of the attic stairs, she tucked the spoons in her apron pocket and took a moment to look in her bedroom for the hair combs her sister-in-law Lydia had sent her last month from Saint Louis. She set them on the dressing table, for she planned to wear them the next evening when she and Reuben hosted a small dinner party. A very small party. Anything larger would have been in poor taste, considering their recent loss. She pulled herself up. She had done enough crying for the past year.

To think these combs had been made from the horn of a buffalo. Astaline's brother Curtis did so enjoy taking Lydia with him when he traveled on business, and Lydia always found the most amazing souvenirs to send to Astaline and Reuben and the children.

Tomorrow would be the first time since the death of their two eldest daughters that Astaline and Reuben had entertained. Had it really been a full year? Mary Etta and Electa. Astaline ran her hands over the filigreed combs and imagined her daughters, each of them wearing one, perhaps on their wedding days. If they had lived long enough to have a wedding day. To have a beau. To have a life.

She sat on the side of the bed and gave in to her tears. She did miss them so.

2000

DEE OPENED THE hatbox she'd already removed from the stack and held up a faded sunbonnet. "Oh! My grandmother had one just like this."

Sadie chuckled. "I had one of those myself."

"So did I," Rebecca Jo said. "It's probably still around some-where."

"We should look in your attic," Dee said, "once the storm is over." I waited for her to add *Or in your laundry room*, but she didn't. She simply turned the bonnet and inspected it on all sides. "This really does look practical with such a wide front brim. If you have one like it, you might want to start wearing it again." I could tell she was being facetious, but I thought about those sunny gardening days when I could use something more effective than my wide-brimmed straw hat.

Sadie pointed to the back of the sunbonnet. "All that fabric in back is there to shade the nape of your neck from the sun. And this one has done a lot of shading, for sure."

"How can you tell?"

Sadie cupped her hands above her eyebrows, mimicking the wide brim. "The bonnet is a real pale blue, right?" We all nodded. She rotated her hands so the palms faced forward. "Now look at the under-neath side of the brim."

Dee turned the rim up. "Wow! Look at that. It's such a dark blue, it almost seems like a totally different fabric."

"That dark blue," Rebecca Jo said, "is what the entire bonnet looked like to begin with."

"Really?" Dee slipped it on. It enveloped her head. "How could you stand it? It's like wearing blinders."

Sadie motioned her to come closer. "You need to gather all this extra fabric and tie it back in a pretty bow with this drawstring." She held up the narrow band that protruded on either side. "That keeps the bonnet from riding too far forward, and makes it drape nicely at the back of your head. Like this." Once she'd made the necessary adjustments, Dee turned to study herself in the cheval mirror.

"This is a keeper." She looked at me with a question in her eyes.

"Be my guest." I supposed I could always make one for myself if I truly wanted one for gardening. There was probably a pattern floating around here somewhere. In one of the trunks, maybe? "Everything you take out of here is one less thing I have to deal with."

"Keep the museum in mind, though," Maddy warned. "We may need to ask for it back."

July 1863

IRRAIAH SURRATT MARTIN felt exceptionally angry with Tobe. "You cannot mean to take a boy of only ten years into battle," she argued yet again, even though her husband refused to take her objections seriously. "What if he is injured? What if you should run short of rations? What if he …" Her breath caught in her throat, and she straightened her shoulders. She had to face this possibility. "What if he should die, husband? You would have that to live with for the rest of your life."

"I am glad indeed that you seem to assume that I will survive the fighting."

His half-humorous tone irritated her no end. "If you bring about the death of our son," she said with a great deal of heat, "you may wish it had been you instead."

He laughed and put his left arm around her shoulders, but she shook it off and turned away from him. Men always seemed to think they were invincible, but her son—her son.

"I courted you," Tobe said, "because you had more valor in you than any of those other pallid women in this town. My spirited wife." He laid his right hand on her arm, and this time she let it remain. "He will

229

stay safe behind the lines." His voice had lost the tone of amusement. "He will be naught but a drummer boy. You know I would not allow my son to come to any harm."

"How could you stop it if your company is attacked? How could you possibly shield him?"

"With my own body, if necessary," Tobe said. "Morgan is not a babe in arms any more. He deserves a chance to see what we are fighting for."

"He is but ten, and this fight will bring no solutions," Irraiah said, but without any real hope that he would understand her now any more than he had understood her before.

Her aunt, Grace Surratt Hoskins, had been the first person Irraiah had ever known to have questioned the reasons for this war. "There should have been a way," Aunt Grace had said, when it became evident that there would be armed conflict at some point, "for the men to come to an understanding. There should have been a way two centuries ago to avoid such evils to begin with. There should be a way other than bloodshed to end them now, for I fear the end of the conflagration will bring naught but dissension."

Irraiah had wanted to ask her more about these ways that Aunt Grace seemed to think might have been possible, but just then Tobe had walked into the room and Aunt Grace had turned aside and donned her sunbonnet. "I must go," she had said after a sideways look at Tobe. "Arthur will be wanting his noonday meal." Nothing Irraiah could say would change Aunt Grace's mind.

For now, Irraiah picked up her own sunbonnet. "I will walk with you as far as the edge of town," she said, even though she did not want to appear to be in favor of their going. The truth was that she did not want to lose sight of her first-born son as long as she might hold him in her eyes even a little longer.

Young Morgan was more than pleased with his small drum. He had almost driven his mother to distraction with his practicing for the past week, and she had shushed him repeatedly. The quiet had never lasted for long, though, as his enthusiasm for the drum overtook all other thoughts. Now, Irraiah wished for nothing more than to hear his noise all day long, every single day, as long as it would keep him here at her side, keep him safe.

Morgan opened the pouch he had strung about his waist, the pouch she had sewn for his drumsticks when she realized the inevitability of his going. "I must be ready, Ma," he said, his voice still the high piping of a child, "ready for when my drumming is needed."

"Not now. Not here in the house." His father ruffled Morgan's hair, and Morgan shied away from the affectionate touch.

"I am no longer a baby, Father."

"No indeed," Tobe said. "But save your mother's ears and leave off the drumming for now. There will be plenty of notice when your services are needed."

"May I drum as we march out of town, Pa? May I?"

Irraiah could see the pride in her husband's eyes as he agreed to that proposal. She only hoped his pride would be enough to shield the boy from harm.

Morgan threw the strap of his drum over his neck. He settled it on his shoulder and positioned the drum just so.

They joined the train of men and boys. Only a few of them were younger than fifteen, she noted. At ten, Morgan would be the youngest in the group. They all marched bravely down the lane, carrying their weapons lightly, joking with each other. Most of the women, the wives and mothers and sisters and sweethearts, were silent as they accompanied their men. At the bottom of the hill, near the river, the men—and her precious son—turned to their left to join yet another group of would-be soldiers.

"Morgan," Irraiah called as her other, younger children swirled about her skirts.

But it was Tobe who turned aside to pull her into his arms for a brief embrace. "Let the boy be, wife," he whispered. "He is anxious to show he is a man now, and he cannot do that if he is held by his mother like an infant at the breast."

She laid her hands against his chest and pushed herself away, although she did it gently. "You have set my sunbonnet askew, husband," she said, and reached to adjust the wide brim, managing to hide her damp eyes as she did so.

When she looked again, both Tobe and Morgan had merged into the crowd and were lost from her view. But moments later, from up ahead, in front of the throng of soon-to-be soldiers, she heard the pa-rum, pa-rum, pa-rum-tum-tum as her boy Morgan led the men up the valley. Led them to a war his mother feared with all her heart.

2000

DEE KEPT THE sunbonnet on. I couldn't say I blamed her. The attic seemed to need a bunch of people in it before it warmed up enough.

"Realia," Carol said, then repeated it slowly, emphasizing the long A sound of the second syllable. "Re-a-li-a. That's what your sunbonnet is, Dee."

Dee touched the blue rim. "What are you talking about?"

"Realia are objects used to illustrate lessons, usually in classrooms, the way Sadie just taught us about how sunbonnets were made and worn and used."

"This isn't exactly a classroom," Ida pointed out.

"You have to admit," Maddy said, "we're getting a pretty good education up here, though."

I had to agree with her. A lot of this stuff we were finding was just junk, but there was so much that seemed to have a story to tell.

Dee picked up Ida's journal, the Mary Frances journal, and thumbed through it. "This is realia for sure."

"White gloves, Dee," I reminded her.

She set it down immediately. "In her journal, she almost never capitalizes anything except names and the beginning of sentences, but in that letter she wrote—the one about opening it a hundred years after she died—she capitalized practically every other word, didn't she?"

"I doubt capitalizing was very easy," Glaze said, "for somebody who was left-handed and writing backwards with a quill pen."

"Then why did she do it in the letter?"

"I can answer that," Maddy said. "People used to capitalize all the nouns, so that's what she did in the letter, since she knew somebody would be reading it a hundred years down the line."

"But in her own private journal,"—Glaze picked up on Maddy's reasoning—"she probably saw no reason to follow conventional rules."

"I guess that makes sense."

But I didn't think Dee sounded completely convinced.

"Anyway," Rebecca Jo said, "in the letter, she wasn't writing backwards."

Another impressive moan from the wind rattled around the eyebrow windows. I looked up at the beams, almost expecting them to bend under the weight of all the ice that must have built up on our roof. I hoped the old leaded-glass panes in the front windows would withstand the storm. They'd be impossible to replace. "How on earth would somebody go about building a cabin, when there was nothing to start with?"

"What do you mean?"

"Well, just think about it, Charlie. When those people came here, the valley was probably nothing but trees and wild grasses. I wouldn't know where to start. Would you?"

Pat jumped in. "I can see myself doing a lot of cooking over an open campfire while the men cut trees and pulled out stumps and, uh, did all that stuff."

"Like dressing the logs," Rebecca Jo said. "That's what they called it, I think, when they cut the tree trunks into useable planks."

I shivered, and it wasn't just because of the cold wind outside. There was so much that could have gone wrong back then.

Thursday, 26 March 1741

LOUETTA WASHBURN TARKINGTON gazed with deep affection at her husband. She usually tried to moderate her looks when her brother Lewis was present, but when Avery strode into their unfinished cabin that morning, holding out a bouquet of freshly-picked wildflowers, she stepped carefully past her brother's heavily bandaged leg where it stuck out from the table, and wrapped her arms around Avery's waist. "Thank you, my love. They are truly beautiful."

"As are you, my dear Wife."

Louetta scoffed gently. She knew she was not beautiful, but she could not help but be aware that her husband truly meant his words. To cover her embarrassment, she bent her head to sniff the flowers. As she did, a number of wayward strands of her long dark hair escaped from her cap—as they always had a tendency to do—and she lifted her hand to push them away from her face. Before she could reach them, though,

Avery cupped his hand around her cheek and then smoothed the hair back and under the edge of her cap.

Behind her, Lewis coughed meaningfully. He did not hold with such shows of affection, but Avery merely laughed at Louetta's brother. "You will know what it is like to touch a woman's hair once you have a wife of your own, Lewis."

"I will have scant chance of finding a wife so long as I am laid up with this leg of mine."

"With my Louetta tending you, you will not dare to linger an invalid too long or she will dose you so much you will heal just to spite her."

His words were jaunty, but he seemed to look a question at her. She met that look with a steady gaze, aware that her brother was watching her carefully. There was always a danger where an injury was so severe. Lewis was strong, and her poultices were potent, but the wound had not responded as much as she had hoped it would.

Rather than look at her brother, she lowered her head into the flowers once more.

Many flowers grew abundantly at the foot of the trees that edged their clearing. Louetta had often looked out the door and rested her eyes for a moment or two on their vibrant colors.

The clearing itself—other than the large garden—was less gentle on the eyes. A tall stack of wood planks, surrounded by the sawdust and wood chips that must accompany any endeavor such as theirs, was unsightly but nevertheless encouraging, for it meant they would soon have a real roof rather than the somewhat leaky weaving of saplings and pine boughs that currently dripped needles and sap from above her.

Would that her brother's leg might heal, and heal quickly, for she feared the planks were even now beginning to warp. As if sensing her disquiet, Avery wrapped his arms around her.

Her son, Brand, stepped into the room, took one look at his parents entwined together, and scooted hurriedly back out the door. He was of that age where he was easily embarrassed. Louetta tried not to laugh. She would not wound his feelings. Brand was a good boy.

Behind her, she heard a groan, and turned in time to see Lewis reach for the platter of oatcakes. "Let me serve you, Brother." She released her hold on Avery and hurried to help Lewis, noticing even as she did that his face had a greenish pallor that had not been so evident even this morning. "Your leg pains you, does it?"

"A bit, but it grows better." The words held little certainty, though.

"As soon as we have eaten, I will re-apply the poultice." She raised her voice. "Brand! Bring a bucket of fresh water from the well." She had kept a constant rotation of rosemary, tulip tree bark, balm of Gilead, and magnolia applied to his leg where an axe-head had flown off the handle and cut him deeply, but the wound still festered, and she knew not what to do other than lave it with as many healing herbs as she had access to. She had even tried a salve of oak bark, lemon balm, and marigold, a potent concoction that usually was most effective. Usually. Not now, though.

She felt her husband's eyes on her, but she strove not to meet them, for she knew he would read the despondency she could not avoid.

"I thought to begin the roofing today," Avery said.

Lewis grunted. "I cannot manage. Not yet."

"Ah, but I have my strong boy here to help me."

Brand walked into the cabin at that moment and smiled to hear his father's praise.

IT WAS NOT the roof that Brand helped with, however. It was the digging of his uncle's grave near the edge of the forest. The roof stayed uncompleted, and the waiting stack of wood planks gradually warped even further.

Brand strewed his uncle's final resting place with as many spring flowers as he could find. Uncle would not care, but Brand thought they might bring some peace to his mother and father.

Father liked wildflowers.

2000

I READ A few lines ahead in the diary. "Hubbard sure had his problems."

"Tell us," Pat urged.

Maddy leaned forward. "I feel sorry for him already."

"It looks like Ira had even more problems than Hubbard," I said.

Maddy harrumphed. "Serves him right, the murderer."

Carol held up a hand. "That's my great-great and so on grand-daddy you're talking about."

"He's still a murderer."

Friday 15 May 1741. Will I never leave this confounded town? I have packed my saddlebags on three separate occasions, ready to follow the Martins and reclaim my wife, but each time, Ira's fever raged and I could not—dared not—leave him.

Doctor Farrard spent half his waking hours here at first, tending the blood-leaking stump. He finally tied down what was left of Ira's arm and poured boiling water over it, ignoring Ira's shrieks. He seemed then to wash his hands of the matter. 'Either he will live or he will die,' he finally told me. 'I can do no more for him.'

Although the treatment has left broad scars, it seemed to aid in the healing somehow, for the wound scabbed over and gradually began to be less red, although it remained painful, and I have oft been awakened by my brother's loud moans—sometimes even screams—at night.

The town council meetings demand my time, for Ira is still unable to attend them. Star went lame for several weeks, and it was all I could do to see that my lovely patient mare did not injure her leg any further.

Are the heavens set against me? Reverend Atherton tells me to be patient. Ira keeps insisting he will be able to ride soon, but I know he will not. Not until that stump heals. Meanwhile, the spring will soon turn to summer, and I will yet be bound to Brandtburg by my brother's plight and by my own sense of responsibility. I would that I could let it all go.

Yesterday I walked into the forest far from the town, pounded my fists against an innocent tree, and screamed at God, who did not answer me.

"JUNE TWENTY-FOURTH IS his next entry." I removed the white gloves. Even after having read so few entries, I felt a connection to him that almost hurt.

Why are you hurt?

Marmalade jumped onto my lap and licked my chin, so I

scratched her ears.

Thank you.

"I feel so sorry for him," Pat said. "What do you suppose he did?"

She looked at Carol, who raised her shoulders in defeat. "I don't have a clue, except that he and Ira were there in Brandtburg until at least the fall."

"I've always heard moving is stressful," Melissa said, "but for poor Hubbard, it looks like all his stress came from *not* moving."

Marmalade jumped onto Melissa's lap and kneaded Melissa's tummy.

I like to move.

"What about you, Biscuit? Did you have a hard time moving here from Braetonburg?"

I didn't have to think too long. "Not really, Melissa. It's not like I was going"—I lifted Hubbard's diary a few inches—"all that far. It's only five or six miles from Braetonburg to here, so I see my family often. Then, too"—I smiled at her—"you made me feel at home right from the first."

Glaze grunted. "Meeting Bob over that dead body probably helped, too."

I saw a movement on each side of the circle. Carol and Charlie had both whipped their heads up at my sister's comment. "Somebody was murdered on the library steps," I explained. "That was how I met Bob."

I found the dead man.

"After Marmalade found the body," I added when Marmalade meowed.

Thank you.

"You'd have met him soon anyway," Charlie said, "in a town this small."

"I read somewhere that moving can be as stressful as experiencing a death," Maddy said. "I have to admit I didn't feel that way when I moved here. I was too happy to get away from …" She clamped her lips shut. I'd be willing to bet she'd been planning to say that battle-ax of a mother of hers. "… from Atlanta," she finished.

Sadie turned to face Charlie. "You've had some big moves in

your life. Did you feel a lot of disruption?"

"Not really. I don't have a problem with change."

July 1995

CHARLIE COULDN'T BELIEVE it. One moment everything was fine, except for Mom's cancer thing, but she was doing a lot better. Charlie had been home six weeks into her summer vacation, and now, just out of the blue, paramedics were everywhere, loading Dad onto a stretcher, and somebody was bundling Mom into the ambulance.

"I'll follow," Charlie told her dad, but he didn't say anything.

"You won't be able to keep up with us," the EMT told her. He gave her the name of the hospital, but she only half heard him.

"Take good care of him," she begged.

As they closed the back door of the ambulance, Charlie called, "I love you, Dad!"

She broke every speed limit, keeping as close behind the ambulance as she could, but then she had to circle through the hospital's packed parking lot. In her frustration, she pulled up over a curb, parked on the grass, and ran for the emergency room.

"They took him into surgery," Mom said.

After less than an hour, a doctor approached them. Charlie didn't like the look in his eyes.

AFTER THE FUNERAL was over and the hefty hospital parking ticket was paid, Charlie told her mom she wasn't going to return to college.

"Nonsense," Mom said. "You can't put your life on hold. You still have two more years of schooling. And I'll be fine."

Charlie wasn't too sure about that. Dad's death seemed to have drained Mom.

"I'm not saying it'll be easy," Mom said, "but you and I are both strong Ellis women. We'll keep on doing what we need to do."

That evening, Charlie called Tricia. Her roommate had such a practical approach to life. Charlie felt like she needed Tricia's good sense. But the call went to voicemail and Tricia didn't call her back.

Charlie cried a lot and yelled a lot and swore a blue streak and hugged herself and her teddy bears and her mom a whole lot. But then she gradually pulled herself together.

Mom was right. They were Ellis women, and Dad wouldn't have wanted her to give up her dreams just because he couldn't be here anymore to listen to her, to take her fishing, to see her graduate, to walk her down the aisle if and when she ever got married—but that was the last thing on her mind right now.

She still had a lot of sad times, but nothing stopped an Ellis woman. That was for sure.

1998

HUBBARD MARTIN KNEW he was going to be in trouble if he didn't get back to the house on time. Clara would throw a hissy fit if they were late to Wallace's funeral. He checked his watch again, patted the envelope in his jacket pocket, and peered down the path.

They always met right here. Always at this time. Every month.

He was getting sick of it, but didn't know how he could get out of it. It would kill Clara to find out.

Finally, and not a moment too soon, she came up the path, looking like nothing could possibly bother her. All she did was hold out her hand. The way she had each month for the past year. All he did was hand her the envelope. The way he had each month for the past year.

CLARA SPENT EXTRA time dressing for Wallace Masters' funeral. As the wife of the town chairman, she would be very much in evidence. Everyone would be there. She held up the two coat hangers one at a time and eyed herself critically in the full-length mirror. The black polyester with the plaited leather belt, or the black knit with the drawstring waist? The knit, she decided. When she tried it on, though, it was considerably tighter than it had been just a month or two ago. The dry cleaner must have shrunk it. She'd have to talk to those people, but there wasn't time today.

What she really needed to do was to buy some new dresses, but for the last year Hubbard had been singularly adamant about not spending anything extra. Clara did wonder if maybe business wasn't quite as good as it had been, but Hubbard didn't like to talk about business, and she preferred to leave all the financial concerns to him. He'd been a good provider. Maybe not the first couple of years right after they were married, but ever since then—except for the past year—she hadn't had anything to complain about.

And where was Hubbard anyway? He needed to get ready or they'd be late.

She wriggled into the other dress, cinched the belt—not too tightly. No reason not to enjoy the funeral food.

This funeral was going to be something new for the town. As much as she and Hubbard had objected at the last town meeting, Marvin Axelrod, the undertaker, had insisted that from now on he would not embalm any bodies. No, he was bound and determined to start something called a green cemetery just above the old town graveyard. Burying people in amongst the roots of the trees? Or letting wildflowers grow on the graves? Disgusting, that's what it was.

Clara still could not understand why the rest of the Council had voted to allow it. Especially when she had been against it. And Hubbard, too. His had been the only opposing vote. It was that thought, that he had voted the way she wanted him to, that kept her from berating him when he came dashing into the house just a few minutes later.

THE FUNERAL ITSELF was sweet enough, Clara supposed. Everybody had something nice to say about Wallace. Of course they had. He'd lived here forever, he and his wife Sadie, so people had to say nice things.

At the reception afterwards at Sadie's house, Clara took over the food management, naturally, telling everyone where everything went. Some people had no sense when it came to arranging dishes.

There was one huge vase, rather an ungainly thing in a deep indigo color, that was filled with yellow flowers. Just like everything else in Sadie's house—yellow, yellow, yellow. Clara didn't know how Sadie could stand it. She was surprised the vase wasn't yellow as well. The flowers weren't displayed right. Some of them drooped too much. She pulled out several of them and stuck them back in where they ought to be. Upright, not hanging over the rim like they were tired out.

"I see you've corrected my display."

Clara turned to see Margaret Casperson, who had a pained expression on her face. Maybe she had indigestion. "You're welcome," Clara told her. "I always did have a good eye for such things."

Margaret grimaced again. "That vase is one I commissioned from Connie."

Clara tried to place who Connie was, but came up blank.

"Connie Cartwright," Margaret said, "the glass-blower who moved to town recently? I'm sorry I didn't order it in yellow so I could give it to Sadie."

There didn't seem to be a lot to say to that, but Clara said something anyway. "The last thing that woman needs is more yellow in this house."

Over Margaret's shoulder, Clara saw Bob Sheffield, the town cop, and that wife of his walk in the front door. She couldn't understand any woman who refused to change her last name when she got married. It was the way things were done. Ought to be done. Clara was proud of being a Martin. She adjusted a few more blossoms and smiled tightly at several women who stood by the table, food offerings in hand.

"Put them over there," Clara directed. "And desserts go at the other end. When you're ready, the line forms"—she pointed—"there, where the plates are."

The women shuffled into the places she'd indicted. Behind her, she heard Biscuit say, "Shall we go see if we can find the plates, Melissa?"

Clara whipped around. "Right down that way, Biscuit darling. On the left."

Biscuit said thank you, but Clara had already stopped listening. That woman was entirely too full of herself. Just like Clara's sister. Maybe Clara should see that Hubbard formed a board to oversee the library. Yes, there was no reason Clara couldn't head up another committee. She'd talk to him about it soon. For now, she had a funeral meal to manage.

2000

"HERE," SAID IDA. "Let's see what Mary Frances has to say."

Monday, 25 May 1741

My father died before dawn this morning. He had been almost out of his head with fever during my supposed wedding yesterday morn, which is why my mother did not attend my wedding. I was just as happy not to have her there. After the ceremony, Reverend Russell asked for our family Bible so he might record the marriage, but it was within my mother's wagon and she would not hand it out. I have not written here for some time as we have been pushing to put as many miles between ourselves and the Brandts as we can, and I have consequently felt exhausted near the end of each day. All hope of running away has gone past me. I have feared for the past week that I might be with child—Hubbard's child—for my courses, usually so regular, always with the dark of the moon, did not come this time.

"Dark of the moon?" Dee said. "What's that about?"

Naturally, it was Maddy who answered her. "Before the Industrial Revolution, women always used to have their periods at the same time. All the women in the community. The Red Tent, you know?"

Dee didn't know, so Maddy had to explain all that first.

"It was always during the few days around the new moon, but now nobody holds to that schedule."

"Why not?"

"Electric lights, changes in the way women relate to each other, even what we eat. There are a kazillion different reasons. Life is just different now."

Ida looked at the diary. "That's for sure."

I have felt sickly each morning so that I must rise early and empty my stomach behind a tree. I cannot risk the life of my unborn child—of Hubbard's child—by leaving this camp to search for my husband.

Yesterday morning Charlotte Ellis, the biggest busybody I have ever known, came upon me in the woods. The suspicion in her

242

eyes was terrible to behold.

"See," Ida said. "I told you so."
Dee made a quelling motion. "Shush. Keep going."

Two evenings ago my father, in between bouts of delirium, called Homer Martin to him when we stopped for the evening meal and begged him—I heard them talking in low voices within the wagon—to take me for his wife. 'She mourns her dead friend and her lost home constantly,' my father said. 'She needs a babe in her arms to comfort her.' I would have cried out then to prevent their negotiations, but I felt my mother beside me, and she laid a firm hand on my arm to keep me quiet. Leaning close to my ear, she whispered, 'It is for the best, child.' Did she suspect, I wondered? Did she know I carry a babe within me? I am certain she cannot be aware of my marriage to Hubbard, for she would not condone a marriage—this marriage to Homer Martin—that could not be a true marriage. And would indeed be a mortal sin.

My father paused then and I heard a moan, which he tried to stifle. There are ugly red streaks rising from the leg wound and a constant smell of rot. It is almost more than I can bear, but I have tried to help my mother with the care of him, even as his foot turns black.

"Eww, yuck," Dee said. "That's gangrene."
"Not surprising," Carol said, "with a deep wound like that."

Homer Martin was singularly silent after my father's request. 'She is comely enough,' he finally admitted. Comely enough? Should I have been complimented? I hoped that he would refuse to supplant Myra Sue, his dead wife—my hand closes uncomfortably on the quill as I write those words, for I miss my friend more now than ever—but my hopes were dashed when he said, 'Tomorrow morning, then. Reverend Anders can speak the words after the Sunday service.'

I heard the sound of them clasping their hands as my father sold me away to banish my tears from his presence. My mother tried to comfort me, but I backed away from her arms, my heart too broken for tears. How could I marry Homer Martin when I was already married? It would doom my soul. But how could I tell anyone? How could I face my father's anger?

'I cannot marry him,' I told my mother.

'You must,' she replied, with that surety she exudes when we have no recourse. As she said it, her eyes dropped to my waist, as if she were telling me she knew, although she never said a word about her suspicions—just that one glance, yet I felt certain she suspected. And so on Sunday morning I was married, with tears streaming down my face. As soon as Mister Martin made his mark and I signed my name, I knew that I was damned forever, for no woman can be wed to two men at the same time. I have no doubt that my immortal soul is lost, but that knowledge pales in the face of my deepest regret—that I will never see my blessed husband, my true husband, again.

Ida lowered the book to her lap.

"Holy crap," Pat said. "Mary Frances Martin was a bigamist."

Why is she a big mist?

"That would be Mary Frances. Garner. Brandt. Martin." Dee stressed each surname and squiggled her fingers in air quotes when she said *Martin*.

Why?

"And Homer Martin's son wasn't Homer Martin's son." Ida raised one dark expressive eyebrow.

Why not?

"All these generations of son after son inheriting the title of Town Council Chairman, and it's all been based on a lie," I said, stroking Marmalade, who seemed agitated. "Did Homer and Mary Frances ever have any other children?" Bob would have been able to answer that question in a heartbeat—he was an expert on Martinsville history—but I was a little shaky on the details.

You are not shaky. You are sitting still.

"No," Sadie said. "Just the one boy. John Martin took over as town leader after his father—that is, after Homer Martin—died in 1768. He was only in his early twenties, but I suppose respect for the Martin name carried the day."

"John Martin, though, was actually Hubbard Brandt's son," Dee mused. "Do you suppose Homer knew—or suspected?"

Ida let out a snort. "I doubt he was that smart. She couldn't have been more than a couple of weeks along when he married her."

"So," Glaze said, "this means all the hoopla about how important Homer Martin's line has been all these years is nothing but a crock of baloney."

I would rather have fish.

I couldn't resist. "I wonder what Clara's going to say when she finds out."

"Clara," Carol said, smiling down at Marmalade. "I think Pat mentioned her name before, but I'm not clear as to who she is."

I intended to answer gently, but Ida beat me to the punch. "She's the self-proclaimed First Lady of Martinsville—or she was as long as Hubbard was the council chair." She gave a wicked grin. "Ironic, isn't it? Hubbard Martin is named after his Brandt ancestor."

Carol nodded in thought. "I wonder why the name persisted through all these years. It must be at least … nine … ten generations since the town was founded."

Sadie raised her hand, like a student who knows the answer to a math question. "It's a tradition. The second son in every second or third generation of Homer's line—well, I guess it would be in Mary Frances Garner Brandt's line—is always named Hubbard."

"But I thought it was the oldest son who became the chair," I said.

"I asked the same thing," Melissa said. "We were talking, Carol and Pat and Dave and I, at *Azalea House* before the power went out yesterday morning. Dave told us that this Hubbard *is* the second son. He had an older brother, Cornelius, who died a long time ago."

"That's sad," I said.

"Yeah." There was something in Melissa's voice that warned me. "Dave said he died when he fell out of a tree,"—she strung out that last word so it sounded like it had five or six e's on the end of it—"that he and Hubbard just happened to be climbing at the time."

Pat spoke into the shocked silence. "I know what you're thinking, and I'll bet you're right. Dave thinks Hubbard probably pushed his brother."

"Murdered him, you mean," Maddy said.

I had to object. "This is all just conjecture."

Maddy opened her mouth to answer me, but Rebecca Jo beat her to it. "I heard those rumors at the time, but nobody could ever prove anything. There weren't any other people around when it happened." She rubbed her upper lip, pretty much the same motion Bob uses when he strokes his mustache. "If it's true, then I'd say what happened to him recently just about serves him right."

"Well," I said, "it's for sure he can't manage the council job anymore, and the others haven't met yet to elect a new chair." I paused, feeling a delicious glow. We could change history here. A major revolution. "They're going to have a hard time choosing someone anyway. Clara and Hubbard's son isn't old enough," I elucidated for Carol. "Each time before, the new town chairman has succeeded an elderly father. It's always been quite orderly. Almost preordained."

"Not any more," Dee said with a lift of her upper lip.

"What do you want to bet," Rebecca Jo said, "that Clara's already started campaigning to be named chair in Hubbard's place?"

"Over my dead body," Ida said.

I seconded that.

I do not want your body to be dead.

Ida picked up the book. "There's more to this entry."

That evening, all the colors of the world drained away as night approached, reflecting my despair. There is no joy left. Why has Hubbard not come to me?

Last night I lay with Homer Martin, now my husband in the eyes of all the people around us, with my fists clenched and my jaw tight. He did not even comment on my tears afterwards. He turned from me and fell into a stupor. The fumes of his breath and his constant snoring kept me awake, so my eyes were bleary with fatigue when, some time before dawn, I heard my mother's anguished scream. Mister Martin did not wake when I left my cold marriage bed as quickly as I could and found my father dead in my mother's arms.

We buried him beside the trail and covered the grave with a mound of rocks to keep wolves or bears or painters from digging there. I could not leave my heart with my father, for I had already left it three weeks ago in Brandtburg. I would not choose to leave any part of my heart with my father at any rate, for is he not the one who banished me to this loveless and sinful marriage? Is he not the one who has been the cause of my damnation?

"That answers your question, Dee," Ida said. "It sounds like Homer Martin was so drunk on his own wedding night, he probably never realized his new wife wasn't as *pure* as he thought she was." The scorn in her voice when she said the word *pure* was positively vitriolic. "I can't believe how awful that man must have been."

We all nodded. "Especially when you compare him to how sweet Hubbard sounds," Maddy said.

"You know," Esther said, "I'm not sure we can trust her opinion. Sometimes the one who got away—or who just isn't there—seems perfect in retrospect, but Mary Frances never actually lived with Hubbard, did she?"

I thought I could tell where she was headed with this, but I couldn't find my voice to ask anything because I was still trying to process the fact that Esther had spoken up. She'd been so quiet up until now, except for when she found the fancy hat with the letter about the Titanic.

"They never got into arguments about whether to squeeze the toothpaste tube at the bottom or in the middle," she went on.

"I don't think they had toothpaste back then," Maddy said.

"You know what I mean. All the information we have about Hubbard Brandt is from the diary of a newlywed before any disillusionment could have set in."

I looked at Glaze, who seemed to be studying Tom's grandmother, and I could almost hear the wheels turning ...

What wheels?

... as she wondered if there had been real problems in Esther's marriage. Of course, everybody who's married gets into tiffs now and then, and it *does* take a while to get used to each other's idiosyncrasies. "I think I know what you mean, Esther," I said. "Because Hubbard wasn't there, and because they'd had only that one night together, all her memories of him must have seemed perfect."

"Compared to Homer Martin," Maddy grumped, "anybody would look perfect."

"That poor woman." Rebecca Jo clasped her hands in front of her chin. "I can hardly imagine how horrible it would be to be forced to marry someone you not only didn't like, but didn't respect either. And then to lose her father on top of that."

"Her father's the one who gave her away to Homer," Dee said with some heat.

"But he didn't know," Pat said. "I'm sure he thought he was helping her."

Ida harrumphed. "Some help that was. He really left the poor girl up a gum stump."

What does that mean?

"Up a gum stump," Carol said. "I've always thought that was a fascinating phrase."

"What's it mean?" asked Amanda.

"It came about when the early settlers were trying to forge a way through the wilderness. Sometimes their wagons got hung up on a stump. If it was any other tree, the stumps were fairly easy to dig out—well not easy exactly, but the men could eventually extricate the wagon. But if they got hung up on a stump from a gum tree, they were stuck for a good long time because those suckers were almost impossible to wrest from the ground."

"Up a gum stump indeed," Rebecca Jo said.

Dee waved her hands and lowered her voice. "Abracadabra! Just like that, there's no more Martin line."

"Maybe not through sons," Ida said, fingering the edges of the diary pages. "But Mary Frances must have had a daughter with Homer, because one of my ancestors was Louise Martin. Where else could she have gotten that last name if not from Homer?"

"There might be a way," Rebecca Jo said. "Remember Homer's

brother Silas? Did he have any children? I wonder whatever happened to him? There isn't much about him in any of the town history."

"That's not so surprising." Sadie turned to the card table and continued her earlier task of stacking letters into piles. She and I had both been using the same method, matching the handwriting as best we could. The tallest pile featured a bold hand with heavy strokes of the quill. In another stack, the addresses were written in a light, fanciful hand. "It's usually the oldest son who gets written about," Sadie continued, "often because they're the ones who inherit the land or follow in the father's business."

Maddy scoffed. "From what we've read so far, it sounds like Homer Martin, our revered founder, was nothing but an illiterate drunk."

"Drunk, I'll agree with," Pat said, "but where do you get the illiterate part?"

"Remember in the diary," Maddy pointed with her chin toward the book that lay in Ida's lap, "where it said Mary Frances signed her name to the marriage document, and Homer 'made his mark'? That means he couldn't write. Not even his name."

"Leave it to a writer," Glaze said, "to pick that up."

Ida stretched her arms above her head. "I need a break," she said. "Let's take an hour or so to investigate more of the trunks."

What could we say? Nobody else could decipher the backwards writing, at least not without a lot of effort. She hadn't read enough to be tired, so maybe it was the emotional factor that was limiting her. I had to admit I was curious about all the other treasures that must still be surrounding us.

"Your eyes must be sore," Sadie said.

Ida took a deep breath. "It's not my eyes that are hurting. It's my heart."

I do not want your heart to hurt.

Marmalade jumped off my lap and onto Ida's, and we all laughed. It was almost like she was comforting Ida, but I felt like I could use a little comfort, too. "I expected the journal to be personal—that's what journals are supposed to be—but I didn't expect it to be quite so gut-wrenching."

"Life was harder in many ways back then," Carol said, "so I'm not surprised by the medical problems or the status of women. But

I've read a number of old journals that were nothing much more than a weather report and a list of chores accomplished and funerals attended. This one goes so much deeper."

Glaze rested her hand on my shoulder. "Those library diaries, all the stuff about Faith's death and Charity taking little Hope? I think they sort of prepared me for this sort of thing."

"I tried keeping a journal once," Ida said, "but like Carol said, it turned out to be mostly comments on the weather or on whatever problems we were having with the grocery suppliers, so I finally gave up. Nobody in the future would be interested in reading all that garbage."

I saw a shadow pass across her face, pulling her mouth down. Ida and Ralph had no children. I wondered if she was thinking that nobody would read her words at all.

"One of the things I like about all this"—I swept my arm in a wide circle—"is that I can feel a connection to these people even though I'm not really connected to them in any direct way."

Dee took a step backwards and held up her hands, palms forward. "Too much philosophy for me! I'm going to find something fascinating." She patted one of the trunks, opened the lid, and reached inside.

From off to my left, I heard Maddy let out a long *hmmmm* sound. She watched Dee pull out an elongated wooden box, but I had the feeling Maddy's thoughts were elsewhere.

She is excited about something.

"You know what I could do?" Maddy's voice held a note of delicious anticipation. We all swiveled toward her, as if her words had drawn us in. "I could put all this together—the diaries and letters and such—into a book of Martinsville history, a *real* town history. I bet there's loads more material in here that we haven't unearthed yet."

"It's sort of like digging up bodies," Carol said, and I saw Glaze flinch. Of course, Carol didn't know what had gone on here in Martinsville in recent years.

No more dead bodies, please.

Pat ignored Carol. "I like that idea, Maddy. You know how history is so often written about all the wars—"

"And it's always written—and highly edited—by the winners," Carol said, "so we seldom get the true story."

"But there aren't any wars up here." Pat spread both her arms wide.

I thought about the secret room and pointed toward the back wall. "Just the repercussions of the wars. They must have affected all these women deeply."

"And men," Carol said.

19 September 1863
Chickamauga, Tennessee

TOBE MARTIN HAD seldom in his life felt so frightened, and had never before felt so helpless as now. He bent over the body of his son and tried to shield the boy from the advancing troops. Or perhaps they were retreating. He no longer had any sense of the flow of the battle. Had lost track of where his compatriots were. Marveled fuzzily that young Morgan had managed to keep hold of one of his drumsticks, although the drum itself was long gone. Was only vaguely aware of a pair of boots stopping within his range of sight.

"That your son?"

It took him a moment to register the question.

"Yes. He—" His words were blocked out by the zing of a bullet that whizzed past his ear. He shook his head, the way a horse might do when bothered by a deerfly. "He is but ten."

Why, he thought, in the middle of a battle, am I answering an enemy soldier?

"My son's age," the man said, shouting over the noise of the battle that raged around them. "Pick him up."

The soldier latched onto Tobe's arm and pulled him along, trying to step over the bodies—but sometimes having to step on them. They wove between companies.

What was the magic, Tobe wondered, that kept the three of them from running into more bullets? There was no way to explain the sense of calm he felt, even in the midst of all this chaos.

They reached the dubious shelter of a small copse of beech trees, and the soldier beckoned to Tobe to lay down his burden. "The boy may not be safe here," the man said, "but you can stay with him at least until he dies."

"Why …" Tobe could not form the words. He bit the inside of his cheek and tasted blood. "Why?"

"I have a boy that same age. He was drummer boy to our company."

That one word registered finally. "Was?"

"He refused to stay back in camp."

Tobe nodded drearily. "My boy, too." He did have the presence of mind to realize that the outcome might have been the same even if young Morgan had remained by the campfire. Only then Tobe would not have been with the boy. Was it better this way?

"I wish," the man said, "that someone had let me stay with my son as his life blood drained out of him, but I was carried away from him by the press of bodies. His mother will never forgive me."

Tobe thought of Irraiah, his wife, and of what she would say to him if he should return without their boy. He rose and reached out toward this unknown benefactor. Just as they clasped hands, Tobe felt a bullet tear through his shoulder. The man before him spun around, splaying an arc of blood.

When Tobe regained his sight and his breath, the battle had moved away from them. He found himself sprawled across Morgan's twitching legs. The other soldier lay wide-eyed, staring unseeing at the beechnut leaves above them.

2000

"AND MEN," I ADMITTED. "But what we have here"—I looked around the wide expanse of the attic—"is mostly what women put here, what women left behind."

"That's what I mean," Pat said. "If Maddy writes *this* story, just think of the new perspective it'll put on the town history."

Dee interrupted her. "Look what I found." She held up the box, longer than it was tall. "It has rope hinges, but they look like they're about ready to fall apart."

"I'm not surprised," Carol said. "Rope doesn't usually last, although it would be safer up here in this dry attic than it would have been if you'd had a basement."

"You're right," I said. "There *is* an old root cellar under this house, and the baskets in it were pretty well rotted through when Bob and I investigated it."

"Any dead bodies down there?" Maddy sounded way too hopeful.

"No," I said. "Only in the yard."

Carol laughed, obviously not believing me. "I'll fill you in later," I told her.

"You mean there really was a body buried in your yard?"

"Several. And Glaze dowsed for them."

"It's amazing what people leave behind them when they move." Rebecca Jo sounded almost as dry as Ida.

12 May 1741

THE THIRD TIME a floorboard broke on the second Endicott wagon, the one piled with the belongings of Worthy's four useless brothers, Worthy drew the line. While three of his four brothers argued about how to get the wagon repaired—Sayrle, the next in age to Worthy, had disappeared somewhere, as he was wont to do whenever real work appeared on the horizon—Worthy waded in amongst the wagon's contents and began heaving articles out onto the verdant weeds at the side of the trail.

"You cannot do that," Daniel complained as his chess set joined the growing heap, but after Worthy backhanded him, he kept his whining to himself. Granted, he hardly ever—well, never—played the game, but he had heard it was a game that required a lot of thought, and it never hurt to have people assume you toted a chess board around because you were quick-witted.

His rock collection was the next to go, and he did feel a pang of real hurt over that when Worthy shoved all six boxes of them over the back tailgate. He had planned to use good Vermont rocks for the foundation of his chimney when they reached wherever they were going. He doubted he'd find anything that durable no matter which colony they ended up in.

Joel, the third son, a year younger than Sayrle, learned fast, so he held his council when his stocks of whittled flowers were sent flying, both boxes landing with a crash and scattering the contents far and wide. He had planned to entice young women—any he could find along the way, although he had not found any as yet—with gifts of the tiny wooden birds or blossoms. It never hurt to soften the females up a bit so he could—he hoped—talk them into walking out with him. It had not worked so far, as the young women he had seen on their journey thus far had turned up their noses at him, but Joel had high hopes. He had started whittling an extra-special bird for Mary Frances Garner. She was better than any girl he had seen along the trail, and she was right here almost under his very nose. Now he would have to begin all over again. At least Worthy had left him his extra knives.

He objected under his breath when Worthy heaved out all seven of his fishing poles. Worthy must have seen his mouth working, though, because he told Joel, "Any idiot can fashion a new fishing pole whenever he needs one."

Sanborn, the youngest of the Endicott brothers, had hardly brought anything at all with him—just a few clothes, his bedroll, and his weapons—certainly nothing heavy or bulky enough to draw Worthy's attention, but he kept an eye on everything that was thrown out and quietly gloated at the losses of his brothers. "Sayrle should have been here to help us," he said. "Too bad his books"—he invested that word with a good deal of scorn—"is gonna get left behind." He watched the box of volumes, not knowing or caring that those books would have been treasured by any number of the other travelers, if only they had known what the box contained. Of all the boxes dumped off by Worthy that day, the book box was the only one that did not break open on impact. It bounced off one of the other crates and landed upside down on a dense patch of summer grasses near a thicket of green bushes.

By the time the injured wagon was repaired, the Endicotts were well behind the last stragglers, and they pulled into camp that night tired, disgruntled, hungry, and angry with each other, only to find that Sayrle, the second-born of the five brothers, had bagged a deer and was seated, eating, with the other families.

Sanborn strolled past Sayrle and said, just loud enough for the others gathered around that particular fire to hear, "We had to lighten the load, so those books you stole from the schoolmaster is all gone, big brother." When Sayrle's face went white with anger, all his brothers beamed.

2000

"WHEN WERE ADENOIDS discovered?" There was a moment of silence as all the women absorbed what must have sounded to them like an inane question.

"I have no clue," Maddy told me, "and I'm not sure it would even be worth finding out."

She looked at Carol, who spread her hands. "Why do you need to know?"

"All that talk about Elizabeth Hoskins made me think about Lyle." Heck, I was going to have to explain at least some of this to Carol. "He was Elizabeth's son. And a fairly unsavory character."

Easton let out a snort. "You think?"

She had a right to be derisive, I thought. "He tried to kill Easton," I said in an aside, and heard Carol draw in her breath. "He had one of those whiny adenoidal voices, which is why I wondered about adenoids."

"You're right," Glaze said. "He always sounded downright irritating. I sure wouldn't have wanted to hang out with him."

"He was the one who got the dear-John note from Sheila somebody-or-other, wasn't he?"

What is a deer jonnote?

"That's right, Carol." Rebecca Jo thought for a moment. "I'll be your buddy, I'll be your pal, but I don't want to be your gal."

"You remembered it?" Pat sounded as surprised as I felt.

"Of course," Rebecca Jo said. "Such fine poetry is hard to forget."

Even Easton caught the sarcasm.

"If he was such an awful person," Maddy said, "why would Sheila have agreed to be his pal?"

"Probably it was the only word she could think of that rhymed with gal." Ida turned a thumbs down on the conversation. "It doesn't matter when people found out about adenoids. That kind of voice has probably been around as long as people have been breathing."

"Let's get back to Dee's box," Rebecca Jo said. "No sense wallowing in bad memories. Or questions we can't answer."

"It's about time," Dee said, but she didn't sound as ticked off as her words indicated. She turned the box over, eliciting a clunk from inside it, and inspected the bottom of it.

"Careful," Maddy warned. "Whatever it is might be breakable."

"If so, it's too late," Dee said. "It says Brand Tarkington here on the bottom of the box, so this must belong to you, Melissa."

"What's in it?"

"How would I know?"

"Whatever it is," Melissa said, "I wonder why it ended up here and not at, say, my parents' house."

"The Tarkingtons were here in Martinsville early on," Sadie said. "And usually it was the daughters who saved the family heirlooms."

"Or the family junk," Maddy noted.

"Or junk," Sadie agreed. "Most of those daughters would have married and changed their last names, but they were still"—she nodded to Melissa—"Tarkingtons. You're probably related to half the other families in town one way or another."

"Oh dear. That sounds ominous."

"Sadie's right," Rebecca Jo said. She smiled at me. "Did you know that your husband is related to Sadie?"

"Really? He's never mentioned it."

"He may not know. It's a distant connection—through my husband," she added in an aside to Carol.

"Even so, I'm sure he'll be delighted to find out." I grinned at Sadie. "You might be my other mother-in-law twelve times removed."

She is not removed. She is right here.

Carol must have been amused by my silly comment, because she grinned. "Yes, she is."

She was smiling at me, not at you, Widelap.

"I don't know the dates, and I'm not even sure of exactly which generations were involved," Rebecca Jo said, "but somewhere back along the line, a woman named Lydia Hastings married a Sheffield. I think his name started with a C. Was it Carson? Carleton? No. Curtis? Yes. Curtis Sheffield." She looked over at Carol. "Bob's my son, in case you didn't know. Our last name is Sheffield."

Carol laughed. "Last names? I'm still struggling to remember all their first names. I'll remember Reebok, of course. Playing in the snow together sort of cements a relationship. And he's a Garner. Fits right into my mental map of the original families. But seeing the rest of the men only at mealtimes makes it a little difficult. Father John's easy to remember because of the backwards collar. He's your brother, isn't he Maddy?"

Maddy nodded.

"So he's an Ames. And there's that other minister, the one who's going to marry Tom and Glaze."

"Henry Pursey," I said.

"Yeah. Henry. I just think of him as the minister."

"Maybe we should wear name tags," Rebecca Jo said. "Anyway, Lydia Sheffield's grandmother—or great-grandmother?—was Edna Russell."

"And Sadie was born a Russell," I added.

"Edna Russell," Carol said, nodding. "She was one of the original party. Sixteen, I think, when they left Brandtburg."

"You amaze me," Pat said. "How can you ever remember all those details?"

"If you devote your life to something," Carol said, "you remember a lot."

1750

EDNA RUSSELL HASTINGS was terrified. She knew she was going to die. Charles was no help whatsoever. As soon as her first pangs manifested and she doubled over at the sudden pain, he had disappeared. Her mother-in-law came bustling into the house several moments—an eternity—later. "Charles said your time was come," she said, and set about gathering the necessary materials, a soft blanket to wrap the babe in, the tiny warm cap Edna herself had knitted, plenty of cloths for the cleaning up. She refilled the kettle and swung the cranc over the fire, clucking all the while about the person—unnamed—who had let the kettle run dry. Edna could not be bothered to feel shame at that oversight. She had enough to worry about otherwise.

Edna had seen children being born. A messy business. It wasn't the mess, though, that bothered her. It was the thought of the babies born dead—her own mother had lost five after Edna was born, three in Brandtburg and two on the trail. Even more so, it was the thought of the women who had died a-birthing.

She felt her stomach wrench, as if the babe would claw its way through her very flesh, and she knew she would not care to die. She and Charles had longed for this babe for the two years they had been married. Now, she was not so sure.

Babies disrupted everything. She had seen it often enough. The women who could barely get their chores completed because of a babe who was sickly. Women who were constantly at the beck and call of a fractious child who could not seem to eat enough at each feeding. Women who spent their mornings bleary-eyed from lack of sleep.

Edna had dedicated her life to her needlework. If this babe should keep her from her sewing, how could she endure that? All the patterns she had developed over her years of plying a needle. She prayed the babe would be a girl to whom she could pass on these skills.

And how would Charles react when the screaming of the baby kept him awake at night?

How did she ever get herself into this situation?

How could she ever keep from conceiving again? The pain was more than she could bear.

She doubled over again, just as her mother came through the door. "Charles said you were—land's sakes, child? Why are you carrying on like this?" She wrapped her ample arms around Edna and tut-tutted, coaxing Edna through sheer force of will into walking with her. Walking, walking, walking. Around and around the room until Edna was like to collapse.

And still, the babe would not come.

Edna was only partly aware when her mother whispered to Mother Hastings to fetch Louetta Tarkington Martin.

The tea Mistress Martin forced her to drink was bitter. Too hot. Too strong. Too …

But it was effective. Little Alonzo Hastings appeared like a spatter of bacon grease popping out of a frying pan.

One look, one suckle, and Edna Hastings cared not that this was a boy. There would always be time for a second child, a girl.

1750

MELISSA STRETCHED HER hands over her head and yawned mightily. "My parents never talked much about Tarkington family history. I can tell I'm going to have to read your book, Maddy. When you get it written. You'd better get busy on it."

"I'll need lots of help with the research. Anybody want to volunteer?"

"Count me in," I said, as all the women echoed me.

Everybody except Easton. "It seems like an awful lot of work," she said. "And we'd have to spend a lot of time up here, wouldn't we?"

"I have an attic in my house," Rebecca Jo said, "and there's no telling what's up there. I haven't looked at it in ages, but I know there are at least a couple of old trunks."

"More letters," Easton groaned.

"It'll be exciting," Maddy said, "especially if we can piece together some of the missing bits."

"Like Silas Martin and his story," Ida said. "I'll get Ralph to bring down some of the things up in our attic, and we can have the next session in my living room." The wind rattled around under the wide eaves, moaning like a woman in labor. "After the storm is over," she added.

"Like anybody can tell when that will be," Easton said.

"You know what, Easton?" Sadie sounded gentle, but I could see a certain amount of steel in her eyes, a glint of something indomitable. "You need your own project up here." She scanned the piles we hadn't even touched yet. "How about that trunk under the stack of boxes over there?"

I would have liked to send Easton to the far end of the enormous space, but Sadie had directed her to the trunk where we'd piled the remaining dozen or so hatboxes—the ones we still hadn't gotten to.

Easton groaned. "The whole thing?"

"Yep," said Sadie. "It's all yours. You can share your discoveries with us if you want, or keep them secret. Whatever you choose."

She lowered her voice. "If you want, you can even pick one of those hatboxes."

Sadie sure did know how to work around Easton. It looked to me like Easton didn't want to get caught up in our excitement, but now that she had a stash of her own, her eyes began to glow.

"Here, Melissa." Dee handed her the long wooden box. "The honor of opening the Tarkington Treasure is yours."

Melissa's grinned mightily. She ran her hands over the box. "It's almost more fun to imagine what might be in it than it might be to actually *see* what's there. Maybe it really is a treasure." She sounded like Glaze.

"Quit stalling," Pat said. "This is worse than Christmas morning."

Melissa gave the box a gentle shake. Something went *clunk* again.

"It could be toy soldiers made of lead," Sadie said. "My brother had a set of those, and they were quite heavy."

"It could be some sort of carved animal," Dee suggested, "or a special rock, like a geode or something."

"Maybe a huge marble?" Amanda surprised us all when she spoke—she'd been so silent for much of the time.

Dee shook her head. "It couldn't be a marble, Amanda. Marbles roll around."

"How about a knife?" Carol said. "That's the sort of thing a boy would treasure."

"But he wouldn't put it in a box," Rebecca Jo said. "He'd keep it with him and pass it on to somebody else when he died."

"How about you open the box and find out for sure," Pat drawled. "This guessing game is driving me nuts."

Melissa laughed. "All right, just for you, Pat." She pulled up the lid, peeked inside, and drew in her breath. "Would you look at the size of this sucker?" She lifted a braided leather string of some sort, but paused before revealing what was on the end of it.

"If I start a drumroll," Dee clapped her open palms on her leg in classic drumroll style, "would that help you to cut the suspense?"

"Oh, all right." Melissa lifted the looped string to reveal an enormous bear's claw.

Carol let out a low whistle. "That was one big bruin. Any more of those in the box?"

"No. Just this one and some little carved, uh, animals I guess they are."

"He must have been learning to whittle," Dee said when Melissa set one of them on the card table. "That's what my brother's early efforts looked like."

Melissa pawed through the box a bit more. "Nothing else. It's funny what people hang on to, isn't it?"

"And thank goodness they do," Carol said. "Otherwise we historians wouldn't have much to go on."

Saturday, 23 May 1741
Along the trail

SILAS WONDERED, NOT for the first time, why anyone paid attention to the words of his brother. *Go here*, Homer would say, and people went. *Stop now*, and they halted. *Head this way*, and that was the direction in which they steered their horses.

There had been many times so far on this journey when Silas had scouted the trail ahead, as he was doing now, reported to Homer, and stood back while Homer declared his intention to go that way instead of some other way, as if Homer himself had made the choice. As Silas thought back over the previous month, he saw that he himself had always been the one to choose the path and Homer had always been the one to declare the direction to the community of travelers.

When the shot rang out ahead of him, he reined in his horse. It might be nothing more than someone hunting—deer were plentiful in these woods and meadows, although there had been few homesteads along the way of late—but it did not do to stumble in unawares unless the source of the shot was known.

"Stay and be quiet for once, would you?" Devil—a misnomer if Silas had ever heard one—was one of the most sociable horses Silas had ever encountered. Devil had a tendency to call out any time he sensed a potential new acquaintance in the area, whether the newcomer was another horse, a person, or a varmint of some sort. Fortunately, he never greeted deer, which helped, as Silas was always on the lookout for fresh meat, and it didn't do to advertise his and Devil's presence ahead of time. Several years ago, Devil had learned the hard way to avoid greeting skunks. Unfortunately, Silas had been on the receiving end as well.

He looped Devil's rein over a convenient tree branch, took his own Brown Bess—it was primed and ready, but he checked it just to be sure—and walked carefully along the edge of the trail that wound ahead of him. The trail was wide enough, for now, to accommodate their wagons, but he needed to be sure it wouldn't disappear at the doorstep of some abandoned homestead. At least it seemed to be headed in a southerly direction.

It did not take him long to locate his quarry. Ahead of him—not too far ahead—he heard a woman's voice. "Don't you dare move until I can get this reloaded, you louse-ridden varmint."

Silas moved more carefully, ending up behind a wide-girthed maple on the edge of a clearing before what looked to be a newly built cabin. His quick glance took in the temporary roof of pine boughs thickly interlaced through thin trunks of saplings, but he had little time to consider the house, other than to note that a boy stood on the front porch.

The heavy bulk of a black bear lay on its side two yards from the doorstep with what looked like half its head blown away, heaving its body in what Silas recognized as a gruesome death dance. The legs twitched and thrashed, clawing swaths of destruction along the edge of the kitchen garden.

Even dying as it was, the bear was still a danger. As was the woman with the blunderbuss. It had taken her only a few moments to reload. Silas, expert as he was, could not have reloaded faster. If Silas startled her, she might easily turn and discharge the weapon in his direction. He knew the probable width of the weapon's spray at this distance, and he did not want to be caught even by a stray pellet.

Behind the bear, the bloody body of a man lay in that stillness that only death can impose, his neck bent at an impossible angle. A boy, not more than nine or ten by the look of him, brandished a hunting knife as long as his twiggy forearm. "I'll get him, mama," the boy announced.

"You hush up," she said through clenched teeth, "and stay there." She advanced on the bear, whose movements had become less frantic, but who could still, Silas knew, be a threat. Even if it was only a death throe, one of those enormous paws could rip her leg open to the bone. Silas wanted to warn her, but he dared not break her concentration. He wanted to kill the bear himself, to take the risk himself, but he dared not advance unannounced. He saw that her cap was badly askew.

She aimed for the mangled head. In that moment, Devil neighed a greeting, and she flinched. The sound of her shot still rang in the clearing as Silas ran to the bear, his own weapon at the ready. He needn't have hurried. There was no need. Flinching or not, the woman's shot had been true. He bent over the now lifeless carcass, and the residual smoke from the woman's shot swirled around him.

The bear looked as if it had lived a good many years. The head—what was left of it—was scarred from numerous fights. The shoulder held a long hairless scar. The smells of rotten fish, gunpowder, fresh blood, and dead bear mingled in the chill of the midmorning air.

The woman said nothing, just turned, laid her blunderbuss on the ground, and dropped to her knees beside the contorted body of the man Silas assumed was—had been—her husband.

The boy brandished his knife, causing his flyaway hair to waver in the slight breeze. "Who are you, mister?"

"Silas Martin. I would say *at your service,* but it looks as if you don't need any service from me."

"We don't. I can skin that bear by myself."

Silas admired the boy's bravado, but he knew the weight of even a small bear, and this one was amongst the largest he had ever seen. He would have a hard time skinning it himself, and he was half again the boy's height and probably three times his weight. "I am sure you can." He walked respectfully to the other side of the man's body, so as not to seem threatening to the woman. She held no rifle now, but he would not have been surprised to find she had a knife in the folds of her skirt. And knew how to use it.

"I would be happy to dig the grave for you," he said.

She lifted dry eyes to meet his. "You can help Brand dig it." She lowered her voice. "He will shoulder a heavier burden now, and this is a good way for him to learn that."

The boy, whose hearing must have been exceptional, Silas thought, spoke from the porch. "I am the man of the house now, Mama. I know what my burden will be."

She shook her head ruefully. "Ears like an owl's," she muttered, wrenching off her cap and throwing it to one side, where it landed on the bear-crushed stems of turnips. "Come over here, son, for a proper introduction."

The boy extended his hand and Silas was surprised at the strength of the boy's grip. "I am Brand Tarkington, Sir, and this is my mother."

"I am pleased to meet you, Mistress Tarkington," Silas nodded in her direction, "and Master Brand, although I am right sorry it had to be under such circumstances."

"The bear came behind him while he was carrying a load of firewood into the house," she said, not acknowledging the introduction. "He never had a chance."

"Mama just stepped onto the porch. She saw it happen and yelled to me to grab the knife while she got the rifle from next to the fireplace. She walked up behind that bear and shot him in the head while he was …"

The boy's voice petered out as the horror of what he had seen showed on his face. Silas could imagine. The father's right arm had been almost ripped out of its socket, and vicious claws had raked down the man's face and body. It was not a sight he would have wanted to witness. He hoped the boy would not have bad dreams, but he doubted that peaceful nights would be an option for a long time to come. Bears were seldom so aggressive unless protecting cubs, but this bear was a male. Silas had heard that there were some berries that could make an animal go mad, but he had never before set store by those tales, for he had always assumed a bear would be smart enough not to eat such berries. Now, he was not so sure.

"I had just taken my own load of wood inside." The boy ran his hand through his hair, causing an alarming state of disarray, and Silas was sore tempted to grin. But there was nothing amusing about the boy's words. "If I had not been so quick, maybe I could have … have helped my pa … somehow …"

The boy's mother was lucky indeed that the bear hadn't turned on her. The blunderbuss was not accurate unless fairly close, so she had to have run to within killing range to have shot the bear so effectively. A range where she could so easily have been killed herself. And Silas did not doubt that if she had been injured, the boy would have sprung to her defense and been killed as well. He felt something crawl up his spine as he imagined himself riding into this clearing and finding three grisly bodies.

Silas laid a careful hand on the boy's shoulder. "We can spend a lifetime worrying about what might have been, or we can do what needs to be done now. Shall I help you dig your father's grave?"

The boy nodded, and turned toward a nearby shed.

"While my son is fetching the shovels, will you help me lay the body out so I can clean it a bit?"

Silas moved some of the fallen firewood aside. "You take the legs," he said, feeling for certain that, although he could have picked up the body by himself, this powerful woman would insist on doing her part. "I will handle the head and shoulders." He did not relish the thought of slipping his hand into the bloody, almost-non-existent armpit where the man's arm had once been firmly attached, but he would not ask her to perform such a gruesome task, even though he had a feeling that women were much stronger and more resilient than most men thought they were. It was a feeling born out by what he heard each time a woman birthed a babe. Despite the screams, they carried on. Many a man—himself included—would quail at the idea of going through what women endured.

He looked, with his artist's eye, at the severe lines of this woman's cheekbones, and knew without any doubt at all that she was one of the strongest-willed women he had ever met. He tried to imagine what she would look like if she smiled.

She simply nodded, and Silas noted the way the afternoon sunlight was shadowed under the stark planes of her dark eyebrows.

She reached out gently and ran her fingers along her husband's jaw. The tenderness, the love in that gesture brought a lump to Silas' throat.

Together, they had the body lying straight and on its back before Brand returned, two well used shovels in hand. Silas had twisted the man's arm back into alignment and tucked it beneath a fold of the man's ripped shirt.

"We will dig the grave over there next to Uncle Lewis, on the edge of the woods," Brand said, in a voice far older than his years. "Papa likes wildflowers."

265

Silas said a few words, quoted a few bible passages from memory, and then waited while Brand sprinkled a handful of flowers on the body. There was not the time or the means to build a coffin, for the long wood planks stacked beside the clearing had begun to warp.

"They were intended for the roof," Brand had informed him as they dug the grave, "but my uncle died before he and Pa could get it built."

Instead, the boy's mother had wrapped the body in a well-used quilt. "It is almost falling apart anyway," Mistress Tarkington told him. "I never used it anymore. Brand and I each have two good quilts for ourselves."

She gazed around the clearing. "It seems like we just arrived here, and now we will have to leave."

"Leave?" Brand stared up at his mother with what looked to Silas like an equal measure of distress and excitement.

"You know we cannot stay," she said. "I may be able to kill a bear," she grimaced and a shudder ran through her shoulders, "although I do think I was fortunate in the doing of it, but I do not have the strength to lift roof beams. Your father and I might have done it even without your uncle, but I cannot manage by myself." Her gaze softened as she looked down at her son. "Even though I would have you to help me." Her eyes strayed to a nearby wooden cross, stuck in the ground under a large-leaved poplar that was bedecked with its spring blooms of yellow, orange, and green. Silas had not paid much attention to the cross before, but now he could see that the wood looked fresh hewn.

"My brother, Lewis," the woman said. "He came with us and planned to clear his own land just over the ridge that way, but he cut his leg when an axe head flew off." She lowered her voice. "Despite everything I tried, the wound festered."

She did not need to say any more. Silas had seen for himself what often happened under such circumstances. Had Calvin Garner not died just a short time ago from that knife wound in his leg?

"If you are willing to go with me," he said, "back to the camp where my brother and a number of other families abide, we can see you and your son safely down the road to the next good-sized town." He paused, struck by the curve of her neck and the lightest fuzz of soft hair on the tip of her ear, where the sun struck a spark of gold. "Or you and your son would be most welcome to join our band. There are many women and children who would welcome you into their company on our journey."

She seemed wary. "Who are the lot of you, and whither do you go? And why?"

"We are a group of eleven families, with near to ninety people. We have been on the road for more than three weeks, and we travel toward the south, where we have heard there is good land with mild winters. We carry our livestock and many provisions with us, but the meat of that creature," he inclined his head back toward where the bear still lay, surrounded now by a cloud of flies, "would be a welcome addition."

"You expect the three of us to tote a bear down this road?"

"Does this road continue far beyond your cabin?"

She gestured vaguely behind her. "All the way to Allensburg."

"Then I will go back and bring the entire company to your doorstep. Perhaps we could camp for a night or two in your clearing, and there will be plenty of hands to skin the bear. If you will allow us to stay a fortnight, we will be able to smoke the meat."

He hoped beyond measure that she would not think to suggest that all those men could help to put a roof on her cabin.

"And then Brand and I could travel on with you? That is, what I meant is, with the women in your group?"

"You would be most welcome, and"—he nodded to the boy—"there are many lads in our company about the same age as you."

"What do you say to that, Brand?"

"I thank you, sir. My mother and I would be happy to join you."

Silas certainly hoped so. He deliberately did not smile at the boy's obvious assumption of the right to speak for his mother. All elbows and knobby knees and flyaway hair. The man of the house, indeed.

"As long as I can keep one of the bear claws," Brand added with a return to a more childlike attitude, and beamed when Silas assured him that it was his right. Had not the bear been killed on his and his mother's land?

On the morrow, while the other men built a smoking shed and the women cut the meat into long strips, Silas helped Brand form a cross for his father's grave. *Avery Tarkington*, they carved on it, along with the man's birth and death dates.

THE FOLLOWING MONTH after Silas showed Brand how to whittle, and after he gave up when he recognized the boy's apparent disinterest and lack of skill, he taught him how to put together a wooden box with rope hinges so he could store his bear claw safely during the few times when it was not on the string around his neck.

2000

MELISSA RAN HER index finger over the name carved into the bottom of the box. "Do you know anything about Brand Tarkington? This obviously belonged to a little boy. I wonder if he survived his childhood—so many children didn't."

"I'm sure he survived and went on to have children of his own," Sadie said with certainty.

"How can you be so sure?"

She answered me over the rim of her reading glasses. "There have been too many men with the middle name of Brand in the history of our town for the name not to have been passed on down through the generations. And the name Tarkington obviously survived as well."

"Maybe he had a lot of brothers," Maddy suggested.

"I'm fairly sure he didn't," Sadie said. "At least, I never heard of any."

"I never knew any of this," Melissa mused. "I wonder why not?"

"I never heard you ask about it," Sadie said. "You're probably directly descended from the first Brand Tarkington. I seem to recall he married Parley Breeton."

"The barn baby?"

"That's right, Carol. You have a good memory."

"With a name like that, she'd be hard to forget."

"I feel sorry for the bear," Amanda said.

Carol let out a humming sound. "I imagine a bear that size could have fed the community for quite a few meals. They couldn't afford to bypass a chance for food."

Amanda didn't look convinced.

"What I'd like to know," Dee said, "is why anyone would put away a beautiful necklace like this. Wouldn't you think it would be a treasured artifact?"

Melissa held it up and the light from one of the lanterns glinted off the gray-black surface.

We all thought about it for a moment.

"Maybe," I said finally, "Brand's sons kept it and wore it, but then one of them had nothing but daughters, who wouldn't see it as something they could wear."

"That theory won't work," Rebecca Jo said. "The name Tarkington lasted all the way to Melissa, so obviously there was at least one son in each generation, and I should think each of those sons inherited the claw."

"Women wear things like that," Pat said. "At least, native American women do."

Carol opened her mouth, as if she were going to say something, but Sadie beat her to it. "What about it, Melissa? Are you going to wear it?"

That is not what ListenLady was going to ask.

"If Biscuit will give it up"—Melissa paused, and I waved my hand in a queenly adieu. She set the box on the card table and slipped the bear claw necklace over her head. "I'll wear it until my nephew gets a little older. He's a Tarkington."

"If I were you," Maddy said, "I'd wear it for the rest of forever. You can always will it to him."

"He'd have a long wait then," I said. "Melissa and I are both planning to live until we're a hundred and four."

Marmalade hopped off my lap and onto Melissa's ...

She is very sad now.

... and I could have kicked myself when I saw the brief flicker of pain in her face. I knew my words had reminded her of her nephew's twin brother, who never made it past his seventeenth birthday, much less to a hundred and four. Just a short time after I moved to Martinsville, he was killed by a drunk driver on that steep curve between here and Braetonburg. Tragedy could strike so suddenly.

269

1753

ORRA FOUNTAIN SHIPLEIGH seldom felt at a loss. Ever since she married Colton in January of '42 while they were still traveling, she had felt safe. Secure. Even though her own mother had died the night of her wedding, Orra had not let that cloud darken her sense of rightness about her marriage. Colton might look like a dumpling, but Orra had always known she could rely on him.

Until now.

She called her son's name yet again, hearing her voice echoed by the other villagers who had strung out in a long line, advancing up the valley. Searching, searching, calling, crying out. She had progressed from merely calling, sure that she would tan his hide when he finally showed up, to screaming his name the farther they advanced into the forest.

"Paston! Paston! Where are you!"

The heavy trees surrounding the search party seemed to absorb her words, but did nothing to alleviate her fear.

There had already been searches along the path that led north, the path they had made when the wagons first entered the valley eight years ago, but no trace of the boy had been found. Now, Orra trudged through the dark not twenty feet from the path, but she might as well have been a mile from it. The woods were so thick, she would barely have been able to see the wagon tracks, even if there had been light enough, even if there had been twelve lanterns for each person.

She tried to gauge the time they had been looking. When the boy did not return for the evening meal, she had not been too concerned, until her younger son, sent to fetch his brother home from his friend's house, had returned to say no one had seen Paston all afternoon, ever since he and William had tussled over some slight or other. Paston stormed off to the north of town, around the big barn, beyond the fields, and had not been seen since.

"Paston!" Her voice cracked with fatigue and terror. The lantern she carried—they all carried lanterns—offered little comfort. Beside her Colton huffed heavily at the unexpected exertion, his musket in one hand and his lantern in the other. He called almost as loudly as she did. Orra felt an unreasonable surge of anger at her husband, that he could not find their missing boy.

"Paston!"

"Ma?"

She heard it. She was sure she heard it. Like a traveler to the north star or a pigeon to its roost, she veered in the direction of his voice and lunged forward, almost knocking into Colton. "Paston!"

"Ma! Here! Here!"

"Paston Shipleigh, what are you doing up in that tree? Come down right now." Orra was not sure whether she wanted to embrace her child or slap him for frightening her so. Until she saw the blood.

"It's still here." He pointed toward a dense thicket not twenty-five paces away. "That's where he went after I shinnied up this tree."

Colton was already headed for the shrubs, along with three other men, all of them armed to the teeth with their muskets held at the ready. They stopped when the branches shivered, and a fox staggered from beneath the thicket, foam dripping from its pointed maw. Colton tried to get his musket into firing position, but Edward Surratt was faster, followed almost immediately by a louder shot from Matthew Russell.

Orra thought her heart would stop when the explosions from the guns rocked the small clearing.

Her boy, gangly-legged at the age of ten, almost fell from the tree into her arms. "He bit me, Mama. He bit me." He untangled his hand from where he had wound it into the tail of his bloodied shirt.

The word spread quickly down and up the line, and people returned to their homes, their evening meals, their bedtime rituals.

Orra and Colton took their crying child home, delaying the punishment they had planned to mete out to him for having frightened them so.

Orra bathed his hand and applied a poultice to the swollen bite. That night the boy did not sleep well.

In the morning he complained of his head hurting him. Indeed he seemed hotter than usual. His father accompanied him to the deep pool in the Mee-too-chee River and insisted that the boy dunk himself repeatedly to cool him off.

The following day Paston refused to eat, and his hand turned rigid.

The day after that he could barely swallow and he shivered convulsively throughout the day.

The next morning, he was dead.

2000

"IT WOULD MAKE a great Christmas gift," Pat said, obviously unaware of the undercurrents pulsing around Melissa. "If you ever wanted to give it up, that is."

Melissa clutched at the bear claw. "No way. I agree with Maddy. I'll wear it as long as I'm around."

Pat's mention of a Christmas gift made my tummy clench. Bob and I didn't do a whole lot for Christmas, but I did like to knit something special for each of my grandchildren. The trouble was, I was way behind schedule. They grew so fast, I usually waited until just before Thanksgiving to begin my knitting projects so I'd be sure they'd fit. For some reason—mostly my plans for Glaze and Tom's wedding—I'd gotten sidetracked this year and hadn't yet started the sweaters I'd planned on making. Instead I'd made boxes full of big red bows for the wedding, but with Glaze and Tom getting married here, I wouldn't need even half of them.

All that time and effort wasted.

Phooey.

And there was no chance to knit while the house was overrun with guests.

Maybe I'd knit hats or scarves instead of sweaters.

"Come back to the land of the living, Sis." Glaze's comment cut into my reverie.

"What did I miss?"

"Pat was telling us about the Christmas she got coal in her stocking."

"Coal?"

Everybody laughed at me. Pat wiggled her left hand in my face, and the diamond on her ring flashed in the lamplight. "I guess it started out as coal, but it got transformed a bit."

"Huh?"

You are not alone Widelap. I do not understand, either.

272

"Yeah," Maddy said. "All it took was a hundred thousand years or so and a few million pounds of pressure."

Everyone laughed again. Everyone, I noticed, except Amanda Stanton and Charlie Ellis, the two quiet ones in the group.

I wasn't the only one who noticed. Sadie asked, "Do you have a Christmas story, Amanda?"

"That's my birthday," Amanda said. "My mom was born on New Year's Eve, and had never, ever, in her twenty-eight years had a real birthday party. She told me that the first thing she said to me when I was born that Christmas morning was *I promise you'll always have a party on your birthday.*"

"And did you?"

Amanda's face lit up. "I sure did, Miss Sadie. When the family gathered for Christmas, my mom always baked a huge chocolate birthday cake with all the trimmings. No eggnog or Christmas cookies for us, unless some relatives brought them."

"So you missed out on Christmas," Charlie said.

"Oh, no, not at all. But I always got to open my birthday presents first."

"I didn't have a holiday birthday," Rebecca Jo said, "but when I was little at least, I got to wear a birthday crown all day long. My mother made it out of cardboard covered with aluminum foil. I thought it was the most beautiful accessory in the world."

I made a mental note to make her just such a crown this next year when her birthday rolled around.

"We did that in my family, too," Sadie said. "Except during the war years when aluminum foil wasn't available. Then it was just made of paper. What were your Christmases and birthdays like, Charlie?"

"Pretty ordinary, I guess."

Christmas Eve, 1995

IT HAD BEEN five long months since her dad died, but Charlie still missed him. When she went off to college in September for her junior year, she made it a habit to call home a lot, so Mom wouldn't be so lonely, but every time Mom answered, Charlie wanted to ask if she could

273

talk to Dad. It was like she lost him all over again, with every phone call.

She stuck the star on the top of the tree Mom had insisted on putting up. "Your dad would have wanted us to have a tree," Mom had said.

And Charlie couldn't argue with that, because she was sure it was true.

It was just that it didn't quite seem like Christmas without him. He used to laugh all the way through The Twelve Days of Christmas. The only part of it he could ever remember was the partridge in the pear tree. He used to bundle everybody up to go see the live nativity scene at the church just down the block. He—

"Charlie?"

"Yeah, Mom?"

"There's something you need to know about, and I think this evening might be a good time to tell you."

"Oh, God, Mom!" Charlie scrambled down from the ladder. The tears that were always close to the surface these days welled up in her eyes. "Are you—"

"No, no, no. I'm doing fine. This second round of chemo's doing exactly what it's supposed to do."

"Then what …?"

"It's about the history of the Ellis girls."

"You've told me that a thousand times already."

"Not really. There were a few things I never shared with you because I wanted you to be proud of where you came from."

Charlie reached out and gently poked her mother's tummy. "That's where I came from."

Mom took hold of Charlie's shoulders and studied her for a moment. "Your dad was so proud of you."

Charlie grabbed a tissue.

A little later, Mom went into her bedroom and came back with a sturdy cardboard box, from which she lifted a tightly-wrapped packet.

"Is that what I saw you reading once a long time ago?"

Mom's face clouded, but then she smiled. "I'm surprised you remember, but you're right. It is. This packet belonged to Charlotte Ellis."

"The woman I'm named for?" Charlie snuggled into the corner of the couch and Mom sat beside her.

"I named you for her before I knew anything about the contents of this box." Mom hesitated. "I chose the name because Charlotte Ellis was—or was said to be—one of the founders of the town."

Charlie rocked back against the arm of the couch. "You mean she wasn't?"

"These are her private papers. She liked to make herself sound more important than she was. She had a way of ferreting out secrets, and she spent a great deal of her life blackmailing people."

Charlie gulped, staring at the box that had suddenly become menacing. "So why do you have all this?"

"Your grandmother gave it to me just before she died. I don't know if you remember, but we lived in a really nice house in Martinsville."

Charlie shook her head. "I don't remember much about it except for the stairs—the ones I fell down when I was five."

"Your grandmother, my mother, wheedled the house out of Leon Martin."

"Who was he?"

"He was the chairman of the town council at the time. His son is Hubbard Martin, the current head of the council." She eyed the box with distaste. "You know how the chairmanship of the town council has always passed from father to son ever since Homer Martin founded the town?"

"Yeah, I guess. You and Dad told me about it a long time ago, but I don't think I paid much attention."

"Well, John Martin was Homer's son. He became the second chairman after his father died."

"Yeah." Charlie wasn't sure where this was headed, but she didn't think she was going to like it.

"The original Charlotte Ellis found out that John Martin wasn't fathered by Homer." She lifted the box lid and opened the stiff fabric carefully, revealing a stack of yellowed paper. "It's all in here."

Charlie touched the fabric, almost as if she thought it might be too hot to handle. "Why is this material so hard?"

"It was treated with wax, probably beeswax, to make it waterproof." Mom sighed heavily. "Charlotte figured out that John's father was somebody named Sayrle Endicott, who happened to be Charlotte's brother."

"So she blackmailed John?"

"Not exactly. Or at least, she doesn't mention that in here. When Charlotte died, her granddaughter Jane got the packet. She's the one who blackmailed John Martin's son Jerrod. Jerrod apparently didn't want his grandmother's name besmirched—that's the word Jane uses in here. More likely, he didn't want to lose his position as a Martin, so he used his influence in the town to get special perks for the Ellis girls."

"*Perks*? Was that a word back then?"

Mom smiled. "No. But that's what he did. He went beyond the usual services that were expected when a destitute woman needed help."

"She was destitute?"

"Her mother, Charlotte, had been widowed."

Charlie bit her lip before she could say, *just like you*. "What about the granddaughter?"

"There seems to be a tradition of Ellis girls never marrying."

"But you said Charlotte was a widow."

"She was, but if you read between the lines, you'll see that she murdered her husband and went to live with her sister, who was married to the town minister."

Charlie rubbed the back of her neck, which had begun to hurt. "Are you sure about all this?"

Mom nodded and set the packet on the coffee table. "I often thought it might be a good idea just to destroy all these." She rubbed her hands together and flicked them like she was trying to get rid of something that was not only sticky, but noxious as well.

"But you didn't because it's history, right?"

"Right."

"Is that why you were so happy to take us away from Martinsville as soon as Grandma died?"

"You always were good at solving puzzles," Mom said.

"So Grandma was blackmailing Leon Martin?"

The look on Mom's face gave her the answer, but Charlie was having a hard time believing this. "That's crazy, Mom! Nobody would care about something that happened so long ago."

"Maybe most people wouldn't, but the Martins have run Martinsville since 1745, and those Martin men have always flaunted how they're directly descended from Homer Martin, the founder. He was a very well-respected man."

"Only they're not descended from him."

Mom screwed up her face. "That's right. They're not, and every Ellis girl since Charlotte has cashed in on this knowledge."

Charlie reached out and touched the stack of papers. "You broke the cycle."

"Yep. I did, and I'm proud of it." Mom stroked the side of Charlie's cheek. "It's up to you now to decide what to do with these, although I'll keep them safe until … until it's your turn to hold them."

Charlie ignored her mother's oblique reference to dying. She didn't want to think that was ever possible. "I don't want them, Mom."

"Still, they've passed from mother to daughter for more than two hundred years."

"A museum," Charlie said. "There's got to be a museum that would want them."

Mom wagged her hand. "If they go to a museum, they become public record."

"But it's the truth, Mom. Isn't that important?"

"Uh-huh. I just didn't want to be the one to tell the Martins."

"But they already know, don't they?"

"Well," Mom seemed to be searching for the right words, "Leon and Matilda Martin certainly did, because of my mother, but I don't know if they ever told their son, Hubbard. By the time he became the chair when Leon died in 1979, your grandma was too feeble to get out of the house."

"And you spent all that time caring for her?" Charlie's voice rose. "She was a thieving monster!"

"She was my mother." Mom kneaded the fingers of her left hand and rotated her wedding band several times. "Anyway, I didn't know about all of this until just … just before she died. She's the reason I didn't marry your dad right away. She got sick and I had to stay with her."

"Oh Mom!" Charlie eased herself—carefully—into her mother's arms. "I don't want you to … you're not going to … please don't …"

Mom buried her face in Charlie's hair. "You know I wouldn't leave you if I had any choice in the matter. But you're a woman now. It's time for you to deal with … with this Charlotte Ellis stuff." She reared back just enough so she could meet Charlie's gaze. "I still have a long time to go. Don't you worry, baby. Don't you worry."

2000

"THIS IS RIDICULOUS," Ida said. "I can't stand the suspense. One or two more stories from the Mary Frances journal, shall we?"

"It's up to you," I said. "You're the one doing the reading."

"That's because you're the only one who can translate that chicken scratching," Maddy said, as if we didn't know.

A chicken? Where?

"That backwards writing does look a little bit like what a chicken would scratch in the dirt," Carol said.

Oh. Thank you.

I couldn't figure Carol out. One minute she'd make complete sense, and the next minute she was coming up with comments like that one. Ida gave her a strange look—she must have wondered the same thing as I did—and opened the book.

Sunday 24 May 1741

IT WAS THE dark before dawn on Sunday, the sky just barely beginning to lighten, when Charlotte Ellis peeked from between the edges of canvas that hung down around her wagon and saw Mary Frances Garner creep from her parents' wagon, look around furtively, and scurry quietly toward the woods. Charlotte felt completely justified in following her, stepping carefully to avoid any fallen twigs or any stones that might roll under her feet.

She could not help but notice that Mary Frances Garner had spent quite a long time in the woods for the past few mornings, and that she had needed to rinse her mouth out after each trip.

Mary Frances did not stray very far this particular morning before she bent over behind a thick-trunked oak. Charlotte wished she could close her ears to the disgusting sounds, although she did have to admit that Mary Frances was quieter than some women Charlotte had heard over the years. Charlotte shuddered, remembering how her sister Sarah—usually so fastidious—had been particularly noisy, and messy, almost every morning during the early months of each of her pregnancies.

She debated for just a moment as to whether she should let Mary Frances see her. Let her know that somebody knew her secret. Of course, if Homer Martin were the father, the fact that Homer was marrying Mary Frances later this very day would render Charlotte's knowledge relatively useless. If someone else were the father, though …

Charlotte could not decide just how this might be to her advantage, but she was good at hoarding her secrets—and those of the other people in the Martin clan. She would wait to see when the babe was birthed. Everyone knew that a baby always looked like its father when it was first born.

A quick vision of her brother Sayrle's face as he bent close to Mary Frances that evening soon after they left Brandtburg came to her mind. Could that be the answer? Could Sayrle be the father?

She began to ease back toward the wagons, but then decided she might as well relieve herself as long as she was out here. It would be easier with so few people up and about. Mary Frances was apparently through, for she had begun to straighten to her full height. Charlotte deliberately stepped on a dry stick and was gratified to see Mary Frances whirl around when it snapped.

"Good morning, Miss Garner," Charlotte said as she turned aside toward another massive tree, this one a towering maple. "We had best finish our business—whatever it may be—before the others are awake, should we not?"

Charlotte could almost hear Mary Frances Garner's thoughts. *Did she see me? Does she know? Does she suspect? Will I be safe?*

Ha! Let her worry.

LATER THAT MORNING, when Mary Frances walked forward to join her intended in front of Reverend Russell, Charlotte thought she looked more like someone approaching the stocks or the gallows than someone contemplating marriage. She certainly was not giddy, the way Mary Surratt had been all those years ago when she had married Willem

Breeton. Nor did she giggle uncontrollably, the way Geonette Black had done during her wedding to Call Surratt. Charlotte had wanted to slap both of them for their silliness.

Mary Frances was completely quiet during the short ceremony, even though tears ran freely down her face the entire time. Charlotte, standing as she did at one side of the wagon, could see them plainly. At the end, when Mary Frances and her new husband turned to face the gathering, Charlotte was struck by how very tragic Mary Frances looked. Charlotte was instantly certain that the father of the baby was not the man who stood beside the bride. She scanned the group, but no one man appeared unduly concerned. Of course, whoever he was, he might not know he had gotten Mary Frances with child.

"Poor dear," a nearby woman murmured. "Mourning for her nearly-dead father on her wedding day."

Let everyone else think that.

Charlotte knew better, and she hugged her knowledge to herself like a long-handled bed-warming pan. She knew not how she would use it, but use it she most certainly would. Even Sayrle, if he was indeed the father, would be apt fodder for Charlotte's plans.

2000

THE NEXT FEW entries were fairly routine, and I found myself almost nodding off, until I heard Melissa say, "Tarkington? Is this where they came from?"

I must have been completely out of it, because my head jerked up, to the amusement of everyone there.

"You'd better backtrack, Ida," Melissa said. "I think Biscuit missed this whole entry."

"I think she missed two or three of them," Dee said, running one index finger along the other repeatedly in that grade school symbol for *shame on you.*

Why?

Marmalade rose to her feet, turned around once, and settled back onto my lap. That was probably why I'd snoozed. She was so warm and comforting.

Thank you. You are warm and comforting as well.

"I could stand to hear that last entry again," Sadie said, and I flashed a grateful smile at her.

Saturday, 30 May 1741

Despite the fact that she has been widowed for barely a month, old Mistress Black seems to have set her cap for Mister Richard Hastings. Poor Mister Hastings does not stand a chance, I fear, for anyone with eyes can see that Widow Carolina Black is determined to have him. If I were willing to set a wager—which of course I am not—I would predict a marriage between the two as soon as her year of mourning has run its course. Other than wearing black, however, I can see no hint of deep sorrow in her attitude. Geonette Black Surratt, her daughter, has not seemed to notice the chase, but I have caught Presila Black's eyes several times when she seemed to be laughing at the far too obvious antics of her elderly mother. Presila reminds me of a fairy sprite, very like the creatures in the <u>Midsummer Night's Dream</u> that Master Ormsby read to us. She never walks; she minces. She never sits; she alights. I wonder that she has not married yet. Perhaps she is too ephemeral for any man.

The number of our company has been reduced by one and augmented by three.

Maddy interrupted. "Don't you love her vocabulary?"

"Yes," Carol said. "It's too bad that this century has seen television begin to dumb down the working vocabulary of most of us."

"You'd never hear a word like *augmented* on TV nowadays," Pat agreed.

"That may be one reason why Bob and I don't have a set."

"After these few days in the attic," Amanda said, "I begin to wonder why anyone needs a TV."

"I'd like to get back to the story," Ida said, "if you don't mind dropping the social commentary."

"Yes, ma'am," Maddy said with exaggerated courtesy and even saluted. "Wasn't there an old book that began the first chapter with *As I*

281

was saying before I was so rudely interrupted?"

"It wasn't a book," I said. "I remember reading about this. Some newspaper columnist—"

"William Connor," Carol said, surprising me yet again with the breadth of her knowledge. "But he wrote under a pen name."

"Right. He served in the second world war, during which he didn't write his column. After the war, his first column began with the words, *As I was saying before I was so rudely interrupted, it is a power-ful hard thing to please all of the people all of the time.*"

"Exactly." Ida repeated the sentence that had prompted all this—as she called it—social commentary.

The number of our company has been reduced by one and augmented by three. Geonette Black Surratt's newest babe died last week, just five days after it was birthed, and for a time we thought the mother would be lost as well. Mistress Surratt is inconsolable, although I know from having seen the deaths of many children that she will recover, especially as her other living children need her. They christened the child Corbin Kilban after a distant ancestor of hers. I fear this journey is hard indeed for women who are with child, and I fear for the life of my own unborn babe, particularly since it will be born in the midwinter. Nevertheless, there is naught I can do about it other than try to still my fears and look forward to the birth.

I pray daily that my husband—my true husband—will find me and convey me far away from here. Surely he will not blame me when he finds that Mister Homer Martin has taken me to wife against my objections.

My deepest fear is that he has been here and has seen me retire to Homer Martin's wagon at night. Could he have abandoned me if he thought I was unfaithful to him? Would he not be willing to hear my explanation?

"Of course he would," I said.

"I wouldn't be too sure of that." Carol almost sounded like she believed what she was saying. But not quite.

"He couldn't have seen her, though," Maddy said. "Not yet at any rate."

"Why not?" I thought she sounded awfully sure of herself.

"Because Carol said he and his brother didn't leave Brandtburg until the fall, and here it is only May."

"Oh." She was right. "Too bad Mary Frances didn't know that. It would have saved her a lot of extra worrying."

Five days ago, though, something occurred that allowed me to forget my fears for a time. After a short scouting trip Silas Martin returned with a woman and her son in tow. He then led our company to a cabin where we beheld the body of a large black bear. The meat will be welcome indeed. The men quickly erected a smoking shed, for there was much ready lumber stacked nearby, and we set to work with the skinning and butchering, lest the meat spoil if we tarried too long in our tasks. We potted some of the meat, boiled some, and placed some in brine to soak. We will, of necessity, remain here for the month required to complete the smoking and curing process. There is a well with plenteous water and a creek behind the cabin far from the privy. The clearing before the cabin is large enough for all our company. We gathered together for a feast that first night, and the bear's meat was tasty.

Widow Louetta Washburn Tarkington and her son Brand—

She looked up. "This is where you woke up, Biscuit. When Melissa asked about those Tarkingtons."

I nodded my rather sheepish thanks.

She repeated a few words.

Widow Louetta Washburn Tarkington and her son Brand, a gangly-looking youth of nine or ten with hair that looks like nothing so much as a dandelion in full seed, still seem to be reeling from their drastically changed circumstances. Silas told us all the story of how he had come upon Mistress Tarkington as she shot and killed the bear that had mauled her husband. The admiration in Mister Martin's eyes was wondrous to behold, although Widow Tarkington seemed oblivious of it, as she mourns both her husband and her brother, who died of a festering wound not three months ago. Young Brand now wears an enormous claw from the bear around his neck and will not be parted from it.

"How do you like those apples," Sadie remarked. "You're right. There's your ancestor, Melissa."

Before Melissa could say anything, Maddy laughed. "I love that description of the boy," she said. "Hair like a dandelion in full seed! Can't you just see him? Mary Frances had quite a flair for writing, didn't she? What else does she say?"

"If all of you will stop interrupting me," Ida said, "you'll find out."

Jane Elizabeth Benton Hastings—why do I insist on writing out her entire long name when I know her as well as any of the other people with whom I travel? We have no other Jane Elizabeth in our company and not even any other Jane! She was delivered of a healthy girl child whom she and Mister Hastings have named Clarissa. Fortunately, the babe does not appear to have her father's almost spherical nose.

"Spherical nose." I pulled the silver locket out from under my sweatshirt and dangled it in front of me. "Here's one more piece of evidence that this locket belonged to a Hastings."

Pat crossed her arms. "Why do you say that?"

"Because of the guy in here. Remember? I showed you the picture. His nose is practically round."

"Hush," Ida said.

It seems so strange to travel and travel without the need for tending a garden. This August there will be no harvest of hay and oats and barley for us to take in, no flax for us to prepare for weaving, and this September no pumpkins, squash, or apples to be picked. Still, we women glean constantly along the sides of the road as we journey, and every evening's camp finds us combing through the woods for edibles and medicaments. Widow Tarkington had a ready store of herbs and potions that she has packed carefully to take along on the journey, and conversations with her have shown all of the women in our company that she knows whereof she speaks.

"I wish she'd listed all those potions and herbs," Maddy said, "although I'm not sure I'd know what they were for."

"There's a lot of information available about herbal remedies," Melissa said. "It's merely a matter of research—and we know you're really good at that."

"Do you lie awake at night thinking up new jobs for me?"

Melissa just laughed. "You know you enjoy it, Maddy."

"I still wish she'd given us a list."

"You'd better be careful what you wish for," Pat warned. "She might list something like—what were those things called?—*rubnomes*?"

"Or blewen," Rebecca Jo said.

"Or 44B doms," Amanda and Sadie said at the same time.

"What are you talking about?" Easton asked.

Hadn't Easton been listening? Sadie answered more gently than I would have. "Remember the 1910 accounts list?"

"No."

That was right, I thought. Easton had been downstairs that whole time.

"The next entry is June twenty-eighth." Ida obviously wasn't waiting for Easton to catch up. "How about yours?"

"I'll tell you about it later," Sadie told Easton. "Remind me before we go to bed tonight."

"Mine is June twenty-fourth," I said. I read the few simple lines.

Wednesday 24 June 1741. Ira seems to have given up on ever being able to manage his life on his own, and I am sore tempted to thrash him.

June 1741
Brandtburg

"I NEED YOU to come with me," Ira insisted. "Do you not want to avenge this … my …" Ira seemed unable to voice the words.

"Your missing hand?" It sounded cruel, but the sooner Ira acknowledged his limitation, the better off they both would be. Or so Hubbard reasoned.

Ira slammed his fist, his one remaining fist, down on the table. "I do not need you to make sport of me!"

"No, that you do not." Hubbard knew he sounded more composed than he felt. "You need me to hunt for you and chop firewood for you, to cook for you and roll up your blanket, to saddle your horse and help you into your breeches every morning."

"How dare you insult me like that?"

"Is it an insult to speak the truth? Why will you not be content to remain here and learn to do for yourself? I know you are capable of it if only you would put forth some effort."

"I needs must hunt down Homer Martin!"

"You need to learn to tend to yourself. I am quite capable of tracking the Martins by myself, but I cannot leave you so long as you insist on being helpless as a newborn babe." He leaned across the table, careful to keep his balance so he would be able to jump back out of the way should Ira strike out with his one powerful remaining arm. "You insist on depending on me. Can you not act like a man?"

Ira did not for once lash out. "I am but half a man!"

He sounded anguished, but Hubbard had heard the self-pitying tone too much over the past two months. "You have two legs, your head, your eyes and ears, and all else that a man seems to need. You even have both your elbows. Only a hand is gone. And part of your arm," he added in the interest of absolute truthfulness. "If you would but strive to learn, you could manage to do without it. And without me."

If only his brother would learn to take care of himself, Hubbard could race after his wife, who must surely be in despair, wondering when he would come, if he would come. Surely she knew he longed for her more than life itself.

Soon summer would turn to autumn, a poor time to travel. He would brave the worst of the winter gales, though, if it meant he could reach his wife.

He started to turn away, but stopped when he caught a glimpse of Ira's face.

"You think I am a burden," Ira said, a question in his voice.

Hubbard pressed his palm against his forehead. It took a few moments, but he finally had enough control to rein in the anger he felt. It would serve no purpose for him to lash out. "You are my brother. You would—"

He was about to say *You would do the same for me if our situations were reversed,* but he found himself questioning whether that was true. If he, Hubbard, had lost his own hand, would Ira be willing to help him?

Fearing the answer to that might be a resounding *no,* he turned on his heel and left the room, praying that he would never be in a position to find out what that answer would be. Praying, too, that if he were ever in such a situation, he would do his best not to give up as Ira seemed to have done.

2000

"I'D WANT TO thrash him, too," Maddy said. "Imagine him, just giving up like that."

"I'm not sure I'd cope very well with losing an arm," Melissa said.

Maddy looked chagrined, but only for a moment. "He still should have snapped out of it by now. What's it been? Two, three months?"

Melissa lowered her head, like a hound dog inspecting a nearby rabbit, but when Ida started to read, she took a breath and let it pass.

Saturday, 27 June 1741
I sat this evening across the fire circle from Mister Willem Breeton and wondered how I will ever be able to protect my child

when it is born. Willem continually reached out to touch his son Willy and his daughter MaryAnne, as if to assure himself that they were both still alive. Willy strayed too far from the wagons this evening, investigating a rabbit warren when he should have been gathering wood, and was chased by a painter. MaryAnne, without any thought for her own safety, ran into the forest straight for the painter as it sprang toward her brother.

"The panther," Maddy said. "The letter, the … uh …"

"Right," Dee said. "The one from the guy who stuttered."

I saw where they were headed. "This is what he was talking about. When he wrote that he'd fallen in love with MaryAnne."

Ida ran her finger down the page, as if caressing each written word. "How marvelous. How simply marvelous."

They were saved, miraculously, when a dead hickory tree fell across the path of the painter and pinned it to the ground, where Silas Martin was able to dispatch it quickly with a single shot to the head.

"Good heavens," Rebecca Jo said, and reached out to touch Dee's arm. Not surprising, I thought, since Dee is like a daughter to her.

Beside me, my mother touched my shoulder, and I smiled at her. We all knew how Mr. Breeton must have felt.

The death of those two children would, I fear, have been too much for Mister Breeton to endure, for he lost his wife this past autumn, just months before we betook ourselves upon this journey. I do hope he will marry again, for he is such a kind man. Perhaps my sister Constance—in another year. That should be long enough. How I long to tell my Hubbard of the bravery of young MaryAnne. How I long to leave these wagons behind. Let people—even my sister—marry as they will or no. I care not. I would give it all up in less than a heartbeat if it meant I could be with my Hubbard.

"You look worn out, Ida," I said. "Are you sure you're okay?"
Her eyes are very tired.
"That makes sense," Carol said.
Here was another one of those comments I couldn't figure out. "What makes sense?"
"Reading that cramped, backwards, spidery writing is difficult to begin with," she said. "Add to that the stress of these horrific entries and the low level of light up here. No wonder her eyes hurt."
"You're right," Ida said, but she looked as confused as I was. "Why did you assume it was my eyes, though?"
"Marmalade told me."
Yes, I did.
Ida snorted in derision. "Right. I guess I've been rubbing my eyes a lot. That's a pretty definite clue."
"Wouldn't it be nice if Marmalade *could* tell us things," I mused.
Goat poop and mouse droppings!
Marmalade sneezed, and Carol laughed out loud, an unexpected, infectious sound that filled the attic with a sense of joy. Hardly thinking about it, I joined in, and soon all of us were giggling and laughing and slapping our thighs.
Why are you laughing?
Eventually, Maddy took a final gasp and sputtered, "Why are we laughing?"
That spun us off into another round of chuckles, not quite as vociferous as the first time around, but still enough to exercise my tummy muscles.
"Laughter has healing properties," Amanda noted as we wound down a bit.
"I've heard that," Dee said. "Think of how much healthier we'll all be after today."
"And all the thought we've been putting into ..."—Pat waved her hand around—"into this, will certainly exercise our brains."
"So, we come out of it healthier and smarter," Rebecca Jo said. "Right?"

"My new husband won't know what to do with me tonight," Glaze said.

"Oh, I'm sure he'll figure out something," Sadie said with such a suggestive chortle, it sent us into another spasm of tittering, especially when Glaze blushed the brightest red I'd ever seen on her.

When we finished, Carol asked the room in general, "When did Marmalade meet some goats?"

"Goats?" Pat sounded as incredulous as I felt. "Why would you think she knows any goats?"

"Just a guess."

"Maggie Pontiac, our neighbor up the street, has goats," I said. "I buy my goat milk from Maggie, as well as my eggs—she has chickens, too." I didn't feel compelled to mention that I've always been afraid of chickens, especially Maggie's lead hen Almyra, which I had covertly dubbed *Vampirah,* for the hood of black feathers on her head.

"Maggie is my daughter-in-law," Pat said, "Dave's and mine."

I like HenLady's goats. They are funny.

"Marmalade usually goes with me when I visit," I went on. "But why did you ask about goats?"

"You really don't know?"

She does not, ListenLady. She hears me but she does not know how to understand. Nobody else does, either, but Widelap and Softfoot are the only ones I truly want to talk to. And sometimes SmellSweet and LooseLaces and Fishgiver.

I waited for Marmalade to quiet down. "Know what?"

"Have you ever heard anything about animal communication?"

"I've read about it. I even tried it once, but it doesn't seem to work."

Carol gave me a long level inspection. "The main reason it doesn't work with some people is that we don't *really* want to hear all that our animal companions have to tell us."

"Yikes," Glaze said, studying Marmalade. "I do wonder what she'd say about ... about some of the happenings in my life."

You were very unhappy when you came here to live, but you are happy now. And you were unhappy when FreckleNose left because you missed her, but then you got happy because you did not like walking her each day.

"Would you truly be prepared to listen without resentment?" Carol laid her palms flat on the card table. "It's often easier to hear the thoughts of other people's cats or dogs or horses…"

Or goats.

"That's right, Marmalade. Or goats."

"She said that?" Maddy sounded skeptical indeed.

Yes, I did.

I had to admit, it almost sounded like Marmalade was carrying on a conversation. "Why can't I hear her? I'd like to know what she has to say."

"Truly?" Carol didn't sound judgmental, but something in her tone took me aback.

"Well …" I studied Marmalade. "I guess sometimes I get a little tired of her asking for food all the time."

Mouse droppings!

"Do you think she's asking for food now?"

"Isn't she?"

"Actually," Carol said, "she just gave the catly equivalent of a swear word."

"You've got to be kidding."

"No. When you misinterpret what she's said, sometimes she says *mouse droppings* or *goat poop*. That why I asked when she'd met a goat—otherwise I don't think she would have thought to use such a term."

"She's met a lot of mice, that's for sure," Sadie said.

Yes. It is my job to eliminate those intruders from the book place.

"She takes her job at the library, which she calls the book place, very seriously," Carol said. "She calls the mice *the intruders.*" She turned to Glaze. "She referred to somebody—a dog maybe—called FreckleNose, and said you were tired of walking her."

Glaze's eyes bugged out. "Gracie," she mumbled. "She had brown freckles on her pink nose. I … I guess I'm really not a dog person."

"What you said, Biscuit, about how talking with Marmalade didn't work? A lot of times—I'm not saying it was this way with you—but quite often people think that animal communication is all about the people telling the animals what to do. But it's really more about listen-

291

ing to what the animals want to tell us. Which is often not what we want to hear."

"Okay, Carol," Ida said, "I'm tired of all this mystery. What's really going on?"

Instead of answering her directly, Carol said, "I didn't believe it at first, either. A few years ago, though, my sister Misty had half a dozen cats and sometimes she called on an animal communicator to help her figure out what was going on with them."

Ida raised a most skeptical eyebrow.

"You're right, Ida. I felt the same way. All the advice that woman gave Misty just sounded like common sense. But then one day one of Misty's cats started peeing in the living room, and Misty couldn't figure out which cat was doing it, so she called the communicator, who happens to live in California. Misty lives in Vermont. The woman spoke with each of the cats and finally called her back and said that Polly, the little gray cat, was the one doing the peeing."

"How on earth," Pat asked, "would she have known that?"

"Lucky guess," Ida suggested.

"Those were my sentiments exactly," Carol said, "until this woman, who had never seen Misty's house, said that Polly was upset because Misty had *moved a red furniture*."

"Huh?"

"What do you mean?"

"She said what?"

The questions came from all around.

"That's what Polly called it. Apparently she didn't know the word for *chair*. It turns out Misty had moved a big red overstuffed armchair from her bedroom to the living room just the day before the peeing started. The woman told her that Polly missed being able to sit on the back of that chair where she could look out at the bird feeder. That's why she began peeing right next to the chair. It was the only way she could get Misty's attention."

"You're kidding with all this," Rebecca Jo said. "Right?"

"Not a bit. Misty asked her if she had to move the chair back to where it came from, and the woman said no, but that maybe Misty could move a little table or a cat-tree next to the bedroom window so Polly could use that instead."

"Did she?" I asked.

"Yep, and the peeing never happened again. The woman also told her that Polly didn't like sudden changes. *If you're going to move any more furniture,* she said, *just tell her first so she'll know what to expect.*"

"That has to be one of the most amazing stories I've ever heard," Amanda said.

"Sure made a believer out of me," Carol said, "so I ended up taking a course from a different animal communicator, one who lived in my own state, and I've been able to hear an awful lot of animals ever since then."

"Not just cats?"

"No, Pat. I talked to a lizard once. He was sunning himself on a coiled-up garden hose in my driveway one early spring day. I looked at him and thought, *I sure would like to know what that feels like.* He raised his head and cocked an eye at me. All of a sudden I felt the most delicious rush of heat that went from my chin all the way down the front of my body to the bottom of my torso and along the inside edges of both my arms and both my legs, and my palms, too—just the way the lizard had been wrapped around that sun-heated garden hose. Once he could tell I'd gotten the picture, he put his head back down and the feeling went away."

I studied Marmalade, who looked calmly back at me. Nothing. I couldn't even get a glimmer. Maybe I'd have to take a class, too.

"Did you know Marmalade has her own special names for some of you?"

I couldn't help feeling curious. "She does?"

"You're Widelap, and there's someone called Softfoot."

"Bob," I said, looking at Marmalade in wonder. "My husband. He's always so careful not to step on her, even when she winds around our ankles."

She looked thoughtful. "He's the police chief, isn't he?"

"Uh-huh."

Shifting gears, she said, "And there's someone she calls Smell-sweet."

Glaze sucked in her breath.

"That would be my sister," I said, grinning. "She always smells like a vanilla cookie."

Carol touched Sadie on the arm. "She refers to you as Loose-Laces."

"Oh, dear," Sadie said. "When I first met her, she had a tendency to play with my shoes. I'm afraid my laces are always coming untied."

Sometimes it is because I pull on them.

"Cats are exceedingly honest." And Carol explained what Marmalade had just said. "Your name is CurlUp, Maddy."

Maddy laughed. We all did. And Maddy re-wound her legs underneath her.

"Does she have a name for Tom?"

Of course, SmellSweet. He is Fishgiver. You would know that if you listened to me.

"I feel like a translator at the United Nations," Carol said as she worked her way around the attic, giving Marmalade's names for everyone, including my mom and dad.

SunsetLady and DreamMaker.

"I sure don't see how you could be making all this up," Pat said, "but it still sounds like something out of a science fiction movie."

I would like to take a nap now.

"Maybe we need to give Marmalade a rest," Carol said, as Marmy stood up in my lap, stretched, turned around, and lay back down again. I guess I didn't mind being her Widelap. In fact, it felt rather comforting, knowing how she felt about me.

I love you.

She closed her eyes and gave a sweet little meowing sigh. The sound she emitted so closely resembled what I felt, I wondered if she and I had somehow read each other's minds.

I read yours. You only guessed at mine.

We all just watched her sleep for ten or fifteen seconds, peacefulness oozing throughout the vast room. Of course, it was Ida who broke the reverie. She turned to Maddy. "How about another hat?"

"We have enough hats up here to outfit the entire town," Pat said. "Why on earth did all of them end up consigned to attic heaven?"

"Purgatory, you mean," Ida said. "They're just sitting here waiting it out."

"Until we place them on our heads and turn their attic into heaven?" Maddy sounded like she was teasing, but it certainly made sense in terms of a metaphor.

"I think they're here," Rebecca Jo said, "because hats can easily go out of fashion before they've been worn out."

Maddy giggled and pointed to Ida's white-feather chapeau. "Whoever owned that thing, I wonder what her excuse was."

"I imagine," Rebecca Jo continued without acknowledging Maddy's comment, "the women who lived in this house were frugal enough not to want to throw them away, no matter how out of fashion they were."

"But this sunbonnet didn't go out of fashion," Dee said. "You said yourself that you've worn one."

Sadie spoke up. "Sunbonnets couldn't go out of style, Dee. They were never considered a high fashion item in the first place." She reached idly into the trunk beside her and pulled out a letter. "Look at this. Eighteen-sixteen. New Year's Day."

The Dakota
New York City
1 January 1816
Monday

Astaline Shipleigh Hastings
Beechnut House
Martinsville, Georgia

"Astaline," Melissa said. "That was the name on the hoop. Do you think it's the same person?"

"Could be." Carol strung those two words out, and I was struck again by how careful she was not to jump to conclusions.

She is not jumping anywhere.

"Oh, don't be ridiculous," Pat said. "There couldn't possibly be two women named Astaline in this town."

"I don't know why not," Ida said. "There were two Hubbards."

Without waiting for anyone to say anything else, Sadie kept reading.

My dear sister, for so I considered you even before you married my brother,

I have read in the New York papers that 1815 is being referred to as "the year without a summer." It certainly has felt like that. My husband's business interests continue to keep him here in the city, and I am happy to be with him on these cold evenings, but I would much rather the two of us were freezing in Martinsville. Yes, you can tell I received your last letter with its news of the hardships that have hit our hometown so hard. Surely this weather cannot last through another year. If it does, I fear there will be widespread famine in these United States as the newspapers say there has been in Europe. This grand Dakota Hotel is desperate for guests, as so many formerly affluent men are reduced to penury and are turned out when they cannot pay their bill. Hunger is a great leveler, is it not?

"The year without a summer," Maddy said. "What's she talking about?"

"That was the time after the Tambora volcano erupted," Carol said. "It was even bigger than Krakatoa, and it caused twice as many deaths. The ash cloud spread around the world, just like it had with Krakatoa, and blocked the sunlight so crops couldn't grow. In a time when all food was farmed, and there weren't greenhouses and such, there was a major famine. Cities were particularly hard hit, because they had to bring in most of their food from the surrounding countryside."

"I'd imagine," Ida said, "that farmers kept what little they could grow to feed their own families."

"Europe was really hard hit," Carol said, "just the way she says. Some towns were wiped out, almost as bad as the plague."

"But even so," Pat said, "it sounds like Martinsville had a hard time of it, too."

"Keep reading, Sadie," Rebecca Jo said. "I want to find out what happens."

Sadie frowned at the letter. "There's hardly anything else."

Do give Reuben my fondest greetings. Despite what the weather may bring, Astaline, please remember that I will always remain,

> *your loving "sister,"*
> *Lydia*

"Could this be the Lydia you mentioned, Sadie? The one who was born a Hastings and married a Sheffield?"

Sadie looked from me to the letter and back again. "Could be, although Lydia is a fairly common name. But the timing seems about right." She handed the letter to Maddy. "Top drawer item, definitely." She looked around at the rest of us. "This is exciting. What's next?"

"I'm tired of old letters," Easton said. "Too bad we're almost out of hatboxes."

"You're welcome to all the hats," Dee said. "I'd rather find good letters any day."

"Me, too." Glaze stood and leaned over the trunk she and Dee had been working on. "I'm going to the bottom of this one. That seems to be where all the interesting stuff is hidden." She pulled out a stack of sweaters, and the smell of mothballs wafted around us.

"That sure brings back memories," Rebecca Jo said. "Pulling out sweaters before winter each year …" She shivered. "Horrible smell. I had an aunt who always smelled like mothballs, year round. I think she had them sprinkled all over her closet floor."

I hadn't thought of mothballs in years. "Does anybody even sell those things anymore?"

"They're really flammable," Maddy said.

"Don't tell me," Dee said. "You researched them for one of your books."

Maddy spread her hands apart, fingers splayed. "Of course. They're supposed to repel squirrels, too. Keep them from nesting in your attic."

There are no squirrels here.

"That's nice to know," Carol said. When we all looked a question at her, she pointed to Marmalade and said, "No squirrels here."

"Whatever," Maddy said. "But if there're any mothballs left in there, you probably ought to dispose of them, Biscuit. They're really not safe."

"Wait a minute." Glaze waved a creamy white envelope over her head. "Here's one that looks old."

"Doesn't look that old," Pat said.

"Are you kidding? With this spidery writing? It has to be ancient." She laid it on the table in front of Sadie. "What do you think?"

"That copperplate script definitely dates it," Sadie said. "I'm just not sure when. People wrote like that for many years."

"It looks like the Declaration of Independence," Dee said. "I mean, the style of the writing."

"It's addressed," Glaze leaned closer, "to Marella Martin Farner in care of Mister Jerrod Martin." She looked up. "Does that ring any bells?"

"Jerrod Martin was one of the leaders of the town council. He was John Martin's son."

"Homer's grandson," Pat said. "Or rather, Hubbard Brandt's grandson."

"So," Dee said, obviously trying to figure all of this out, "Marella Martin Farner must have been related to Jerrod. But how?"

"Sister? Daughter?" I was just guessing, of course.

"She must have lived with him for the letter to be addressed the way it was," Maddy said.

"But the Martins never lived here at Beechnut House," I said. "How do you suppose it got to the attic?"

"Passed on to a daughter who married a Hastings, probably," Rebecca Jo said.

"Well," Easton said in complete opposition to her earlier indifference, "don't keep us waiting. Read it."

"Put on gloves first," Carol warned her.

Monday, 30 November 1818
Haven House, Garner Creek

Marella Martin Farner
Martinsville
Dearest Mother,
   I do not know just what the men who pass between our two towns gossip about, so you may have already heard my good news. I write to tell you of the birth of your second grandson a full three weeks earlier than expected. I know you had planned to travel here to be with me the last week of my confinement, but the baby had a mind of his own and came much earlier than expected. It was a surprisingly easy birth, perhaps because he is so small, quite unlike his brother Jerome was! You may travel now with the expectation of holding your new grand-baby in your arms the moment you arrive. I do hope you will come soon.
   I have named him Hubbard John.

   Glaze paused. The tension was almost palpable. "Oh my gosh. Hubbard John."

   Fortunately, my dear husband did not object to so unusual a name, for there is an important reason for the choosing of it. It is a reason I have not shared with you, because I was waiting to see if my child would be a boy, and if he would survive. If he had been a girl, I am not sure when I might have told this story, for it seemed a tale not to be shared lightly.
   You may recall that last May, when you were so ill—probably from the cold winters and summers we have endured for the past two years—At that time, I traveled to Martinsville to see Great-Grand-mother Martin one last time before she died. I am so very glad I did not wait, for sitting beside her throughout her last day on this earth was an honor I hold dear. I shall always remember May tenth.

Several hours before she died, Great-Aunt Constance, who had been with her day and night for several weeks, asked if I would like some time alone with Great-Grandmother. I was so grateful for her understanding. She left, telling me only that she would be in the next room if I had need of her.

As soon as she left, I told Great-Grandmother I thought I might be with child. That news brightened her face. She clutched my hands as tightly as she could—she still had a surprising strength in them, as I am sure you remember. I am fair certain these were her exact words:

"I would have asked this of Marella years ago, except that she never had a son. So now I ask it of you, for you are my great-grand-daughter, Marella's only living daughter. Name your second son Hubbard John. It is in memory of someone who was most dear to me. And tell your first granddaughter to name her second son the same."

"There's the reason for all the Hubbards," Rebecca Jo said.

"Hmm." Glaze ran her gloved finger over the spidery script. "Guess so."

She looked at me then with such an intense countenance, I thought surely her eyes must start from her face. "Promise me this," she said, and did not relax her grip on my hands until I so vowed. She sank back onto her pillows, sighed quite deeply, and said, "His name must never be forgotten in Martinsville." I do think, Mother, that she had forgotten I now live with my husband in Garner Creek, but I did not think it right to correct her at such a time. What, after all, could it matter?

She took a moment and seemed to be gathering her courage, although for what I know not, unless it was that she knew she was dying and had set her sights on Heaven. She told me, "Each grand-daughter must do this. I was"—here she coughed heavily, and I thought she must be on death's door. Then she straightened a bit and said, "His wife." But she sank into a daze then and never told me what Hubbard John's wife said or did that made the memory of the man's name so important to her. His wife and Great-Grandmother must have been the firmest of friends, for her face was suffused with joy at that moment.

I do not know why her words made such an impact on me. Perhaps because she never said another thing after those two final words. She died peacefully—I know I have already told you that, as I told everyone I spoke with at her funeral, but I ask you to keep her final request private, just between the two of us. It seemed—please do not think me silly for suggesting this—it seemed sacred somehow.

I have now fulfilled the first part of my promise to her, and I pray that I might live to see my first granddaughter—your great-granddaughter!—that I may pass on the message to her and thereby keep Great-Grandmother's wish alive. If I should not be blessed with a granddaughter, I will give the message to my cousin Ketchum's granddaughter.

I look forward to seeing you soon,

Your loving daughter
Catharina

Glaze sat back with a sigh. "Her dying words told her great secret. *I was ... his wife.* And Catharina didn't understand her. How sad."

"At least she finally had a chance to say it out loud," Ida said. "No wonder she died peacefully."

Rebecca Jo pulled out her handkerchief. "After this, everything's going to be an anticlimax."

"There are another few lines," Glaze said.

Post Scriptum. Great-Aunt Constance came into the room just shortly before Great-Grandmother died. I was surprised to see her so agile at her advanced age, for she has, as you know, been poorly of late, and sometimes her breath sounds strained. She and I sat on opposite sides of the bed until the end. Once Great-Grandmother took her last breath, Great-Aunt opened the small cabinet beside the bed and removed a number of books—four or five at least—as well as a ribbon-tied bundle of paper and a large packet wrapped in what looked like oiled cloth. "These do not need to be seen by anyone but me," she

301

said. I was too saddened at the moment to question her, but I wish I knew what those books and that packet contained.

Beside me, Charlie shifted in her seat. I knew how she felt. These folding chairs were darned uncomfortable for sitting long stretches in.

"The diaries," Ida said. "Those books, four or five of them, are probably these diaries, wouldn't you say?"

"And the ribbon-tied bundle of paper," Glaze quoted, "might have been those letters to Myra Sue."

"Possibly," Carol said, "but we can't be completely sure of that."

Glaze looked back at the letter. "Maybe we'll find that large packet she mentions."

"Probably not," Charlie said.

I wondered why she sounded so negative. Nobody knew what else was up here in the attic.

Sunday 10 May 1818

WHEN CONSTANCE ENTERED the spartan room in which her sister had always insisted on sleeping, she thought at first she was too late. Catharina bent over her great-grandmother's hand, and even from the doorway, Constance could see the child's tear-stained face.

Before she could ask the inevitable question, Catharina became aware of her—Constance must have made some sort of sound, although she had tried to walk quietly. She was getting ever slower, and had noticed of late that her breathing sometimes sounded like the wind whistling into the gorge at the foot of the Metoochie River.

"She still lives," Catharina whispered, but Constance could see that it would not be long now. There were seemingly endless gaps between her sister's increasingly shallow breaths. They barely stirred the coverlet under which Mary Frances lay.

Constance took the ladder-back chair across the bed from Catharina and lifted her sister's frail hand, shocked momentarily at how much colder those fingers had grown in just the brief hour since she had last sat here.

She had never once entered her sister's room without smelling a whiff of new-mown hay. Even now, a faint trace of that elusive scent wafted past her nose.

"Thank you for giving me this time with her," Catharina said.

The girl looked as if she were going to say something else, but closed her mouth so firmly, Constance doubted any blood reached her lips.

Mary Frances took a long, shuddering breath and subsided in that manner that only death employs, and Catharina sank onto the bed, sobbing.

Constance stood. "Sit with her for just a moment, child. There is something I must do." Catharina nodded dumbly, and Constance turned to the small table beside her sister's bed. When she opened the cabinet door, she was surprised to find a sizable handful of hay, wrapped tidily with a piece of white ribbon. This was obviously the source of the scent. What on earth was Mary Frances doing with hay in her room?

And that left-handed sickle, leaning against the back of the cabinet. It had been two years since Mary Frances had been able to do any work whatsoever on the harvest, and then it was only a bit of threshing. Why had she kept the sickle when she could have let someone else use it? Constance cast her mind around the town, looking for another woman who was cack-handed. Rose Hoskins, Astaline's girl. She used her left hand, did she not?

She removed the packet of her sister's journals, the stack of ribbon-wrapped letters, and the other one, the one Mary Frances had given her instructions about.

"Do not read these," Mary Frances had said. "Swear that you will never read any of these. Burn—"

Before she could finish her instructions, though, she had been overtaken with a coughing fit that left her too exhausted to speak. Constance did not know whether she would be bound by that last word, and decided that perhaps she would not. Surely Mary Frances could not have wanted her to burn books that she had treasured for so many years. Constance had oft seen her writing in them in that strange backwards way of hers. And this packet was so carefully wrapped. It was obviously intended to last forever.

She took the stack with her when she left the room. She left the hay behind in the cabinet. She would clean it out later. She would give the sickle to Rose, and that would be the end of it.

CONSTANCE WAS SO caught up in the funeral and the cleaning out of her sister's belongings—Rose had been delighted with the sickle—that she did not untie the strings around the two packets until almost three weeks later. First she inspected the tied stack of letters. The salutation on all of them was to someone named Myra Sue. Nobody in Martin's Village held that name. It was the same name as the woman who had been killed in the north so many years before, but the dates were far more recent. Unable to parse such an enigma, she re-tied the stack and set it aside, feeling reluctant to intrude on her sister's privacy, particularly since Mary Frances had chosen not to send them, even though tinkers regularly visited the town and could have initiated the journey of any number of letters.

She recognized the small books, of course. Had she not often seen her sister writing late at night by candlelight? Constance found herself of two minds, one that had no desire to try to read her sister's diaries, for that writing was far too difficult to decipher. But there was that piece of her that longed to know more about the inner thoughts of her very private sister.

She thought back to her sister's words. "Swear that you will never read any of these." Constance had not sworn, though. It was a fine point, she knew, but surely if she had taken an oath not to read them, she never would have considered it. But she had not sworn.

She knew the writing would appear incomprehensible to most people, but it was simply a matter of tracing each line from right to left. She opened the first one and read the first entry.

Putting aside all thoughts of propriety, she pulled her chair closer to a window where the light was better. It took her more than a fortnight to read through all the entries in each of the books.

When she was through with them, she tied them back together. She could not bring herself to throw them away, but no one must ever read these. Not ever.

It was only after she had tucked the letters and the journals away where they would not be seen by casual eyes, that she turned to the final packet. The one wrapped in oiled paper. It tempted her. At night she could almost hear it calling to her. 'Read me. Read me.'

When Mary Frances had said *Burn*, had she meant all her papers, or only these? Constance did not know. Should she burn it? What could it possibly contain?

Perhaps just one brief look, just enough to help her decide how to handle this burden. Now that her dear husband Willem was dead and her grandchildren so well-grown, she had far too much time on her hands. She waited for a rainy morning when she was sure she would not be disturbed.

She untied the heavy twine that bound the heavily-waxed packet. The cloth was heavily creased, showing much evidence of having been opened and closed repeatedly. Constance unwrapped the first layer to find a second waxed fabric layer inside. Whoever had bound this up had certainly wanted to be sure it was protected.

She unwrapped that layer to reveal a yellowed page headed in spidery writing.

The Knowledge of Charlotte Endicott Ellis.
To be given to my eldest daughter at the time of my death.

But, Charlotte Ellis had died years ago. Why had this packet been in the keeping of Mary Frances Martin? Louisa, Charlotte's older daughter was dead now as well, but Louisa's daughter, Jane, one of the first babies born on the trail, was alive.

Constance compressed her lips. Jane had continued the Ellis Girls' 'tradition' of birthing a daughter out of wedlock. Still, what was right was what was right. And giving Jane this packet that had belonged to Charlotte Ellis and should have belonged to Louisa Ellis—that was the right thing to do.

It took Constance a good half hour to steel herself to re-wrap the package without reading any further. That afternoon, she took it to Jane's meager house and delivered it into her hands, saying only that it had been entrusted to her.

"When my mother died, you mean?"

Constance did not want to lie, so she simply bowed her head and left, feeling justifiably righteous for having done the proper thing. That evening, she found herself regretting that she had not taken even a peek, a tiny peek, at a page or two. Or three.

Within two months, the town council, at the urging of Jerrod Martin, voted to use town monies to improve the sagging house of Jane Ellis and her daughters. "It lies along the road into town and looks an eyesore to people who travel this way," Jerrod reasoned, and of course the council members went along with his suggestion. He was a Martin, after all, and the leader of the council. As grandson to the great Homer Martin, surely he knew what was best for Martin's Village.

Constance, like most of the townsfolk attending the meeting, was baffled, but the town flourished, and it made sense to help those in need.

Tuesday, September 26, 2000

"IT MAKES SENSE to help those in need," she told Hubbard Martin as he handed over yet another envelope. There was hardly any irony in her voice. Hubbard thought maybe Charlotte Ellis actually believed it. This was almost the first time she'd said anything to him at all. Usually she was silent. What, after all, was there to say?

As always, she turned and walked away from him down the path.

Just a few feet past the towering trees that marked the entrance to the path that wound down from the cliff, she paused, looked toward the tree to her left, and—he could see it from all the way up here—she smiled. Then she kept going.

What was that about? He didn't have to wonder for long. Once Charlotte was completely out of view, Clara stepped from behind the tree.

"Hubbard Martin! What is going on? Why were you sneaking around up here with that woman?"

Hubbard tried to think of something—some excuse—some reason—some lie—that would get him out of this. He should have planned something to say in case this ever happened.

But he hadn't, and he couldn't think of a thing.

So he told her.

"BLACKMAIL? SHE'S BEEN blackmailing you?" Clara could hardly believe her ears. She'd suspected Hubbard was having an affair. That was why she'd followed him up here and hidden that way. That would have been better than this. "Why did you ever agree to put up with it?"

"I did it for you. I know how much it means to you that I'm a direct descendant of Homer Martin. I've known that all along."

"But to pay blackmail? Is this why I haven't been able to buy any new dresses for the past three years? The money's been going to *her*?" She embedded that word with as much scorn as she possibly could.

Clara could tell she'd hit a nerve. Hubbard stared at her like he'd never seen her before.

"You want me to stop, then? Okay. Tell you what, Clara. I'll pull those fangs of hers. I'll march into the council meeting next week and announce that I'm not a descendant of Homer Martin. Neither was my father or his father or anybody else back up the line. We're all descended from Sayrle Endicott."

"You wouldn't dare."

"I wouldn't? Just try me. Her grandmother may have been able to blackmail my father about it, but I'm a better man than he ever was. I'm sorry I let it go on for this long. Once everybody knows, she won't have any sort of hold over me, and then you'll have your precious money." He stopped and seemed to put some effort into collecting himself. "I did it for you. Everything I've ever done has been for you, only you're never happy."

Clara had never clenched her fists as tightly as she did now. She felt her nails digging into her palms, but she didn't care. "You did it for me? So I can trail around in dresses that are three years old?" She had to pull herself together. She had that library board meeting in less than an hour. Still, she couldn't help asking, "What's going to happen to me if everybody knows you're not really a Martin? How will I ever hold my head up in public?"

"At least your dresses will be up-to-date."

"Cornelius was five times, ten times the man you are. I wish you'd been the one to die, instead of him." Clara had never hit anybody in her entire life, but she struck out, fueled by every ounce of anger she'd held in for years.

December 7, 2000
the Attic

"GREAT AUNT CONSTANCE," Pat said. I could see her working out the context. "She would have been Mary Frances' younger sister?"

"That's right," Carol said. "Good for you for remembering."

Glaze looked at the stack of books that still sat on their gingham wrapping on the table next to Ida. "So that means Constance is the one who saved all the diaries."

Carol held out a hand and Glaze handed her the letter. "Didn't you tell me earlier that Ketchum Martin was one of the hereditary town council chairs? That name's hard to forget!"

We all nodded. I wondered where she was headed with this.

"So, Catharina must not have had a granddaughter."

"I'll be darned, you're right," Sadie said. "The Hubbard name passed down through Ketchum Martin's family. He and his wife—Janet I think her name was—had a daughter named Aleeza. I love that name. I think that's why I remembered it."

"So-o-o"—Pat was still trying to fit the pieces together—"if Catharina had had a granddaughter, then the name Hubbard would have stayed up in Garner Creek? Right?"

"Uh-huh." Glaze tucked the letter back into its envelope and handed it to Maddy. "Another top drawer treasure."

"This is incredibly confusing," Easton said as she turned away from the group. I couldn't believe how dismissive she seemed to be. Surely, with a last name of Hastings, she was as much a part of this town's intertwined history as any of the rest of us, but she seemed to bounce back and forth from interested to indifferent. I couldn't figure her out.

Before I could worry too much about it, she picked up a rather bedraggled-looking hatbox that was considerably wider than the others had been. "This must have come from the time when women wore those huge, wide-brimmed hats that blocked the vision of everybody in back of them." She looked around at our puzzled expressions. "I saw it in an old movie once, where everybody at a theater couldn't see because of all the feathers and bows and flowers and ribbons in the rows ahead of them."

"It must have been a comedy," Sadie said, obviously making an effort to step out of the somber mood Catharina's letter had left us in. "Let's see what sort of concoction you have there."

Easton peeked in the box, then opened it with a flourish.

The hat she displayed certainly qualified as a sight blocker. When she lifted the hat, a stiff ribbon of some sort—it must have been heavily starched to hold its shape like that—dangled off to one side of the wide brim. On its end was a star-shaped piece of fabric.

"It looks like a shooting star," Maddy said.

"Or somebody's skewed idea of what a shooting star is," Pat said.

"Who on earth would wear a monstrosity like that? It's too ugly to be fashionable." Ida gestured toward the bottom of the box. "Is there a name or anything?"

"Something better than that," Easton said, and I was surprised at the excitement in her voice. Was she finally being enticed into the attic ethos? "There's an evening bag." She drew it out of the hatbox, but groaned when she saw the ugly white multi-pointed star stitched onto the side of it. Balancing the hat in one hand, and with her other hand holding the reticule dangling from its tasseled cord, she looked like blind justice with her scales. I told her so.

Marmalade jumped into Carol's lap.

Who is Bline Justise?

Carol murmured something, too low for me to hear.

"It would be pretty," Pat said, "if it didn't have that horrible star thing. Is it embroidered on?"

Easton handed the hat to Amanda. "Tiny stitches." She passed it back to Easton.

"My mother liked to carry a reticule on Sundays," Sadie said. "Anything in it?"

Easton curled her lip, but dutifully set the hat down and spread open the reticule's gathered top. "There's a letter. No envelope. It's just a note, I guess."

The questions came from every side. "Who's it from?" "What does it say?" "Can you read it to us?"

We passed the hat—if you could call it that—around the circle. Easton opened the single sheet of paper.

I know you will not listen to me if I try to tell you this in person, Emma, so I am taking the liberty of writing you this short letter, which I will leave on your front porch tomorrow morning. You know you will never wear that hat more than this one time, and I should not have to mention how ridiculous you will look if you dare to put it on. Our family will be a laughingstock. Even if you take off the comet trim, the hat will look out of balance. Why ever did you put so much effort into making it? You will not possibly be able to dance wearing it tonight, for it would endanger the eyes of any dancers passing near you. That amount of starch is a peril. Nor does the hat even look like Halley's, at least not what I have seen of the comet on the few cloudless nights we have had. Knowing you and your sister as I do, I daresay she has a hat just like yours, but you were ever the instigator. Please be sensible for once. If you refuse to wear yours, Caroline will not dare wear hers.

Easton frowned at the note. "It's not signed or anything."

"Too bad the writer had such a hard time expressing her opinion," Ida said.

Sadie snickered. "She sounds just like you, Ida, except you're not that mean-spirited."

"I wouldn't have kept such a snippy note," Pat said.

"You have to admit"—I reached out and jiggled the head of the comet—"she had it right. I wouldn't be caught dead wearing something like this."

Do not be dead!

"It's okay, Marmalade," Carol said. "That's just a saying."

Amanda wiped her palms on her thighs. "I bet it hurt her feelings to receive a note like that."

"She was probably used to it," Easton said, and I wondered what brought that on. Over the past few years, Bob's told me a little bit about Rupert Hastings, Easton's alcoholic father. Maybe early on Easton got accustomed to hurt feelings. If it truly was her father who did that—and this was a flash of insight I wasn't sure I could trust—maybe Easton had needed so much to have a father to love her, maybe that was why she chased men the way she did.

"I don't know," Sadie said. "I think it might be fun to wear a crazy hat like that, even if it was only once."

Dee ignored the rest of us and spoke to Sadie. "You could wear it for Halloween, maybe."

"The name in this note is Emma," Maddy said. "And Caroline, Emma's sister. Has anybody heard of people by those names?"

"I haven't," I said, "but that doesn't mean much. When did Halley's Comet happen? Does anyone know?"

We all looked at Carol. "Eighteen-thirty-five," she told us. "And nineteen-eighty-six. It comes around every seventy-five years."

"Wait!" Maddy waved her hands around. "I've got an idea. Emma makes the ridiculous-looking hat in 1835 to celebrate Halley's comet, and somebody writes her that note. Emma crumples up the note and decides to wear the hat anyway, but on the way to the dance she drops dead of a heart attack—or maybe she's set upon by brigands and she's murdered. Anyway, she's dead and all the note-writer is left with is the hat and the note, which she finds tucked into Emma's purse—"

"Reticule," Carol corrected. "It would have been called a reticule."

"Okay." Maddy waved her hand in a *whatever* gesture. "So these are all the note-writer has left and she enshrines them up here."

"In a hatbox," Ida said, her voice dripping with sarcasm, "consigned to an attic?"

"Maddy's a writer," Glaze said. "You've got to give her some leeway for an overly stimulated imagination."

"I do not have to give her leeway for something that ridiculous," Ida said. "Nothing even vaguely like that could possibly have happened."

1835

WHEN SHE WOKE so suddenly, Rose Hastings Hoskins thought the world might be coming to an end. There was a furious pounding on the front door, loud enough for her to hear it all the way upstairs. The pounding was followed almost immediately by the sound of the door being thrown back hard enough to crash against the wall. It was a wonder the glass had not cracked. Frenzied footsteps thumped up the stairs.

"Auntie! Uncle Baxter! Come fast! Hurry!"

Rose drew the cover tight up underneath her chin. "What is it, Ben?"

Beside her, Baxter, who was always slower to awaken, muddled his way into a semblance of sense. "What are you talking about, Benjamin? Why are you yelling at us?"

They had been awake late, for the dance last night had lasted longer than they had expected, and Baxter had not wanted to leave while there was still cider to be had. Rose knew the cider had contained extra ingredients, for Baxter's speech had become increasingly slurred throughout the evening. Normally he drank only small beer. Anything stronger than that was, according to Baxter, an affront to the Heavenly Father, but he seemed unable to tell when his beverages at parties had been altered, and Rose had never felt it was her duty to educate her husband. He always snored like a thunderstorm after he had been drinking to excess. Why of all nights, had Benjamin chosen this one to disturb their sleep?

"It is Mama. She's taken a very bad turn. Papa sent Howard to fetch the doctor."

"And I suppose he thought nothing of having you waken us at this late hour?" Baxter peered out through the cracks in the shutters and heard a rooster crow from up the street. "Early hour. It is still dark outside."

"Do not rail at the boy, Baxter. What is wrong with my sister?" In the hall behind Benjamin Rose could see her son Arthur, the legs of his sleep-tangled nightshirt wound around his knees, hair sticking out at all angles the way it always seemed to do on young boys.

"What's wrong, Benny?" Arthur stifled an enormous yawn.

"Casiah thinks Mama may be"—the boy clutched at his heart.

He was Emma's youngest and tended to live his life as if he were starring in a melodrama, although not quite as bad as his oldest sister, Casiah. "She thinks Mama may be dying."

Rose had already whipped herself out of bed and behind the tall dressing screen. It took her no time at all to don a sturdy dress and a heavy shawl. Baxter would have to stay with Arthur and Zenus.

She would never have trusted Casiah's opinion alone, but if Humphrey had seen fit to send for the doctor, Emma must be in bad straits. Humphrey was not one to panic. "Arthur," she called over her shoulder to her son, "go back to bed." Why had she even bothered to say that? He was at the age when sleeping as much as possible was a given. He had already turned away from her and from his frantic cousin, probably too sleepy to care.

She arrived at her sister's house to find her oldest niece almost hysterical. "Mama is going to die. She is going to die. I know it."

Rose briefly considered slapping Casiah, but refrained for fear it might make matters worse. "Take your sister into the kitchen, Benjamin," she directed the boy. "We don't need this amount of noise. Casiah, pull yourself together and put on the kettle for some tea." If the girl had a task to keep her hands busy, then perhaps she would quit the wailing.

Upstairs, she found Humphrey bent over his wife, who writhed on the bed, her body curved around her hands as they clutched the right side of her abdomen, her nightgown drenched in sweat. On the other side of the bed, Caroline dithered about, unable to make up her mind whether to embrace her twin, bathe her forehead with the contents of the nearby ewer, or simply stare in consternation.

"Did Emma eat something that disagreed with her?"

"No, I do not think so." Humphrey, usually a competent fellow, had never sounded so helpless. "She woke about an hour ago. Every time I try to touch her, she cries out. I sent Howard for the doctor, but I doubt she will let him examine her. She is in so much pain, she cannot seem to unbend."

Rose could certainly see that, even in the uncertain glow of the overly dim lanterns.

"I am glad you sent Benny to fetch Caroline, but he should have come to me first."

Humphrey looked up in some confusion. "I did not …"

"I knew." Caroline touched her sister's shoulder and left her hand there. "I knew, and I came as quickly as I could."

Rose did not have to wonder about such a proclamation. Emma and Caroline had always known each other's thoughts, known each other's moods. Rose had been surprised sixteen years before that the two had taken time away from each other to marry and to move away. Of course, *away* was a relative term. Caroline's cottage was barely a dozen steps from Emma's verandah.

Emma screamed, cutting short any further thoughts.

The doctor, when he arrived, pronounced a bowel inflammation.

He recommended cold compresses, hot teas, and an aperient, all of which Rose administered with grim efficiency.

Emma died two days later, just before dawn. Baxter blamed the doctor for not knowing an effective treatment, but Rose said that anyone could make a mistake. After all, appendicitis could easily look like any number of other conditions.

After the funeral, Rose turned her sister's reticule over and over in her hands, as if the simple act of keeping such a frivolous piece of frippery in motion could negate the fact of Emma's loss. The silly white star Emma had appliquéd onto the side of the reticule glimmered, even in the dim late afternoon light. Casiah had begged her to take the reticule—it and the hat. "I could not possibly use them, Auntie," she had said. "They would remind me too much of Mama."

Rose had her doubts about that. She knew Casiah's true reason was that she would not be caught dead wearing *The Hat*, which is how Rose had come to think of the monstrosity. Nor would Casiah want the bother of picking out the closely stitched threads that edged the lopsided star-shaped comet, despite how fine a reticule it had been before Emma maimed it.

What was she going to do with it? Baxter, of course, would never let Rose use anything as fancy as Emma's reticule, even without the star on it.

"Why are you bothering with that thing?" Baxter sounded particularly testy this rainy September afternoon, but she knew it came from a sense of helplessness. She was fairly certain he dreaded the thought that someday Rose herself might die in agony, and he would be unable to do anything to save her, in the same way that Humphrey had been unable to save Emma.

"She did not deserve this, Baxter." Elizabeth could not summon enough energy to infuse her words with the anger she knew she ought to feel at the sheer waste. "Emma was not even fifty yet. She should have lived another twenty years at least."

"Do not tempt Fate," Baxter cautioned her. "Your sister had a long and happy life."

"Not long enough." Rose removed the contents of the reticule once again. *Why did I ever write her such an unloving note?* Her fist closed around the carefully folded paper, crumpling it into a tight wad. *Why did she keep it?*

She could imagine Emma smiling over the note, sharing it with her twin, the way they shared everything. They always had.

Why did I not just laugh with everyone else when she and Caroline wore their ridiculous hats through that first dance of the evening? Emma brought such merriment to life, and all I could think to do was quash it.

Sighing, she flattened the note as much as she could, replaced it in the reticule, and folded the whole thing flat. After laying it underneath the Halley's Comet hat and tucking the lid of the hatbox firmly in place, she retreated up to the old attic and placed the box close to where she had secreted her mother's silver necklace and Baxter's pocket watch. She could not bear to look at the hat any more, but neither could she tolerate the thought of throwing it away.

As she turned back toward the stairs, she noticed a flash of gold in the dull stream of light from her lantern. When she looked closer, she found the two necklaces that Father had given the twins on their sixteenth birthday. The golden chains were tangled tightly. Rose had often wondered what had happened to them. If she had known they were here in the attic, she could have separated the two and buried Emma in the one with the blue stone—the one Father had given to Caroline, thinking she was Emma.

Rose could not help herself, she laughed aloud as she remembered the way nobody could tell the two girls apart. Nobody except Rose. Until they had reached their early forties, when Emma's hair developed streaks of gray. Rose stopped laughing. Whatever was Caroline going to do now without her twin?

CAROLINE HASTINGS BLACK sat with her arms around her folded up knees, staring at the rungs of the ladder backed chair across the table from her. The chair where her sister always sat when she visited each day.

Could she have done something? Something to save Emma?

Emma had not been quite herself at the dance. They both had laughed, donning their hats, taking their husbands' arms, and sailing forth, scattering the other dancers left and right, as everyone—everyone except Rose and Baxter—applauded the *Comet Twins*. No one had dared to follow too closely behind them. Those bouncing comets were truly treacherous. But for only that one dance. They had been such fun.

Still, Caroline had known that her sister was not laughing quite as hard as she might have. Was not dancing quite so enthusiastically as she was wont to do.

Maybe, if Caroline had insisted on consulting with Doctor Garner. He and his wife had been at the dance. He had not been drinking the excruciatingly potent punch. He might have helped. If only Caroline had said something.

She groped for the cup of tea on the table before her and gripped it tightly, not even noticing how the heat of it almost blistered her palms. She did not drink it.

She was never going to forgive herself.

2000

"DID YOU SEE Halley's Comet," Carol asked, "when it passed by in 1986?"

"I was just a teenager," Maddy said, "and my dad drove me and my brother out away from Atlanta's lights one night when the sky was clear. It was amazing."

"I saw it, too," Ida said, "but I was considerably older at the time. I didn't think it was all that impressive. Of course, 1986 was the year the Challenger Space Shuttle exploded. Now *that* I do remember, and Halley's Comet seemed … seemed to pale in comparison. I can even tell you exactly what I was doing when I first heard about the Challenger."

"Okay," I said. "I'll bite. What were you doing?"

"Rearranging the broccoli heads on the produce aisle. What were you doing?"

"Walking along Main Street, right in front of the Beauty Shop. Sharon hollered at me through the open front door. She'd just heard about it on the radio. Whenever I think about the Challenger, I remember the overpowering scent of hairspray."

Ida looked sideways at me, so I added, "I don't mean to sound disrespectful."

"No harm done," Ida said. "Sharon's hairspray should be banned, like DDT."

"And mothballs," Maddy said.

"I saw the comet, too," Sadie said. "I thought it was marvelous. What about you, Carol? Did you see it?"

Carol shook her head. "It was visible for only a couple of weeks, and every time I went out at night, everything was clouded over. We're talking Vermont, remember."

"We have cloudy spells here, too," Rebecca Jo said, "but not usually for two weeks at a time. It's kind of sad that you've never seen a comet."

"But I *have* seen one." The lift in Carol's voice was almost tangible.

"Tell us about it," I said, since she so obviously wanted to.

"It was right after Christmas in 1973. I don't remember the exact date, but I do know the sky was spectacularly clear. It might even have been early January in '74. At any rate, my sister Misty and I drove her Jeep out away from town, left it in a parking area near the Appalachian Trail, and pushed our way through snow that was thigh-deep. She lives in a little mountain tourist village called Hamelin, where most of the men wear kilts—although not in weather like that. There aren't too many city lights around there to interfere with skywatching. We ended up at the top of a steep hill. We had on long johns and sweats and snowmobile suits—they're warm and snugly even if you don't have a snowmobile."

"And we certainly know that snowmobiles can be exceedingly helpful," my mom said. She looked at Glaze with such an outpouring of love, it stopped conversation for a moment. "I'm so very glad you wanted us here for your wedding, Glaze."

"We can't have it without you, Mom."

"Did they keep you warm that night?" Obviously Ida wanted to get the conversation back on track. "The snowmobile suits, I mean."

"Oh, yes. We stretched out on the snow near the top of the ridge—we were practically at a forty-five degree angle, so we didn't have to strain our neck muscles in order to look upwards. Then we braced our elbows on the ground in front of us, and trained our binoculars on the sky, searching for Comet Kohoutek."

"I thought Kohoutek was a bust," Dee said. "I lived in Atlanta at the time, and I never did see it."

"Nobody who lived in or near city lights could have seen it," Carol admitted. "And even people out in the countryside might have been disappointed. It wasn't very bright. But the longer we lay there watching it and the longer the silence seemed to soak right into us, the more I realized the … the absolute majesty of it. The head was off a bit to my right, and the tail arced up to the left, all the way across the sky as far as I could see. It started as just a fine white line, but it widened steadily all along the tail, until it was …"

She held her arms straight out in front of her, palms together, one on top of the other, and gradually widened the space between them until her upper arm was a good two feet above the bottom one. I could almost see the sweep of the comet's tail.

"Sort of like a contrail," Maddy said, a question in her voice.

"Except that it was more indistinct, filmy-looking. I could see background stars through it."

Marmalade jumped off my lap and put a paw up on Carol's knee. *I like seeing the stars.*

She paused as Marmalade meowed softly.

"I like them, too, Marmalade. Stars, that is," she said to the rest of us. When she began talking again, her voice held a note we seldom encounter. Complete awe, I thought.

318

"After we'd lain there for maybe a quarter of an hour or so, just scanning from the head of the comet to the tail and back again, I began to *hear* it."

The silence in the attic by this time was breathless. Ida, of course, was the one who broke it, but even she sounded reverential. "What did it sound like?"

"Imagine the most beautiful symphony you've ever heard, and then double, triple, quadruple the beauty. Far away, though. Barely discernible, like the sky was singing way far off. I could never reproduce the melody—if there even was a melody. Maybe there wasn't one. I don't know. It's so hard to describe. One thing I thought of as I listened to it was the words from that old hymn—*This is my father's world, and to my listening ears all nature sings, and round me rings the music of the spheres.* I think whoever wrote that hymn must have seen a comet and heard it singing."

"Wow," Maddy said, mirroring the awe and the longing I felt. How I would love to have heard such a sound. The music of the spheres.

I hear the stars all the time because I truly listen.

Carol bent down and scooped Marmalade up into her lap. "Lucky cat," she said.

Glaze turned to me. "Do you remember when Dad took us outside that night in the fall of 1957?"

"Yep, I sure do. But I think it wasn't night. It was just before dawn."

I like the time before dawn. That is when the birds wake up.

"I remember it," Mom said. "He snuck out and left me sleeping. I was so upset with him after I heard what you'd seen."

"That's right," Glaze said. "It turned cloudy for a few days after that, didn't it? I remember you grumping about it."

"Don't leave us hanging," Pat said. "What did you see?"

"Sputnik," I told her. "It had been launched a month or two before, and you could see it, blinking across the sky."

"Blinking?"

"Something about its orbit," Glaze told Pat.

"No," I corrected her. "Not its orbit. For some reason Sputnik tumbled end over end, causing the rays of the sun hitting it to seem to blink on and off."

"Who woulda known," Dee murmured. "Was it like Kohoutek? Could you hear it?"

Glaze and I looked at each other. "No," we both said. "But it was pretty impressive anyway."

"Nowadays," Rebecca Jo said, "the average person seems to take space exploration very casually, but back then it was a really big deal."

"What do you suppose people back during the 1700s were in awe about?"

"Let's find out," Sadie said. "There's bound to be some awe somewhere in this attic."

Not that I was expecting anything awesome in that trunk of ours, but I delved around in it for a while. And came up with absolutely nothing. Giving up, I went to one of the old metal bed frames and picked up a sort of hamper-like box I'd ignored before this. The bed springs were covered with one of the ugliest bedspreads I'd ever seen. I wondered if it might have belonged to Lyle when he was a boy.

There was so much stuff up here in the attic, it was easy to by-pass all sorts of interesting items. But I knew we'd get around to investigating everything eventually—maybe not during this one ice storm, but maybe over the next few months. Or years.

I sighed.

There wasn't room for the box on Sadie's and my card table, so I sat down on the bedspread—the squeaky metal springs seemed to object—and held it on my lap for a moment. It was heavy enough for me to think it might hold promise.

What it held was four oversized leather-bound journals.

I hollered for everyone to gather around. Gold lettering flowed across each of the covers.

Winifred Glancey Millicent

"Old Grandma Millicent?" Sadie held out her hand for it and looked at the cover with a great deal of wonder. Here was that sense of awe she'd said we'd find. "Mrs. Millicent lived in the Millicent Mansion when I was just a little girl. I think she was a widow. Do you remember her, Rebecca Jo?"

My mother-in-law nodded. "I've heard of her, but I never met her. I think she might have died, though."

"You think?" Pat asked. "An old lady that long ago?"

Rebecca Jo frowned at Pat's sour tone, but before she could say anything, Sadie handed the book back to me, and I opened it. Centered on the first page were several lines written in a cramped script.

Winifred Glancey Millicent
4 January 1763 - 18 October 1783

"This is really weird," I said. "You know how a lot of time the death date is written in another hand, like somebody filled it in afterwards?" I held up the book so everybody could see. "The ink is a different shade, but I'd swear that October date was written by the same person."

"Winifred Glancey Millicent." Sadie reached for the book again. "The dates are wrong. I have no idea who this woman was. She certainly wasn't the one I knew as Grandma Millicent."

"You don't suppose," Rebecca Jo said, "that this could be the woman who hanged herself? For years people said the Millicent Mansion was haunted by her ghost."

"How awful," Maddy said.

"The stories vary," Sadie said, "but there was apparently something about her being jilted."

"I heard her fiancé was killed in a car wreck," Rebecca Jo said.

"That's pretty lame," Maddy said. "There weren't any cars in the seventeen hundreds."

"You know, you're right. I never thought about it."

"It's crazy the way rumors get started," my mom said.

"And they just keep growing," Dee put in.

"Grandma Millicent—the woman I knew—her daughter was the last Millicent to live in the Mansion." Sadie turned to Carol. "She's the one who willed the house and all their books to the town to be used as a library."

She ran her finger under the first entry. "Listen to this. It sounds very much like what Mary Frances wrote at the beginning of her journal. *These journals will be the ongoing story of my marriage to Albert*

321

Rockingham Millicent. That's the same thing Mary Frances said, except she was talking about Hubbard Brandt."

"What's the date?" Dee asked.

"For this first entry? It starts in May of 1783." She read a couple of lines to herself. "All about getting ready for her wedding. It looks like Albert had these books made up for her with her married name on the cover."

I opened the other volumes, one at a time. "They're all blank."

Sadie ruffled the pages of volume one until she found the last one Winifred had written on.

18 October 1783. I have already written in the date of my death on the first page. It is not often given to us to know the date we will die, but as I accomplish this through my own act, I have that knowledge. I feel no remorse in leaving this life to join my dear Albert and my dead child.

Rebecca Jo counted on her fingers. "She'd been married only five months when she killed herself. No wonder we all thought the house was haunted."

"It sounds like she had a miscarriage," Pat said, "at around five months."

"And her husband," I said. "He was dead, too."

"The poor woman," Glaze said. "She sounds like she was totally depressed. I wonder if she had anybody she could talk to."

"I don't know about the rest of you," I said, "but I don't think I can face reading this right now. I'd much rather deal with Mary Frances and her problems—"

"And Hubbard and his problems," Dee said.

"Right. If it's okay with everybody, could you put these in the museum drawer, Maddy? Maybe we can read this one some other day."

I handed her the stack. At the dresser she set down the stack and opened the top volume. "There's something in here. Well, look at this." She withdrew a folded piece of paper and handed it to me.

I had no idea what it was, but Sadie solved the mystery. "It's a pattern for a sunbonnet!"

Dee grinned. "There you go, Biscuit. You can make your own now."

Tuesday 25 May 1802

THE MILLICENT'S HOUSEKEEPER looked with some exasperation at her thirteen-year-old granddaughter. "What on earth do you need a pattern for? Any fool can sew a sunbonnet."

Maria bent her head over the sheet of butcher paper that held her meticulously-drawn pattern. Mrs. Surratt could see the girl's forehead drawn tightly into a most unbecoming furrow. "Raise your head child and straighten your back. You'll be bent as a shepherd's crook by the time you're twenty if you cringe like that. Show some backbone for once."

Maria straightened obediently, and she stuffed her pattern into her apron pocket, but her face remained contorted.

"You will not cry," Mrs. Surratt ordered her. "Surratts do not cry. Tears are most unbecoming. Wipe your face and help me set up the tea tray. We cannot keep Madam Millicent waiting."

Together they transferred one china cup and saucer to the tea trolley, then added a linen napkin, the second-best silver teapot, and a tray of delicate biscuits and cream-filled eclairs.

"Quit your pouting, Maria. Your lip is stuck out so far I could stand on it if I wished to."

"Yes, Grandmother."

"You know what to do? How to unload everything carefully?"

"Yes, Grandmother."

"Place it all on the mahogany table next to Madam Millicent's cream brocade chair."

"I know, Grandmother."

"Be sure the cup is well back from the edge."

"Yes, Ma'am."

Mrs. Surratt accompanied the girl to the hall just outside the morning room. If the child did well—pray do not let her drop anything!—she would be promoted.

"Where is Mrs. Surratt?"

She heard the peremptory voice from inside the morning room. Her granddaughter stuttered a reply, and Mrs. Surratt stepped inside to forestall any disaster. "I am here, Madam."

"I plan to purge the attic, but I do not want to work in dust and mess."

"I can set the girls to mopping and cleaning right away." She thought of the chaos upstairs, and added, "It may take several days."

"Just so it is done. I plan to begin on Friday. Mrs. Hastings will be here to help me sort."

Mrs. Surratt could just imagine how much sorting Madam Millicent would do. She would stand at the top of the stairs and say *yes* or *no* to everything that was carried in front of her.

"Is there anything else, Madam?"

"No. Yes. I need to write a letter to Mrs. Hastings. Send one of the boys up to deliver it."

Mrs. Surratt ushered her granddaughter and the tea trolley out of the morning room, gathered a number of maids, and organized a frenzy of cleaning.

While Maria was mopping, she took the pattern out of her pocket and stuffed it inside an old leather book that sat on a lopsided chest. So Grandmother thought any fool could make a sunbonnet? Maria vowed she would never wear a sunbonnet again as long as she lived.

2000

"BEFORE I SEW a sunbonnet," I said, "I'd like to get back to the diaries." I closed the basket and left it on the bedsprings before I joined the other women as we seated ourselves around our circle.

Wednesday, 21 October 1741
I am becoming ponderous with my pregnancy. I long to have it finished. Sarah Russell is particularly encouraging, for she predicts a large and healthy baby, although others in our company urge her not to say such things for fear she bring undue attention onto my

head. In a Christian company such as ours, I fail to see how any such kind words from the mouth of the preacher's wife could possibly hex me. My child is without sin. Without any sin whatsoever. If there are any repercussions on my babe's health, it will be because of my sin, and my sin alone, not because of anything Mistress Russell might have said. I cannot fathom though how God could blame the child, conceived by a lawfully wedded mother, even though He must deplore this second false marriage of mine.

"That poor woman." Ida rubbed her forehead, as if simply reading about Mary Frances and her doubts had given her a headache.

"She sounds pretty feisty, though," Pat pointed out.

My babe will be born after the Yuletide, and I pray we will have traveled far enough by then for the weather to be milder, for I would not want the difficulties of keeping a newly-born child warm through a blustery cold winter.

"I can't imagine what women back then went through," Maddy said. "I've never had a baby, but I can't believe traveling with one is easy."

Understatement of the year, I thought, feeling the unspoken agreement of every mother in the room.

There is much dislike among the women of this company for the rowdiness of the three youngest Endicott brothers. Their frequent fights and even more frequent shouting—often when some poor woman has just managed to rock a fractious child to sleep—is beginning to fray the nerves of all of us. I pray that my child will be healthy, and will sleep soundly despite the Endicott's yells. Sayrle continues to avoid me, as he has done ever since I told him I would not marry him. Surely he cannot think that I wanted to marry Mister Homer Martin. He could not think so little of my intelligence as that. I have seen him often watching me, but he will not quite meet my eyes. I *suppose that is just as well.*

"I kind of feel sorry for Sayrle," I said. "It had to be really awkward for him. They must have been running into each other all the time."

"Nope," Ida said.

I raised an eyebrow.

"She says he's avoiding her."

I had to concede her point. "I still feel sorry for him, and it couldn't have been that easy to avoid somebody when the company was that small."

"Wait," Ida said. "Listen to this."

There have been several instances when Sayrle has approached me, although never as if he would talk with me. Each time it has been when his sister Charlotte has been in my vicinity. It is almost as if he were trying to protect me from her, and I wonder again at the warnings he gave me about not accepting any gifts from her or any food from her hand.

Ida looked over at Charlie. So did I. So did everybody. Charlie had her elbows on her thighs and her chin resting on one fist. She looked like she was bored out of her gourd. Obviously it didn't bother her one bit that the original Charlotte Ellis was such a wacko.

Monday, 2 November 1741
Brandtburg

FINALLY! HUBBARD SADDLED Blaze first. Thanks be to Providence that Blaze had a steady gait that would not jostle Ira's still-tender arm overmuch. Hubbard had for months despaired of ever leaving Brandtburg. Now, with the onset of winter's cold, it was the least favorable time to travel, but he could delay no longer. His wife had already been almost seven months upon the trail. Every day that passed took her farther away from him, so when Ira suggested once again that they go after the Martins, Hubbard readily agreed.

He added Ira's saddlebags and bedroll. Star would carry the extra canvas. They would need a tent for shelter along the way.

He paused for a moment, wondering why he had never thought beyond the time when he would carry his wife away from the Martins. On the return trip he would have Ira, a wife, and one tent. That is, if Homer Martin did not shoot Ira the moment he set eyes on him. Irritated with himself, but grateful he had thought of it before they left, he rummaged around the barn and selected another length of canvas to add to Blaze's load.

Ira had done precious little to help prepare for the journey. Hubbard felt fortunate that the wound had been to Ira's left hand and not his right, otherwise Hubbard would be feeding his brother as well as dressing him, to say nothing of the countless other chores Ira would not attempt.

Once both horses were saddled and loaded, Hubbard led them to the front of the house. He helped Ira mount, ignoring his brother's clenched teeth—at least Ira had stopped shouting at the least disturbance to his stunted arm—and raised his hand in an abbreviated goodbye to the Grants who had come to wish them Godspeed. He had no doubt that the Grants' second eldest son would take over the house. He had said something about "keeping it safe for your return." Hubbard could just hear the young man's thoughts—*hoping you never return.*

Hubbard almost smiled to think that the young Grant would have to dig a new privy hole. And probably build a new outhouse as well, since the one Homer Martin had not tipped over had begun to sag dangerously. The door would barely open. Once open, it was nigh impossible to close.

Hubbard ignored the tears in the eyes of the Grants' eldest daughter. Ira seemed not to notice them at all.

He was surprised to see other Brandt neighbors along the cold path from town. He tipped his hat to the few women and nodded at the many men, each of whom wished them well on their journey and success at their task. He could almost read the blood thirst in their eyes. *Death to the Martin,* some of the men called out. Had they forgotten already that it had been Ira who had murdered Homer Martin's wife?

He nudged Star into a trot through the light covering of frost that had accumulated overnight and could hear Blaze behind him matching their speed. As soon as they were out of sight of the town, though, he turned in his saddle and saw Ira's pasty skin and clenched teeth. Slowing to a walk, he read the relief on Ira's face.

This would be a long slow trek indeed.

Pray God that the Martin clan had been delayed along the road.

2000

"I WONDER IF he turned out to be a Christmas baby," Sadie said. "Does anybody know when John Martin was born?"

"That would be John Brandt." Maddy practically spit the words.

"Now, dear." Sadie put out a restraining hand. "I know you feel a kinship with Hubbard Brandt—you've made that quite clear—but John Martin was known as John Martin all his life. That's the name he would have been christened with, too."

Maddy made one of those sounds that expressed disgust, repugnance, loathing.

It is a snarl.

She almost sounded like Marmalade did the day that man attacked me on the cliffs above town.

"Well," Rebecca Jo said, "no matter what he was called or when he was born, I hope along with Mary Frances that he was a sound sleeper. It seems like he'd need to be, surrounded as he was by that Endicott crew."

"Brrr," Sadie said. "Can you imagine having a baby outside in the middle of winter?"

"I can't imagine doing anything outside in the middle of winter." With perfect timing, a huge gust of wind punctuated my words.

Except feeding the birds.

Except feeding the birds.

Tuesday, 17 November 1741
Somewhere along the trail

THE FIRST THING Hubbard did after helping Ira dismount—he still had to steady his brother every time—was start a fire. Next came setting up a tent shelter nearby. He always tried to situate their stopping places beside a stone wall or a heavy bank of trees and dense shrubs, as he had done this day, so the heat of the fire would reflect back into the tent. He cut and spread a thick layer of pine boughs to insulate their bedrolls from the cold ground, and draped one of the blankets around Ira's shoulders, where he sat on a log near the fire, his back to the steadily-stiffening breeze.

Only after those chores were accomplished did Hubbard prepare food. This particular evening he roasted squirrels he had snared. Despite this first snowstorm they had ridden through most of the day, the squirrels had been out in abundance, chattering at the two men as they disturbed the quiet of the wide path. It made a pleasing change from the Johnnycakes they had been subsisting on.

"This snow is damned inconvenient." Those were the first words Ira had spoken in hours.

Hubbard could barely hear him over the whine of the wind. "We should perhaps be glad the snow has held off as many days as it has. It could have followed us all these many miles since we left Brandtburg."

Ira merely grumbled low in his throat.

Ten days they had been on the road. Ten interminable days. Hubbard hoped he would be able to refrain from throttling Ira for the next two months, for it would surely take that long for him to overtake the Martins and reclaim his wife. If only Ira could ride faster.

2000

"I DON'T KNOW about you," Dee said, "but I'm ready for lunch."

"You think the guys will have it ready and waiting?" Maddy asked.

"No," Ida said, "but if we go down and sit around the table, maybe they'll get the hint." She set the journal aside, a little reluctantly, I thought.

"We'll have to clear off their cards, first," Pat said.

Amanda held up her hand. "Are we going to tell them about … about all this Mary Frances and Homer stuff?"

I sank back down onto my chair. "Maybe we should wait until we know more about how this all turned out. What do you think, Rebecca Jo? Sadie?" As the two senior women, and the two magnificent role models that I had come to love so much over my time in Martinsville, I respected their judgment.

Sadie took a deep breath. "They'll come to know about it eventually." She grinned and looked around her. "Once Maddy has the museum up and running."

"Not here," I said, remembering Bob's advice about a particular two-letter word. I must have spoken more loudly than I intended, because Marmalade woke with a start.

What is a tooletter word?

"Well, wherever." Maddy brightened. "Maybe we could take over that side wing of the town hall?"

"And don't forget," Dee said, "Maddy's going to write up the history of Martinsville. Maybe that's when we let the word get out, once the book is published."

Of course, I knew darn well I'd tell Bob all about this long before the museum was started or the book was written.

"Speaking of the book," Ida said, "I'm with Dee. My tummy's gurgling. Any chance we can get some lunch now?"

I tilted my head and looked at her sideways. "What does lunch have to do with the book?"

"Not much, I guess."

"If those husbands of yours have gotten around to putting it together," Dee said. "Let's go light a fire under them."

Fires would hurt them.

"Sounds like Marmy's hungry, too," Glaze said.

Mouse droppings!

But before everyone else rose, Maddy reached forward and touched the cover of the journal almost reverently. "All the horror stories I've been writing over the years, and now I find the real horror is right here, with somebody we always thought was a hero who turns out to be a complete louse."

"I think," said Melissa, stroking her bear claw necklace, "that the men will be so interested in this Tarkington bear claw of mine, they won't even ask about anything else."

"Take the box along, too," Maddy suggested. "It looks like it has its own story to tell."

"Wish we knew what that story was," Rebecca Jo muttered. "At least we know where the bear claw came from."

"Yeah," Pat said. "Louetta Tarkington, the Bear-Killer," and I could hear the capital letters in her voice. She high-fived Melissa. "What's it like to be descended from stock like that?"

Before we reached the stairs, Dave bellowed from below. "Time for all of you women to congregate in the kitchen!"

"Coming," Pat called back at him.

"Good timing," Glaze said, and I wondered if her thoughts were running along the same line as mine were. "Maybe we won't have to wait too long for lunch."

"You just want to see that new husband of yours," Pat teased.

"He's not my husband yet." Glaze looked at her watch. "Not too much longer, though."

"Whatever," Pat said.

"You're right, though. I'm ready to see him. After that rotten stuff about Homer and the Endicott boys"—she gestured back over her shoulder—"couldn't we all use some interaction with good men?"

And so, with light hearts and an unspoken agreement to keep the weightier contents of the journal between ourselves for now, we trooped down, wondering what we'd find awaiting us.

By the time we made it to the kitchen, after plenty of side trips to the various bathrooms on the second floor, and a detour on my part into the living room to be sure the kettle was on the stove so we'd have hot water later for the washing-up process, the men had lunch all laid out. I sent up a fervent thank-you that our water hadn't frozen and that the generator for the fridge was still working.

"Why am I not surprised," Ida asked her husband, "that you've done nothing but put out sandwich fixings?"

"Sandwiches are good lunch food," Ralph said in a placid tone.

Ida made one of those noises somewhere between a snort and a cough that said what she thought of that sort of reasoning.

"Looks good to me," I said, although there was no mayo, no lettuce, not even any cheese. But everything else was spread out in an inviting array, including lots of luncheon meats. And lots of mustard. I wondered why Tom, our resident chef, hadn't corrected any of the deficiencies, but I didn't worry about it for long. My tummy rumbled. Even moldy cheese and dry bread would have looked inviting at this point.

I will accept some fish.

Tom welcomed us into the fold. He bent to put Marmalade's dish on the floor. and I noticed, not for the first time, the small scar at the base of his right ear. He and Bob had been climbing a tree when they were kids and tried to stand on the same branch at the same time. They never did that again. "Here you go, Furball," Tom said. "A little treat for you."

Thank you, Fishgiver.

Ida headed for the fridge and, I assumed, the mayo and such.

Bob wrapped his arms around me from the back. "What did you women find up there? Anything else as exciting as the liberty hoop?"

"This," Melissa said, and uncrossed her arms, revealing the bear claw in all its glory. I enjoyed all the gasps of surprise.

"And a letter about the Tambora volcano explosion," Maddy said.

"And another letter about Mary Frances on her deathbed," Dee added.

The bear claw was a resounding success, but none of the men asked about the volcano explosions. Just as well. Those cold years reminded me too much of this current ice age we were living for ourselves.

I went to sit down, and had to move the folding chess set off my chair. "Has chess invaded the poker table?"

"It was about to," my dad said, "but we got hungry."

"Very hungry." Bob pulled out the pocket watch, opened it, and ran his thumb over the face. "It's past lunchtime."

I was glad he was using it.

Sadie sent Easton upstairs to retrieve the letters, and the journals too, so we could review the last entries for the men. Ida read the pertinent part of the journal about Louetta Tarkington and her son Brand.

While we ate, the discussion turned to how the journey two hundred years ago had progressed.

"If Carol's right," Ralph said, and I watched Carol bristle, just a little, "then Hubbard and Ira were months behind the Martins. Wouldn't the trail have been hard to follow after that long a time?"

"Maybe Mary Frances was like Hansel and Gretel going into the forest and finding the gingerbread house," Maddy suggested. "She might have left a trail of bread crumbs."

"The birds ate those," Ida said. "Remember?"

Maddy was undeterred. "So maybe she tore little pieces off her petticoats."

Ida snorted. "For a thousand miles?"

Monday, 23 November 1741

HUBBARD SPOTTED THE black queen first. The day had been bright, and the winter sun must have melted the snow from the four-inch-tall carved chess piece. He reined in Star and heard Blaze behind him whiffle a question. It was not time to stop, for they had barely put three miles behind them since their noon break.

Ira had strengthened considerably during the past fortnight. The enforced traveling seemed to be doing him good, although Hubbard could have done without the freezing cold. Still, today was not too uncomfortable. The bright sun had warmed the air considerably. Star blew out her breath, and the air before her nostrils was not the misty cloud it had been for so many days.

He swung down from the saddle and approached the little queen slowly, scanning the bumps of snow for other indications that someone had passed this way. It did not take him long to find them. Amongst a pile of heavy rocks, he found the other chess pieces and the shattered box that must have contained them. Long poles most likely intended for fishing, an assortment of small whittled figures—were they animals, flowers? He could not tell for certain.

And then he saw a box that appeared to be unbroken.

"You are wasting time," Ira complained from above as his gelding edged closer and snuffled around the little queen. Blaze found a mouthful of grass and chomped it vigorously.

"This may tell us for certain whether the Martins came this way."

"Of course they did. Have we not seen only narrow trails branching off this one? Nothing wide enough to accommodate the Martin wagons."

"It never hurts to make sure." Hubbard pulled his knife from his belt, righted the box, and pried open the lid. What he saw took his breath for a moment. Books. He lifted them reverently, one at a time, and cradled them on his lap. Eight of them. This was a treasure trove indeed. Only the one that had been packed on the bottom, and had therefore covered the other books as the box lay upside down in the rain and snow, was damaged beyond reading. He was able to decipher the name and little else, for the pages were soggy. *An Epistle from a Nobleman to a Doctor of Divinity* by John Hervey. Reluctantly, he laid it aside and opened the next book, which was little more than a few pages. *Advice to a Lady* by Baron George Lyttelton. The third book, the most substantial of the lot, had been written by Isaac Watts. Hubbard had heard of Watts a full year ago from a tinker who had quoted one of his poems in response to one of the women of the town who had disparaged the itinerant's worn coat and bedraggled wig. Hubbard thought back. When he had it, he said it aloud.

> *The tulip and the butterfly*
> *Appear in gayer coats than I.*
> *Let me be dressed fine as I will,*
> *Flies, worms, and flowers exceed me still.*

He hoped the entire poem would be in this volume, but with a title like *Philosophical Essays,* he doubted such frivolity would appear therein.

"What sort of nonsense are you spouting?" Ira sounded irascible as always.

"Just a bit of poetry to lighten the journey. It was written by a minister."

"We need no poetry, by a minister or anyone else. We need to be on our way."

Hubbard ignored Ira and studied the next book, a drama of some sort. *The Miser*, translated from the French. Well, that should be entertaining at least, far more than Watts' essays.

He checked the other three volumes for excessive damage, but found them whole. Fortunately none of the books would be too large or too heavy to preclude his inserting them in his rucksack. Two of the books, James Hammond's *An Elegy to a Young Lady* and *The Honest Yorkshireman*, another drama, this one by Henry Carey, were, like the Baron's book, mere pages, the covers of which took up almost more room than the contents. Finally there was a volume Hubbard was sure he recognized. The schoolmaster in Brandtburg had owned a copy much like this of the works of Alexander Pope. In fact, he had quoted from the well-known poet frequently. The schoolhouse and the tavern had been about the only two places the boys and later men of Brandtburg gathered together, although in both places, they had seated themselves separately, the Brandts on one side and the Martins on the other.

Hubbard had a few favorite lines from Pope. He propped his knee on a convenient rock and thought about them.

> True ease in writing comes from art, not chance,
> as those move easiest who have learn'd to dance.

> Be not the first by whom the new are tried,
> Nor yet the last to lay the old aside.

> Education forms the common mind.
> Just as the twig is bent, the tree's inclined.

Before he could get caught up in such memories, for the ground was cold and his brother impatient, he thumbed open the cover and saw the inscription.

> *Ex Libris*
> *Francis Ormsby*
> *Schoolmaster*

"They came this way," Hubbard said, standing to show Ira the writing in the book.

"So they are thieves as well," Ira said.

"Thieves?"

"Mister Ormsby did not travel with the Martins, did he?"

Ira was right. Master Ormsby was one of the many cousins of Hubbard and Ira's parents. He was a Brandt. He had remained with his schoolhouse in Brandtburg. Hubbard could not imagine Master Ormsby giving away so many precious volumes. So someone must have stolen these books.

How could anyone have thrown books to the side of the trail? Hubbard finished adding the seven intact volumes to his carry-sack and pulled himself onto Star once more. This would have been a good place to camp for the night, but they needs must put more miles behind them before they could afford to stop. Mary Frances was closer each day, for two men and two horses could travel far faster than the slow Martin wagons. Even so, Hubbard regretted that he and Ira had gotten so late a start on their journey.

Saturday, 18 April 1741
Late at Night

SAYRLE ENDICOTT HAD NOT wanted to listen to his younger brother, but Joel could be particularly persuasive when he wanted to be. "You know as well I do," Joel had said, "that old Ormsby will not come here tomorrow or Monday either. He already said the school will be closed on Monday since he and his sister want to watch all of us leaving."

Sayrle nodded at that. Having that extra day would add to the safety of this expedition. Still, he felt obliged to argue. "Master Ormsby was good to me when I was his student."

"His number two student," Joel reminded him with a smirk.

Sayrle's grimace was not one he was proud of.

Joel jumped on it. "Hubbard was always Ormsby's favorite. Probably because they're both Brandts."

Sayrle had to admit Joel had a point.

"I have seen Hubbard visit the school often, both during and after classes. He is definitely a favorite. Sometimes I have seen him take a book home with him and return it days later."

Sayrle lowered his eyes at that. He had never thought to ask Master Ormsby if he could borrow one of the books. He wondered if it might even have been possible.

"You know Ormsby has never locked away his books. Just leaves them on that old rack up front, like he doesn't even care about them."

Sayrle knew that was not so. Master Ormsby treasured his books. He used them so frequently in the classroom, it made no sense to put them under lock and key. But, then again, he had let Hubbard Brant take them home.

"Think of it as a loan," Joel crooned. "We will come back some day and you can return them then."

By the time Sayrle agreed, the moon had set, and the brothers had only starlight to guide their steps to the schoolhouse. The schoolhouse Sayrle had always enjoyed and Joel had always hated. Sayrle carried a sturdy wooden box. By the time they left the schoolhouse, the box was considerably heavier.

By the time they left Brandtburg on the following Monday, the box was buried beneath piles of other paraphernalia in one of the Endicott wagons.

2000

NATURALLY, OUR LUNCHTIME discussion eventually devolved into comments about the weather and how long everybody would be stranded here and whether we thought the food would last. Marmalade stretched across my lap and proceeded to lick her paws, one after the other.

I like to stay tidy.

"That's about the last thing you have to worry about," I said, thinking of my packed pantry and all the food Melissa and the Petersons had brought with them from the B&B and from the grocery store.

"I don't think I would have wanted to be in charge of meals on the Martin's wagon train," Dee said. "We know this ice storm will be over soon. Well, maybe not soon, but at least the inconvenience won't last four years."

Charlie Ellis spoke from down the table—the first time she'd said anything during the meal. I'd actually forgotten about her. "Four years. That's kind of like a college education on the road."

"That's rich!" Dave laughed a little louder and a lot longer than necessary. I didn't think it had been that clever a comment.

Apparently Charlie didn't think so either. The glare she shot at Dave would have stopped anybody else who wasn't so oblivious. Good old Dave. Kind of like an overgrown puppy. Obnoxious at times, but relatively harmless, although I would hate to have to put up with him for too many days in a row. I wondered idly how Pat managed, but then I had the answer. Pat and Dave had one big thing in common. She loved Dave, and Dave loved Dave. For some reason I thought of Nick Foley and wondered if he and Dave were related somehow.

Carol spoke over Dave's noisy chuckles. "I imagine the education the Martins got was a lot more daunting than anything we run into in a university."

Charlie just nodded and settled back into her chair.

I got to thinking about some of the things I'd learned outside of college. Carol was right. A lot of our education came from life experiences. I was glad indeed that I hadn't had to take a four-year, continent-long trek in order to get my degree.

What is a degree? Where is it?

Especially since the Martin clan hadn't had a generator or fridge or wood-burning stove.

Next door, Matthew Olsen's House

CLARA WASN'T SURE. She might have been imagining it. She looked around at the other people picking over the bowls and plates on Matthew's dining room table. There was precious little food to be divided. Clara couldn't possibly have toted any food along with her. She'd had enough to do just getting Hubbard here. You'd think if Matthew was going to invite them here, he would have arranged to have enough to eat on hand. The Foleys could have brought food. But all they'd brought was a couple of sandwiches. How completely thoughtless of them.

Matthew didn't have enough chairs for everyone to sit there for a meal. She couldn't imagine why anybody would make do with only three kitchen chairs and no proper dining room. What food he had was on the table and everybody had to help themselves. Once their plates were full, the five of them scattered to whatever seating they could find throughout the house. Well, the four of them. Hubbard was already installed on one of the couches near the wood stove.

Clara hated balancing a plate on her lap at any time of the year, but for now, what with her having to keep an eye on Hubbard, feeding him small bites so he wouldn't choke himself, she hardly had a chance to enjoy any meal. She always had to wait to eat until after she'd fed Hubbard and cleaned him up and settled him down with a blanket over his legs—or tucked him up in bed for a nap—before she could manage to eat. And by that time, everybody else had already finished eating and there she was all alone juggling a plate and a coffee cup. Anita Foley had offered to help her feed Hubbard, but Clara doubted anybody else could do it as well as she could. After all, hadn't she been married to the man for thirty-two years?

The days weren't too bad. At least she could lead Hubbard to the toilet. He was slower than the dickens, but at least he could walk. But at night she had to diaper him, and then there was always such a mess to clean up the next morning. It was even harder here at Matthew's house, what with the bathroom across the hall.

This was just her fate. Just her lot in life. She sighed audibly, said, "Open up now," and lifted another small forkful of mashed-up lasagna to Hubbard's mouth. It reminded her of feeding a baby. She had to be sure the food was soft. She found herself opening her own mouth, the closer the fork got to his lips.

She put her other hand under his chin, ready to push his mouth closed. Just as she was about to press the fork against his upper teeth and pull the lasagna off the fork and into his mouth, his eyes flicked up to hers.

Again, she wasn't sure, but this was the second time this day he'd actually seemed to look at her for just a split second. Surely, he couldn't be waking up. Not after all this time. Not here and not now, not with all these other people around.

He raised his hand and rested it against his shirt pocket. Clara didn't think anybody else noticed. The Foleys were too involved in some sort of discussion with Matthew.

Please. Please. No.

WHAT WAS HIS name? Where was he? Who was he? The warm stuff in his mouth tasted … glue? gob? gun? g-g-good. It tasted good. But who was she? The one with the fire? form? ford? f-f-f-fork. The one with the fork? He shifted his arm and felt the … the … the thing in his front pocket. G-g-good. Seef … sof … safe.

the 1960s, 70s, and 80s

DAVE PONTIAC WAS accustomed to getting his way. That was what made it all the harder when his little brother Joe grew taller than Dave and stronger and—well, Joe'd always been smarter than Dave.

Then, when his brother ended up at the same university as Dave, it didn't take long for the professors to start referring to Dave as *Joe Pontiac's brother.*

Dave tried only once to get Joe to write part of an English term paper for him, but Joe refused. "I've got to work on my advanced calculus," had been Joe's excuse, but the look in his eyes had told Dave he'd better not try that again. It wouldn't have been cheating, Dave convinced himself. It was just one brother helping out another. Only Joe wouldn't do it.

Dave graduated, although it took him several summer sessions and an extra year to do it. That meant the two of them walked up onto the stage one after the other. Dave to get his BA, Joe to get his Bachelor of Science, Summa Cum Laude. At least D came before J in the alphabet, so Dave got his degree first.

Now, though, after all these years, the two of them had evened up. They both had been successful in their fields. And Dave figured he'd learned a lot more on the job than he ever had in college.

Joe, for his part, never mentioned how Dave tried all those years ago to get Joe to cheat. And Dave did his best to forget it altogether, especially when his company took off and the profits went through the roof.

Joe asked him for a loan once, to help with funding some special research. Just one brother helping another. Dave refused.

When Hubbard Martin phoned Dave that February day with an offer—a demand, really—Dave thought about asking his brother's advice. Should he cave in? Should he refuse? But Joe was too stuffy. Anyway, Dave didn't want Joe to know about what had happened way back when.

1952

IT HAD TAKEN all Hubbard Martin's powers of persuasion to convince his brother to leave Clara behind that day, to sneak out the back of the house. The boys knew Clara could see their front door from her house across the street.

"You don't want anybody to see you climbing a tree," Hubbard reasoned. He knew his sixteen-year-old brother had a reputation to maintain, and a boy that age—almost a man—had to uphold his dignity, even when his younger brother challenged him to a tree-climbing competition. Corndog wouldn't want Clara to see him doing kid things like climbing a tree. And Hubbard certainly didn't want her anywhere nearby.

They ran into Dave Pontiac at the corner of Fifth and Juniper. "Dare you," Corndog called.

"Dare you both," Dave yelled, and beat the two of them to the old oak they'd all been climbing for years.

"Where's Nick?" Corndog yelled.

"Dunno," Dave called back. "He didn't show up."

It wasn't fair, Hubbard thought as he struggled up the tree, trying to pass Corndog. Dave, with a head start like that, had already made it as high as his long legs and sturdy frame could carry him. The tree was old and broad and the branches were thick, but even Dave wasn't stupid enough to try those skinny branches at the top. Corndog edged his way around to the other side of the trunk, obviously planning to work his way higher than Dave.

Hubbard didn't have a chance of winning. He thought about climbing back down. He could make it home—Mom was baking cookies this morning—and he could get an extra share before his brother made it back. He glanced up in time to see Dave stomp on Corndog's hand. "You can't beat me," Dave yelled.

Corndog let out a squawk that made Hubbard laugh. Until Corndog crashed past him, bouncing off one heavy branch after another.

Hubbard made it down first—well, first after Corndog. Dave joined him and they looked at the body. Corndog twitched a couple of times and groaned. He almost looked like he was sleeping, only his neck was kinda twisted.

"He lost his grip and fell," Dave said. "That's what happened."

"No! I saw you. I saw what you did."

Dave grabbed Hubbard's arm and yanked, hard. "He lost his grip, right?"

"No!"

Harder, harder, until Hubbard yelped. "Okay, okay. I gotta go get Mama. She can help him."

"Swear first."

So Hubbard swore he'd never tell anybody what really happened—it was an accident, really, it was. That was what he'd say. But he knew Corndog would say different when he woke up.

By the time he got back to the oak tree with Mama, Corndog was all alone, and Corndog wasn't moving any more. His neck looked even worse than Hubbard remembered, his ear was practically on his shoulder. Hubbard tried to forget about it. But he could never really forget, could he?

2000

DAVE DEVOURED HALF his sandwich in only a few bites. "Everybody hunted back then, didn't they?"

"Not necessarily everybody," Carol said. "Most of the men hunted, but there were some professions that were—maybe not exempt, but at least where the men were less likely to be hunters."

"Like what?" He took another huge bite.

"The minister." Carol acknowledged the grins of Henry and Father John. "The schoolmaster, too. He was usually fed by whichever family he boarded with, and all the families with school children paid him with whatever they had available to give."

"But I thought you said they didn't have a schoolmaster on the trail." Rebecca Jo looked around at the group. "What was his name? The one in Brandtburg?"

"Ormsby." Maddy and Carol spoke at the same time.

Sadie took up the answer. "That's true, but they obviously got a schoolmaster once they arrived here. We have the old schoolhouse as testament to that."

Carol sat up straighter. "You still have the original schoolhouse?"

"Don't get too excited," Sadie said. "It's on Clara and Hubbard's property, and it's in pretty bad shape."

"Couldn't the town do something to refurbish it?"

Melissa gave one of those seesaw motions to her hands. "Like Sadie said, it's truly dilapidated. It would take a lot of work, and I don't think anybody's too interested."

"If you're looking for one more project for the M-Money," Glaze said. She looked a question at Dee and Maddy, her two employees at the Martinsville Foundation, and they both nodded.

"You'll have to find somebody to head up the project," Dee said, "but don't ask me to do it."

"Not me, either."

There was no doubt in anybody's mind that Maddy and Dee both meant what they said.

I wasn't about to volunteer. Clara and Hubbard owned that land. Refurbishing the schoolhouse would put me in constant contact with Clara—the last thing I wanted.

Marmy quit her grooming and looked at me. Now that I knew she could understand my thoughts I felt strangely unnerved. And strangely comforted.

Dave single-mindedly went back to the topic of food. "Bear meat, venison. What other kinds of meat would they eat?"

"They probably tried to conserve their ammunition as much as possible." Carol lifted her shoulders. "There were always rabbits."

"You'd have to be a pretty good shot to kill a rabbit without messing up the meat."

"You're right, Dave," she said. "That's why they quite often used snares. It was a skill the children learned early on."

"A survival skill," Maddy said.

1 December 1741

HUBBARD BRANDT TIED together the legs of the two hares he had trapped and field dressed just that morning. They would make a fine meal once the brothers stopped for the evening.

He managed to keep to his feet on the uneven floorboards of the small cabin when Ira shoved him, but he was just off-balance enough that he couldn't spring back out of the way when Ira's right fist came up with lightning speed.

Even though they had traveled hard and had been on the road for such a short time, Ira had already consumed the flasks of whiskey he had secreted in his bedroll and saddlebags. Hubbard had hoarded what little ready money they had, refusing to give any to Ira for the purchase of liquor along their road. Hubbard was glad to have a brother who might be cantankerous from lack of spirits, but who was also more clearheaded as a result. Even clear-headed, though, Ira's idea of entertainment—as always—involved shoving and riling.

His bullheaded approach to life seemed to get worse the longer they were unsuccessful in overtaking the Martin clan.

Now, Hubbard righted himself quickly after Ira's punch. For a one-armed man whose stump had not yet healed over completely, Ira was disconcertingly powerful. "You did not need to do that, Ira."

"It keeps you on your mettle."

"My mettle is just fine, thank you, without your bashing me about." He reached to his left for the bucket of water to extinguish the hearth fire, but the bucket was empty.

Ira held up his stump. "Let us just say I am keeping in practice with my one good hand until I find that bastard Homer Martin."

"Why do you not practice on a tree trunk instead of on my jaw?"

Ira laughed aloud, his belligerent mood shifting almost instantly to one of benevolence. He looked around the disreputable cabin they had sheltered in last night. There were holes in the badly thatched roof of pine boughs. "Did I not find this hospitable place where we both could rest out of the night chill?"

"No. If I recall, I am the one who led us to it, when I saw how several deep ruts veered off the trail we were following." Hubbard set the empty bucket back down and made a vague gesture over his left shoulder toward the heavy woods. When they had come into the clearing around the cabin late yesterday evening, he had hoped that some kindly settler would offer them a well-cooked meal. His hopes were dashed, though, when repeated halloo's failed to rouse anyone. He should have seen right away that there was no smoke from the chimney.

There were two wooden crosses near the edge of the encroaching wood, two crosses above two mounds of dirt, and he had inspected them, afraid to find that one of them might have held the name of his wife, but one was marked with the name Lewis Washburn and the other Avery Tarkington. Both graves were still high-mounded, so they could not have been old. Otherwise they would have sunk down to the level of the ground around them. Tarkington's death date confirmed his guess. He had died but six and a half months before.

Hubbard wondered who the dead men might have been and what had happened to them. Had their wives and sons—they must have had wives and sons because who else would have buried them?—had they gone with the Martins down that broad trail that headed south from here? He wondered, too, why they had left behind a shelter full of firewood, a smoking shed, and a perfectly good bucket, one that he had filled with clean water from the well in front of the house.

The water had refreshed them as they ate their evening meal of roasted hare, and Hubbard had refilled all of Ira's flasks with the clean, clear water, prompting Ira to grumble about the lack of spirits.

"You may yet be grateful for this water, Brother," Hubbard had told him. "The rains have been plenteous, but there is no way of knowing what sources of water we will find along the trail."

"There are streams aplenty here," Ira complained.

"Here, yes, but as we travel farther south, who knows what we will encounter?"

Ira continued to object, but Hubbard ignored him.

Now he took the bucket outside again, lowered it into the well, and brought it up brimming over with fresh water. He would use it to douse the hearth fire. Despite the rains, he knew a fire could spread quickly to the surrounding woods, for the winter-dry grasses had grown tall around the cabin and would serve as ready tinder. Star and Blaze both munched contentedly, not caring how tall the grass was.

Inside, he set down the bucket and watched as Ira gathered up his bedroll and looped a rope around it with some difficulty. He slung it over his shoulder and picked up his saddle. "Let us go now, brother. I feel we are closing in on them."

Hubbard was constantly surprised by how quickly—once they left Brandtburg—Ira had adjusted to life with only one hand. He managed his daily routine well enough, but Hubbard knew Ira's anger over the loss of half his arm boiled just below the surface. He certainly hoped he would be able to prevent bloodshed if and when they did catch up to Homer Martin.

Hubbard's real reason for leaving Brandtburg with Ira, of course, had been to steal his beloved wife away from her family. He doubted now that he and she would return to Brandtburg, not with the way Ira was so dead set against anyone in the Martin clan. Would finding his wife mean losing his brother?

Hubbard rubbed the sore spot on his jaw where Ira's meaty fist had surely left a bruise. Just as long as Hubbard was able to retrieve his wife, he cared little what might happen to his brother. No doubt he would feel differently tomorrow, would find that the camaraderie between him and his brother had returned, but for now, especially with this lump on his jaw, he cared naught.

It would be a minor miracle if Homer Martin and his friends did not kill Ira as soon as they set eyes on him.

Hubbard closed his eyes and imagined Mary Frances Garner Brandt when he had last kissed her, when he had last held her, and when he had watched her climb in through the window of the Russell house so she could be with her friend Myra Sue Russell on her wedding day.

"Are you asleep on your feet, Hubbard? I said it was time to go."

"Let me be sure the fire is out."

"Leave the fire." Ira dropped his saddle with a decided thunk. "It will burn itself away."

"Unless something disturbs the coals and they burn down the

house."

"It would be little enough of a loss."

Hubbard bent down beside the soot-darkened hearth and blew on the coals. They flared up a deep red. As red, Hubbard thought, as the comb on a rooster. "I will not leave live coals unattended, brother."

"And I say you will." Ira's anger burst forth once more, and he slapped his brother so hard on the shoulder, Hubbard went reeling face first onto the glowing bed of coals.

The End
Not quite.

Thus ends **BLACK AS SOOT.** The story will continue in **PINK AS A PEONY** and **WHITE AS ICE.**

The Original Families on the Trek

MARTIN
(descended from Albion & Lucelia Sabriss Martin through their son William)
Homer (marries 1. Myra Sue Russell / 2. Mary Frances Garner)
John (born to Mary Frances on the trail)
Silas (marries widow Louetta Washburn Tarkington)
Brand Tarkington (son of Louetta)
Louise (barn baby, daughter of Silas and Louetta)

BREETON
Willem Breeton & 1. Mary Surratt Breeton / 2. Constance Garner Breeton)
MaryAnne (marries Thomas Russell)
Pioneer (marries Bridgett Hastings)
Susan (became a spinster)
Willy (marries Nell Surratt)
Parley (barn baby, born to Willem & Constance) (marries Brand Tarkington)

GARNER
Calvin Garner & Augusta Hastings Garner
Nehemiah
Wilbur
Mary Frances (married to Homer Martin on trail)
Constance (marries Willem Breeton on trail)
Able (marries Anne Russell)

HASTINGS
Robert Hastings, innkeeper & Jane Elizabeth Benton Hastings
Charles (marries Edna Russell)
Bridgett (marries Pioneer Breeton)
Lucius (marries Fionella Surratt)
Clarissa (born on the trail)
Cordelia (born in Martinsville)
Robert's father Richard Hastings (the original innkeeper)
Jane's elderly mother

RUSSELL

Reverend Anders Russell & Sarah Endicott Russell
- Myra Sue (marries Homer Martin)
- Thomas (marries MaryAnne Breeton)
- Anne (marries Able Garner)
- Abner (bachelor)
- Edna (marries Charles Hastings)

Matthew (blacksmith) & Abigail Downes Russell
- two sons, Mark and Luke, apprentices

SURRATT

Call Surratt & Geonette Black Surratt
- Nell (marries Willy Breeton)
- Fionella Surratt (marries Lucius Hastings)
- Edward (bachelor)
- Barnard (barn baby)

Widow Black & Geonette's siblings (Sergeant & Presila)

ENDICOTT

Chauncey (elderly brewer) & his wife

Worthy Endicott & Eunice Surratt Endicott
- Isabelle
- Jonathan
- Rufus
- Ellen (born on the trail)
- Herman (born in Enders)

Charlotte Endicott Ellis, widow (first daughter of Chauncey)
- Louisa (unmarried)
  - Jane (born on the trail)
  - Adele (born on the trail)
- Martha (unmarried)
  - Alice (born on the trail)
  - Tansy (born on the trail)

Sarah Endicott Russell (Rev. Russell's wife)
Sayrle (bachelor)
Joel (bachelor)
Daniel (bachelor)
Sanborn (bachelor)

EVEREST
Joseph Everest & Arinda Surratt Everest, with five children

FOUNTAIN
Peter Fountain, wife, and eight children
Marcus Fountain (marries Juliana Stickney)
Orra Fountain (marries Colton Shipleigh on trail)
Alan Fountain (fiddler)

SHIPLEIGH
Elias Shipleigh & Anthina Surratt Shipleigh
Colton (marries Orra Fountain on trail)
and six daughters

STICKNEY
Timothy Stickney & Adah Kellogg Stickney with various children
Juliana Stickney (marries Marcus Fountain on trail)

=======================================

BRANDT
Ira Brandt & Felinda Merchant Brandt (deceased)
Ira Marcus
Ira Alonzo
Ira Prentiss
Ira Samuel
& 3 daughters
Hubbard John Brandt

Children of Beechnut House

Robert & Jane Elizabeth's children:
1. **Charles** m. Edna Russell
2. Bridgett m. Pioneer Breeton
3. Lucius m. Fionella Surratt
4. Clarissa (born on the trail)
5. Cordelia and Emeline

Charles & Edna's child:
Alonzo m. Margaret DeWitt

Alonzo & Margaret's children:
1. Lydia m. Curtis Sheffield
2. **Reuben** m. Astaline Shipleigh
3. Ethan m. Naomi Russell

Reuben & Astaline's children:
1. Mary Etta
2. Electa
3. **Rose** m. Baxter Hoskins
4. Emma and Caroline (twins)
5. Lilian
6. son
7. son

Rose and Baxter's children:
1. Zenus Hoskins m. Melanie Surratt
2. Kathryn
3. **Arthur** Hoskins m. Grace Surratt (sister to Melanie, Elspeth & Delilah "Dolly")
4. Euston
5. Timothy

Arthur & Grace's children:
1. daughter (stillborn)
2. **Gideon** Zenus Hoskins m. 1. Leonora Martin 2. Eliza Russell
3. daughter
4. son
5. son

Gideon & Leonora's children:
1. son
2. Ellen
3. son
4. Rachael
5. **Young Gideon** m. Amelia Stockwell

Young Gideon & Amelia's children:
1 - 4. daughters
5. **Perry** m. Elizabeth Endicott
6. Myrtle m. Frank Snelling

Perry & Elizabeth's child:
Lyle

Town Council Chairmen

Homer Martin (b. 1721) m. Mary Frances Garner
John (b. 1742) m. (wife's name unknown)
Jerrod (b. 1772) m. Betsy Surratt
Ketchum (1800-1893) m. Janet Russell
Tobe (1822-1912) m. Irraiah Garner
Morgan (1851-1924) m. (wife's name unknown)
Obadiah (1883-1946) m. Irmagarde Hoskins
Leon (1915-1979) m. Matilda Shipleigh
Hubbard (1940- 2000) m. Clara Black

Inhabitants of Beechnut House

Richard Hastings (the original innkeeper)
Robert Hastings, builder of Beechnut House, m. Jane Elizabeth Benton
Charles Hastings m. Edna Russell
Alonzo Hastings (son of Charles) m. Margaret DeWitt
Reuben Hastings (son of Alonzo) m. Astaline Shipleigh
Rose Hastings (daughter of Reuben) m. Baxter Hoskins
Arthur Hoskins (son of Rose) m. Grace Surratt
Gideon Hoskins (son of Arthur) m. 1. Leonora Martin 2. Eliza Russell
Young Gideon Hoskins (son of Gideon) m. Amelia Stockwell
Perry Hoskins (son of Young Gideon) m. Elizabeth Endicott
Lyle Hoskins (unmarried)

Who's in Biscuit & Bob's House

Biscuit McKee, librarian & her husband **Bob** Sheffield, town cop and, in alphabetical order by first name:
Amanda Stanton, neuromuscular massage therapist
Carol Mellinger, visiting professor
Charlotte Ellis, relative newcomer to Martinsville
Dee Sheffield, employee of M'ville Fdn., Rebecca Jo's daughter-in-law
Easton Hastings, redhead
Father John Ames, priest at St. Theresa's, brother to Maddy
Glaze McKee, Biscuit's sister, head of the Martinsville Foundation
Henry Pursey, minister at The Old Church
Ida & **Ralph** Peterson, grocery store owners
Madeleine "Maddy" Ames, would-be thriller writer and employee of M'ville Fdn.
Melissa Tarkington, owner of *Azalea House B&B*
Nathan Young ("Doc"), town doctor, and **Korsi**, the office cat
Pat & **Dave** Pontiac, guests at Azalea House
Rebecca Jo Sheffield, Bob's mother
Reebok Garner, Martinsville Deputy
Sadie Masters, widow and role model to Biscuit
Tom Parkman, restaurateur and Glaze's fiancé
and me! I'm Marmalade

Latecomers:
　　Frank & **Sylvia** Parkman, Tom's parents
　　Esther Anderson, Tom's grandmother
　　Ivy & **John** ("Mom" and "Dad") McKee, Biscuit's parents

In Matthew's House:
Matthew Olsen & his parakeet, Mr. Fogarty
Hubbard and **Clara** Martin
Nick & **Anita** Foley